Douglas Armstrong

Even Sunflowers Cast Shadows

iUniverse, Inc.
New York   Bloomington

iUniverse books may be ordered through booksellers or by contacting:

iUniverse
1663 Liberty Drive
Bloomington, IN 47403
www.iuniverse.com
1-800-Authors (1-800-288-4677)

ISBN: 978-1-4502-5873-9 (sc)
ISBN: 978-1-4502-5875-3 (hc)
ISBN: 978-1-4502-5874-6 (ebook)

Printed in the United States of America

iUniverse rev. date: 10/18/2010

For Mom

One

When he was fifteen, my brother, John B., balled up a fist and knocked my sister Eileen down in the parlor, chipping off a front tooth. Eileen probably had it coming—who can say—but it terrified me, Johnny yelling that she was a tramp and a troublemaker before Mom stepped in to separate them. The bottom seemed to be falling out of everything. How far were we all going to sink?

Many years later, my sisters and I looked back on the horrid turn things took that day and debated the root cause of it. It was pretty clear to me that the blame should be laid at the Berns' door. But my little sister, Sue-Sue, pointed out that none of it would have happened if the Drummonds hadn't moved in behind us four summers before. Eileen said if you were going to argue that way, you might as well go back to when our ancestors dropped down out of the trees, since that was the origin of monkey business. Funny she would put it like that, since climbing a tree outside her window played such a big part in the trouble.

Eileen had been late to develop, like all of us Starkey girls, and I suspect John B. was secretly disappointed when she began giving up her companionable tomboy ways and wearing her patent leather Mary Janes even after church and sometimes on the occasional weekday, too. I know he wasn't ready later for her to transform into a young lady, that he missed the days when they ran barefoot together in Grandpa Starkey's pasture chasing Phelps, the horse. Spooking the old stud made it fart—every time. As it panicked and fled, it really let 'em

I

rip. We'd all laugh until we had tears streaming down our faces and stitches in our sides.

My God, what passed for entertainment back then. We were just a bunch of hicks who didn't know a thing about the world beyond our hometown of Cornucopia, Kansas—except El Dorado Springs, Missouri, where Grandma Hainline lived. When you get right down to it, we didn't know that much about Cornucopia either. John B. claimed it had been burned to the ground by the Confederate rebels in the Civil War for helping the slaves to escape to the North. "Why somebody'd bother to rebuild it is beyond me," he'd say. Which was more typical of John B. Always a card.

Rather than go clear back to the monkeys, I'll start with the sultry July day in 1922 when the Drummonds moved into the house behind ours on Cherokee Street from faraway Michigan. John B. was eleven, I'd just finished kindergarten and life brimmed with excitement. Over a shallow creek that separated our yards, Margaret and Rach Drummond told us stories about the world beyond Kansas in their sophisticated Yankee accents. But we thought they were making stuff up to impress us.

Even the first time we were together, Rach was at the center of things. He was a string bean of a boy with skinny ankles shooting out the bottom of his britches and a cowlick like a tornado in his straw-colored hair. He bragged about a manufacturing plant where his daddy had worked in Detroit that made "an automobile a minute."

"Bull," John B. challenged. The boys were the same age, but my Johnny was a half foot shorter than Rach. "Does not."

"Does so," Rach shot back. There was something wiry and pugnacious about him that I immediately admired.

John B. smiled. "Y'all talk funny."

Rach laughed. "And *you all* don't?" Then everybody laughed.

So we became thick as thieves. We just couldn't get enough of each other. Rach had a certain swagger that you had to keep your eye on, and I could see that Eileen, who was nine at the time, was getting her money's worth. Margaret Drummond was my age. She could cross her eyes harder than anyone I ever met, before or since.

She'd pull them in and down until practically all that was left was white. Sometimes she'd set them that way with her lids closed and open them up on someone. It scared the bejesus out of little Sue-Sue the first time. Margaret never got to enjoy the full reaction of her victims, of course, because she'd have had to be able to look out her nose holes to do it.

Our two houses were situated at the edge of town. The Drummonds were the last house on Cherokee Street and we were around the block at the very end of New York. Cornucopia being a river town, it was just a short hop from either place through a little wooded glen to a cool swim on a hot summer afternoon. So that's where we all headed for a dip below the dam that first day to get acquainted. Us and the Drummonds.

New York Street wasn't paved in front of our house in those days, but there was a nice sidewalk across the road that ran past Old Lady Rogers' place. If you wanted to roller skate, it was your only option. But Old Lady Rogers was meaner than skunk stink and didn't want anyone on *her* sidewalk. I didn't bother telling Margaret about that the first time we strapped on our Flyers and lit off down that concrete strip. We hadn't any more gotten onto the old lady's property than she was out her front door, shaking a broom, and screaming at us. Margaret might have stood there and argued with her—she could be stubborn—but she had seen me flee up the block and quickly followed.

"Hey! What kind of town is this?" she demanded to know.

"Not much of one, my brother says."

In those days, Margaret sometimes elected to stay at our house for lunch. John B. was never thrilled about it, so Mama often made us up a picnic to take outside. Mama always favored John B., and little wonder, everything he did for her and us girls.

It was picnicking on an old rug out on the front lawn where I first acquainted Margaret with the neighborhood. I told her, "Yonder is Max Nix's place," pointing to the next intersection, "that little house, kitty corner."

She interrupted. "Max Nix seems like a funny name." And she went back to munching on a carrot.

"That's cause his real name is Gustav Heitzelpfarrer—or something. But if you can't pronounce it, he always says 'Max Nix,' which means something in German. So that's what us kids call him." Then I repeated it imitating Max's accent, *Mox Nikts.*

Margaret frowned and I continued.

"Dema lives there, in that place next to Old Lady Rogers. She's our age. Got more freckles than Carter has pills. And her brothers are twins! Can't tell 'em apart. They even have the same halitosis. One's Harvey. The other's Harlan. They all go to Catholic school."

"Who lives there?" She pointed down the next block to the house with the trellis out front. "That one with the new car in the driveway. Looks like the kind of car my daddy used to make."

"Oh, that's the Berns. Tommy is in John B.'s class. He's a big, ugly cuss. Got a big mole on his face with hairs sticking out of it. But his daddy owns the drugstore, and you can get a piece of candy for nothing there if you smile real nice."

On the afternoon we met Margaret's big sister, Reno, for the first time, she offered to take us all swimming. I was surprised when Mama let little Sue-Sue go along. Even though Reno was sixteen, she acted more like an Atlantic City bathing beauty than a baby-sitter. She was obviously all grown up, and proud of it. That nursery she was toting around under her swimsuit filled it to stretching. Right from the get-go, Reno gave the neighbor ladies plenty to cluck about.

At the river, she attracted the attention of some older boys and they went off to swim above the dam, leaving us kids in the shallows below. We watched as they swam out to the island and didn't come back. John B. had to stick near the shore after that to watch Sue-Sue.

"Anybody ever dive off that bridge?" Rach asked him. It seemed to loom over us, though it was some distance away. It was the only bridge over the Neosho for several miles in either direction.

John B. scoffed. "Are you kiddin'? You'd break your neck. You'd have to be crazy to do that."

Rach floated on his back and looked at the bridge and smiled. "What you're saying is," Rach taunted, "you don't have the guts."

When my brother was in sixth grade, he was susceptible to any dare.

I was out over my head in the river when I heard this chatter. I don't think I meant to do it, but I suddenly swallowed a big gulp of the Neosho and began coughing and sputtering like crazy. In my panic, I lost my stroke and went under, thrashing for air. My short legs were unable to find the bottom in the murky water.

In a flash, John B. had me up on the riverbank pounding hard on my back. When I finally caught a breath, the first thing I did was yell at him to cut that out. Then I coughed out a bit more ooky river, wheezed in a couple gulps of air, wiped my nose on my wrist, and said in my most plaintive voice, "Johnny, you got to promise me you won't ever jump off that bridge."

He blinked. "Okay, Emmy. I won't."

I had no way of knowing if he meant it at the time, so I insisted. "Promise?"

"Promise," he vowed.

As it turned out, John B. didn't keep his word. He couldn't really, not faced with those dire circumstances four years later. I shake my head over it still, eight decades later, realizing that when you're six, you don't know how lucky it is that you can't see the future.

Two

My fast and furious friendship with Margaret Drummond almost came to a halt the day we started first grade together. That's when I found out she already knew how to read. She told me about it just as we lined up outside the door the first morning. That streak of summertime silliness, which I loved in her, had misled me as to her basic nature. She was actually very studious, and plainly, she was way ahead of me. *The little smarty pants.* I was pretty certain she wouldn't want me for a friend if she thought I was stupid.

"Oh!" I exclaimed, thinking quick on my feet. "You can read, too?" I saw Margaret's expression pinch liked she'd sniffed a bad odor. "That's great!" I exclaimed, and grinned at her. She smiled weakly back.

I felt like running, but I was stuck there. Mama and Mrs. Drummond were already pushing their baby carriages home after walking us to school. Little Alice Drummond, who was six months old, sat up in hers all smiley and cute, while my baby sister, Mary Ellen Starkey, just lay there and bawled. She smelled bad besides. Were the Drummonds better than us at everything?

I made up my mind I would catch up to Margaret as fast as possible, and without her knowing I'd ever been behind. I thought I could do it, too, since I'd already learned the alphabet from Eileen. I could recognize all of the letters written in big block capitals and small letters on the blackboard when we got into Mrs. Graham's room. Eileen had taught me those along with the alphabet song when she was a first grader. How hard could the rest of it be?

I found out when the readers were handed out after lunch the first day. I opened mine up and saw it was gibberish, like some secret code. The pictures were nice, but I didn't get the rest. Mrs. Graham explained to us what the cover and the first page said. She had us watch as she pointed out each word. I still didn't get it. Then she turned us loose to copy down the first story inside, letter for letter, onto a sheet of blue-lined paper. I turned and saw Margaret copying diligently. She stopped for a second and, without looking up, she smiled knowingly at something she'd read. I hated her. I let a little time go by and then walked up to Mrs. Graham's desk with my reader, having paged noisily through it. "You got anything harder?" I asked. Loud enough for Margaret to hear.

"Sit with me a moment, Emma," she said, pointing to a chair next to her desk. "Let's go through it together."

Well, I walked right into that trap. Still, I'd paged through it and seen the pictures and I thought I could spin out the yarn I expected they'd printed in the word part. Until Mrs. Graham stopped me. She had a narrow face that easily radiated suspicion.

"What's this word?"

I dithered. "Which one?"

"This one," she said gently.

I looked at her and I could see she meant no harm. So I asked, "Could I talk to you a minute in the hall?" We went out and shut the door and I gave her my best pitch about it being an off day for me, and maybe we could try it again tomorrow. In the meantime, would it be okay if I just stuck to the assignment she'd handed out. She agreed, and sent me back to my desk to continue copying.

In the school yard later at recess, Margaret wanted to know what all the fuss had been about.

"I had to explain to Mrs. Graham how my sister Eileen learned me to read."

Margaret made a face. "Really. Is that so? Then why do you go over to that man's house up the block and have him read you and Sue-Sue the comics?"

Max Nix. Dang. I had told her that. "Well, like I said, he gets the Kansas City paper and we get the one from Wichita, and, actually, I'm the one reads those comics to Sue-Sue. And to *him*, mostly. 'Cause he stumbles on the words."

"Is that right?" She got all prissy sounding. "Okay then, why did you make up a story instead of reading the one that was in the book?"

I was so mortified that when I got home, I told Mama I had a whopper of a bellyache and probably wouldn't be able to go to school for a week. Boy, was I mad. I promised myself that I would never walk to school with Margaret again. I would walk with Roberta Grubbs, the colored girl up the block. Even if she wasn't any fun.

As usual, when a day got as cluttered up with bad things as that one had, I stalked off to bed early to sulk. John B. turned up a little while later, and I pulled the covers over my head so he couldn't see my face. John B. could make anybody grin. Except maybe our dad, Thad. I wasn't sure Thad knew how.

"I know you're in there," John B. said, and his strong fingers clutched at my sides through the covers and squeezed a big laugh out of me.

I yelled, "Don't! It's not funny!" I used my flintiest voice on him. But he did it again and dug his chin into my ribs for good measure until I squealed with laughter at the delicious torture. "Stop!" I pleaded. "Stop!"

"Not until you tell me what's wrong," he said.

"All right! All right!" He let up and I told him. "It's not fair," I concluded. "She got a head start."

John B. agreed. "Yeah, those Drummonds are clever, all right. Not sure they fit in here in this backwater town."

He scratched his chin like he had whiskers, then disappeared for a few minutes. He came back with a scuffed and dirty McGuffey reader. The whole back cover was torn off. Some pages were crinkled and wouldn't lay flat, and a few were ripped loose inside when I opened it. "I told them I lost it," John B. explained. "Me and Zeke Wilhite kicked it around the school yard one day just for the fun of it, and I figured I'd catch it worse for doing that than losing it."

"What am I supposed to do with it?"

"Practice! Learn! You're sharp, Emmy. You can figure it out."

Some help that was. Later, Eileen came up to do homework and saw me glowering at a page of Johnny's beat-up reader, puzzling over the scramble of alphabet letters. She sat on the edge of my bed and offered some advice.

"Your tongue should be like the needle on the Victrola and the letters like the tiny bumps in the groove," she explained.

"Huh?"

"Look here." She pointed. "Sound that out. *B* sounds like 'buh' *B—buh*."

"So we should call him John Buh?"

"Dang it, Emmy. Be serious for once. *B—buh*. The *O* sounds like 'oh.' Put them together and they sound like what?" She hesitated a tick. "*Bow*, right? Now you got this last letter here, *Y*. *Wye-ee*. Buh-oh-wyee."

"*Buh-oh-wyee?*"

"Just say it fast. Buh-oh-yee ... boy-ee ... boy!"

"Well, why didn't you just say so?"

"What do you mean, why didn't I *say so*?"

"Why not just say *that* word is boy? B-O-Y."

"Oh! But see, you've got to learn to use your tongue like a needle on a Victrola and sound things out for yourself."

"Sure, Eileen," I said. "Thanks." I meant it. "At least I know one word now."

"Naw, you already know lots of words. You just don't realize."

"That's right, I don't. 'Cause I don't know ANY!"

She left the room and came back with an unopened bar of soap. "What's this?"

"Soap."

"What kind?"

I looked at the label. "Ivory. It floats!"

She pointed to the letters on the package "I-vuh-oh-ree. I-voh-ree. Ivory!"

"Wow!" I had to admit.

Somehow, that gave me confidence. I was excited by the idea and eager to be left alone to sound out some more words for myself.

After a night of practice, some of it under the covers with a flashlight (until Mama took it away from me for laughing out loud at the line, "John must not tear the book"!), I returned to school with a sense of confidence, eager to show Margaret just how well I could read, even if it was only two pages. Only she wasn't in class that day. Or the day after.

I finally asked Mrs. Graham about it. "Is Margaret sick or something?"

"Not that I know of, Emma. She's not in our class anymore, you know. She was promoted to the second grade."

"Don't that beat all!" I complained at recess to Claude Barnett, a *b-o-y* I knew. Claude was a bit of a slug, but he could do impressive tricks on the monkey bars. "That confounded Yankee shows up here out of the blue and gets to skip to second after only going to first for one day! That's not fair!" I pictured Margaret zooming ahead of me in everything. How could she be my best friend if she did?

Claude's front teeth stuck out of his grimy little face like a rabbit's. "Yeah, it's stoopid." On impulse, I invited him to play at my house after school. Only when we got there, all he wanted to do was chase the chickens around inside the fence in our backyard, shrieking as they ran squawking and flapping their useless wings. I couldn't wait for him to go home. So I said, "Hey, Claude, want to see something queer?"

"Queer?"

I dragged him three blocks over to Pecan Street, where he got his first glimpse of Rex chained to the tree in his front yard. It wasn't a moment later Rex tilted his head and made his funny high-pitched yell that sounded like "Ha-pa-pa-pa-pa-pa," something my sister Eileen could mock to perfection.

Only it scared Claude, I think, and he got all offended. "They got a man chained up like a dog!"

"That's so's he won't run away," I explained. "Tolden ya it was queer."

Claude did not seem mollified, so I said, "They sent him away once to the loony bin, you see, only my sister Eileen says he missed his tree so much, he had to come back home." Sue-Sue and I thought that was hilarious. Not Claude. He scowled.

Gosh, there were a lot of fools in Cornucopia to snicker at, Claude being one. Only I didn't find Claude (or Rex) amusing just then. If a slug like this rabbit-toothed *b-o-y* could pity a grown fool chained to a tree, instead of laughing at it, it would only make me sadder. "Claude," I told him, "I'm going home now. You go home, too."

Once Margaret was promoted, I became the star reader in Mrs. Graham's first grade class at South School. The satisfaction I might have taken from this was always dimmed by the pestering knowledge that Margaret was one step ahead of me and moving fast.

Three

*T*had always sat in the middle of us kids at church so he could reach down the back of the pew and thump anyone who giggled or misbehaved. Sue-Sue and I sat on one side of him, Eileen and John B. on the other. Mary Ellen was in the nursery and Mama was always up front in the choir.

I must admit, I'm a talker. Always have been. Sometimes it's just plain hard for me to keep my mouth shut. And on the first Sunday in October, when I saw that snooty Margaret Drummond in a new store-bought dress unexpectedly parading down the center aisle of *our* church with her family, I just had to blurt out to Sue-Sue (in a breathy whisper), "Oh, no! It's Little Miss High and Mighty herself and ... Youch!" The sting of Thad's flick on the back of my neck made my cheeks tingle and the little hairs on my neck and arms stand up.

I looked down at the washed-out pattern of my homemade, hand-me-down dress and fought back tears. I was not under any circumstances going to give my dad or that girl the satisfaction of seeing me cry. I gritted my teeth, lifted my head, and put on a sunny smile to swallow my anger and envy—anger and envy being two things that are generally frowned upon in church. Not that it necessarily stops anyone.

Why is it always so tempting to be naughty in church? Is it the solemn pageantry that goads you? One time, John B. let a belch get away from him. There was a scattering of sympathetic chuckles around us but Thad was furious. No thump on the neck this time. You just knew the strop was coming when we got home.

I watched Mrs. Drummond sit down, a jaunty, fashionable hat perched at an angle atop a beauty-shop hairdo. The Drummond children, Reno, James, Rach, and Margaret, were dressed to the nines, too. It seemed like these people were made of money. Why come to our church then? It didn't have an organ or stained glass windows or a carpet running down the aisle. There were grander churches in nicer neighborhoods. A sigh started in my chest and ended up as a snort when Mr. Drummond came marching up the center aisle in a robe with the rest of the choir, following the minister in the processional as we all stood. I saw Thad's hand coming toward me for the snort and I ducked away. This was bad. The Drummonds had obviously made up their minds to join our church. Which meant I'd have to put up with Margaret on Sunday mornings, too. It wasn't fair. My family was here first. This had been *our church* for as long as I could remember.

My gaze followed Mr. Drummond until he reached the choir bench. His dark, deep-set eyes and sandy-colored hair reminded me so much of Rach. There was a cockiness about him, too. Here he was, in our church for the first time, and you'd have thought he owned the place. It irked me, like the night I slept over to Margaret's house and he insisted on tucking in and kissing everyone, including me, despite my attempts to duck out of his way. My dad never went in for that kind of stuff, and it made my armpits sweat when Mr. Drummond pulled it.

The Drummonds were peculiar in other ways, too. Their house stunk to high heaven of sauerkraut, which they made in a barrel and kept in the pantry. But Mrs. Drummond fixed the best fried potatoes I ever tasted. I sure hadn't minded eating over to their place when Margaret and I were still friends. You hardly ever saw Mr. Drummond around at mealtime. He was usually late. His job with the cement plant was the kind where you got to wear a suit and tie and travel out of town.

He beamed broadly now at his family, lined up like royalty in the pew across the aisle, as we all sang the opening hymn. I made an attempt to follow along with the big words in the hymnal, but I was having a time of it because I couldn't concentrate. I must have scowled pretty good because Mama gave me one of her warm smiles like a gentle nudge. *It's okay.* I guess she figured I was just puzzling over the words.

Sunday school after church was mandatory at Cornucopia Presbyterian, like paying your taxes, and on the day that Margaret arrived, she got lumped in with the rest of us little kids on account of her size. "In God's house," I told her, "there are no skips or free passes." Children out of earshot of adults and off to themselves at church were free to revert to school yard taunts.

Margaret refused to look at me the rest of the morning, which was good, since Sue-Sue and I only pretended to drop the pennies Thad gave us into the Sunday school offering plate. We liked to hang on to ours to buy candy with later. We were heathens, I know, but it had never bothered me before. Not until the sanctimonious Margaret was in the same room. She was spoiling everything.

The whole thing was so upsetting that I spent the following week trying to plot a way to avoid having to see Margaret again at church the following Sunday. But nothing came to me. Instead, I was saved by an accident. (I know what Mr. Freud would say. My mother said it before him. "That was *no* accident!")

You see, there was always so much hubbub at our house on Sunday mornings. John B. had to lead the cow to pasture and the rest of us had to pitch in to help with breakfast and other chores so we could get out the door to church on time. You never missed church after your Saturday night scrub in the tub, even if you were dog-tired as I was on that particular Sunday morning, having read under the covers half the night. It was my turn that day to tote the bedroom thunder mug to the outhouse and empty it. I was hurrying down the stairs, that fragrant bowl sloshing in my hands, as I thought about a way to skip church. And then it just happened. I stumbled, and some of the chamber pot contents slopped onto my Sunday-go-to-meeting outfit. Mama's temper flared. She *shouted*. I was in no condition now to go to church and I could look forward to a switching when she got home. "On the Lord's day?" I said. "But I didn't mean to!" And to think Johnny got away with telling her he'd learned a new line of scripture every week when all he could ever quote was *Jesus wept*. But Mama cooled down after a morning's reflection.

"I know I promised you a switching," she said in a cold voice when she returned. "But I have something else in mind for you instead. I'm very disappointed in what I'm hearing, Emmy. You used to like Margaret Drummond. What happened? What is this silly feud that the two of you have going?"

My explanations fell on deaf ears.

"You know, you're prettier than she is. And you're more graceful. God doesn't hand out all His gifts to just one person. Would you really want to trade?"

God got it all mixed up with the Drummonds, I thought, when he made Rach pretty instead of Margaret. I thought about being as clumsy and as homely as Margaret Drummond with her close-set eyes and pigeon-toed walk, and I whispered, "No."

"Now, the way you've been behaving toward her has got to stop. I don't want any more incidents like the one this morning. And even though this is the Lord's day, as you so pointedly reminded me, you are going out to the well house this afternoon and wash that urine out of your good dress. After that, you're going to go over and apologize to Margaret Drummond."

As soon as Sunday dinner was finished, at a time I'd rather have been out playing with my friends or going off to Grandpa's farm, I plunged that stinking dress in cold sudsy water up to my bony elbows and scrubbed it clean in the gloomy old well house. Then I cranked it through the ringer, which was hard work, but I managed it by picturing Margaret's head going through between the rollers instead.

I'd been happy to hear she was miserable in second grade, shunned as a funny-talking little stranger from out of town. It was no worse than she deserved. And I'd be gosh darned if I was going to go over to her house and eat crow for something she started.

I went over there at half past three under threat of more punishment, but I didn't go to their door. I sat down instead in their yard and put my back against the upwind wall of their outhouse and read a book, figuring Margaret would be along sooner or later.

It was Rach who showed up first. I heard his piddle splatter at the bottom of the stink hole and then the creak of the hinges after it stopped. He must have said something to Margaret as soon as he went back in the house because she was out there a moment later.

"What do you think you're doing?" she asked.

"Reading," I said nonchalantly.

"I can see that. Why are you reading out next to our privy?"

"My mama sent me over to apologize. So there, I did it." I stood up and turned to leave. "That's all."

"Where'd you get that?" She pointed at my book, *The Lost Princess of Oz*.

"Birthday present from my grandma," I said defensively. I felt like I'd been accused of something.

"I didn't know you liked Oz books," Margaret said. "I've never seen that one. Is it good?"

In truth, I was finding it tough sledding, and on impulse I held it out to her. "Why don't you read it? I'm done with it. I was just reading it a second time."

"You sure?"

"Sure," I said. "Just tell your mother we're not fighting anymore so she'll tell my mama and I won't get screamed at again, okay?"

Thus was struck what I thought would be the everlasting truce between Margaret Drummond and me.

Four

Once Margaret and I patched things up—sort of—Mama decided it would be all right to have Margaret's big sister, Reno, come over and baby-sit us on the folks' card night out. None of us ever told Mama what happened at the river the time Reno took us swimming. Perhaps we should have, considering what happened next.

Reno arrived smelling like a whole Sunday school and shooed us out of the parlor the moment Mama and Thad left. It didn't surprise us. She had never seemed particularly keen on being around little kids, shunning even Margaret and baby Alice in her own family. So we occupied ourselves as though she wasn't there, until the doorbell rang.

I ran to answer it, loving the novelty of the new electric bell in our house. There stood a man in a raffish suit, the type that door-to-door salesmen wore, and before I could say, "Sorry, we ain't buyin' any," he tipped his hat and said, "Is Miss Drummond here?"

"Charlie!" I heard Reno call as she came up behind me and pushed me out of the way. "Come in, come in!" She giggled and showed him into the parlor, where Charlie fished into his pocket to produce a couple of big, shiny quarters. "Y'all go buy yourselves ice cream, you kids," he said. "And don't come back in the house to eat it neither. You hear me? It's too messy. Y'all play in the yard 'til Reno calls you in. Savvy?"

We all knew this was no time to go for ice cream. With Charlie's quarters safely tucked into John B. and Eileen's pockets, we could buy cones any time we wanted. What was important now was to see what was going to happen next between Reno and a stranger she had just invited into our house. So we sashayed back and forth past the parlor door, looking busy, but trying to watch. Was this Charlie guy really Reno's boyfriend? A grown man?

Charlie glowered and quickly put an end to our spying. He called us together and said, "I gave y'all money for ice cream. Now go on! Scram!" He swept the back of his hand at us.

Out the front door we went, pretending to head off toward town, but circling back around the block at Second Street to cut through at the Drummonds'. I held Sue-Sue's hand as we leapt across the little creek that separated our yards. We worked our way around the side of the house with John B. and Eileen in the lead, moving as quietly as we could. Then my brother signaled me over to him and hoisted me up on his shoulders. I bounced and rocked up there as he awkwardly moved over to the parlor window.

"What are they doin'?" John B. whispered.

"Can't see nothing," I whispered back. "The shades is pulled. Let's try the porch."

It took some time, but Eileen and I slowly scooted into a position where we could see them on the divan, kissing. "Hoo, boy!" Eileen whispered. "Did you *ever* ...?" Reno had taken her shirt off. I had never seen a man touch a girl's breast before or seen a girl stick her hand down the front of a man's pants, and I was wondering why they would, since they were both moaning like they were in agony. My throat tightened watching them and a warm, tingly feeling spread though my belly and between my legs. Eileen scooted away giggling after a time so John B. could have a turn, but I couldn't take my eyes off of them. Suddenly, Reno looked my way and I ducked. I stayed down a few seconds before stealing another peek, and by then, Reno was pushing Charlie off her and covering her breasts.

Charlie turned now and saw me. He jumped up, cussing. He went for the door and came after us. We ran screaming and laughing in four different directions, and when I looked back, I could see he wasn't chasing me or John B. or Eileen. He was going after the smallest and slowest, Sue-Sue, who promptly tripped and fell.

He got to her and snatched her up. Sue-Sue squealed like a pig headed for slaughter. "You little snoop!" he shouted. "What do you brats think you're doing?" He shook her like a rag doll. Sue-Sue stopped squealing and her eyes got big as saucers. "I'm going to teach you a lesson you won't soon forget!" Charlie shouted. Sue-Sue started squealing again as this stranger kneeled down and threw her over his leg, like he was fixing to paddle her scrawny behind. It was all so unfair. Sue-Sue didn't care about Reno and Charlie. She'd pleaded with us to go for the ice cream cones. I watched as she squirmed and fought him. He spanked her rear end but I couldn't will myself to go to her rescue. My skin turned all prickly under my shirt.

From around the corner of the house, John B. came running with Mama's garden shovel in his hands, gripping it high over his shoulder like a baseball bat. He lifted it in a swinging arc while he was running full tilt and still two or three strides away. Then he brought the flat blade of the shovel around and connected it full swing with the back of Charlie's noggin, and it made a sound like a bell in the courthouse tower had gone off. I was startled to see Charlie topple like a sack of potatoes. Had John B. killed him? From the upstairs of our house, Mary Ellen began crying in her crib. She'd been left there by Eileen when the excitement began. And between the sound of Mary Ellen's cries and the clang of that shovel, the fun drained out of the escapade.

"Hey!" Reno called. She was standing on the porch now, tucking in her blouse. "What do you think you're doing?" John B. threw down the shovel, scooped up Sue-Sue and ran toward the back of the house. He needn't have hurried to get away from Reno because she ran directly to Charlie, who was still crumpled on the ground. It took a moment but he came around and staggered to his feet, stumbling in the direction of the porch, where he sat down on the steps and squeezed his temples between his palms. Reno put an arm around him.

"Are you all right, Charlie?"

"No thanks to you, you little tart," he said, shrugging her off. "Get my damned hat and coat. I'm leaving!"

Mary Ellen wailed upstairs as Reno fetched Charlie's hat. Reno watched Charlie walk away before turning her angry attention onto Eileen and me. By then, we were the only two standing in the yard.

"Get over here," Reno ordered us. What a strange and frightening creature she was. It had excited me in a dreamy way to see what she was doing with Charlie, but I was upset and scared of her now, and Mary Ellen's cries were getting more insistent. How could Reno not go and calm her?

I worried about John B., too, and the trouble he might be in for what he'd done. Was Charlie going to the police right now? I took a step toward Reno, but Eileen grabbed my arm and shook her head. John B. and Sue-Sue had yet to come out of hiding and the evening was still being disturbed by Mary Ellen's cries. When we didn't move, Reno sprinted across the grass toward us. Eileen pushed me in one direction like a signal and took off the other way around the house. I stood there frozen a second as Reno closed in on me, her painted nails out like bloody claws. At the last opportunity, I made a feint in one direction and took off in the other, dodging her. As fast as I could I ran zigzagging away from this madwoman cussing at my heels. Eileen and I met up again in back—my sister out in front—and we leapt the little creek. Reno shouted something. The sound of her voice was further back now. I stopped running, and turned to look. She stood at the edge of the creek, hesitating. I felt she would not cross and follow if I went to her house. So I made a move that way and Reno took off and ran north.

Mama and Thad came home at the usual time that night and found us all over at the Drummonds playing Parcheesi, refugees in the sauerkraut odor zone. Mary Ellen was asleep on the Drummonds' carpet, wrapped in a blanket. Later, I heard from Margaret that her mother waited on Reno's bed that night for her daughter to return, and confronted her when Reno snuck into the house in the wee hours. There was a lot more to the story than that, but I wouldn't learn about it for some time to come.

Five

*T*he week after Thanksgiving, Margaret and I began to chatter incessantly about Santa Claus and candy canes and extravagant presents we imagined with our names on them under the tree. Margaret started wishing hard for a bicycle one morning on the way to school that week, and I noticed Roberta Grubbs, who was walking with us, got very quiet. So I told Margaret she should hush up about Christmas for once.

Anyone with eyes could see Roberta's winter coat was frayed and one sleeve mended and that the buttons didn't all match. I would have gladly given her the old thing off my back if it wasn't destined to be handed down to Sue-Sue when I was done with it. Roberta's father had two jobs. He was a janitor at the cement plant six days a week and a night watchman there on weekends. They were the only Negro family in the neighborhood.

That afternoon when Margaret and I went up to my room to cut pictures of the people out of an old Sears and Sawbuck catalog for paper dolls, I put the issue to her.

"We need to get Roberta something for Christmas," I told her. "Ain't right that Sandy Claws don't stop at the coloreds' houses."

"Who told you that?" She stopped cutting around a tall, smiling, blond-haired woman in a long apron holding a dishtowel.

"Thad. He takes a box of our old stuff over to Grubbses' every year about now. He says Sandy Claws don't stop there 'cause the jolly old elf is white and Grubbses ain't."

"Ain't isn't a word, Emma."

23

"Double-dog dang it, Margaret, stop changing the subject."

"Okay, but what would we get her anyway?"

"How 'bout a slingshot?"

"What? A slingshot!" Margaret scrunched up her already pinched-up face and shot out her weak chin. "How we gonna do that?"

"We could write to Sandy Claws and ask him for one, like it was for us, only we'd take it over to Roberta instead." Margaret got a funny look on her face like I'd said that cows could fly. I thought she probably had a point. So I said, "Yeah, you're right. You can't fool the jolly old elf. How 'bout we buy her a pack of gum instead?"

She went back to cutting. "You got the money?" She pushed her bumpy tongue out the corner of her mouth as she cut around the catalog figure's tiny feet.

"Do *I* have it? You're the one gets an allowance."

"Yeah, but I'm saving up to get something special for Rach."

Saving up. Now there was an idea. Margaret was using her pointy head. *Saving up.* I'd never considered that. Whenever I had a penny in my pocket, I spent it before night fell. I could try to save the offering penny Thad gave me each week, since I only bought candy with it anyway. If I managed to save them all for a month, I'd have almost enough to buy Roberta a pack of gum by Christmas. "Margaret, you're a genius!"

"What?" She wasn't following.

"Oh sure, I'll have to flamboozle Sue-Sue somehow," I said, paying no mind to Margaret's pinched-up face. "Get her to pitch in. But … better to give than receive. Isn't that what they tell us in Sunday school?"

"*What* are you talking about?"

"The gum, silly. Why aren't you paying attention?"

Thad's old household slippers had nearly fifteen years of foot odor trapped in their dark recesses. To be in the same room with him when he had them on was enough to make your eyes water. Fortunately, my dad usually smoked a cigar when he wore them, which helped to cut the smell. The Sunday afternoon I snuck into Mama and Thad's room with my stolen offering penny in my hand, unfortunately, my nose didn't have that cigar to run interference. The stink of those dang slippers came right through the closed closet door and flew like a wasp up my sensitive nose. It was like something had died.

I pinched my nostrils tight and raced through the room, my eyes working the nooks and crannies like a bug, hoping for a good place to hide the penny. I settled on a spot behind a radiator leg that fell into a natural shadow. Why not hide it in my room, you ask? Well, I thought if I stashed the loot in Mama and Thad's room, there'd be less chance I'd go for it in a weak moment to buy candy. Plus, if the folks found it, they'd think one of them dropped it. In my room, a stray penny would raise questions.

On my way out, I was tempted to grab Thad's slippers from the closet, run them to the biffy out back and drop them down the stink hole. Be done with that awful smell forever. But Thad would ferret out the culprit, and I would feel the strop across my backside, holiday season or no holiday season. Besides, it might spoil Thad's holiday mood.

Christmas was the one time of year he was not so gruff and grouchy. In fact, he'd get as excited as a kid and practically as giddy. He'd even wiggle his ears. It was a sideshow trick, those big ears wobbling while the rest of that hard face was set in stone. He'd do it for us on Christmas morning after a couple glasses of eggnog. Eileen once told me that John B. could wiggle his ears, too, but he refused to because he didn't want to be like Thad.

And who'd want to be Thad with his sinister sunken cheeks, leathery skin, and dark eyes? He like to never smiled. Mama smiled enough for both of them. It would be years before I understood that my father was unhappy, that he was a man with big plans that could not materialize. Instead of arriving at the day when he could buy a ranch out West and raise prize steers, he was stuck like a bug on flypaper supervising Mr. Osborne's lumberyard.

"It's a big job," Mama told us. "Your dad has his hands full."

I managed to save four cents for Roberta's gum real quick, thanks to John B. and Eileen, who each chipped in a penny when they got wind of what I was up to. As soon as I had all four pennies, I ran to the store and bought a pack of Juicy Fruit Gum before I could change my mind. Its sweet fragrance leaked out of my pocket and later bloomed in my underwear drawer, where I hid it. That scent made my stomach rumble. Before long, it was about all I could think about. I didn't want to give in to temptation, but I didn't want to give Roberta her present too early either. Willpower, I told myself.

Then something came along that took my mind off it completely.

Three days before Christmas 1922, at the start of our school holiday break, my baby sister, Mary Ellen, had a seizure. I didn't understand what had happened, but I could read in Mama's face that something was seriously wrong. Christmas cookies sat half finished in the kitchen. "Mary Ellen is very sick," Mama said, "and we need to be quiet so she can rest. Mrs. Woods is up with her now."

Inez Woods, who was my friend Dema's mother from up the street, stayed the night with Mary Ellen. Mrs. Woods was meticulous and efficient, her hair drawn up tight in some secret sort of way. I suspect she'd been a nurse at one time, because she seemed to know how to handle it when my sister went into a spasm. She would immediately insert a spoon into her tiny mouth. "Why's she doing that?" I asked Mama.

"So she won't swallow her tongue," Mama said. I'll tell you, that scared me, and the sound of little Mary Ellen's crying jags chased away my excitement about the coming of Christmas and Santa Claus.

Mary Ellen had only just learned to sit up and take in all the activity around her, and we had gone to any length to coax a gurgling laugh out of her little, pink, bowlike mouth. Sue-Sue and I liked to take her for rides in the old wicker baby buggy, strapping a bonnet on her and bundling her little body up in a wool shawl against the cold. Eileen liked to feed her solid food in her high chair and laugh when she spit out what she didn't like.

But now she'd gone back to being a crying baby, and you could tell this time she was miserable.

The seizures kept on, and on the day before Christmas, Grandma Bethany, who liked to be called Thaney, drove in from the farm with Grandpa Joseph, whom we called Pa Joesy. They offered to help Mama take care of the house and the baby. John B. gave up his room to give our grandparents a bed, and he moved to the cellar to sleep on a cot next to the furnace with all its creepy pipes jutting out every which way from a bulging white firebox. I don't know how he did it. It was like a room in hell with a white octopus for a roommate, but Johnny smiled and said, "Hey, it's the Ritz—for spiders!"

Despite our sagging spirits, we strung popcorn and cranberries and a bit of tinsel on our tree that year. Electricity was still new to the house. So we had no lights for the tree, and Mama refused to let us use candles. After we placed a few ornaments here and there, our tree looked beautiful. It smelled wonderfully fresh indoors. Trimming the tree was usually a joyous time, but Thad refused to lend a hand that year and Mama was distracted. Preparing for the holidays ran against everyone's mood, but the rest of us pressed on without Thad. John B., Eileen and I tried to help Mama put her troubles aside, but then Mary Ellen would make herself heard from upstairs, and Mama would go running. It was an awful soup of feelings.

The folks traditionally waited until the night before Christmas to do their shopping, and did not return until we were asleep so they wouldn't have to wrap or hide anything. Thaney was around that year, and she wouldn't cotton any nonsense. So Johnny and Eileen didn't get into one of their customary Christmas Eve donnybrooks. In a way, I missed it, another tradition gone missing, even though their arguments and wrestling matches usually scared the heck out of me and Sue-Sue.

On Christmas morning, I was so excited I ran downstairs, forgetting about Mary Ellen. But the air rushed out of me when I discovered a lump of coal in the bottom of my limp, empty stocking. Even Mama looked shocked. She shot a hard look at Thad, who growled, "I guess that's what girls get who steal money from church offering plates."

The dam on my sorrows and fears burst. I ran shrieking from the room, bounded up the stairs to my room, where I grabbed that pack of gum for Roberta from my underwear drawer, tore it open and wadded all five pieces into my mouth. I worked them around with my dry tongue until I thought I would choke. Then I spit it all on the floor, crawled under the bed and cried.

Only then did I remember about Mary Ellen's troubles and cry harder at my foolishness. I buried my face in my arms and asked God what kind of birthday party He thought He was throwing for his son, Jesus.

Hours later, after I'd fallen asleep, Mama came up, knelt down next to the bed and spoke quietly to me. "Emmy, come out of there now. Our dinner's ready and everybody has gathered around the table."

"I'm never coming out," I vowed.

Mama said, "John B. told me what you were trying to do, and that was a very nice thing. But you should have asked one of us to help instead of going about it in a sneaky way." She paused. "Anyway, I think Santa really wanted you to have this."

She pushed a doll that I had been hoping for under the bed.

I cried again at the sight of it, "I don't want a present," I whined. "It's not really Christmas, not with Mary Ellen so sick. All I want this year is for her to get better."

Mama's strong arms reached under the bed and drew me out into her warm embrace. Her face was wet with salty tears, and her voice turned husky. "Your lips to God's ear, Emmy."

Six

O n a cold day that February when I was home from school
nursing one of my miserable earaches, my baby sister died in
the room across the hall. Thaney, ramrod stiff and distant,
brought me the news. "The Lord has seen fit," she said. I was glad
she made no move to hug me, because I would have only had to push
her away.

Even after all the seizures and wailing, I was shocked. I'd been
sure Mary Ellen would pull through. Her suffering had been horrid,
but her death felt absolutely cruel. How could such a precious, young
life be stolen away? Death was for old people, like Thaney. I sank into
a pit of misery and cried until my pillow was wet.

A mourning wreath went up on our front door, and there was a
funeral at our house two long days later. Folks gathered around the
tiny white coffin in our parlor. Thad gently blew warm cigar smoke
into my aching ear and stuffed it with cotton before we started. It
gave some temporary relief so I could help set up dining room chairs
and card table chairs and kitchen chairs and the old rocking chair
with worn arms from the folks' bedroom. Thaney would sit in it.
John B. dragged up a stained stool from the basement that Mama
covered with a sheet for Sue-Sue. Still, many people had to stand
when everyone arrived.

Mama made me look at Mary Ellen in the box before it started.
"You need to say your good-byes now," she said. "It's the last time
you'll see her." I couldn't bear it. Her skin was the color of ashes, and
there were no wiggles left in her. The rigid stillness of her little body

scared me. What was this spirit we had that could be here one minute and gone the next?

We dressed up in our Sunday finest and clung to each other like survivors on a raft as we sat before Mary Ellen's coffin. I held Sue-Sue close on my lap and John B. kept a firm grip on my shoulder and his other arm around Eileen. You could feel the strength of sympathy in hugs from Grandma and Grandpa Hainline, who drove over from El Dorado Springs. I had never seen them so grim. Grandma's wrinkled mouth was a quivering line. Shirttail relatives arrived at our door from distant places to pat our backs and muss our hair.

For the service, Ada Jensen, the soloist from our church, sang "The Old Rugged Cross," accompanied on our piano by Nora Demet, who liked to roll the chords for flourish. Her playing always made Old Man Davidson cry in church, which used to make us laugh. But hearing the roll of the chords put a lump in my throat, and I felt like I might owe Old Man Davidson an apology. Margaret's dad sang a duet of "Nearer My God to Thee" with Mrs. Jensen that made Mama's spine go soft. Thad had to prop her up. Her hair, jet-black the week before, began turning milky white almost overnight.

"Mary Ellen has gone to be with God, her maker," our preacher, Pastor Richeson, said in his rich, mellifluous voice. "She was such a sweet, adorable baby. She's probably sitting on God's lap right now." For some reason, I took comfort in that idea, I'm not sure why. I've sometimes thought how startlingly old she would be today if she had lived, and I've wondered what kind of person she would have turned out to be. We had but a few short months to discover what we could about her, and all that was left after that was a small tombstone and memories.

I didn't cry once during the solemn proceedings. I must have been cried out by then, but I would go on moping for months afterward. The funeral seemed to go on and on, and everything—the day, the room, the mourners—began to feel peculiar to me, people bowing their heads respectfully over a tiny baby who had never spoken a word. They didn't really know her. They hadn't held her in their arms like we had or heard her tiny cries. What were they doing here making our parlor insufferably hot? Mary Ellen was ours and ours alone, and now she was gone.

Mama told me at the last minute that it would be a mistake for me to go to the cemetery in the frigid February air with my earache, so I had to stay behind with Thaney, who had me lie down so she could pour warm olive oil into my ear. It created a sound like I'd gone swimming. "You watch, this will clear it right up," she said. But it didn't. The pain persisted, just as Mary Ellen's seizures had.

For a while, everything safe about my world vanished. Bad things had been cascading down for weeks, as unstoppable as the bitter wind howling at our windows, a thief trying to break in. I was suddenly frightened. Could my spirit desert my body without warning too? Was there a little white box and a graveyard hole in my future? I said, "Grandma Thaney, can you die of an earache?"

"No, missy," she replied, as if I had said something funny. "You'd be the first."

You could see where Thad got his warmth.

Things were not the same for a long time after Mary Ellen died. For one thing, Pa Joesy went back to the farm and left Thaney behind to keep an eye on Thad and Mama and us kids. Little did we know that this was a preview of things to come, that Pa Joesy's health was already starting to fail.

All we knew was that it was unpleasant having Thaney in the house. She offered to help with the chores, but when we saw her drop her false teeth into the dishpan to scrub them before she started in on the dinner plates, we wanted to puke. We made sure she never got her old lunch hooks on our dirty dishes again.

Thaney was a meddler, too, and she treated Margaret rudely on her visits to the house. She didn't care for the Drummonds or their "woods colt," as she called little Alice. "That family's not right," she insisted, without saying why. I decided Thaney was stuck up. She liked to say proudly that she was "a Methodist *and* a Republican." One of us kids had to accompany her to church every week. We took turns. John B. didn't mind because it got him out of Sunday school, but I felt like an intruder being dragged into that place. Some of that Methodist worship was like ours, but the music and prayers were all different, even the Lord's Prayer. I tried to sing the hymns, but I didn't know the words, and I couldn't keep up with what was printed in the hymnal. So I tried humming, guessing what note was coming next, until I felt I had to stop because people were shooting me funny looks.

Some Sundays we sat next to Mr. Osborne, who owned the lumberyard where Thad worked, or behind Tommy Bern and his gray-haired druggist father. There were a lot of big shots in that church, and you could tell that Thaney was completely unaware that she didn't fit in, that she was a plain, old farmer's wife in a homemade dress and a straw bonnet with velvet roses that was ten years out of date.

I'm pretty sure Thaney didn't care for my Negro friend Roberta either, only Roberta seldom came around. When I saw her right after Christmas, I could not look her in the eye, not after chewing up her gift and spitting it out. I felt guiltier still when Roberta's mother handed us apples to eat on the way to school the morning after Mary Ellen's funeral. "Heard about yo little sister," Mrs. Grubbs said. "Gone to God, child. Gone to God."

"I never knowed nobody who died before, Roberta," I said as we walked. I tried to sound like it was okay with me now, like the way the adults spoke about it, but it was hard since I was fresh from fighting back tears after Mrs. Grubbs gave me that apple. I said to Roberta, "That funeral gave me the heebie-jeebies."

Roberta said, "Had a sister die, too. She weren't but two year old, neither."

I realized then that I knew next to nothing about Roberta's family, that they kept entirely to themselves and didn't entertain the likes of us at their place. I asked, "Wha'd she die of?"

"Flu, I s'pose."

We walked on in silence, but I could see from Margaret's expression that she was surprised, too. After a moment, Margaret asked, "What was her name?"

"'Liss-peth."

And so we continued on to school on that cold bright February morning, nobody saying another word, the sound of the last two syllables rattling around in our brains, along with images of babies who had vanished and gone to live with God.

Seven

We were eager to put a depressing winter behind us the day spring arrived on a warm westerly breeze. So we slung an old rope over the branch of a stately oak along the Neosho River and launched ourselves out into the water.

John B. and Rach were daredevils, flipping and twisting in the air, each trying to outdo the other's acrobatics. Eileen briefly joined in the competition before retiring to the shore, where she bent and stretched and held one hand to her lower back. She finally lay down with a groan on a towel alongside Margaret, who scarcely glanced up from the book in her lap.

I was content with flying once off the rope, going high above the water and dropping like a stone with a cannonball splash. I was surprised at how much that stung and how cold the water was, an icy reminder of the winter just suffered. I got out fast and hurried up the riverbank to join Margaret and Eileen in the sun, and I wrapped my blue gooseflesh tightly in a towel to stop a convulsive burst of shivers. Then I lay back to stare up at the budding April trees shimmering in the intense afternoon sun.

But I couldn't take my eyes off John B. and Rach's antics for long. More than once that summer when I saw Rach do some reckless trick or other, I wondered what it would be like to kiss a boy. That day on the riverbank, I watched as he immodestly pulled off his undershirt, exposing the line of his flexing shoulders and upper arms when he gripped the rope and swung out over the water. Each time he climbed out of the river, his swimsuit clung to his buttocks and made me want to giggle. Rach glanced over at Eileen from time to time, but she would pop an eye open only if she thought he wasn't looking.

A noisy truck rumbled across the bridge high above in the distance, the growling sound of it amplified in the hollow of the river. We paused to watch black smoke puff into the blue sky as it passed, and I felt a sudden itch to get moving.

"Want to go explore the ditch?" I asked Margaret, trying to pry her loose from her reading. "Have you seen all those big pipes? We could go crawling through 'em!"

"I have to be home for supper shortly," Margaret said, never taking her eyes off the page. "And I don't want to crawl through a dirty sewer pipe in the meantime."

"Hey," I said, "it's not like they been used, you know. Jeez Louise."

I wondered if I could convince Eileen or John B. to come along instead. The workmen had begun digging up the street just west of our house. We would have to go around the hole on our way home for supper later, and when we did, I looked in at the two colors of dirt—darker on top and lighter on the bottom—and asked John B., "You want to come back later and explore?"

John B. loved tunnels. The previous summer, he had discovered an animal hole along the riverbank and we took turns crawling into it on our bellies. It was filled with spiders and roots, one of which I mistook for a snake and clambered back out of there as fast as I could, screaming.

"Rach and me are playing keepers marbles later," Johnny said. "Besides, I already seen it with Zeke."

Eileen turned me down, too. "I'm baking with Mama tonight. What about Sue-Sue?"

"Aw, she's too little," I said, feeling deflated.

I'd been wanting to explore that ditch for a week, so I decided to go by myself at twilight. There were several children clambering on a silent steam shovel and on the stacks of heavy pipe when I got there. Still more were down in the ditch that the workers had abandoned for the night. I didn't know any of them. One older boy had planted himself squarely behind the controls of the shovel and was pulling on its dead levers. It looked like fun. In the ditch, disputes broke out over who was king of the tunnel and some of the children looked big.

I backed away disappointed and turned to go home. Then I saw a tall pile of dirt up the block where a connecting street was also being dug up. There was no steam shovel at this one to act as a magnet. I ran over to have a look just as three boys climbed out of the ditch. I scooted in behind the pile of dirt, out of view. I didn't want anything to do with them.

"That's no fun," I heard one of them say. "Let's go back to the other one."

I slipped in the loose soil when I finally slid down the embankment, and the rocks in the dirt skinned my elbow and hand. But I pressed on after I'd spit on the red, raw skin, and I made my way into a much larger concrete pipe that was tall enough for me to stand inside. Off in the distance, light was pouring into the pipe through an opening, and I decided to walk that far just to experience the enclosure of the manmade cave. I got to the manhole just as a boy scrambled down a ladder from the street, startling me.

"Hey!" I shouted.

He was a North Side boy my age I'd seen before on the town square with his family at band concerts. I remembered his red hair, his freckles, and the smile you couldn't trust.

"I'm going to fuck you," he said. His eyes were green and demented.

He scared me. I didn't know what his strange word meant. Only it sounded like a threat. I felt cornered. The boy had landed in the pipe between me and the opening I'd come through. There was nothing but blackness the other direction.

"You're not doing *nothing*," I replied, and I turned on him and made a fist with my left hand, holding it high with my elbow bent, the way John B. had showed me. "Show a guy that," he said, "and then smack him a good one with this hand." Meaning my right. That was Johnny's advice. The red-headed boy leaned back out of reach when

I raised my fist, but he kept on talking. What he said next sounded so preposterous that I thought it must be another Sandy Claws yarn like the one I'd fallen for until the lump of coal in my Christmas stocking prompted Margaret to spill the beans about Santa. What a bunch of hooey!

"I'm going to stick my man thing in your girl thing. Then you'll have a baby." The green-eyed creep was acting like a know-it-all.

"Shut up!" I said. I couldn't think of anything else to say. I was at a loss. I didn't know what a "girl thing" was. And I didn't want a baby. Once I'd seen John B.'s boy thing when I was little and wondered why I didn't have one like it. I even felt around down there to see if I'd missed something, and I figured mine must be stuck up inside me and ready to pop out at any minute. But it never did, and I hardly gave it another thought until right then in that shadowy sewer. I decided not to sucker punch this creep. Instead, I ran right at him and pushed him down. Then I ran back down the pipe.

But I could not get my thoughts away from those disgusting ideas. It was like spoiled, spilt milk tainting everything for days with its stink. Was it true? Did people really do that to make babies? Had Thad and Mama? It was unimaginable. But in the bathroom that night, I checked and found that I might have a girl thing. It was like my very own tunnel I hadn't known was there. Did that make it true?

John B. seemed surprised to see me early the next morning as he led our cow out of the barn to take her to pasture at the vacant lot Thad leased near town. I asked to tag along, and John B. said, "Not walking with your friends this morning?"

I put my hand up on Tallulah's rump and felt the awkward pull and yaw of her muscles as she strolled down the street. "Naw," I said. The cowbell clanked softly as the old gal trudged along. The ripe, dewy smell of the spring morning was spiked with the stink of cow haunches.

"Something eatin' you?" John B. wanted to know.

Never could put anything past him. "John B., is it okay if I ask you somethin'?"

"Sure."

So I told him what the boy had said, choosing my words a little differently.

"Birds and the bees," John B. replied, and shook his head when I had finished. There was color in his cheeks and his forehead was pinched as he made an effort to fuss with the rope around Tallulah's neck.

"You mean it's true?"

"Facts of life," he said, still not looking at me. "Ask Mom, okay?"

"But I can't! How could I show my face if I tried? Did you talk to Thad about it?"

"Huh-uh. Naw, Zeke told me. He had a little pamphlet like." Johnny turned toward me. "Look, Emmy, try to understand. It's just natural. Like when Thad rents a bull to spend time with Tallulah here and in the spring we have the calf."

My God, even our cow did it? I was dumbstruck.

"Listen," John B. said, "don't worry about it. You're too young to be thinking about that stuff. Just pretend like you never heard it. You'll be okay."

Pretend I hadn't heard it? Be okay? Not in a million years. But John B. made it sound like he was ending our discussion, so I said, "Okay. Sure."

That summer, Rach pledged his undying love to Eileen and told her he would marry her some day. I couldn't believe how angry that made me with Eileen, until I thought about them pushing their privates together to make a baby in some sewer someplace, and I decided to spend less time hanging around with my sister and Rach. I also vowed I would never let a boy touch me that way. No, sir.

Eight

*T*he neighbor us kids called Max Nix never shifted his Model T Ford out of second gear when he drove it around town. You could hear that old car grinding up the street from three blocks away, picking up speed, then slowing down, then picking up speed, then slowing down. Even as little kids, we knew what an awful driver he was. When he pulled alongside Sue-Sue and me on Bridge Street one spring afternoon, bouncing over the curb to come to a stop, I was so mortified, I prayed I could become invisible on the spot.

"Get in, *meine Kinder.*" He smiled a lopsided smile. "I geebt you the ride."

Mama had sent Sue-Sue and me to the grocery store for a sack of flour, and it was starting to get heavy. We had stopped and set it down on the sidewalk so I could waggle my arms. Sue-Sue said, "I told you we should bring the baby buggy."

"Nuh-uh," I said, under my breath. I never wanted to touch Mary Ellen's rickety, old baby carriage ever again. I cupped my hand at the edge of my mouth and said, "We're walking home, got it?"

It was okay to read the funny papers with Max Nix when it was just us in his front room on Sundays, but I had no wish to be seen riding around with him in that Tin Lizzie. Max opened the passenger door. "Come, come. You go. I take."

"No! Thanks, anyway. We better be getting along now." I picked up the sack. Max Nix adopted a hurt look. I said in my cheeriest voice, "See you on Sunday, okay? See what happens to those Katzenjammer Kids?"

He brightened some. "Ja, ja, Katzenjammer. Those rascals!"
Then his smile faded and he gave us the eye. "Vy you say no? Zack
iz hard, yah?"

Hard, yes, but nothing compared to the humiliation of being
seen riding around in Max's Model T. Then, in an instant, I realized
how much it could annoy Thad if he saw us with Max Nix, and how
Mama would have to defend us since we were running her errand. So
I changed my mind on the spot.

"Okay, then. We'll come with you," I said, ignoring Sue-Sue's
look. I was angry with Thad for my Christmas lump of coal. He never
admitted it was his idea, of course, but it was. "Santa Claus knows
when you been naughty," he said. He never admitted how unfair he'd
been either, how he hadn't bothered to check the facts.

Max patted Sue-Sue's behind as she crawled over the seat into
the back. He couldn't ever seem to keep his hands off her. I was
surprised that Sue-Sue didn't mind, even when Max insisted she sit
on his lap and he gave her little hugs as we laughed at things we read
in the comics. Max smiled and clamped his hat down on his round
bald head now, and off we lurched, bounding off the curb and down
the street in herky-jerky fashion. Soon Max's eyes were on the road
and Sue-Sue and I covered our mouths and giggled. Only it didn't
take long for my plan to go awry. Instead of Thad seeing us, two boys
from school came running out from a backyard to watch us careen
down the street. I grabbed Sue-Sue and pulled her down onto the
floor of the Model T, where we stayed until we were safely in front of
our house. Then we jumped up, let ourselves out, and fled, shouting,
"Thanks for the ride!"

Unfortunately, Thad was not around, and as far as I know, he
never found out.

That afternoon, I told Margaret what we'd done when she
wandered over to watch Sue-Sue and me try to catch crawdads and
frogs in the creek between our houses.

Sue-Sue realized I would start talking to Margaret now and
lost interest in the fishing. As soon as she went back in the house,
Margaret blurted out the most surprising news.

"My mother's marrying Reno off," she said.

"Marrying her off?" *Could your mother do that?* I exclaimed, "But she's sixteen! How can she get married and still go to school?"

"She's not. She's quitting school." Margaret shook her head and said bitterly, "She never did very well anyway."

I couldn't believe my ears. Reno, quitting school and getting married! Dangnation! "Can your mother really make her do it?"

"I guess."

A breeze rattled the leaves in the maple above us. I lay back in the grass and looked up at the strong, arching limbs. This was news. A mother making her daughter get married. And I thought the worst parents could do to you was whip you and send you to bed without supper. Margaret jumped over the creek and sat down beside me. I said, "So is it that guy who came to our house? What's his name, Charlie?"

"No, not him. Somebody else. Some friend of my dad's. He looks like a bull."

I thought of the bull Thad hired for Tallulah and didn't like the picture that came into my head of Reno and some guy who looked like a bull. I said with emphasis, "I'm never getting married."

"What?" Margaret lay down next to me and stared up too. "Why not?"

"Because. I'm never going to do that, you know, that whatever it is. That's why."

"Why do you always talk in riddles?"

I got up and grabbed Margaret's arm. "Come on."

"Where we going?"

I led her into our barn, which stood behind our old house from its farming days. The barn was home to Tallulah and the Saxon now. Margaret followed me up the splintery ladder into the hayloft.

"What are we doing?" she wanted to know.

"Just give me a hand here." We pulled some hay bales together in a makeshift wall and scooted in behind it. After I'd peeked back over to be sure we weren't followed, I said, "Margaret, what do you know about this facts-of-life business?"

She made a face like somebody caught in a lie before she even told it. "Nothing."

"Nothing? Don't give me that. You know. Now tell me, what's this thing married people do to make babies?"

She sighed. "Why you askin' me that?"

I could have tried my sister, Eileen, of course, but where would she have heard anything, I wondered? Margaret's sister, Reno, on the other hand, was much older. "Because I don't get the whole shebang," I said. "That's why. It's too strange." I told her what the little red-headed creep from the North Side had said to me. She didn't act the least bit surprised.

After a moment she said, "My mother says it's not entirely unpleasant."

Her mother? "Your *mother* talked to you about it?" I asked. I couldn't believe it. Her mother told her something like that when mine hadn't even hinted at a thing! Again, Margaret looked as if she'd let something slip. I said, "Come on, you talked to Reno, too, didn't you?"

This appeared to make Margaret more nervous. She waited a tick and giggled. "Reno says it's like sticking your finger into an electrical socket. Everything comes on at once and the juice really starts flowing."

I said "Eeew!" and giggled without knowing why. Mama had warned us about sticking anything into one of our new sockets. It could kill you, she said. I was staring down at my toes, so I wiggled them. "Margaret, your family is strange, you know?" I wished I hadn't said it after I heard it come out. So I said, "I need to find out more about this facts-of-life stuff so I can decide whether to run off and join a circus before my folks marry me off to someone who looks like a bull."

Margaret laughed at that. "But you can't walk a tightrope or tame tigers!"

"I know. What's it matter? I can sell popcorn, can't I?" After a bit, I fixed my eye on her. "So tell me, what the heck's a *girl thing*?"

I got invited to supper that night at the Drummonds'. Reno didn't seem very happy for a bride-to-be. When baby Alice fussed and pushed her tiny spoon away, Reno threw it down in the bowl of warm cereal and screamed at the poor little thing. "Shut up, you little snot!" Then, before anyone could stop her, she was out the front door with a bang. Mrs. Drummond's delicious fried potatoes turned cold on my plate.

"Let her go, John," Mrs. Drummond said, when her husband started to get up.

He gave a half shrug, hung one arm over the back of his chair and settled his silverware on his plate. I glanced from the cleft in his chin to Rach's plain chin. Rach sat across from me. He was off someplace in thought. Margaret, too, lowered her head, almost like she was praying.

"Supper is delicious, Mrs. Drummond," I said so they'd remember I was there. I thought maybe it might cheer her up, too.

None of us neighbor kids would be invited to Reno's wedding, which only fueled the curiosity. But all that was eclipsed for me by something Margaret told me when she drew me aside after dinner that night and led me back out to our barn and up into the haymow. The burden of a secret she'd been keeping was finally too much for her to bear.

"I'm not supposed to tell you this," she said, "so cross your heart and hope to die if you tell someone." She stared hard at me when she said it. I crossed my heart and said, "hope to die," and was surprised when she looked away before she said something I could barely comprehend.

"Baby Alice is not my sister, really," she said.

"She isn't?"

"She's my niece."

I was completely baffled. Margaret wasn't old enough to be an aunt. Aunts wore corsets and smelled of lilac talcum and had big, squishy bosoms. Margaret was a runt kid like me, even if she did have an oversize brain. "What are you talking about, Margaret? How could she be your niece?"

"My mama didn't have baby Alice," she said. "Reno did."

Nine

The Drummonds' little secret was worse than a stolen offering penny burning hot in my pocket that night when I crawled into bed next to Sue-Sue. As usual, she asked me to make up a bedtime story for her just as soon as we settled under the covers. I usually took inspiration from something that had happened during the day. But the only thing on my mind that night was that baby, and that it was Reno's, and that I had promised not to speak of it. Dangnation.

Then I remembered about the wedding. That wasn't a secret.

"Okay," I said, "listen to this. Once upon a time there was a naughty princess whose name was Reno." I could feel Sue-Sue squirm with anticipation for that setup. "And one day the Queen came to her and said, 'Princess, you must marry.'"

"Marry a prince!" Sue-Sue said.

"Not just a prince," I replied, "but a king! The King of the Pasture. The Bull!"

Sue-Sue let out a shriek that shattered into a delighted laugh. "Yes! Yes!"

"Because only a Bull King could tame such a wild girl." Sue-Sue grabbed my hand and squeezed, like she was hanging on for dear life. I adopted a squeaky, whining voice. "'But I want to marry Charlie,' the princess cried. 'He's dreamy!'"

Sue-Sue became still and rigid at the mention of Charlie's name. The memory of his angry shouts and the grip of his hands remained fresh in her mind. So I shifted direction.

47

"'No!' the Queen said. 'You cannot marry an evil commoner! Never! Marry King Bull and I shall give you the most beautiful wedding dress ever made!'"

"Made of real silk!" Sue-Sue put in tentatively.

"'And it shall be sewn up with pearls and rubies,' the Queen said. 'And it shall have a train as long as U.S. 66. And the veil will be gozmur like the wings of a dragonfly. And it shall have a flap in back with buttons so you can hurry off to the biffy if you drink too much wedding punch and get excited and have to go—*real* bad!'"

Sue-Sue squealed with laughter.

"All right, girls," Mama called. "That's enough. Time for sleep now!"

We pulled the covers up and I continued the story under them in a whisper.

"So the Princess agreed to marry the Bull King. And all of the Kingdom was invited. And the church was decorated with roses and gardenias and dandelions and hog thistle." I had to stop and clamp my hand over Sue-Sue's mouth just before her giggles could erupt into guffaws. Then the force behind her bottled-up glee snorted out of her nose in a thin steam of snot, and that made me yell "Eeew!" and laugh out loud, too.

Mama called again, "Girls, that's enough now! Time to stop! Get some sleep."

I wiped my wet knuckles on the blanket and listened for any approaching footsteps. Hearing none, I continued in a lower whisper. "And the Princess sent a messenger to 107 New York Avenue to summon a young girl known far and wide as Sue-Sue the Pretty. And she was brought to the castle and measured for a special dress that she would wear as the flower girl in the wedding. And all of Sue-Sue the Pretty's friends were green with envy that she should get to walk down the aisle before the royal couple scattering rose petals in their path. And one of these friends was a wicked prankster who was so jealous she snuck in and switched the basket with one filled with marbles!" Sue-Sue laughed again. I had to raise my voice slightly so she could still hear me. "And Princess Reno and the Bull went skidding like dogs running on ice, slipping and sliding and ..."

The light snapped on, the covers were snatched back and there stood Thad. Sue-Sue threw her arms around me and trembled.

"I thought I heard your mother say it was time to be quiet," he said with his customary gruffness. He had the evening paper in his hand, and it didn't take much to imagine him rolling it up to smack us like a couple of dogs.

"Yes, sir," I stammered. "We're going to sleep now."

He switched off the light and I heard Sue-Sue chuckle softly and later give a little sigh. When her whole body twitched a short time after that, I knew she had gone right to sleep. I got up and made a contribution to the thunder mug, and crawled back into bed. Then I lay there for the longest time listening to sounds in the house and thinking about why I no longer felt like laughing. In fact, I felt like crying. It was poor baby Alice. She might never know who her real mother was. What if she found out that her grandmother was not her mother? That she was the daughter of crazy Reno.

Maybe the Drummonds had moved to Cornucopia because of that baby, I thought, and maybe people back in Michigan knew all about it. Was that what Thaney meant about a "woods colt"? They sounded shameful, those words, so snide and cutting. Had she been talking about baby Alice? What was a woods colt, anyway? And how would Thaney know about it?

Just when you think you've got a handle on this world, it changes on you. You think you've grabbed a piece of cake and it turns out you're holding cornbread. I was trying my best to deal with all that I had learned recently about Santa Claus and what people's privates could do, but it felt like the world kept shifting on me. How could you set a course if you didn't know where you could step without the ground shifting? A high school girl having a baby. Who ever heard of such a thing?

I snuggled in close to Sue-Sue and listened to her slow, steady breathing, and before I knew it, it was morning.

I could never look at baby Alice the same way again after that. She seemed like an orphan in her own house. The Drummonds treated her like dirt, too. It took every ounce of restraint I had to keep my big mouth shut when Eileen remarked on it one night at dinner. "Why are the Drummonds so mean to that baby?"

I looked for a hint in my mother's eyes that she knew what was going on or that she suspected. I could see something in her run for cover and slam a door behind. "You haven't eaten your turnips, Eileen," she said. "We're having peach cobbler for dessert. If you want some you'll clean your plate."

I went on thinking about baby Alice. What had she done to hurt anyone except be born? It seemed all topsy-turvy. A family that loved its baby like ours lost her forever, and one that didn't love its baby was stuck with her.

Ten

My Aunt Fern was just what our gloomy old house needed that summer. She was bubblier than seltzer and sweeter than syrup—the absolute opposite of her dour brother, Thad. When she came for a visit, she transformed the entire household with her lively ways and cheerful chatter.

She arrived in the middle of June and presented each of us girls and Mama with a fancy new bonnet, each in its own special box. Fern was a milliner by trade, and her work was top-notch. I was thrilled. For once, I looked forward to church on Sunday. The dark green satiny hatbox that came tied up with a ribbon was beautiful, too, as nice as anything I'd received in a long time. I kept it for years after I outgrew my wonderful new hat, storing baby teeth, picture postcards, a trilobite I found and a spool of thread I'll tell you about later.

My spirits were sky high as I dressed for church that Sunday. For once, we would give those fancy pants Drummonds a run for their money. But as I presented myself downstairs that morning, I saw Fern's eyes sink from her splendid creation to my faded, hand-me-down dress. Her smile sagged. It was the only Sunday dress I had.

"We look like a bunch of chair makers," she said before we got in the car to go. Itinerants, she meant. Gypsies. She said it with a bright laugh, but I felt like turning around and going back up to my room.

Before I could, she pulled me aside.

"First thing Monday morning, we're going to town and pick out some material and make you a new dress, young lady." Well, I

51

practically floated through church that morning beaming at everyone, the generosity I felt spilling over as the offering plate was passed. I dropped Thad's penny right in.

That night, I scarcely slept, and I barely touched my breakfast in the morning. Butterflies flapped freely in my stomach. What kind of dress was Fern going to make me? When were we leaving for town to pick out a pattern and fabric? Finally, Thad said he'd drop us off on his way to work.

"Which do you like?" Fern asked after we sorted through dozens of Butterick & Co. packets of patterns at the dry goods shop. I went through a handful of the packages again, studying each of the drawings.

"I like them all!" I said, too overwhelmed by my good fortune to pick one.

"What about this?" It had short sleeves, a gathered flounce and a sash. Very grown-up looking. Fern said, "It's relatively simple. Which is good, since we're going to make this together."

"We are?"

"Yes, we are."

I'd had a lot of practice cutting out paper dolls, but the thought of taking scissors to smooth, unspoiled material and risking a mistake that might ruin my new dress was scary. I'd watched Mama work with Eileen and heard the tension. I vowed to leave the critical parts to my aunt. I'd hold back to do the grunt work, like rocking the treadle on the sewing machine or holding the material while she guided and cut—a seamstress's assistant.

"Let's pick out a fabric," Aunt Fern said.

"Can we get organdy?"

"For the sash. Yes. That would be perfect."

She seemed to have a thousand things in mind as she inspected bolt after bolt of colorful of cloth, shaking her head, holding some up to my chest. "No. No. Close. No." I surprised her when I pointed out a navy blue that I liked. "This is a summer dress," she cautioned. "The color should be light, but if that's what you want." She quickly went through a few more. "What about this?"

It was beautiful. It had a soft print of coral flowers on a background of creamy white. Far better than my choice. "Yes," I agreed. I adored it.

"And we'll need buttons and thread," Aunt Fern told a clerk. Again, there was a meticulous search until she found perfect matches. Then we headed home and set to work.

We chatted excitedly as we stretched the fabric out on the long dining room table, carefully arranging on it the filmy, tissue-paper pattern sheets with their mysterious markings.

"The notches show how the pattern goes together," Aunt Fern explained. I couldn't see it. "The three plus marks show edges to be placed on a fold in cutting." It was confusing, but she guided me along with a gentle hand.

During a lull, I had the courage to ask a question about something that had been on my mind since I'd seen Fern and Thad together. I said, "When Thad was a boy, was he like John B.?"

Aunt Fern shot me a look. Pins were lined up between her lips, and she pulled one out to attach a piece of the pattern paper to the cloth. "Yes and no," she said out of the corner of her mouth. Then she reached for another pin, and before she fixed it to another corner of the piece, she said, "Why do you ask?"

"Just wondering." I couldn't see how all of these odd little pieces were going to fit together into the dress I thought we were making. I made a face.

Fern let all of the pins drop from her lips into her hand, and I stopped what I was doing and looked at her. She said, "Your daddy grew up a cowboy, you know."

"A *cowboy?*" This was news to me. "He did? Did he fight Indians?"

"No." Her laugh was musical. "He punched cattle on our farm in Ohio with our brothers when they were growing up, too. Your dad spent a lot of time by himself tending those steers. Being out there alone became a part of him from a very early age. As a result, he's just naturally—how should I put this—taciturn. You know that word?"

"No, ma'am."

"Reticent. A man of few words, mostly gruff."

That was Thad to a T, I thought. But I couldn't get past my surprise. I always thought my father wanted to buy a cattle ranch in order to do something different, to get away from the city and the lumber business, to drag his children along and take us away from our friends that he didn't like. All along, it turned out, he was hoping to step back into a world he'd grown up in. I tried to picture it and couldn't. My dad wore a bow tie and suspenders to work. Could he have once worn chaps and spurs and a Western belt? The only time I'd seen him on horseback was when he jumped on the back of Phelps the Farting Wonder Horse to hurry him back to the barn before an approaching storm. Picturing Thad as a boy with a lasso never came into my mind. And I couldn't see Fern roughing it on a ranch either.

"Why aren't you ... tass-a-turn too, Auntie?"

She laughed again. "I was the baby of the family, four years younger than your daddy, and the only girl. I didn't go out to herd cattle. I stayed in the house to bake biscuits and make shirts and dresses like we're doing now, only with my mother—your grandmother, Bethany. Now, let's have you pin that piece of the pattern down, right there."

When it came time to cut, Aunt Fern showed me the proper way to hold the scissors and the correct technique to create a straight, smooth cut. Then she had me go first on my precious, shimmering fabric. It was not a bit like cutting something from the Sears catalog, I'll tell you. I could feel every fiber of that material shear between the blades as I slowly squeezed.

"You're doing fine," Aunt Fern encouraged. "It doesn't have to be perfect. See this seam allowance built into the pattern?" There was an extra bit of material next to the stitching line. "That gives us plenty of margin for error. And if the cut isn't straight, it won't show. Understand?"

About that time, Eileen wandered through and asked how it was going with a smile that said she thought the truth would be pretty funny. Aunt Fern smiled back. "Your sister is a natural, Eileen. I believe she might grow up to be a milliner like me." Eileen nodded wide-eyed, said "Great," and vanished.

Later, Mama had to pull Sue-Sue out of the dining room and banish her to the backyard after she refused to be shooed away. She couldn't stop touching everything and mixing up the pieces. I told her to leave, and she snapped, "I got just as much right to be in this room as you have, Emma Starkey!"

As she steered Sue-Sue away, cajoling and threatening, Mama turned back to look one more time at the fabric. "What a beautiful dress that's going to make!" she said.

After the pieces were finished and stacked, Aunt Fern said, "Come on. I'll show you how to thread the bobbin on the sewing machine."

Aunt Fern had a name like "hip yoke" for each piece we sewed, and I tried to remember them as we went along and a real dress began to emerge from all those oddly shaped pieces.

Then we made our way to the porch after lunch on a fine afternoon to hand sew the buttons and hem. John B. strolled by before dinner leading Tallulah home, her bell clanking past the house to the barn. Aunt Fern laughed at the sight of them.

"What's so funny?" Johnny wanted to know.

"Oh, nothing. Just that cow. She's named for the woman your father dumped to marry your mother, Tallulah Hayes. I can't for the life of me figure out why your mother would have wanted to name her that. Still, there *is* something about that cow's eyes . . .." She laughed again, but she had made me uncomfortable. I wasn't sure why, but it scared me to think of Thad with someone else.

At dinner, everyone wanted to know how my dress was coming. Even Thad glanced up.

"It's turning out wonderfully," Fern said. "Emma is a quick learner. I'm thinking of letting her finish on her own."

I nearly choked on my drumstick. "You were?"

She aimed a sly wink my direction.

I said, "Oh, of course, if you think I can do it."

We went back to our hand sewing after dinner. By the time we set everything down, the sun was setting, the crickets singing, and reflections off the river lit the underside of the trees down the block.

It felt cozy there on the porch. "Does everybody have secrets?" I asked, glancing at my aunt.

"Everybody *I* know does," she replied. She rocked a moment in the porch swing, as though sorting out something she didn't plan to share. "What would life be without a little mystery, Emmy?"

"I s'pose," I agreed. I shoved my hands into my overall pockets. "Could I ask you something silly, Aunt Fern?"

"Why sure."

"What's a woods colt?"

"A woods colt? Where did you hear that?"

"Grandma Thaney."

"Oh, dear." She stared into the gathering darkness. "Well ... how should I put this? What do you know about where baby animals come from?"

"Not much."

"Well, baby colts, you know, have a mama and a papa—grown-up horses. Only the papa is not around to help raise the baby. Just the mama." She stopped, and I could tell she had sidetracked herself. "Sometimes, Emmy, a mama horse has a colt after she's run loose in the woods for a time, and nobody knows who the colt's father is. Was your grandmother referring to someone in particular?"

"I'm not sure. But there's a little baby at the new neighbors."

I could see Aunt Fern nod in the dark. She was quiet for a time. "Well, I wouldn't worry about it if I were you."

But I did worry. "How's a woods colt s'posed to feel?" I demanded. "Wouldn't she want a daddy like anybody else? Shouldn't a dad care if he had a daughter, too?"

"Missy! This is eatin' you up, isn't it?" She scooted over, put her arm around me and pulled me close.

I was sorry now that I'd mentioned it. Sometimes I don't know what is going to come flying out of my mouth. "It's just confusin', that's all," I said. "It's not important."

"Oh, but it is important." She emphasized the sentence with a little squeeze. "Each of us is God's little miracle, Emmy, a one-in-a-zillion chance. If your daddy hadn't married your mama instead of Tallulah and his daddy before him hadn't married your Grandmother Thaney and on ad infinitum, you wouldn't be here or be who you are. That's the blood that's in you."

I'd never thought of that before. It seemed like another scary thing to worry about.

"And that baby is here for a reason, whoever her father is," Fern said.

"Even if her father doesn't care about her?"

"I wouldn't be too sure about that. You can never know what's in a man's heart."

Horsefeathers, I thought. Of course, you could. A lump of coal told me everything I needed to know about what was going on in Thad's heart.

When I slipped into that new dress the next morning and gawked at myself in Mama's big vanity mirror, I could not believe how glamorous I looked. If it hadn't been for my straight hair and straight-cut bangs, I might have been a picture right out of a slick magazine.

"It's a little big for you," my aunt said, turning her head this way and that. A little air escaped from my balloon. She put me back up on a chair to make another adjustment to the hem. "But that only means it will probably fit you again next summer."

"It's the bee's knees," I said, and smiled.

"The cat's pajamas," Aunt Fern agreed.

My pleasure was overwhelming. I'd never had a dress to be proud of before. Not just one I wanted to be seen in, but one I had helped to make. It couldn't have been any more special. "It's as good as one you'd find in a store," I chirped.

"Better," my aunt replied, "when you add in all the love that went into it."

I hugged her tight, and I swallowed hard around the lump in my throat.

I was surprised to find Fern's suitcases packed and ready to go in our front hall later that afternoon. "Do you really have to leave so soon?" I whined.

"Yes, I'm afraid I have to get back to my shop," she said. "People will be wanting their hats. And your Uncle Arthur will be coming back from his sales trip to Iowa and he'll want to know where his dinner is." I couldn't imagine how great it must be to earn a living making stylish hats or watching over a man like my Uncle Arthur, who lived on the road most of the time as a tractor salesman.

Before she left, Aunt Fern had one last parting gift for us. A phonograph record.

"John B., crank up the Victrola. We're gonna cut a rug."

And boy, did we.

"It's the Charleston!" she said, launching into an arm-tossing, leg-kicking, fast-paced dance that made my jaw drop. Here was my Aunt Fern, as old as my mother, out there twisting and kicking like she was some East Coast flapper we'd heard about.

"What are you waitin' for?" she said after dancing alone for a minute.

Eileen didn't hesitate another second. She began hopping and flapping and kicking up her heels in an almost perfect imitation of what Aunt Fern was doing. When Fern stopped to help Sue-Sue, I, too, copied the steps and moves as she demonstrated them slowly and deliberately. John B. just folded his arms and leaned against the wall.

All of us girls stopped dancing immediately when we saw Thad standing in the doorway, but the music kept playing and Aunt Fern kept on dancing. She acknowledged Thad's presence without missing a beat. "Come on, brother," she said brightly. "Step on out and I'll show us how it's done."

I was shocked to see my father blush. It was the first time we saw him wiggle his ears when it wasn't Christmas, and a funny little grin turned up the corners of his mouth, as if it had awakened out of a slumber.

Then he danced with Aunt Fern while all of us backed away in shock.

Eleven

Workmen were back in our house that summer with noisy hammers, saws, and drills as they installed our indoor plumbing. They carved out a new room at the end of the upstairs hall by poking a shed dormer out through the hip roof in back. The sweet smell of fresh-cut wood from the lumberyard where Thad worked spread throughout the house when it was hauled up the back stairs. The wonderfully pleasant aroma was spoiled by the B.O. fumes of workmen who lugged in an enamel-coated metal tub, huffing and grunting and cursing it up each step as they clutched it by its lip and claw feet, tipped on its side. Mama had to shoo us out of the house when the air turned blue.

Running water in the kitchen seemed such an extravagance after years of having to fetch it from the hand pump in the well house. We turned the tap on and off just to hear it whoosh and clang. But it was the new bathtub that was nothing short of a miracle. It could be filled with steaming hot water at the twist of a handle.

The first time I got a chance to be alone in it with the bathroom door closed, I felt like lying there forever, watching soap scum ripple across the surface, ducking my head under like I was at the river—only much warmer. What a difference from the cramped galvanized tub in the kitchen, bathing with Sue-Sue, cocooned in our roomy nightgowns. I'd never been alone and naked for so long. It felt somehow shameful. I took a long, curious look at my stubby body in the water as I soaked and tried to picture a woman's hourglass figure popping out of it. Then I passed a little gas just to see the bubbles.

I lay there daydreaming, discovering what a great place a bathtub was to think about stuff. I thought about the Drummonds and how ugly surprises had a way of popping out when they were around. And I thought about how hard Margaret was to figure out.

We were spending more and more time together. The Urchin Club, John B. called us. Little misunderstandings that had separated us in the past were long forgotten. To her credit, Margaret never lorded it over me how much smarter she was. That was a big part of it. We were as friendly as two girls could be. But close? It was like the real Margaret was always hiding something. Like when I wanted to teach her the Charleston.

We were on one of our walks into town that summer to look in shop windows and we were talking about saving up to buy a new phonograph record together because there was only religious music at my house, except for the Charleston record, and it had gotten all scratchy. The Drummonds had only warbly opera aria records that Mr. Drummond loved.

"Hey, Margaret, how about I teach you to Charleston?"

"I don't think so," she said.

I was sure the dance was something Margaret could get, so I said, "Don't be bashful. You can do it." But it turned out that wasn't it. It was her folks she was worried about.

"They don't want us dancing," she said.

What did that mean? "Why ever not?"

She shrugged. She was also an expert at changing the subject. "Feel like going to the library?" See? Secretive.

"Again? No!"

When we got back to my house, I dragged her to our parlor and put on the record. I did some quick steps to demonstrate, and then I sent Sue-Sue on a bogus errand so Margaret and I could sneak off to the barn.

Margaret was a fast learner, as usual, and we danced to our own singing until we were exhausted. Then we lay down in a cool breeze in the haymow and yakked, mostly about the start of school the following week. She would be blazing her way through third grade with hard-nosed Mrs. Gutchow while I went to second with Mrs. Arndt.

On the first day of school, I got out a pair of hand-me-down overalls from Eileen and checked the mirror to see how far in my new front tooth was. Then I walked to school alone with Roberta, as Margaret said she had to go in early. When Roberta and I passed the Berns' house along the way, Tommy was suddenly on the sidewalk yelling at me. He was the same age as John B., four years older than us, and the only kid I knew who wore hair tonic that smelled like flowers. His clothes were starched and ironed. I never cared for him, and it wasn't just that he was fat and ugly. More than once I'd caught him sniffing his fingertips and wondered where they'd been.

"Emma Starkey, what are you walking to school with a pickaninny for?" he demanded. I sputtered and couldn't make anything sensible come out. He said, "You better watch yourself or you might not be welcome in my dad's store."

I felt my face go hot. How dare he say nasty things about Roberta like she wasn't standing right there? I yelled, "Just you shut up, Tommy Bern! You're mean!"

That's when he slapped the lunch right out of my hand.

I had planned to eat it with Margaret at school that day instead of coming home. Mama had wrapped a sandwich up in wax paper that now lay open on the sidewalk, butter and ham and white bread flecked with specks of dirt after skidding across the pavement. I walked over and stomped on that sandwich as if it were Tommy Bern's head. Like that'd show him. Afterward, my socks and pant legs were spotted and streaked with grease and my shoe made a squishing sound when I walked.

Tommy glared at Roberta, spit at her feet and walked away.

It took me a moment to settle myself, and when I was calm again, I noticed how absolutely still Roberta had become. Like a stone. I said, "Oh, don't pay Tommy Bern no mind. He's just stuck up."

Roberta shook her head slowly. "Naw, that boy were no good."

I agreed, but didn't want to say so. I was sorry for what had happened, but I discovered I was peeved at Roberta as well. She had never caused me any trouble before, but she felt like trouble now. Mama always said that we were all the same in God's eyes, but right then I thought God could use a pair of specs, because anyone could see how different Roberta and I were. "Let's get goin'," I said. "Don' wanta be late the first day."

I picked up the rest of my lunch, but the bag had split, the apple was bruised, and my cookies were crumbled and dirty. So I kicked everything in the street.

Roberta said something quietly behind my back. I turned and heard, "My daddy run that boy off t'other night. He were lurking in our yard round sunset. Took hisself away mighty quick at the sound a my daddy pumping a round into his shotgun."

I wasn't sure what to say. It was all too thrilling and scary sounding.

After our run-in with Tommy, Roberta and I began taking a different route to school. Sometimes, Margaret and I went to Roberta's and we'd go the long way around to Bridge Street. Other days she came to my house and we'd cut through Drummonds' yard over to Cherokee. I found myself hoping that Roberta would tire of sneaking and stop coming with us and I could be free again to walk up my own street. Put an end to it.

I still liked Roberta. She was so quiet and undemanding. She could be very funny when she tried, too. But I began to fret. And in quiet moments in church, I prayed that I could find a way to stray from our friendship without violating God's rule that we love others as ourselves.

I was fretting about it one Sunday in October as Ada Jensen sang "How Great Thou Art," and I almost didn't notice how nobody in the choir except Mr. Drummond would look at Ada Jensen. Mama had her eyes down, and Mrs. Hodge next to her had one of those deep stares going, as if she'd been hit by a two-by-four.

Only Mr. Drummond watched, and his eyes had a dreamy, faraway look in them. I chuckled thinking about him getting that way when he listened to his ridiculous opera records. I enjoyed my little joke so much I forgot to lean forward, and Thad caught me a good one on the ear for giggling.

I rubbed the sting and looked around to see if Margaret was snickering about her father's moment of rapture too. She always got a kick out of the things he did, like scratching his back on a tree in their yard as if he were a bear. But I didn't see Margaret in church. Or Rach. Or James. Not even Mrs. Drummond. That was odd. They were always there. I was craning my neck to make another survey of the pews when I saw Thad's hand scooting toward me again and I swiveled my head back to the front faster than you can say cock robin.

Something definitely felt wrong, but I have to say I didn't expect what was waiting in the wings, a Thing that the women's fellowship chairman, Mrs. Sterns, said there wasn't enough perfume in all of Kansas to take the stink off.

Mrs. Drummond was waiting out on the sidewalk when church let out. And when she saw Ada Jensen sharing a laugh with Mr. Drummond about something on the steps, Mrs. Drummond advanced on her, fingernails first. She got hold of Ada Jensen's hair and would not let go, using it to try to pull the screaming woman down onto the sidewalk.

"Hussy!" Mrs. Drummond was shrieking. "Home wrecker! Hypocrite!"

At first, no one moved. With all the squalling and scratching, everyone was too startled to react. Then the minister and his wife stepped in before Mrs. Drummond could yank Ada Jensen's hair clean out, and they managed to pull the two women apart.

"Let's take this discussion inside," Rev. Richeson suggested.

"This *discussion* is over," said Mrs. Drummond. She wheeled and stormed off, Mr. Drummond in her wake, palms up, pleading with her to listen.

Ada Jensen sat down on the church steps and wept, her forehead and cheeks streaked white where Mrs. Drummond's nails had scraped her skin. She was still sobbing as Mrs. Richeson steered her away and called back to the muttering crowd: "Time for everyone's Sunday dinner, I expect. Time everyone went home."

Twelve

Everybody was in a state of shock after Mrs. Drummond went cuckoo. When I didn't see Margaret all day, I began to worry about her. After supper, I went out to the creek between our houses and stared at the lights in the Drummonds' back windows. The night air was cool, and I sat down in the damp grass and wrapped my arms around my knees to fend off the chill. It seemed oddly quiet and peaceful at the Drummond house, but I didn't think I could risk going over to find out why.

From behind me, voices arose in my house, Eileen and John B. arguing. It added to my sense of unease. Restlessness overcame me and I got up to go in. Then there were footsteps in the grass coming fast around the barn and past the chicken coop. Out of the dusk, Margaret turned up.

She thrust her hand forward. "Hide this," she said in a half whisper. "Please!"

Then she ran home, jumping the creek without breaking stride, and quietly let herself in her back door with a tiny wave that seemed to say she was counting on me.

I couldn't see clearly in the dark, but I could tell it was a photo that she'd given me. I unbuttoned my jacket and tucked it inside my overall top before going in the back door. Then I made a beeline for our new, well-lit palace of privacy on the second-floor and its porcelain throne. I latched the eyehook to keep everyone out. Almost immediately, there was a knock.

"No. 2," I yelled. "Go away!"

"Hurry up!" John B. said, trying to sound gruff like Thad. "I gotta go bad."

"Use the old biffy out back," I said. We were still waiting for it to be taken out of the yard and the hole filled in.

"No, you use it. That'd be better for everybody." I could tell he just wanted to tease me.

"Too late!" I said, making a sound like a grunt.

John B. laughed. I sat on the lid and listened for noises outside the door, and when I was satisfied he had gone away, I pulled the picture out and looked at it. It was a snapshot of Mr. Drummond standing alone near a cabin in the woods with a big smile. There was a jaunty hat on his head with fishing lures dangling from it. He held a fishing pole in one hand, his other hand perched smartly on his hip.

Why was this something to hide? I wanted to understand what was going on at the Drummonds'. When we had driven home from church that day, John B. had asked whether Mr. Drummond was stepping out and Thad had responded that the fight between Mrs. Drummond and Ada Jensen was "no business of children." My imagination ballooned. Adult secrets were always the juiciest. But I worried that Margaret's mother had lost her marbles, like Rex, the man chained to the tree, and that Margaret might get hurt. It was a side of Mrs. Drummond nobody had ever seen.

There was another knock at the bathroom door, and this time it was Thad. "What's the holdup?" he growled. I imagined him out there clutching his folded-up newspaper.

"I'm finishing up," I said quickly. "Hold on a second."

I tucked the picture back into my overalls. I noisily yanked some toilet paper off the roll and threw it into the bowl. Then I flushed and washed my hands. I thought there was a suspicious look in Thad's eye as I tried to duck under his gaze going past and off to my room. Maybe it was because I still had my jacket on. "Lots of people in the family," he called after me, "only one bathroom."

"Sorry," I called back.

When Sue-Sue went to brush her teeth before bed, I pulled the photo back out of my overalls pocket, took another long look at it, saw nothing new, and then hid it in my hatbox under my new hat.

Sue-Sue expected a story at bedtime.

I struggled a bit for an idea, not happy having to make one up, so I said, "Once upon a time, there were three little kittens who liked to fish for crawdads in a creek by a river. And the mother cat would lick her kittens when they found a crawdad and that made them very happy." Sue-Sue's eyes were wide as she lay on the pillow.

The month before, a stray cat had turned up in our barn and given birth to a litter of adorable kittens. Thad had carted them all away over our strenuous objections and all of our pleading, saying they'd harass our chickens and kill the chicks. But that wasn't what my story was about. I continued, "But the mother cat had a terrible secret. She was really a ferocious lion in disguise. And one day she caught a bird that was singing in the branches of a bush and she—"

"—Emmy," Sue-Sue interrupted. "I don't think I like this story—"

"—and she plucked the feathers off of that bird and threw them on the ground—"

"Emmy!"

"—and gave a mighty roar. And the lion picked the kittens up in her powerful jaws—"

"Stop!" Sue-Sue shouted, loud enough for everyone to hear. "Stop it!"

"Girls!" Mama called.

"What's the matter?" I whispered harshly.

"I told you," Sue-Sue said. "I don't like that story."

"I don't like it either. But it's the truth!"

The truth. What was the truth? I wasn't exactly sure—not then, and not even after I overheard the adults talking about the Drummonds' dirty secrets.

These new revelations surfaced on Friday night when the card party couples came to our house. J.B. and Liddy Silica were there with Junior, their youngest child, who was my age. Also playing cards were Nora Demet, the church pianist, and her husband, Lute, who sang in the choir. Tim Barber brought along his housekeeper as a playing partner. He didn't have a wife for some reason, but he did have a young daughter.

"Let's spy!" I suggested to Junior. Like me, Junior had a naughty streak in him. He eagerly agreed. All of the card party members went to our church, so I figured they'd almost certainly have to talk about Mrs. Drummond and Ada Jensen before the night was over. And I wanted information. Adult information.

I led Junior down the back stairs to the kitchen and through the narrow pantry that also connected to the dining room. I eased open the swinging door. The muffled voices from the parlor became louder and more distinct, but it was still hard to hear everything. So I dropped down to my hands and knees, motioned for Junior to do the same, and we crawled across the carpet past the table of snacks and desserts Mama had set out for her guests, inching our way into the living room, which was across the front hall from the parlor. There were ample hiding places there. I waited until the cards were dealt and everyone at the two tables was busy sorting hands, then I pointed Junior to the space behind an armchair while I scrambled and took a spot concealed by the platform rocker that was Pa Joesy's favorite.

"Lute! Please! You could see he was sweet on her from the moment he joined the choir," Mrs. Demet said. "You men, always defending each other."

Tim Barber's housekeeper must have found this funny, for she giggled. Mr. Barber, however, was not amused. He grumbled, "A man can't tip his hat or open a door for another woman without everyone jumping to conclusions."

"Are you saying he wasn't slithering around with Ada Jensen?"

I held my breath. Was slithering around the same as stepping out? Had Margaret's dad gotten all lovey-dovey with Ada Jensen, smooching her and stuff in secret, even though he was wedded to Margaret's mama?

"He drove her home a couple of times. What's the harm?" Mr. Demet asked.

"Other than the Seventh Commandment, you mean?" Mrs. Demet asked with sarcasm. "Or the Tenth?"

"Whose bid is it?" Mama asked politely.

Mrs. Demet said, "You recall that they liked to hang around together after choir practice on the pretext of rehearsing a solo or duet, don't you? But when I offered to stay and accompany them ..."

I remembered suddenly that Ada and Mr. Drummond had sung a duet at my baby sister's funeral, and it made me hot and prickly and kind of queasy.

"What's your bid there, Barber?" Junior's father wanted to know. Mr. Silica had thick black eyebrows and a tone of voice that suggested they were pinched together just then. He said, "We've heard about enough of this hanky-panky nonsense."

I edged out to look at Junior. *Hanky-panky?* He shrugged.

"Will you let your children go out on Halloween, Liddy?" Mama asked.

"It's hard to keep them in, you know, but ..."

Mrs. Demet interrupted. "I hear she sent the lout packing, Mary Drummond did." She would not let the subject drop. "I also heard that *he* cleaned out their bank accounts before he left."

You could almost hear heads swivel toward J.B. Silica, who was president of Citizen's Bank. I looked at Junior, and he nodded meaningfully.

"Bank business is confidential," Mr. Silica said. "You wouldn't want me blabbing your financial affairs around, would you?"

Then Mrs. Silica spoke up. "Let me just interject, Daddy, that it's going to be tough sledding for Mary Drummond for some time to come. The poor woman, what did she do to deserve this?"

J.B. Silica, who could stick out his belly and sound important at the drop of a hat, made a little speech. "One never knows everything about these things, *dear*. They are seldom clear-cut or one-sided."

A silence drew out.

"Maybe we could do something to help," Lute said, "as a Christian fellowship. As a church."

"Good luck with that," Mrs. Demet replied. "I hear Mary Drummond's left the church."

It was some time before I saw Margaret again. She was making herself scarce. When I caught up with her one day at the entrance to the library, I wasn't sure what to say. *How have you been?* would have been stupid. I knew the answer to that. *Awful*, of course. Fortunately, Margaret spoke first.

"Did you hide the picture?" she asked.

"Course," I said. "Said I would, didn' I? Hey, what's so important, anyway?"

"Nothing." Margaret looked at her feet.

"Why'd you have me go and hide it then?"

Without warning, she burst out crying. "Oh, Emmy, I don't think my daddy is ever coming back!" She blubbered and moved toward me and I put my arms around her. I never dreamed I'd ever feel sorry for Margaret Drummond—or any of the Drummonds, for that matter, except pitiful baby Alice. Margaret whimpered, "It's the only thing I have to remember him by! Mama took everything else away and burned it! You *do* have it, don't ya?"

"Yes! Jus' said I did, didn' I?"

"Could I come over and see it?"

"Course." This was really exasperating. And I felt very sorry for her. "Oh, Margaret, what's your family gonna do without a dad?"

"I don't know," she sobbed. "I just don't know."

Thirteen

*T*haney and Pa Joesy were two completely different people to me after Aunt Fern's visit. Her stories lifted them out of the distant obscurity of grandparenthood. They might be crabby old Kansas farmers now, but they'd once been rugged cattle ranchers and frontiersmen. In my mind, they'd gone from relics to living legends.

I wanted to ask them about everything. But what I discovered was that it was hard living with legends. Besides my grandfather being deaf as a post by the time I learned the pertinent facts, he was nearly blind. He moved slowly around his old house, knocking things off tables on his wobbly walks. His shuffling feet turned up the edges of rugs. Thaney steered me away from him. "Your grandfather can't really hear you, you know." Or she'd say, "Not now, he needs a nap."

Pa Joesy harvested one final crop that fall with hired help, and then gave up the farm to move into town with Thaney and live at our house. In the future, his fields would be leased out to a neighbor, Jefferson Mock, who would also look after Phelps, the horse. The house, the summer kitchen, and the tool shed were empty now on the Starkey property, but everything still stood ready for picnics on summer weekends.

It was crowded under that one small roof on New York Street after my grandparents moved in. Now there were eight of us. Thaney and Pa Joesy always took the best seats in the living room, too. Thaney would read the paper to my grandfather through his ear trumpet, which looked like a black snake that had swallowed a funnel and froze up dead. Thaney spoke into the bell part at the end, and we all became better acquainted with current events.

Pa Joesy's hearing horn fascinated me. I liked to tell him things through it. "Dinner's ready, grandpa," I'd shout. He'd fumble for my hand, clutch at it with his trembling, leathery fingers, and squeeze like I was a lifeline. "Lead on, little girl," he'd say in his scratchy voice. "Lead on."

I wondered how anyone so frail could have ever wrestled steers. I tried to imagine him scorching a branding iron onto the flank of a bucking bull, but the picture refused to form in my mind. I had to admit that I didn't really know Pa Joesy—or Thaney—that I would probably never know them, that they'd made themselves unknowable in the way adults sometimes do. It was frustrating. Why would you hide all the wonderful stories about once being a cowpoke?

"Him?" Margaret said when I told her. I could see her trying to put my words together with the gentle, slumping figure before her eyes. "And his name is Josie?"

"Joseph, actually," I corrected. "I been callin' him Pa Joe-sy since I was a baby."

Margaret stared. There was nothing in Pa Joesy's stooped shoulders or blank face to suggest I might be telling the truth.

"Honest!" I said. "My Aunt Fern told me. She grew up on the ranch."

Margaret was deeply skeptical. And I think my grandmother frightened her a little. Maybe she'd gotten wind of what Thaney had been saying about the Drummond family, how they weren't respectable. Thaney's opinion had softened slightly in the wake of the marital split. She had taken pity on Mrs. Drummond as "a woman left to fend for herself and her five children!" It didn't hurt that Margaret's mother had also "found religion," as Thaney put it, having landed with the Methodist flock after fleeing Ada Jensen and the Presbyterians. Bottom line, however, the Drummonds remained "danged Yankee Democrats," as far as Thaney was concerned.

She cast a fresh eye Margaret's way, I noticed, as if taking some secret measure of her character to keep entirely to herself. But if she was plumbing my friend for traces of Reno, I thought, she was wasting her time. Margaret was a brick.

When Margaret tired of spying on Pa Joesy the cowboy that day, I said, "C'mon. Let's go to my room. I think there's some kids in Western outfits in the last Sears and Sawbuck we can cut out." There were, and we played ranch with them in my room, talking in a drawl and pretending to spit "ta-backy" the rest of the afternoon.

One bright fall Saturday morning, Thaney decided I should be in charge of walking Pa Joesy downtown to the barbershop before one of his rare visits to church. I had the hateful suspicion that Thaney liked to trot the poor man out once in a while on a Sunday for respectability or sympathy.

"Make sure he don't get hit by a car or wander off," she told me in her lecturing tone. "And make sure he gets a decent shave for church tomorrow!"

I stared at the short white beard on Grandpa's chin and wondered if she meant for him to cut it off. Her eyes narrowed and she reached up to Pa Joesy's face and rubbed the sandpapery whiskers near his cheekbones. "There!" she said. "And have them catch those wild ones growing out his ears, too." Like Grandpa was some sheep to be shorn.

The long, slow walk downtown would have been a good time to ask for some cowboy lore, except that I would have had to shout my questions out on the public sidewalk for all the neighbors to hear. Instead, I let my imagination wander as I had when I made up stories for Sue Sue about it. "Cowboy Joesy could lasso a steer with his left hand or right. Sometimes he'd rope two at a time by using a lariat in each hand!"

After we arrived at the barbershop and took seats to wait, Pa Joesy reached deep into his pocket and pulled out a shiny dime.

"Tell ya what," he said in his crackly voice. "Grandma Thaney is partial to those soft white peppermint candies. Now if you'd go get a nickel bag of those, you'd have a nickel left over to get something for yourself, now wouldn't ya? What do you say?"

"Yes!" I shouted. I'm pretty sure that Pa Joesy heard me because his grin revealed gaps between his long brown and yellow teeth all the way to the back.

Once she was situated in our house, Thaney became a new voice of parental disapproval with which we all had to contend. "Young ladies don't cross their legs in that fashion," she'd tell us. "Chin up and shoulders back. Remember girls, *posture!*" John B. was instructed to "always hold a chair for a lady." And Thaney's pool of aphorisms seemed inexhaustible. "Never count your chickens before they're hatched." "A fool and his money . . ." Worse, a lot of the rules we'd been given were suddenly subject to change.

Eileen grew defiant. "I'm not curtsying to her every time she gets an idea into her head," she said to Mama after one Thaney upbraiding. Eileen was nearly as tall as Thaney, and the first to call her Thaney *Insane* behind her back. Thaney's maiden name was Sain, you see. Eileen said to Mama, "Since when do we have to listen to her?"

"Since now," Mama said firmly.

In retrospect, I can see the awkward position Mom was in, forced to present a united front with her cranky mother-in-law, but at the time what mattered to us was whether Mom was for us or against us. And she wasn't *for* us.

Then Thaney stepped over a line with me and it became a catalyst for a serious confrontation between the two women. The whole incident was so shocking that the admiration I'd recently felt for her as a cowboy's wife vanished faster than cookies at Sunday school.

The first I knew that something serious had come up was when Mama called me into my bedroom. In the weeks after Mary Ellen's death, her hair had gone as snowy white as a cloud, while her expression had darkened. Thaney's hair remained iron gray, like an Army helmet, and a scowl on her was nothing new. As I entered my room, she stood near the end of my bed with a look of triumph mixed with bewilderment, as if she had expected something bad of me, but not this bad.

I hastily reviewed in my mind my recent mischief and could come up with nothing that would account for a feeling of doom that hung in the room. Surely pilfering a handful of cookies from the jar earlier in the week was not sufficient cause.

"What's wrong?" I asked Mama, a picture of innocence.

"What are your feelings toward Mr. Drummond?" Mama asked evenly.

This surprised me. "What?"

"Mr. Drummond. Do you like him?

Like him? It felt like a trick question. "I s'pose. Why?"

She stared over my shoulder for a moment and pushed her glasses up her nose. "Was he ever … affectionate toward you?" Her eyes locked on me.

I thought a minute and remembered his icky good night kiss at Margaret's sleepover. I sensed honesty was required in the circumstances. "Well, he kissed me."

Thaney clucked her tongue and Mama gave her a meaningful look.

I moved a little farther into the room, suspicious about what was happening. That's when I saw my hatbox on the floor beside the bed, the lid off. I was immediately indignant. "Who's been snooping in my things?!"

Mama held out the photo of Mr. Drummond. "Why have you got this?"

"Hey! Give me that!"

Mama pulled it back with a warning look. "Why do you have it?"

"I can't tell you," I said, angry and worried that Margaret's secret was being betrayed, that her only picture of her dad was no longer protected in my safekeeping.

Mama took a minute. "How many times did Mr. Drummond kiss you?"

"I don't know! What does it matter? Give me that picture back! It's none of your business!" I turned on Thaney. "You did this! Didn't you? You were poking around in my things! <u>My</u> things! Private things!"

The lines of worry deepened on Mama's face. "Sit down," she ordered. She gestured toward the bed. "You need to explain."

"About what? About Grandma Thaney stealing stuff that doesn't belong to her?"

"Emma! You mind that mouth. Now sit down! Right this minute!"

My eyes and throat were hot, and I felt the tears welling up.

"This is not fair!" Once I heard myself say it, the dam burst and the waterworks came. Mama's large, warm arms took me in. "I didn't do anything wrong!" I hollered. "She did! Thaney did. This is her fault!"

"Emma," Mama said when my outburst subsided, "you have to tell me what's going on. Why do you have a picture of Mr. Drummond hidden away?"

I said, "Margaret gave me that picture to hide so her mother wouldn't throw it out with everything else. She likes to come over and look at it once in a while when she's feeling blue."

Mama held me at arm's length. She waited until I looked her in the eye. "And that's the truth, is it?"

"Yes. I promised her I'd keep it secret for her. Now look!"

Mama drew me back into her arms and rocked me, and I heard her clear her throat like she was crying now, too.

"Thank you, Emma. Now, you go downstairs and get a glass of milk. I want to have a talk with your grandmother."

As I left, the bedroom door closed behind me.

Before I turned in that night, Mama took me aside and handed me the photo.

"You go on and keep it safe for Margaret," she said. "It's important. I'll not mention you have it to anyone, and Grandma Thaney will not touch your things again."

I took a deep breath and hugged Mama tightly.

Thaney spent several days in her room, indisposed with a headache, not taking her meals with the rest of us. Eileen read the news to Pa Joesy from the paper, and Mama sent Thad up with a dinner tray every night. It came back untouched every time.

Fourteen

*M*argaret still had her baby fat when she first moved to Cornucopia. I'd noticed her cheeks were pudgy and her arms doughy. Then, shortly after her father left, it all began to melt away. Several months later, the difference was dramatic.

"Did you shoot up an inch or something?" I asked her. "You look taller."

"Might have," was all she said, like *what did it matter?*

Since her family couldn't afford an indoor bathroom after Mr. Drummond left, Mama invited Margaret to bathe in our large new tub the Friday night before Easter. She spent a long time in there, and when she came to my room to get dressed, she dropped the towel she'd wrapped around her and I saw her ribs stand out. The girl was nothing but skin and bones. For some reason, I still didn't put that together with the changes at her house. No one ever thought someone could go hungry in Cornucopia, Kansas. It was too preposterous.

"When did you get so skinny?" I asked her.

John B. started cutting up out in the hall about then, cupping his hand under his armpit to make farting noises by flapping his arm to amuse Eileen and Sue-Sue.

"Hey! We're trying to talk in here," I yelled.

"Don't get your bowels in an uproar," John B. replied. Eileen must have thought that remark was particularly hilarious given the raspberries he was making, and she rewarded him with another big howl. John B. got to goosing his armpit good then and yelling "Bowels

81

in an uproar!" to milk the joke. From the sound of it, Sue-Sue was laughing so hard she was in danger of wetting her pants. Margaret hurriedly dressed before my little sister had to burst in to grab a dry pair. Margaret said, "I gotta get home. Thank your mama for letting me use the tub. It's really nice."

Margaret never once complained to me about being hungry. If I'd known she was not getting enough to eat, I would have done something—I'm not sure what—but something. I was already worried about her for what was happening at school.

One day, the door to the second grade classroom swung open and there she stood, accompanied by the principal, one hand resting on Margaret's shoulder as she walked her to the front of the room to make an announcement.

"Margaret Drummond will be rejoining her former classmates in second grade. Please make her feel welcome."

I tried to catch Margaret's eye, to see if her expression could communicate something about what was going on, but Margaret turned pink and her eyes dove for her shoes. Mrs. Arndt escorted her to an empty desk. "We're very happy to have you in our class, Margaret," she said with a tinselly brightness. Then she announced, "Now children, Margaret is an excellent student, and I think she deserves a big welcome."

A couple of classmates clapped besides me, but I heard whispering and snickers go around the room, and I quickly swiveled my head to try and identify the culprits and hear their snide remarks that were going to require payback later.

"Hey, Drummond, I think you forgot your dunce cap in the other room."

"That will be enough, Cliff Barnhart," Mrs. Arndt said, her face a mask of sternness. "And that goes for the rest of you. Unless everyone would like to stay in for recess." Her eye scanned the room like a searchlight. "Very well. Open your readers."

Margaret sat down and stared out the window, something I saw her do a lot over the next several months as cruel remarks were addressed to her back.

"Hey, pointy head, whyn't you try stickin' your brains in the pencil sharpener?"

"Your mama gonna pull the principal's hair out next?"

Margaret's Yankee accent did her no favors. It sounded stuck up. But all I heard on those rare times she spoke aloud was an unfamiliar listlessness in her voice.

I would look over at her during lessons and catch her doodling on a sheet of paper. I supposed that she had already learned her addition and subtraction tables and how to write in cursive, so maybe she didn't need to pay attention. But it seemed to be something worse, as if she'd lost interest in the things that had once excited her, things like books and riddles and math problems. Had she stared out the window and doodled instead of paying attention in the third grade, too?

"Why do you suppose God hates some people?" she asked me one day as we sat in the dirt of the school yard, off in a quiet spot away from the monkey bars. A game of stickball was going on and a circle of children were playing Apple Core, Baltimore.

"I didn't know that He did," I replied. I sketched a flag in the dust with a stick.

"Isn't it obvious?" she said.

"No." I studied her face. "Wait a minute, Margaret. Are you saying you think God hates *you?*"

"I must have done something to deserve this." She looked away.

"No!" I objected. "That's not true!" Boy, the way that girl's mind worked sometimes. You never knew where the next strange notion was coming from. Had she never heard the *Jesus Loves Me* song at Sunday school? What were they teaching her at the Methodists?

I said, "You're bein' silly. You ain't done nothin'." Now Reno, I thought, there was a different story. But I didn't say so.

"It's just so darn gloomy around the house," she said. "The smallest things make my mother cry. Do you know the saying 'Don't cry over spilt milk'?"

"Yeah," I said. "I'm pretty sure Thaney told me that."

"Well, the other night, Alice knocked over a milk pitcher and I thought Mama would never stop crying."

Margaret looked so forlorn that I wasn't sure what to say. "Hey," I ventured, "maybe your mama could use a good joke." I was hoping to turn it around, offer her one. But now, it seemed, it was Margaret's turn to cry. And when I tried to pat her back, she got up and walked away.

One week later, she turned up at school a completely different girl. It was if she'd gone back to being herself, but overshot. She had too much energy now. Sparks practically shot out of her.

"You're mighty chipper," I told her.

"I am?" She blinked. "I am!"

"Did something happen?"

She gave me a grin then, and something about it scared me.

"What's with you?" I asked.

She said, "Can't a girl smile without you givin' her the third degree?"

I was looking out our bathroom window the next morning as I pulled up my overalls and buckled them and I saw Margaret stuff something into a gunnysack and deposit it behind their shed out back. She looked around quickly, as if she was checking to see if anybody was watching, but she didn't look up at the second story of our house. Then she ran to her back door and let herself in.

The grass was starting to turn green and the new buds on the trees made it hard to see what she'd put in the gunny. I left the upstairs window and scampered down the back stairs two at a time, racing across the kitchen linoleum for the door.

"Wait! Emmy! Wait! Where do you think you're going?" Mama said as I opened it. "Sit down and eat your breakfast."

"In a minute."

"No, now please."

"Uh," I said. "Uh. I got to feed the chickens. It's my turn."

"All right. But hurry it up. Your eggs will get cold."

I pulled the gunnysack out from a pile of wood along the back of the shed and untied the string that held the one end together. It surprised me to find clothes, a book and a diary inside.

"Hey! What do you think you're doin'?"

I turned to see Margaret racing toward me. So I asked her the same thing right back. "What do you think *you're* doin'?"

She stepped closer and lowered her voice. "I'm going to go live with my dad."

"You're what?" I was stunned. It didn't sound natural. Mothers took care of kids, not fathers. And if I'd been given a choice between living with Thad or Mama, it wouldn't have been any contest. "What's your mama say about this? Is it okay with her?"

"It's none of her business. It's between me and my dad."

"Wait. Didn't you tell your mama?"

"No," she said. She had a serious expression on her face as she extended her hand for me to shake. "Well, Emmy, it's been nice knowing you. You've been a true friend. I'm not sure what I'd have done without you." She pulled the bag out of my hands.

"Cut it out, Margaret! You're not leavin'." This had to be a bluff.

She squinted slightly at that. "Oh, yeah? Just watch me." Then she turned and marched away.

"Margaret, wait a minute!" I ran to catch up. It scared me to think she might be serious, and I had to stop her if she was.

"Where does your dad live?"

She turned on me. "Why do you want to know?"

That startled me. "Well, I dunno. How will I know where to write to you?"

"You won't," she said, and turned to walk away, the gunnysack dangling from her hand.

"Hold up! I want to talk with ya," I called.

"I don't have time. I've got a bus to catch."

Fifteen

A silver and blue bus rumbled to the curb in front of Bern's drugstore downtown with a card in the front window that said "Joplin Mo." The bus's front grill, choked with dead bugs, seemed to snarl at everything on Bridge Street.

Margaret hung back until the driver stepped off and went into the store, where Mr. Bern sold bus tickets. With the bus door open, she began to move toward it, but I grabbed her gunnysack away from her. She yelled, "Hey!"

"You're not goin' anywhere, and that's final," I said.

She looked like she was ready to punch me as I lifted her bundle high above my head. She stared at the gunny a second, stomped her foot, and said, "Okay. All right. Fine! You win." Then she turned in the direction of home and I smiled and followed. An instant later, she had snatched that sack away from me and was racing back toward the bus. I gave chase but couldn't catch her before she was up the three steps and into the inside. The air in there was close and the light oddly colored. I pursued her down the center aisle past ten rows of seats as heads swiveled our direction.

"Your mama'll wonder where you went," I said, scooting in beside her.

"No, I left her a note." That confused me. So she told her mama?

"You can't do this!" I whispered urgently. "Your mother needs you!"

"She's got my brothers."

"They can't watch Alice! You know how it is." They were mean to her. So was Reno.

"Tough," Margaret harrumphed.

I'd never been on a bus before. It was big *and* confining. My hands started to sweat. What was I doing here? How could I talk Margaret off before the bus left? "Please," I pleaded. "We need to get to school now!"

A Negro man approached the door and the driver hurried out of the drugstore to intercept him. When the man produced a ticket, the driver inspected it closely, took a hard look at the man's face and finally allowed him to pass. The Negro came down the aisle, eyes lowered. His shoulders twitched slightly when he saw us sitting low in the backseat. He quickly shifted his eyes away and took an open seat across the aisle, as close to the window as he could move. I smelled nervous sweat.

Then suddenly the driver was back behind the wheel, closing the door with a worn brass lever and grinding the gears worse than Max Nix. The bus lurched away from the curb and started to roll down Bridge Street, its engine racing. I stood up and Margaret grabbed my arm and pulled me back. She hissed, "Not now."

"But I got to get off!" I hissed back. The Negro man squirmed slightly in his seat, and I noticed his nostrils were flared and white showed in his dark eyes. But he never turned his head our direction. His face stayed rigidly forward.

"Sit still!" Margaret whispered. "They don't like stowaways on buses. They'll put you in jail." That scared me. I scooted back in and ducked low in the seat. She leaned in close. "And keep quiet."

I couldn't. "You don't have a ticket, neither."

She pulled a wrinkled envelope out of her overalls and produced a printed piece of cardboard from it. I felt my stomach sink. Margaret lifted her index finger to her lips to silence me, and suddenly the railroad tracks rumbled under the bus's wheels and I knew we were practically out to the highway.

The sound of brakes screeching as we approached the highway intersection scraped against my frayed nerves. The driver stopped to look both ways. Then he accelerated out, and farm fields began to fly by out the windows.

"Holy Jesus," I whispered. "Mama's gonna switch my legs raw."

We hadn't traveled far when an old lady in a dark dress got up from a seat close to the front and jostled her way back toward us, gripping seat backs as she came. She had a large straw bag swinging from one arm. Behind spectacles, the old lady's eyes were hard. Her hair was tucked up into an elaborate hat that would have turned the Astors' heads at an Easter parade in New York City, and she gave off a sweet fragrance that made me queasy. She stopped at our row and glared down at us, then in the direction of Margaret's gunnysack.

"You girls come out of that Jim Crow seat this very second, and you come sit up front where you belong. D'you hear?"

Margaret and I exchanged a quick glance.

"Yes ma'am," Margaret said.

I shook my head urgently. Margaret had a ticket. I didn't.

"Come on, now. Let's go." The old lady's bony fingers dug into my elbow and she practically yanked my arm out of its socket.

I saw the Negro man watch us now with the same impassive face as we made our way up the aisle. The driver's eyes appeared in a mirror mounted above the windscreen, too, a surprised expression in them. He hit the brakes hard and veered to the right, the tires spitting gravel along the shoulder. I grabbed a seat to keep from falling. Margaret stumbled into me, however, and the next thing I knew, the bus was stopped, I was on the floor, and the driver was standing over me.

"Wha'da you kids think you're doin'?" he demanded.

I just stared at him. Then I saw Margaret's arm come up from above and behind me, ticket in hand. He snatched the strip of cardboard away and checked it closely.

"Where's hers?" he asked, pointing the ticket at me.

Margaret said, "She left it in her other pants."

The driver's laugh was hollow. "Now there's a new one," he said. "Only it doesn't work that way, young lady. No ticket, no ride."

"It's okay," I said, about to offer to get off and walk back to town.

"That's right, driver." The old lady adjusted her hat and opened her bag. "How much is the fare?"

He looked surprised. "One dollar and fifteen cents, ma'am." He reached down to help me up. "This your girl?"

"For the moment," she replied.

"Let's go," one of the passengers groused as the driver fumbled in his pocket for change. "We ain't got all day."

Once we were seated again and the bus had bounded back onto the pavement, the old lady was on us like a cat on a bird.

"Now you two are going to tell me what's going on," she said. "What are a couple of ragamuffins like you doing on a highway bus by yourselves?"

I have to hand it to Margaret. She was a quick and effective liar.

"My grandpa died and we're going to his funeral."

"What? By yourselves?" Incredulity gave way to indignation. "Where are your folks?"

"There wasn't room for all of us in the car," Margaret said brightly.

The old lady's eyes got large behind her specs. "And they sent you off alone?"

"Yes, ma'am. They couldn't very well send the baby. Or little Todd."

I suppressed a smile. I was enjoying this. I couldn't wait to see what Margaret would say next. It was like being in a play without a script, Margaret making everything up as she went along. I listened carefully, needing to know what role I was supposed to perform and what my character should say.

"Todd has a bad cough," I offered.

Margaret shot me a look that said she expected me to keep my yap shut.

"Wait," the old lady ordered. "You two aren't family." There was no mistaking our accents. And I felt I had spoiled Margaret's perfect little scene. But she'd read a lot of books with a lot of strange doings in them.

"Sure, we're family," Margaret countered. "We're cousins. Emmy here lives in Cornucopia. I'm just down for a visit. From Ohio. Where my dad has a spread. Horses mostly." I sensed Margaret was enjoying this now, seeing how far she could stretch it all. "Well, it's a goat farm, actually. We don't have much." She patted her gunnysack.

"I'd say!" the old lady agreed. "Looks to me like you're not eating very well either."

I suppose I could have told the woman the truth then, and put an end to Margaret's running away. The temptation flitted somewhere around the edge of my thoughts while I waited to hear how Margaret would deal with this accusation. She must have thought the old busybody had it coming, because she laid it on thick again.

"It's sort of a family curse," she said. "We're all skinny. Well, you'll see. My fa ...."—and here she stumbled for the first time, I thought—"my, uh, uncle is meeting us at the bus station."

This was news to me. I'd been worried about what would happen once we got there, and how I'd get home. But Mr. Drummond could take care of it, I was pretty sure. I watched the old woman's creviced face, which was rouged and powdered. I wondered if she was buying any of this. I could tell she had her doubts.

"Very well," she said. "And what grade are you girls in at school?"

Margaret could have probably convinced her that we were in college, but she said second grade. The woman shook her head.

"Parents these days," she muttered. "Honestly." She squinted slightly at Margaret. "I'm going to speak to that uncle of yours when we get there about turning second graders loose on interstate public transportation! And letting them sit in the Jim Crow seats. I never!"

I must have frowned at that, because the old woman turned on me.

"That's right, dearie," she said. "We shall see what he says to that!"

Sixteen

Margaret bolted from the bus the instant the driver opened the door at Joplin. She'd been sitting on the aisle and it afforded her a clear path of escape. Before she ran, she gave the old lady her freakish crossed eyes. I hadn't expected any of it, and before I could get up and run too, the old woman had seized the strap of my overalls. She yanked on them as I stood up, and it pulled me right to the floor.

"Not so fast," she said. She must have figured that Margaret had made a fool of her, and she was sputtering mad. "Somebody is going to pay for your fare, you little vagabond." She grabbed my ear as I started to scramble to my feet. Wow, did that hurt!

"Ow, ow, ow!" I yelled. My ear like to tore off if I moved, so I stood stock still, bent at the angle dictated by the level of her vise-like fingers. I wanted to say that I hadn't asked her to pay my fare, that I would have been happy to get off the bus and walk home, but I didn't get the chance.

"Don't think you can run out on me, you little thief. I didn't teach school for forty-two years for nothing!" She made a little sound of triumph in the back of her throat. "Now, Emma, you're going to tell me your last name."

I couldn't think how she knew my first name was Emma until I remembered how Margaret had referred to it when she was passing me off as her cousin. I mumbled my answer, and the old lady yanked harder on my ear. Again, I yelped. "Ow! Ow! Ow!!!"

"Come, come, girl. What is your name?"

I couldn't believe how low it was of Margaret to abandon me this way. The dirty double-crosser. "Starkey!" I said, louder. "Emma Starkey."

"Where is your grandfather's funeral? And where is this uncle of yours?"

"I don't know. Ouch! I don't know, I tell ya!"

She kept twisting my ear as a means of extorting an answer, so I yelled, "It's a lie! There ain't no funeral. She made that up!"

"Ha!" the old lady replied. "I thought so."

I was close to tears as we came off the bus. I vowed I would fix Margaret's wagon when I caught up to her. See how she liked it when somebody grabbed her ear and tried to twist it off.

"It would appear that your young confederate has left you to face the music alone." My ear was free of the old woman's strong, gnarled hand now, but she had my overall strap firmly entwined in it instead. "I'm going to teach you a lesson you won't soon forget."

I couldn't imagine what she had planned for me—nasty ruler slaps or maybe abandonment in some secret, hidden dungeon someplace. How would Mama and John B. and Eileen and Sue-Sue ever know what happened to me? Tears welled in my eyes. Why had I ever bothered with that low-down Margaret Drummond? So what if the little snot ran away from home. Let her. What did I care?

Joplin, Missouri, was strange and unfamiliar. It frightened me. Where was this place? Was it anywhere near El Dorado Springs? If it was, maybe I could reach my Grandma Hainline and ask her to come with some money. I tried to ask the old schoolteacher about it, but she had a scary, Thaney-like streak in her that refused to listen.

"You hush up!" she hissed at me. "I've had enough of your deceit and prevarication to last me a month. We're going to find us an officer of the law."

Her head was swiveling, taking in the scene on the busy street, looking for a policeman. "Just listen!" I pleaded, trying another tack. "I can get the money. My mama will bring it." I didn't want to go to jail.

"Not another word from you," she said. "If you have a mother, she's certainly not caring or responsible enough to count on for that."

That did it. I'd had it with this loony old hag. I thought about hauling off and socking her one right in the belly, just as hard as I could. Watch the old prune fold over and try to catch her next breath. Only reason I didn't, where would I run? I'd quickly be lost on the unfamiliar streets. Then somebody would find me and turn me in, and I'd be in deeper trouble. So my anger and frustration vented a different way. Sassing.

"If I'da had you for a teacher, I'da plugged my ears insteada listening to your cockeyed lessons," I said. "You're probably the worst dang awful schoolteacher that ever lived!"

At this, the old woman slapped my face.

I heard a man say, "Hey! Hold on a minute there."

"You stay out of this," the woman shot back.

But the approaching man did not. "No. You let go of her!" he said. I watched him stride forward with purpose. He was a tall man, younger than Thad, in a nice suit and polished shoes. He reached for the old lady's hand to pull it free of my overall strap. "Is this your grandchild?" I heard him ask. Then I saw the old woman's shoe shoot out from under her dress and clip him hard on the ankle. "Hey! Ouch!" he yelled. And she kicked him again. "Hey!" he shouted again. "Cut that out!"

I saw my chance, tore free, and took off on a run. Margaret was up the block, watching the whole thing from the safety of a shop doorway. I ran *at* her as much as *to* her, and when she saw the fire in my expression, she turned and skedaddled like a jackrabbit.

But she'd never been very fast, and she had the gunnysack to slow her down. I caught her within a block. I grabbed for the back of her overalls the way the old lady had done mine and Margaret skidded down to the pavement yelping. She tried to get back up and pull away. "Stop it!" she shouted. "Whatcha doin'? We gotta git!"

"You lousy stinkpot! You ran away and left me!" I drove my fist into Margaret's side and heard the air rush out of her. "First you drag me off to God-knows-where. Then you run off so I have to answer to a crazy woman?" Boy, was I angry. I grabbed her ear and started pulling. "How do you like that, huh? Huh? How's that feel?"

When she could finally suck down a breath, she held onto it for only an instant before she let it rebound as an ear-piercing howl. I realized my mistake as soon as she did it. And before I could clamp my hand over her mouth, I could hear the approach of running footsteps.

"Oh, boy," I said, seeing what looked like an approaching posse.

We were in front of a butcher shop, and I pulled Margaret up and dragged her inside. There was a long, refrigerated display case filled with scarlet cuts of meat and prices on white cards jabbed into them, including several slabs of crimson liver, which I detested. Behind the case, chatting with the women shoppers, making them laugh, was a short, heavyset man in stained white shirt, hat, and apron. He yelled, "Hey, where do you kids think you're going?"

Pell-mell for the back, as anyone could see. I put my hand out for Margaret so we didn't get separated again. "Hang on," I told her. "Coming through!" I yelled. I dodged a couple of women holding numbers, waiting their turns, and arms flew up like there was a robbery in progress.

A curtain over an opening to the back yielded to my swatting hand, and I never broke stride going through or continuing toward a screen door at the rear of the building. But my hip clipped the sharp corner of a desk in the dark space where a woman was making entries in a ledger in a pool of light from a small lamp. I'd thought I could get past, but the impact spun me around and I went down hard, letting go of Margaret's hand to grab at this new stab of pain. "Ow! Ow! Ow!"

Margaret's voice was urgent but controlled. "Ma'am, you gotta help us. My mama's old boyfriend is chasing us. I think he's going to try and take us someplace bad."

Without a word, the woman helped me up and steered us toward a wide, heavy wooden door, which opened at the metallic click of a huge metal latch. Cold air poured out as the door opened. We peered in at slabs of dead cow and pig hanging from hooks on metal frames. An aroma of curdled blood and cold fat made my stomach churn.

I felt a hand in my back push me forward and then the door closed behind us. I bent over and wretched. My throat burned, but almost nothing came out. I wondered what I'd puked, since there was no breakfast in there.

"Eew," Margaret said.

I had to take several gasping breaths to get the wave of nausea to pass. After I did, it got quiet enough in the cooler to hear the steady hum of an electric motor. I gripped my upper arms and shivered.

"Listen," Margaret said, setting down her sack. "I knew that old lady on the bus wasn't going to let us go, and I needed to tell my dad to pretend he was our uncle. Tell him about the funeral. Don't you see?"

I saw. But I thought I was going to be sick again, and the cold air was rank and miserable. I was still angry at Margaret, too. Wasn't it her fault my hip was throbbing and my tortured ear was burning like it was on fire in that icebox?

Margaret said, "And that man who came to rescue you? I sent him. I told him that a crazy woman had kidnapped—"

"Wait," I commanded. "Where is your dad?" I was resting my hands on my knees, still bent over at the middle, thinking I could use a glass of water.

Margaret shrugged. "I don't know. He said he would meet the bus."

I got all hot in that refrigerated air. "What the Sam Hill do you think you're doing, Margaret, jumping on a bus and going someplace far away without knowing exactly what's going on? Why did you think your father was meeting you? Or is this just some wild goose chase?"

"Don't yell. They might hear you." She spoke softly now. "My dad'll buy you a ticket."

"Yeah, how's he gonna do that? I don't see him." I looked around mockingly at the hanging carcasses. "You know, Rex used to run away too, Margaret, until they chained him to his tree."

"Take it easy. I got my dad's address. Maybe he just got stuck in a meeting or something. Or maybe he overslept."

"What's the address?"

She fished the envelope out of her pocket. Written in the corner underneath a printed return address that had been crossed out was a Joplin street number on Wisconsin Avenue.

"How we gonna find that?" I asked.

Margaret shrugged again. "We'll manage."

I said, "Well, you better figure it out quick 'cause I gotta get ahold of my mama. Tell her where I am. I didn't leave a note saying I was moving to, to—what's this place?"

"Joplin."

"Yeah, Joplin. My mama's probably worried sick about me. Unless she's talked to your mama and they've figured it out." A kind of distant stare came into Margaret's eyes when I said that. I asked, "What is it?"

She looked down and spoke even softer. "I didn't leave my mother a note either."

"You mean nobody knows where we are?" Again, I was yelling, not caring who heard. "Boy, Margaret, when you mess up, it's always a doozy."

Seventeen

At the click of the cooler door latch, we stopped talking and edged out of sight behind a long, greasy carcass with exposed white ribs. It twisted slightly on the hook, and I wanted to steady it, but my hand jerked back at the slimy, cold touch of dead flesh. I quickly wiped my fingers on my overalls.

"It's all right," the woman said. "You girls can come out now."

Margaret peeked out and whispered, "Is my mama's boyfriend gone?"

"Yes. He's gone. I told him you ran through the store and out the back. He went on through to the alley. I checked. It's okay. Come on." She motioned to us.

The air was warm and heavy outside the cooler, but the chill lingered in my clothes and there was a stink to them that I didn't like. The woman snapped the door shut. She was nicely dressed. Her hair was raven, her eyes green, and her smile warm.

"Now, who wants to tell me what's going on?" she asked.

I looked at Margaret, and she looked back at me as if it were my turn to cook up a whopper. But I didn't have the stomach for it. I was ready to throw myself on the mercy of this lady as the first friendly, interested adult we'd met since we left home. She had, I thought, what Mama called a good heart. I was trying to figure out where to begin my explanation of the whole mess when she spoke up again.

"Why aren't you girls in school today?"

Margaret jumped in. "I'm changing schools, and my dad is supposed to take me to the new one." I was growing accustomed to her lies by now, so even this hint of the truth sounded like a lie. Margaret went on. "But he's tied up, I guess. My mama's boyfriend must have followed us in a car." She pulled the envelope from her pocket. "Could you tell us how to find this place?"

"Whose address is this?" I could see her eye take in all the writing.

"My dad's."

The woman's carefully plucked eyebrows shot up. "And you don't know where it is?" She apparently didn't expect an answer to this question because she immediately asked another. "Is this where you girls live?" she asked, pointing to the main address on the envelope. "Cornucopia, Kansas?"

"Yes, ma'am. At least I *did*. But my mama sent me here to live with my dad."

My head swiveled toward Margaret to examine her expression. She was completely composed and natural. Was she always this dishonest? How could I trust anything she told me ever again? The question wouldn't matter if she was moving away. Only I couldn't tell how this was going to turn out.

"Come on," the woman said. "This isn't far, but the directions would be confusing. I'll give you girls a ride." I had the sense she suspected a pack of lies and was snooping around now to see what we were up to.

Before we left, she poked her head through the curtain into the shop and said, "Herb, I'm runnin' out for a couple minutes. Catch the phone, will ya?"

"What?" he hollered. Without another word, she had us in tow going for the screen door and out into an alley. It reeked of garbage. Flies buzzed nearby. The brilliant sunlight hurt my eyes, and I put my hand up to shield them. When I did, I saw reflections off a shiny black coupe parked along the brick wall next to a dirty loading dock.

"Hop in the back, girls," the woman said. The seat was hot and narrow and cluttered. "Just move those boxes out of your way. There you go. Good. Now, I'm Natalie, and you are Margaret, right? And you?" She looked right at me. "We might as well be able to call each other by our names, don't you think?"

"Emma," I said uncertainly. Why had I been so eager to trust this woman?

"Okay." She started the car and eased down the narrow alley to the side street, where she waited for traffic. "Do you know much about Joplin?" she asked.

"It's in Missouri," Margaret said.

Natalie laughed. Something about her reminded me of Aunt Fern, as if the possibilities in front of you were always limitless and exciting. Natalie said, "At one time it was the lead and zinc capitol of the world."

I wasn't sure what to say, just that I should say something. "That's nice," I said. All I wanted to do was find Mr. Drummond and go home. Maybe get a little drink of water. I was dying of thirst.

"This is a nice little town," Natalie said. "You'll like it here, Margaret."

Margaret stared silently out the small window in back. We made some turns past brick office buildings with gold-lettered names of dentists and lawyers printed on upstairs windows. I was lost and glad that I hadn't made a run for it. We crossed an open space with a creek in the middle and turned down a residential street.

"So why was your mother's boyfriend chasing you girls?" Natalie asked.

Margaret's shoulders had slumped slightly. "I dunno," she said.

"Does this boyfriend have a name?"

"Yes," Margaret said, as if it were a stupid question.

Again Natalie laughed. "All right, did he know where you were headed?"

"Oh no," Margaret replied. "I don't think so."

"Give me the house number again," Natalie said.

It belonged to a graying white frame house with a large front porch and an elm tree in the yard. For some reason, Natalie pulled out a compact and checked her makeup in the mirror. Then she lit up a cigarette. "How about if I go to the door with you?"

Margaret had grown unresponsive. She stared silently at the house. Then she stood, reached over the front seat for the door handle and pinched through the gap and out the door, dragging her gunnysack out with her.

Natalie and I got out and followed. Natalie had a smart, sprightly step, and her heels clicked rapidly up the cement walk. "Looks like a boarding house," she said. She took a drag on her cigarette and held it aloft between two slender fingers. "Swell place," she added, I thought, for Margaret's benefit.

A dowdy woman in an apron and a babushka answered the chime that could be heard on the porch where we stood waiting.

The woman looked annoyed, as if we represented trouble. "Yes?"

"Is Mr. Drummond here?"

"Nope."

"Can she come in and wait?" Natalie asked, indicating Margaret.

"Be a long wait, sweetie. He moved out. Left yesterday. Off to Wichita, I think, looking for work."

"N-no!" Margaret stammered. "He wouldn't do that! He told me to come. He told me he'd meet me!"

"Don't know nothing about that," the woman said, scowling.

Natalie intervened, "Did he leave a note or anything? This is his daughter." Natalie tried to put her hand on Margaret's shoulder but Margaret shrugged it off.

The woman said, "No. No note. No g'bye. No kiss my foot nor nothing. Heard everything I know about it from my other boarders. Hey, what's this all about?" She shifted her considerable bulk in the doorway. "I don't need no family squabbles here."

I'd never seen Margaret so angry before. She threw her gunnysack down and ran silently to the safety of the backseat. I raced after her and climbed in too, patting her shoulder as weeks of trouble cascaded out of her in great gulping cries and streams of tears. She was inconsolable. I thought she'd been a fool and said so.

"Oh, Margaret, what ever did you think you were doin'? You couldn't just go off and live with your dad."

She took a couple of hiccup breaths and gave me a defiant, "Why not?"

"Well, for one thing, he went and smooched up another woman!" I shuddered again at the thought of one of Mr. Drummond's slobbery kisses.

"No he didn't!" she screamed. "That's just some story my mama made up."

I was taken aback. "But why would she do that?"

"She's crazy." But it didn't sound very convincing the way Margaret said it.

Through the front window of the shop, we could see Natalie speak to Herb, the butcher. He jabbed a finger at her when he replied, and waved a hand toward the back. Natalie lifted her wrist and pointed at her watch. She pointed back at him and jerked her thumb in the direction of the car on the street where we waited. Herb poked at the air between them some more and Natalie's mouth opened wider the next time she spoke. She wagged her index finger at Herb then braced two fists against her hips. Herb shook his head, sliced his arm through the air in the direction of the street, and Natalie stormed out.

"Men," she said when she got to the car and slammed her door.

I snickered at this. Margaret turned her face away. I felt sorry for my friend and sorry too that I'd unloaded on her, but I was thrilled that we were headed home to Cornucopia.

"You girls are something," Natalie said after she'd driven a ways. "How'd you even make it onto an interstate bus alone?"

"Margaret had a ticket," I said. "I guess I snuck on, without meaning to."

"Didn't they catch you?"

"Oh, they caught me all right, but Margaret tells terrific fibs."

Natalie laughed again. "Like the one about her mother's boyfriend chasing you?"

Margaret grunted and burrowed her face into the corner of the backseat. She thought she had fooled a lot of people, but I think she saw her web of lies now as shredded cheesecloth.

Natalie said, "I thought her mom's boyfriend was kind of cute." She glanced back at us with a smile. "I was kind of hoping we'd run into him again." Getting no reaction to that, she asked, "So, Emma, what did you do when they caught you without a ticket?"

"Some crazy old schoolteacher paid my fare. Then she liked to pinched my ear off when we got to Joplin. Boy, was she nasty. She had these awful, scary eyes. One of 'em pointed off towards Joneses sometimes."

I heard Margaret chuckle into the upholstery. I smiled.

"You could never tell exactly what she was looking at," I said. "It was like she could see anything and everything at once! Except what an old battle-ax she was."

Margaret laughed, and I felt even better. But she made a face and turned back to the corner to hide it. When she kept her face pressed into the seat, I turned and read billboards and watched cars coming from the other direction as we sped down the highway. The cars would get larger and roar past close by, just beyond the broken white line, engine sounds and gusts of wind coming in through the top of Natalie's window. There were Fords and Studebakers and Packards and once in a while a Saxon like my family's. I tried to picture the driver before we got a glimpse of a face in a windshield.

And then I saw Thad behind the wheel of our car. The sight of his stern jaw sent a shiver through me. He roared past, and you could hear the high-pitched whine that car made only when my father was running her full out. I said, "Uh-oh."

"What's wrong?" Natalie asked.

"Nothing!" I said. I didn't want her to stop and turn around. I couldn't face Thad at that moment. Not alone. I needed my mother nearby to watch over us when the time came to answer to him.

How peculiar, I thought. Here Margaret had been chasing after her father, and now I was running away from mine.

Eighteen

Mrs. Drummond was drinking coffee at our kitchen table with Mama when we arrived. Her face had the sallow, jittery look of someone recuperating from a serious illness, but a fire smoldered in her eyes every time she looked at Margaret. I braced myself for hysterics. Nobody said a thing about a letter sitting open on the table. Everyone was polite and circumspect with Natalie there, a civility that would be scrapped the second she left. You could tell.

"We can't thank you enough, Miss Pierce, for everything you've done," Mama said to Natalie. "Really, I'm not sure what to say. It's been quite a day. Would you care to stay for dinner?"

Natalie seemed to be out of place just standing in our worn-out kitchen explaining things after dropping us off. I was not surprised when she declined my mother's humble hospitality. "That's very kind," she said. "But thank you, no. I have to get back. I left some things on my desk, you see, and I have to finish them before tomorrow." She turned to us. "It was a pleasure spending time with you girls. Maybe I'll see you again one day?" She winked at me, and I wanted to hug her, but some invisible force held me back.

I looked to see what Margaret would do and saw her clomp across the linoleum to pick the letter up off the table. Her hand shook after she read the first line. "This is to me!" she shouted. "You opened my letter?"

"Yes," Mrs. Drummond said. "We were frantic with worry, Margaret. I could see it was from your father. I know it's not the first. This has all been very foolish, but we'll talk about that later."

It became very still as Margaret continued to read, and I jumped a bit when she threw the letter down and glared at everyone in the room. Sue-Sue, who had wrapped her bony arms around my waist and clung to me since the moment I arrived, tightened her grip. Margaret stormed out of the kitchen, down our front hall, and charged up the stairs. I tore loose to run after her.

"What does it say?" I called as she ducked into my room.

"Do you still keep the photo in that hat box?" she demanded.

I lowered my voice. "The one of your dad, you mean?"

"What else!" She snatched the box out from under my bed, yanked off the top, and dumped everything out.

"How could he do this to me? My own father!" she shouted, plucking the picture up and waving it in my face. "I never want to see him again! He's no good! He's a bum!" She tore the photo in half and flung the pieces aside. Then she fled from my room.

I didn't chase after her again. Instead, I stooped to pick up the photo pieces, sat down on the edge of my bed to line them up, and tried to understand what had just happened. An ache formed in my chest. When I glanced up again, Mama was standing in the doorway with a switch in her hands and a determined look on her face.

"Emma Faye Starkey, do you have any idea the trouble you've caused? You scared this whole family half to death! Your brother John B. was out searching for you all morning. He was frantic with worry. All of us were. Sue Sue was hysterical. Your father didn't go to work so he could look for you. We were just about to call the police when the mail arrived and Mrs. Drummond rushed over here with that letter from Mr. Drummond." I held my breath, wondering what it said. "Your father is in Joplin right now trying to find you. Believe me, he will not be happy when he returns." She paused for a breath. "On top of which you skipped school! What in the world were you thinking?"

"Nothing," I admitted. "What did the letter from Mr. Drummond say?"

She paused a moment, staring at me. She shook her head. "That is their affair, not ours," she said. She shifted the switch to her right hand. "You've got one coming, you know."

"But Ma ..." I grappled for an excuse, an argument. "I tried to get off the bus, Ma. Really. It's true. Margaret wouldn't let me. I didn't mean to go."

"It doesn't matter what you tried to do or what you didn't mean to do. It's what you *did* that matters. And what you did was the most foolhardy and dangerous thing you've ever done, Emma Faye Starkey. I don't wish to leave the slightest doubt in your mind that you will never, *ever* be tempted to do something like that again."

She made me take down my overalls. The lash licked at my legs and back until I cried out in pain. "It's not fair!" I hollered. "What should I have done?" The lash paused.

"You should have told me or Mrs. Drummond that Margaret was running away."

"But she'd have been gone by then and I didn't know where she was going! She wouldn't tell me!"

"Turn back around. We're not done here."

I imagined Thaney in her room listening to me cry out and nodding her head in satisfaction, so I refused to yell again. Instead, I clamped my teeth tight and turned each cry into a grunt. I squeezed the bedspread tightly in my fingers.

Mama's voice turned deep. "It's always easier to blame someone else than take responsibility for your own actions," she said. It sounded like something Thaney would say. My stomach ached real bad, but I said, "Yes, ma'am," hoping a show of submission would get her to stop. It did, and I crawled between the covers and pulled them over my head. This was all Margaret's fault. Thanks to her, I'd suffered unfair pain and humiliation. How could I have ever been her friend?

The next day, John B. handed me the letter I'd seen on our kitchen table. "Make it quick."

The cream-colored envelope had "The Commercial Hotel, Enid, Oklahoma" printed on it. That had been crossed out and *J. Drummond, 1712 Wisconsin St., Joplin, Missouri* was written beneath it. It was addressed to Margaret. My hands shook a little. I started to ask, "But how ..."

"Do you want to read it or don't ya?"

"Yeah," I said. I pulled out a letter that was written on both sides of a sheet of scratch pad paper. It had a railroad emblem at the top.

"Get goin' then," John B. ordered. "We're a little short on time here."

The penmanship was loopy. My eye stumbled and had to backtrack some.

My precious Margaret,

Stay home. Do *not* come to Joplin. I've thought it over and your coming here is a serious mistake. I have no way to raise you on my own. You belong with your mother.

Keep the bus ticket. You might need it again someday under happier circumstances. I'm moving on tomorrow, and I won't be writing again. It's no use pining for something that can't happen. It's time we faced up to that.

Promise me that you will grow up to be a fine young woman, one I would be justly proud of, even if I'm not there to watch you or admire you along the way. I know this is difficult. Try to understand. Try, too, to forgive.

Be my good girl now and watch over the family. I'm counting on you.

Love, Father

I read it through twice, smoothing out the words the second time after I'd figured out Mr. Drummond's loopy penmanship. He made his *t*'s and *l*'s funny, not the way we were taught. When I finished, I handed it back to John B.

"Thanks," I said.

He nodded and left.

From my upstairs window, I watched him slip the letter to Rach in the yard. Rach was still angry with his dad. Maybe he thought the letter made him look bad, but I wasn't so certain.

I wondered whether Margaret had gotten a thrashing when she got home. She never said one way or another, and I don't know if I'd have believed anything she said after Joplin.

She deserved a worse one than I did for being the cause of it all, that was for sure. Much later, I had second thoughts about that though. What had Margaret done really? Tried to be with her dad. Should a mother whip a daughter for that?

After the "Joplin escapade," as John B. began calling it, Margaret reformed her ways at school. She paid attention and did her work. But it was harder to make her laugh or to get her to talk. And I never saw anybody read so many books. Or so fast. Lord, you could feel a breeze from her turning the pages.

Nineteen

*D*evilry made a healthy return that summer after school let out. Eileen started imitating Thaney when she wasn't around. John B. followed her lead, taking the role of Pa Joesy.

"Pity the plight of a poor pale parsnip on a plate," Eileen would say in Thaney's grating voice, picking up some comment from dinner the night before. "It's gone cold! And still, it must be eaten. That's what comes of being finicky, child. Eat up!" She pointed a bent finger at Sue-Sue.

"Ick," Sue-Sue said, joining in the fun. "It tastes like a carrot in vinegar."

"Quiet! Children should be seen and not heard," Eileen said, even mimicking the clack of Thaney's loose dentures.

John B. cupped his ear and said, "How's that? There's a sheen on the herd, you say?" How was any of us to know, laughing at Grandpa's deafness, that it was only a matter of years before my own hearing would be gone?

Often, the Drummonds were the audience for these shenanigans out in our yard. Eileen threw herself into the role, especially when Rach was there. She was a born actress, and she had Thaney's mannerisms, inflections, and bromides down to a *T*.

You could tell that Rach adored it. And more than just the stories, too. When Eileen was out in the yard, he'd always wander over. And Eileen usually found an excuse to come out if Rach was there. The Reports from Our Dinner Table and Parlor, as John B. called them, were just a convenient excuse.

While Rach was partial to Eileen's mockery, he did not warm up to Johnny's.

"Even a blind squirrel finds an acorn sometimes," Rach liked to say to belittle John B. if we'd all laugh at a good one. Rach used a voice like Eileen's impersonation of Thaney when he said it. Mimicry once removed. His remarks never quite captured my grandmother, however, and I wondered why he tried. Maybe it was his way of saying the Starkeys didn't have it any better than the Drummonds, that simply keeping a family together didn't make everything peaches and cream.

"Never shit a shitter," Rach said once in his crackly old lady voice. There was a nervous pause before John B. laughed, then Eileen. I was too shocked and in no mood to laugh. Where had Rach heard such a disgusting phrase? I immediately thought of Bull.

"Your mother ever wash your mouth out with soap?" I muttered to myself.

Rach imitated Pa Joesy for a change. "Wha'd she say?"

Eileen responded in her Thaney voice. "She said, 'Lie down with dogs and you wake up with fleas.'" That got a laugh, and then we all looked at John B., who had cupped his ear. "Say again? You lied to the dog and he woke up with a sneeze?"

Rach's dungarees smelled like machine oil and firecrackers that summer. I asked John B. about it, and he said I had a nose like a bloodhound. It was true. I always smelled everything first. Absolutely everything. It was a kind of a curse.

I'd noticed that Rach was different in other ways, too. Harder and meaner, I thought. He looked tougher. With the type of skin that sunburned easily, his face and arms were often a pink blotchy mess, as if they'd been in a nasty fight with the sun and lost.

"What's going on?" I persisted when John B. dodged my question.

"Nothing," John B. said. "Rach is just doin' a little huntin' is all."

"For what?"

This got a laugh. "For dinner." He said it with a smile, and I couldn't be sure he was serious.

Eileen overheard us. "That boy has ants in his pants," she remarked in her Thaney voice. "And his sister has a dang bee in her bonnet."

"You want me to lay out some poison, Thaney?" John B. said.

One morning, Pa Joesy didn't come down to breakfast and Thaney unearthed an orange from somewhere. My eyes got big. I loved oranges. The only time we saw one was in our stockings at Christmas. Thaney wasted it though by mashing the lovely thing with her bony fingers to make a very small glass of orange juice. "Grandpa Joseph is a bit under the weather," she announced. "Be right as rain in a day or two."

It was another of her expressions that I never understood. What did it mean? Right as rain? What was right about rain? When we were kids, everything about rain was wrong. Except the puddles it left for splashing.

I went up to see him after breakfast, but the poor old guy could barely open one clouded eye a slit to nod back at me as I patted his hand. I listened to his ragged breathing a moment and then picked up his ear horn to shout in a few words. "You get better, Pa Joesy, okay?"

Mama was keeping Eileen busy in the kitchen with chores in those days, so the job of helping Thaney work in the garden fell to me. She had completely taken over our yard the summer after she moved in, ripped up perfectly good lawn in back for a vegetable garden, and rudely pulled out Mama's flowers in front to plant her own favorites. Thaney was partial to moss roses, red dahlias, carnations, sheep shower, and black-eyed Susans. She dug at the driveway entrance and placed "sentinels" there. Mama called them yucca, which I misunderstood to mean she thought they were ugly too.

"A garden is a friend you can visit anytime," Thaney told me one morning, but I was certain her garden was no friend of mine.

She brushed aside my skeptical frown. "No need to scowl," she said. "She who plants a garden plants happiness!" Then she muttered, "Of course even sunflowers will cast shadows," and cackled.

I was reminded for some reason of something that Margaret had told me, that there were huge black spots on the sun you couldn't see with your naked eye. "And you better not try," she'd warned.

As Thaney droned on one afternoon about taking pride in calluses while we worked on the weeds in a row of turnips, Eileen arrived at the edge of the garden and summoned me. I dropped my hoe and bolted. "Tell her Mom wants to talk to you," she said in hushed tones.

"About what?"

"Just tell her. Then get back here."

I could see I was being given a lie to tell, but I did it because I was pleased to be rescued from Thaney and grateful that Eileen was showing an interest in me. She was usually too busy competing with John B. or showing off for Rach or helping Mama to pay much attention to her little sisters.

"Come on. We're going to follow the postman," she said.

"What?" I said. "For heaven's sakes, why?"

"You'll see. You won't believe this."

We trotted down New York Avenue to Second Street. and turned south. When we got to Cherokee, we saw our postman up the block in a short sleeve uniform, mailbag slung over one shoulder walking the path to someone's front door.

I was about to say, "So?" when Eileen slipped into the backyard of the corner house, running crouched over from hiding place to hiding place. I followed along. We had to leap a couple of short fences to catch up to where he was, and then we sped ahead across two more yards and stopped at a house with some wash out on a clothesline.

"Perfect," Eileen said. "C'mon."

We took cover in some shrubbery near the back corner of the lot.

"Eileen," I started to say.

"Shhhh. Try to show some patience for once."

I'd never paid the postman much notice. He had a thick belly and stubby legs and the shadow of his round, broad-brimmed helmet hid his eyes and much of his bulbous nose. When he appeared around the corner of that house, I was completely surprised. What was he doing in the backyard? And how had Eileen known he'd go there?

We crouched very still in the bushes near the crisp, white wash drying in the sun: fresh sheets, dishtowels, and underwear. My imagination told me what those clean sheets would smell like, but all that was reaching my nose at that moment was the dampness in the soil beneath our bare feet and the sun-dried sweat on my own forehead and arms. I watched as the postman looked around. Then he advanced quickly toward the hanging wash and stopped at a pair of the underwear, pulling it toward him.

"What's he doing?" I whispered.

"Can't you see?" Eileen whispered back. "Sniffing the crotch!"

"Why?"

"*Why?* Because he's crazy! Like everybody else in this town."

Something must have alarmed him—maybe he'd heard us, I don't know—but he suddenly turned and hustled back toward the street.

"Holy smokes!" I said a little louder after he'd gone. Eileen was laughing, but I felt uncomfortable and upset, as if I'd secretly watched somebody take a poop. Eileen looked at me and rolled her eyes, disappointed I guess that I didn't think the whole thing was every bit as funny as she thought it was. "He's a pervert," she said, wiping the tears out of her eyes from holding back laughter. "He sniffs bicycle seats, too." I made a face. Eileen said, "Oh, grow up." At that moment, I wasn't happy that she had finally taken an interest in me. She might be ten, but that didn't give her the right to drag me off to watch something disgusting and then mock me for not thinking it was funny.

"Thaney's going to wonder where I went," I said, and ran for home.

I waited at dinner that night to see if Eileen would say something about the incident and try to use me as a witness. I think I'd have crawled under the table to hide before I'd have admitted spying on such an abomination. Fortunately, John B. spoke up and asked Thaney if he could use Pa Joesy's hunting rifle. This pretty much dominated the table conversation for the rest of the night.

"What do you need it for?" Thaney wanted to know.

"Rach asked me to go hunting with him," John B. said. "I don't have a gun."

Thad broke his policy of eating in silence. "What does Rach hunt?"

"Rabbit mostly. Some squirrels."

Margaret's family ate squirrel meat? I nearly gagged, and when I did a p-tooey spitting out my potato, Mama scolded me.

I scooped the pieces back up. "Sorry."

Thad glowered. "You'd need somebody with you at first," he told Johnny.

Mama got a worried look on her face. This comment sounded as good as an approval. And I sided with Mama. I didn't want John B. toting a gun around. Apparently, Thad had noticed Mama's expression, too. "Your mother and I will discuss it," he told John B., as if that were that. But John B. turned and pleaded his case directly to Mama and you could see how expertly he knew how to soften her up by pouring on the charm.

I got up and went outside, and sat on the porch steps, unwilling to listen.

I thought about getting older and how I didn't really want to. I liked things the way they'd been before—before I knew what adults did to make babies and what Mr. Drummond snuck around doing with Ada Jensen and what the postman got into when he thought nobody was watching. I wanted to forget about all that. But after what I saw, I stood guard in our backyard whenever Mama hung our wash out until I was absolutely certain the mailman had gone past our house and was clear out of our neighborhood. He wasn't going to sniff my underwear. No, sir. Not if I had anything to say about it.

Twenty

When Pa Joesy didn't get out of bed for a week, the worry that had been silently building in the house began to spill out.

"Is it time to call in a doctor?" Mama asked Thaney.

"He's about to turn the corner," Thaney assured her. I sighed. How could you believe her? She'd been saying that all along. But I did want to believe her.

Sue-Sue and I helped Mama get Grandpa out of bed and over to a spindle-back chair in his room that Monday so that she and Thaney could change the sheets. He smelled as sharp as mustard plaster. "Time for a sponge bath, Joseph," Thaney said.

I wasn't sure he heard her, and he seemed too weak to cooperate. He slumped in the chair as Sue-Sue and I held onto his arms to be sure he wouldn't fall over. His nightshirt drooped on his sloping shoulders revealing his bony chest and muscles like melted wax, making it even harder to picture him as a once-vigorous cowboy.

I wanted to say something to him. Let him know who it was who was holding him up. I just wasn't sure quite how to go about it.

"It's me, Grandpa," I shouted next to his ear. "You want a glass of water or anything?"

He made a sour little grunt that left me wondering whether he meant yes or no. I was struggling with what to do next when Thaney spoke up.

"He's too confused just now to understand what you're saying," she said. "Come on. Let's get him back into bed."

We pulled him up onto his feet, and he nearly toppled over as he staggered a few steps to the bed with us holding him up. His nightshirt rode up over his knobby knees and his smooth, hairless legs when we got him up on the mattress. Rivers of blue veins were mapped out under the papery skin, which was as faded and thin as old wallpaper. I was afraid his business might pop out at any second, so I turned my face away. Mama lifted his wooden limbs into place on the sheets. We all worked up a sweat by the time we got him under the covers.

"A doctor might be good, I guess, if you don't mind spending the money," Thaney said to Mama.

The doctor arrived within the hour. He was a tidy man with a dark beard and rheumy, tired eyes. He took his black valise into the room and closed the door. "Joseph!" we heard him shout. "I'm Dr. Frederick. How are you doing?" A grunt or a moan came in reply. "I need to sit you up for a moment. I'm going to examine you! Ready? Here we go!"

"Run along, girls," Thaney said. "There's still plenty to be done. Idle hands are the devil's playthings."

Idle hands? Who had time for idle hands? When I wasn't getting dirt under my nails helping Thaney dig up weeds or plant seeds, I had them plunged into dishwater for Mama, whose time was monopolized by the ailing Pa Joesy.

We took Pa Joesy's sheets and others that we stripped from the upstairs beds out to the pump house for Mama to put through the wringer washer later. I wanted to hang back and lurk in the hall near the door to Pa Joesy and Thaney's room, hear what Dr. Frederick was discovering about my grandfather's ailment.

When Mama and I came back in from the pump house, Thaney was talking to the doctor at the front door. Their heads turned our way and the conversation ended abruptly. Then the doctor offered her his hand to shake with the sort of overt sincerity the minister used at the church door on Sundays. Then he turned to leave. The lines on Thaney's face said the rest.

Mama had been standing behind me.

"Why don't you girls get on your swimsuits? It's a beautiful day and I'll bet the Drummonds are already down at the river. Eileen!" She listened a second for a response. "Eileen!" she called. "The girls are going swimming. I want you to take them."

Whenever Mama put Eileen in charge of watching us, mostly at times when John B. was off hunting with Rach or playing ball with Zeke Wilhite and the boys, Eileen relished the opportunity to be boss. She swooped down on us from the stairs. "Emma, Sue-Sue, come on. Get your swimsuits on. Come on! Hurry up!"

"Chop-chop!" I said. It was an expression of John B.'s, and while it made no more sense to me than some of Thaney's, I liked it better. Especially because it made Eileen look annoyed.

Two days later, Mama came out to call us in from the yard in the early afternoon. Once we were inside, she said, "Your grandfather is dying." Her words, while not unexpected, startled me with their nearness to finality. Had his time really come?

We trudged up the stairs and tiptoed into the bedroom to gather around him, hands folded solemnly in front of us.

It was too eerie to feel like crying, nothing like it had been when our precious baby girl, Mary Ellen, was taken. You could see how the old man's body was worn out. I was curious and watchful as we stood there, surrounding Pa Joesy's bed, looking helpless. I wondered, did Mama intend for us to do nothing else until he passed over? She had said on the way up that his grandchildren should be with him when he died. I didn't ask her when this might happen. And now it was as if nobody wanted to break the silence, even Thaney, who was never at a loss for words. Her jaw was set, like a monstrous test was coming.

Thad stood near the head of the bed, ramrod straight and glassy-eyed, barely glancing down at his father. He had the look of someone mesmerized by the distant drone of a fly.

I started to get antsy, listening to his labored breathing, thinking about Pa Joesy's white, hairless legs and splotchy chest under the sheet as the moment stretched out longer and longer, like a rubber band being pulled beyond its limit. I was afraid John B. might do something to make me laugh. He had that power over me. I had a feeling he found this gathering as peculiar as I did, and just thinking about that was enough to put a tickle in my throat that wouldn't go away. Then it began eating at my brain. I decided I had to move before I forgot how I was supposed to be behaving.

I stepped away from the wall and sat on the edge of the sheet. I reached for Pa Joesy's hand, which was lying on top. It was cool and dry. He couldn't hear me, I knew, but I thought he might feel my touch. So I interlaced my small fingers between his large, thick ones. This was the way I had held his hand when I walked him to the dinner table and the day we walked together to the barbershop downtown.

At the moment, I had a lot of questions I didn't feel I could ask. Did Pa Joesy know he was dying? Did he want to say good-bye and couldn't? Was he scared? I squeezed his hand. Pa Joesy didn't move, but his wheezy breathing stopped immediately, almost as if the pressure I'd applied had stopped it. It was suddenly very still in the room. You could feel an electricity. I snatched my hand away and looked at Mama. And then, Pa Joesy took another noisy, gasping breath that was almost a snort. It startled me, and I jerked. I had thought he was dead. I made the mistake of looking impulsively at John B. There was a mock rebuke in his eyes, pretending he was disappointed in me, and it made me laugh aloud. My face immediately blazed hot. How could I do such a thing?

Mama pulled me away without reprimand, and Thaney finally spoke.

"It's the death rattle," she said with gravity. The term raked across my brain like the bristles of a steel brush and left a scar that restless thoughts would poke at for years. It drove me into a sort of daydream trance, and thus I was not really paying attention when my grandfather passed a few moments later. *Death rattle.* I associated it with the tail of the venomous snake, a ragged, warning drumroll before the lights went out. I would say those words—*death rattle*— to Sue-Sue with hushed urgency after that whenever it suited my storytelling purposes.

My first chance came that night at bedtime, the last night Sue-Sue and I would spend in our own bed for several nights to come as Starkeys poured in from everywhere for the wake and funeral. Our aunt and uncle took over our room. In the story I made up, an old elephant went to the secret place where elephants go to die. The young elephants tried to follow the old one but came to a river that only the old elephant could cross. This made the young elephants anxious. "How will we know where to go when our time comes to die?" one asked. "It will come to you when the *death rattle* begins," said the dying elephant's mate.

Our neighbor, Mrs. McVey, arrived around bedtime to sit with Pa Joesy's body overnight in our parlor. It seemed an odd thing to me, but somehow reassuring also. What if Pa Joesy started breathing again and nobody was around to notice? We didn't want him to get buried alive accidentally.

My Aunt Fern arrived the following afternoon. In her dark silk dress and black veiled hat, she made my heart race. I hugged her with all my might. I had the expectation of long stretches of time together, as during the previous summer. But I discovered I could barely get her to look my way. She was always with her brothers, who doted on her. Or she was taking care of domestic duties that mushroomed as the house filled up with people.

I'd never really known my uncles and I had expected them to be like Thad, having grown up as cowboys too. But they weren't taciturn. In fact, Uncle Roy was a talkative and funny man, and a hat maker to boot. He'd introduced Fern to the profession.

After they all had pinched our cheeks, patted our heads, and given us hugs and kisses, Johnny, Eileen, Sue-Sue, and I might as well have been pieces of furniture. The conversations between adults got going in earnest and we were shut out. The family hadn't been together for a while, and there was a lot to catch up on. Juicy stuff, too. Without intending to eavesdrop, I learned over the course of a few days that Uncle Walter was a drinker and a Christian Scientist, that Uncle Frank had money troubles, and that none of my uncles' wives had had children. Theories about why abounded. But when these discussions really got going, somebody thought to send us outside to play.

"Do you have to touch him or anything?" Margaret wanted to know.

"What?" We were up in the haymow, where I had told her about my grandfather's open casket in our parlor, lying there in his Sunday suit, looking like he was napping, the only difference being his color, which like Mary Ellen's had gone all gray. "Touch him? No! Why?"

"Well, I read once that in some churches, they line you up and everybody has to kiss the dead person good-bye. On the lips!"

"Eeew! You're making that up!"

"On a stack of Bibles, I swear it. But I don't think it's the Methodists that do it."

Thaney had insisted on having a funeral at the Methodist Church, and the Drummonds apparently were planning to attend. Margaret and the Drummonds were still new to the Methodists.

"Well, if they do that kissing thing, Margaret, you won't have to do it 'cause I won't be doin' it neither. We'll just sneak out the back if it comes to that."

Margaret looked relieved. "Good. 'Cause dead people are cold, you know. And they're creepy. Sorry, no offense to your grandfather. He was nice. I liked him."

None of that sounded very sincere to me, but I accepted it as an apology.

"It's okay, Margaret. I hardly never kissed him even when he was alive."

Twenty-One

*I*t was a cry for attention that got me into trouble on the day of Pa Joesy's funeral—the first time at least. I had taken advantage of the hubbub as everyone hurried to get ready and put aside my good dress to slip into the one Aunt Fern and I made together the previous summer, a dress I still loved.

"Wow!" Fern said when she saw me. "Look how you've outgrown that!" I'd hoped she'd notice. Lordy, it cut me hard in the armpits. What I was hoping she'd say next was it was time we made a new one.

I hadn't worn the dress in months, not since Mama took it away and made me wear an Eileen hand-me-down instead. It took some time to hunt it down. I found it in a box in the cellar among the clothes to be given to Grubbses the next Thanksgiving. That made me angry. How could they give away the only dress I'd ever made myself?

"Emma! What are you doing!" Mama appeared from nowhere. "Go up to your room and get that dress off. You put on your good dress and stop this foolishness. We're all going to be late! What would your grandfather think!"

That's the kind of thing everybody had been saying for days, and I was sick of it.

"Pa Joesy didn't go to church!" I yelled back. "He didn't care about it. And he didn't care how I dressed, 'cause he couldn't see me. He told me the only thing he really liked about church was hearing the funnies read before and eating Sunday dinner after!"

Company or no company, Mama came after me with her hand raised. I never ran up the stairs so fast in my entire life. But I was still angry when I got to my room, and I slammed the door and stormed through the mess my aunt and uncle had made in there. When I finished taking off that dress, I threw it out the upstairs window.

"Ha!" I yelled. "See how anybody likes it now!" I couldn't tell if the Grubbses heard me or not. I hoped they did.

As Pa Joesy's next of kin, we had to sit down front in the first pew, right under the Methodist minister's skinny nose, craning our necks to stare up at his pulpit in a tiny little balcony. I bet Pa Joesy was glad they closed the lid to his box and he didn't have to hear what was said because it was all way too sappy.

I loved old Pa Joesy, and I missed him already. But he never complained through the whole ordeal of getting old and his body falling apart. He never begged for sympathy, unlike Thaney, who couldn't get enough. What would he think, indeed?

I was pretty sure Thad wouldn't thump me in a strange church, so I looked around to see who had come. I was surprised to see Max Nix sitting next to Mama's and Thad's card friends, J.B. and Liddy Silica, Lute and Nora Demet and Tim Barber. I saw Mr. Osborne, who owned the lumberyard. Some of the Methodists I recognized were there, too, not just the Drummonds, who were only pretending to be Methodists like I did once a month. It seemed like a pretty good turnout for my old grandfather.

As the service wore on, I thought I smelled dog poo, and I began wondering who might have stepped in it and was still walking around with it on their shoe. When I checked my own, Thad thumped me, and then I sat there and tried not to smell it, which was impossible once I had.

"Let us remember Joseph Starkey in our silent prayers," the minister said. Everybody bowed their heads. Other than "God bless Pa Joesy," I couldn't think of a dang thing I could pray. So I prayed that about a hundred times before the minister finally said "Amen" and we could all quit.

When the service ended, us Starkeys walked solemnly down the center aisle, everybody staring at us as we followed the coffin out of the church. Rach Drummond sidled up to me at the entrance just as Pa Joesy's box was being loaded into the hearse. "I hear you were very brave," he said.

"What do you mean by that? Who said I was brave?"

"John B." Rach put a serious look in his eye. "He told me you laughed in the face of death." Then a smile began to spread on his face. "Right there on your grandfather's deathbed!"

I had not gotten over being embarrassed and angry about that stupid mistake, and now John B. had gone and blabbed it to Rach. And it was John B. who'd made me laugh! I shot Rach a dirty look and without a word walked over to where John B. was talking to Uncle Walter and slugged him as hard in the kidneys as I could.

"Hey!" he yelped. He wheeled around, one hand reaching for where I'd hit him, like he was trying to get hold of something. Then he said, "Wha'd you do that for?"

"Tellin'!"

"Tellin' what?"

"About making me laugh. That was all your doin', wasn't it!"

I had hoped that Aunt Fern wouldn't hear how I laughed on Pa Joesy's deathbed. But there she was, looking somewhat shocked, standing next to Mama, who seized my wrist and dragged me around the corner and up the block, bending down to put her face in mine before she exploded.

"What's gotten into you, Emma Faye Starkey? This is your grandfather's funeral, and you are making a spectacle of yourself! I can't believe how ashamed I am! Now you stop behaving this way right now!"

I started to speak, to say I was very sorry, that everything was going so horribly wrong, but I couldn't get much out before tears came hard and fast. "I'm sorry! I'm sorry!" I sobbed. "Poor Pa Joesy!"

I'd never seen so much food. Ham and beef and fried chicken, sliced tomatoes, baked beans, corn on the cob, potato salads, biscuits and bacon and jams and jellies and loaves of bread, plus Mrs. Drummond's fried potatoes, which I heaped liberally onto my plate. At the center of the dining room table was a spray of flowers from the Grubbses' yard that Roberta's mother had brought over, along with a pan of warm cornbread. I took several chunks of that, too.

The line for food snaked through the kitchen and dining room as folks loaded up on their choices while Mama, Aunt Fern, Inez Woods, Mrs. Sterns, and Mrs. Drummond edged around to refill the serving dishes and trays as the food disappeared. Thaney was the widow behind a black veil in the living room with her somber sons, visited by a stream of mourners stopping to pay their condolences.

I took my plate out in the backyard with Margaret and watched huge black storm clouds gathering in the distance. "It's gonna be a gully washer," I said, repeating one of John B.'s expressions, even if I was not past being mad at him.

I took a bite of buttered cornbread, which practically melted in my mouth. Margaret chewed on a drumstick.

"Margaret," I said, "what do you think happens when you die?"

She set the chicken bone down on her plate and wiped her hands in the grass. "What do you mean? You *know.*"

"Well, for instance, do you think we'll go to heaven? Or ... or ..."

"Or hell? Naw. Come on, Emma. We're not going to hell. Least I'm not."

"Hey, that ain't funny! You're the one thinks God hates you!"

"Not anymore."

"Well, what if He switched over to hating me when He stopped hating you? And what if Pa Joesy went and told Him that I laughed about him dying, right in his face?"

Margaret stared at me like I didn't get it. "What difference would that make? God already knew. He's better at seeing things than Santa Claus."

She was right. So, He'd seen all of the bad things I'd done that day, things Mama called "disrespectful."

"So He knows I slugged John B. in church? And even that I was thinking about dog poo when the minister was reading the Scripture?" Then I remembered something else I'd practically forgotten. "And that I threw my favorite dress out the window?"

"You what?"

It was hopeless. I'd gotten onto a bad path, and I wasn't sure how to get off it. I stared up at the dark clouds, which were moving fast now, some of them breaking away from the main pack and gathering speed over Cornucopia. Like black smoke billowing right out of God's angry ears.

"Do you suppose if I hang onto my soul real tight, I can keep God from yanking it up to heaven and passing judgment on me after I die?"

"Nope. Nobody's stronger than God. He'll pry it loose, right out of your best grip. No, I'd say your only hope is to repent. You gotta make it up to Him."

"How do I do that? I can't take it back, 'cause I never once thought it was funny to begin with. Sure, it was evil to laugh, I know, and I ain't never going to forgive myself for doing it. But I didn't mean it. Not at all. So what do I do?"

"You got me," she said. She bit into a tomato slice she held in her fingers and looked up at the blackening sky. "But maybe you better figure it out before He strikes you with lightning."

Twenty-Two

I vowed to hew to the straight and narrow after that, praying there was still time to atone for my errant ways and skirt the scorching fires of hell. This eternal damnation business was far too scary to ignore. If reforming meant spending some extra time tending Thaney's garden or finishing everything on my plate at dinner, even the stuff that made me gag like rutabaga and Brussels sprouts, so be it. I'd throw in a moratorium on nose picking as well, and make doubly certain I flushed the toilet and fluffed up the hand towel in the bathroom when I used it. And all without being reminded.

After my reformation, I made it a point to correct Sue-Sue whenever she got off a snide remark about Thaney. "I'm sure Grandma *does* need to take all those pills and all that special tonic every day, Sue-Sue. Otherwise she wouldn't be doin' it. We wouldn't want her to end up sick like Pa Joesy now, would we? Come on, let's make our bed."

Sue-Sue was not happy. "No!" She folded her arms. "I'm not doing that stuff anymore. You do it." Maybe I'd pushed her too far. She said, "I liked you better *before*, Emma Faye."

Before, I was virtuous only on short binges near Christmas and my birthday. That might have fooled Thad and Mama, but you couldn't fool God, according to Margaret.

Or John B.

"Putting on quite the little show, aren't you?" he asked me one day. He had ball bearings in his hand and was juggling them with his fingers to make them clack. "All this *yes, ma'am* and *beg pardon, sir.* You'll be quoting us the Scriptures next, I suppose."

"I'm not putting on any show. It's just the way I am now. I turned over a new leaf. And I like it this way just fine, so leave me be. It's good to be helpful, I'll have you know. You might try it sometime." That last part just sort of slipped out, and I winced after I said it. It was like I couldn't completely reform and be nice, even to my beloved brother. It was like the devil really did have the upper hand in me.

"Sure. Okay," John B. said. "Being helpful is good. As it turns out, I could use a little help myself, Em. My Sunday shoes could use a good polishing, and I don't have very much time this week. What say you spiff them up a little for me? Maybe just until you can see your virtuous smile in them."

Boy, I walked right into that one. I could see by the grin he tried to conceal that he thought he'd tricked me good. But I'd show him for trying to turn me out as a hypocrite when I was truly reformed. "Okay. Right after I've done the dusting for Mama," I said, neatly masking my irritation. "Just leave them by my door."

I thought the shine turned out pretty good actually, even though it took me days of scrubbing to get all the shoe polish off my fingers.

It wasn't a day later Mama was yelling at me. "Emma Faye Starkey, you get in here this minute!" Her tone suggested that I not seriously think about dillydallying, although I had my hands full just then. I put down the pair of scissors I was using and told Sue-Sue not to move, that I'd be right back.

When I got to my room, Mama pointed. There on the bedspread were two black outlines in the shape of John B.'s shoes where I'd accidentally smudged the polish a bit. Mama demanded, "What in heaven's name is this? How did this happen?"

"I polished John B.'s shoes for him."

"I can see that. And you ruined a perfectly good bedspread in the process. Heaven help me! What were you thinking?" She glanced around the room, just looking for trouble. "Wait! More on the curtains? How could you possibly get shoe polish on the curtains?"

I had, hadn't I? I could see it now. "Holy cow. It must have rubbed off when I took them over to the window to look at 'em better if I'd missed anywheres."

Mama walked in a tight little circle looking up at the ceiling and came back to face me again, one eye cocked. "Think hard. Did you by any chance break a little glass figurine in the living room. A little Eiffel Tower that my sister gave me for Christmas? Maybe when you were dusting?"

"Maybe."

"Maybe?"

"I mean, I might have. It might have fallen." Heck, I wasn't even dusting it when I heard it hit the floor. How could that be my fault?

"*Might* have?" Mama demanded. She wasn't buying it. "We are going to have to have a talk, young lady. This can't go on."

"All right, but can it wait 'til I finish cutting Sue-Sue's hair?"

"What! You're cutting her hair!!??"

I was trying to get back in my sister's good graces, and she had jumped at my offer. We were doing it up fancy with the pinking shears. "It's only a little trim," I assured Mama. Then Sue-Sue came down the hall from the bathroom and into our room to see what all the fuss was about.

Mama screamed.

I didn't need her to explain to me right then that my plan for redemption was backfiring badly, but she stepped up and delivered a big lecture anyway. I waited her out as long as I could, but she seemed determined to go on and on.

"Mama," I said. It took a couple of tries to get her to stop. "Mama? Mama!"

"What is it, Emma?" She snorted with exasperation.

"I have another idea. Is it too late to register for Bible Camp?"

"What did she say to that?" Eileen wanted to know. My big sister had a mixing bowl tucked under one long thin arm while the other was slathering something gooey and sweet smelling around in the bowl with a spoon. There was a small streak of flour on her cheek. I watched for a time. Fixing something sweet looked like fun.

I said, "Mama told me it was too late for a lot of things, and then she just stomped off to take Sue-Sue to the beauty salon. What do you suppose she meant by that?" Mama was a lot closer to God than me, and her assessment of my situation sounded dire.

"She's had it with you." Eileen shook her head. "Listen, why don't you stick around with me for a bit and stay out of Mom's hair."

I wished she hadn't put it quite that way, but what she proposed sounded like a level-headed idea, even if it was suspicious that she would suddenly want to take me under her wing. "Okay," I agreed, and waited for the other shoe to drop.

"I'm making some muffins to have with our dinner. Check the recipe for me on the table. What does it say about folding in blueberries?" I read it to her and she set the bowl down. "You want to try it?" she asked, pointing with the spoon. She'd seen me watching her.

"Sure." And together we finished making batter and poured it into muffin cups. I blinked at the cloud of heat that pushed into my face as we opened the oven. The batter was still squiggly in the cups, but it would miraculously puff up in the heat soon.

Eileen closed the oven and took a step back. "What's Thaney doing?"

"She's taking a nap," I said.

Eileen appeared to give that some thought. "Would you be okay staying with the muffins for a few minutes while I run out?"

"Sure," I said, "where you going?"

She hesitated. "We need sugar. I want to sprinkle some on the muffins when they come out. I'll just go borrow a cup from Mrs. Sterns. But if I'm not back in twenty minutes for some reason, take the muffins out, okay? Think you can do that?"

Twenty minutes seemed like a long time to go for sugar at Mrs. Sterns' next door, but I was happy to be put in charge. "Sure," I said. Who *couldn't* do that?

Eileen handed me a potholder and took a coffee cup down from the cupboard. "Okay. Don't forget twenty minutes. Got it?"

I looked at the clock and said, "So I take them out at five minutes after four?"

"That's right. If I'm not back." Eileen studied my face. "Okay? Okay. Bye."

"Boy, something smells good," Margaret called from the back door.

"Blueberry muffins," I announced when she let herself in. "Eileen and I made 'em." I threw my shoulders back, proud. "We could have a couple when they're done."

"Sure, but I gotta go look for Rach first," Margaret said. "Have you seen him? Did he and John B. go off hunting?"

"I don't think so. John B. walks Tallulah home about now."

Margaret got a worried look. "My mama wants me to find Rach real quick. Think you could help me?"

"I got to watch these muffins 'til Eileen gets back."

Margaret pinched up her face a moment. "You could turn the oven off now and then turn it back on when we get back."

Margaret always had a clever way of dealing with any problem. "I s'pose," I said. "Yeah, that'd work." I looked at the dial on Mama's new gas stove. Eileen hadn't showed me how to run it, but I could see the word "Off" around a ways as I turned the dial past 550. It stopped a little short of Off, but it was close.

"There," I said to Margaret. "Let's go. I didn't want to be hanging around waiting for Eileen anyway."

I saw one of our coffee cups sitting atop a fencepost out back and wondered about it. Margaret was saying, "I've been to Wilhites' and to the park and I didn't find him. Where do you suppose he is?"

"Let's try Howard's house," I said, but after the two-block walk, it turned out that he wasn't there.

"Maybe he went swimming," I suggested.

"By himself?"

"Maybe he met somebody."

We made a beeline for the river, where it surprised me to hear Eileen's distinctive laugh. It came with an echo, like she was hiding under the bridge. Margaret and I exchanged a look that slowly turned into a pair of grins. With a nod, we silently agreed on a plan. I went first, sneaking down the embankment next to the concrete bridge abutment until I could get close enough to peek around the corner.

When I saw Rach and Eileen lying next to each other in the sand, I pulled my head back and whispered, "He's there with Eileen. They're lying there together. Eileen's cheeks are all pink." I clamped a hand over my mouth and giggled.

Margaret made her way down and pulled me out of the way so she could look. We exchanged another smile. I crawled under her and stuck an eye around the corner. Then Margaret yelled, "Hey! What do you think you're doin'?" Eileen popped up like a pin had pricked her, and Rach's head turned our way, a slow burn starting on his face. I took off on a dead run, knowing there'd be hell to pay if he caught us.

Margaret and I zigzagged along the riverbank squealing and laughing as we shrieked encouragement to each other. "Don't stop! This way!" Every time I looked back, Rach was gaining on us. Then there were sirens, like the cops were chasing us too. I squealed as we shot through the woods and broke out into the open on the other side. In the clearing, I saw smoke rising from the direction of my house. I stopped running and Margaret slammed into me.

"Oh, God," I said. "Look! That's my house on fire."

Twenty-Three

Black smoke billowed out of our kitchen window. A ladder was propped up to Thaney's bedroom window upstairs, and thin hazy smoke drifted out of it as well. Thaney was next to the ladder on the lawn, bent over, coughing, a fireman supporting her. I wanted to run and hide, to pull something over my head and not come out for a month. When I did come out, it would only be with an excellent disguise. But my feet began sleepwalking in the direction of my house, moving along as if they were barely touching the ground.

"Holy cow!" I heard Rach exclaim behind me, still panting from the run.

"Thaney, are you all right?" I asked when I reached her side. She had soot on her face and clothes, and she smelled like the char from a woodstove.

A trembling hand came my way, landed hard on my shoulder and she tilted her face up to mine. "Eileen nearly killed me," she croaked. "The little fool ran off and left something to burn up in the oven! She'll be getting a piece of my mind! You can count on that! Happily, I'm going to live, thanks entirely to Mr. Odum here." She looked toward the fireman, who wore a big smile to go with his wide yellow suspenders, big rubber boots, and big black overalls. He leaned in my direction and tipped his chipped red helmet. "Afternoon, Miss." He needed a shave and a swish of Listerine. He had halitosis bad. Thaney said, "Mr. Odum carried me down the ladder when I couldn't make it out through the smoke."

There was shouting at the back of the house, someone barking orders as firemen turned valves out front on the pump engine. It belched black smoke of its own out a red chimney. Two fire hoses were snaked through our yard. Kids from all over and many of our neighbors had gathered in the street. Other than Granny Rogers, who was sweeping her sidewalk to keep gawkers off, everybody was watching our house as if it might explode at any second.

"Is my house going to burn down?" I asked Mr. Odum, picturing Thad thrashing me with a strop the way he did Johnny sometimes when he was really furious.

Mr. Odum laughed. "No, little girl. Just a kitchen fire. We probably got her out already. That smoke's gonna cause a stink, though. Count on it. And she did some damage, she did. Plus all that water is gonna leave a stinkin' mess."

My knees gave way at this news, and I dropped to the grass and buried my face in my hands. Oh, I had really done it this time. The oven had not really turned off, and I had nearly burned the house down with my grandmother in it.

"I'm sorry," I said, speaking directly to the grass. "I'm really, *really* sorry."

"What's that, girl?" Thaney said. "What in tar-nation are you blubbering?"

When I lifted my face toward her, my eyes flooded with tears. "I said I'm sorry! This is all my fault. I left the house when I was supposed to be minding Eileen's muffins."

I heard the Saxon honk in the street just then, and it struck a note of instant terror in me. Once again, my feet seemed to be making decisions of their own, and this time they took flight to the back of the house before Thad could maneuver the car into our driveway through the throng of onlookers.

I raced to the barn, scrambled up the haymow ladder, and threw myself down in the straw. What a pathetic, bone-headed idiot I was! Would I ever do anything right ever again?

A minute or two later, I heard someone on the ladder. I held my breath and let it out only after I saw it was Margaret hoisting herself into the loft. She had a stricken look.

"Emma, ohmigod! This is terrible!" she said.

"Yes," I said, "*Terrible*. My dad is going to skin me alive."

"But why? It wasn't *your* fault!"

"Sure it was. Of course it was. I must have left the oven going. If I'd done what I said I'd do, everything would be just fine right now."

"No, that's my fault. I told you to leave the muffins, remember?" Sure, she had suggested it, but who'd have known it would lead to this? She said, "It's really Rach and Eileen's fault, if you think about it. If they hadn't gone sneaking off together, none of this would have ever happened."

That was a good point. But if I was so innocent, why was I feeling so guilty?

I heard Tallulah's cowbell clank as John B. led her into the barn. Margaret and I paused our discussion as Johnny urged the old cow into the stall, cussing softly at her before closing the gate.

"Why don't you ask your brother whose fault he thinks it is?" Margaret said before I could hush her.

"Emma?" John B. called. "You up there?"

Margaret answered for me. "She's up here."

The ladder creaked and John B.'s head popped up in the loft. "What the heck happened?" he wanted to know. He stood on the ladder staring at us.

Margaret explained things while I sobbed and hid my face.

"So whose fault do you say it is?" Margaret demanded.

"Seems like there's plenty of blame to go around, if you want to know." Something about the way he said it left me with the impression he wasn't excluding himself in his sweeping indictment. "I'm going to go find Thad and talk to him. You wait here, Emma. Don't budge."

We couldn't stay in the house that night. Even after the firemen hauled out the burned, mangled stove and dumped it in the backyard, you couldn't hardly breathe in the place. Soot and fumes had gotten into everything. Months later, when I pulled my winter coat out on the first day of frost, I could smell once more the horror of that awful fire.

"We have to be out for a couple of days," Mama said. Sue-Sue told me later that Mama had run the last three blocks home when she heard her house was on fire. I couldn't picture her running. Not at all. "You two behave yourselves," Mama said, lifting a finger in the direction of John B. and me before she closed the car door and they pulled away.

We'd been foisted off on Drummonds while Thad took Eileen, Sue-Sue, Mama, and Thaney out to the old farm that night. John B. still had the cow to milk and pasture, and Mama thought it best to keep me and Thad separated for the time being. I think she also wanted to get Eileen away from Rach.

Eileen took the brunt of the blame for the fire, but I was not off the hook.

"The firemen said several of the muffins exploded because the oven was turned up as high as it would go—almost to 600 degrees," John B. told me. He'd taken fifteen cents of the money Mama had given him to help buy groceries for the Drummonds, and spent it on a huge ice cream soda he shared with me. It was the first one I'd ever had, and I felt like Mrs. Astor's plush horse. None of us kids had ever had more than a nickel ice cream cone from the counter before. That day, Johnny and I sat inside in the sweet shop's big, cushy horseshoe-shaped booth looking out at the downtown square.

"But I turned the oven off!" I said as I spooned out vanilla ice cream and soda from a tall tulip glass. The cold slurred my words. "How could it explode?"

"I dunno," John B. said. "Maybe you turned the dial the wrong way. It was set to 600." He sipped the soda. "Hey, Em, it's okay." He reached over to pat my hand. "Nobody ever showed you how it worked. And Eileen should never have left you there alone."

"It was a dirty trick. She lied to me."

From the fleeting little smirk that crossed his face, I could see John B. actually found something to admire in this. He said, "She's all moony-eyed over a certain someone just now. I think her brain has turned to mush."

"Mush is right!" I laughed. "It turns my stomach."

John B. laughed too.

"Do you think they'll grow up and get married?" I asked. John B. shrugged and looked around the sweet shop as though he was hoping he might see someone he'd have to get up and go say hello to. He refused to look at me, even after I said, "Margaret says they're gonna—get married, that is."

"Margaret."

"Yes. And she says they will have five children. And they will name them all after us—little Margaret, little Emma, little John B. Like that." I didn't tell him the rest. That Margaret thought Rach would go kissing some other girl someday and leave Eileen and the children.

I asked, "Do you think Rach is mad at me?" It seemed like he was getting meaner everyday. He was going on thirteen now, and his sweat smelled all sharp, like a man's. He had some little hairs starting to sprout out of his chin and along his jaw.

"That's just the way he is. Doesn't mean a thing." I thought John B. should know. He and Rach were close. They seemed to be able to tell each other things without speaking. Margaret or I would say something to each other at the Drummonds' dinner table, and Rach would look at John B., and John B. would look back at Rach, and then they'd go back to eating.

John B. set his spoon down now and licked the ice cream off his lips. I could see he'd planned to speak about something and been saving it up. "Listen, Emma, this whole business got out of hand. You know, Pa Joesy dyin' and you laughin'. You were right; it was my fault. I did try to make you, 'cause I was trying not to laugh too. And I shouldn'a tole Rach nothin' about it. So if anybody is going to hell, it's me. So you can just stop worrying about it, and give up this quest for sainthood."

I took the straw out of my mouth. He looked me in the eye, all seriouslike. I nodded, and a tiny little grin formed at the corners of his mouth.

"But you have to admit," he said, "that whole death rattle business was pretty cockeyed."

It was a good thing I'd swallowed or I might have spit ice cream soda everywhere in the huge laugh that burst out of me—the first one in days. The image of Thad standing there like a cigar store Indian and Thaney working her dentures and none of us knowing what to do, standing around thinking about Pa Joesy's disgusting old body. And then he lets rip with some scary snort after we think he's already gone!

"Pretty funny," John B. said, "except the part about Grandpa actually dying."

That remark sort of killed the fun.

"You s'pose Pa Joesy is mad at us?" I asked. "Up there in heaven?"

John B. moved his shoulders in a way that said he didn't know, but out of his lips came a flat denial. "Naw."

I had trouble falling asleep in a strange bed at Drummonds' the first night, my mind teeming with ideas for bedtime stories to tell Sue-Sue, stories I was sure I'd forget before I saw her again. In one, she was a hero, saving people from a burning house. On the second night, I switched myself into the hero role and fell asleep in an instant.

Twenty-Four

In the week it took to make our house fit to live in again, John B. and I marked time at the Drummonds'. I had plenty of opportunity to reflect on what I'd done. In my dreams, Grandma Thaney chased me with a stick, and I couldn't get away because the air was like molasses. I probably had it coming. I was pretty sure Eileen was peeved, too, being stuck out there, away from her friends, away from Rach, Sue-Sue around to pester her constantly. Even a rip-snortin' Phelps fart couldn't make her laugh if that was the case.

Occasionally I saw Thad when he would drop by our place to check on the laying of the new kitchen floor or on the repainting or on all the other things that had to be done to the house, but we never spoke because I ran the other direction when I saw him. Once, as I was watching workmen unload our shiny new stove off the truck, I must have been transfixed by the shiny handles and white surfaces because Thad was suddenly there, getting out of the Saxon. Only the workmen setting the stove down and tipping their hats alerted me to my father's presence, once again home to supervise. I ducked away quick before he could decide to club me.

Seeing that new stove and then going right back over to the Drummonds' where they had a sooty old iron clunker made me think their house really belonged out in the country nearer to Thaney and Pa Joesy's old farm. The Drummonds had no running water or electricity, and the furniture was from another century. And although Mrs. Drummond kept everything spotlessly clean, I grew more troubled during our stay about what Mama called the

Drummonds' "circumstances." I hadn't realized just how humble their circumstances were with Mr. Drummond gone.

James, the oldest after Reno, had quit school to go to work as a laborer in the cement factory. He had also taken the place at the head of the table where his father had once sat. His hair was gray at the temples with cement dust where his hard hat and breathing mask didn't cover it. He spoke magisterially to his brother and sisters from his lofty perch, as if he were truly a man.

"Alice, don't play with your food," he ordered.

I could barely look little Alice in the eye. No one ever offered her much affection. She wore hand-me-down rummage, and her hair was as unruly as straw in a March wind. She was stick-figure thin, skinnier even than Margaret was, and jumpy as a frog in a skillet.

"Stop that infernal wiggling," James barked.

One night, when Rach and John B. returned empty-handed from hunting, Mrs. Drummond put mush on the table for our dinner. I immediately wished my mother wasn't still out at the farm, and I felt stupid for having pigged out on an ice cream soda with some of the grocery money my folks had given us. It would have paid for a bit of meat. I stared in disbelief at the glob of mush on my plate. John B. caught me at it and threw an elbow into my side, but I don't think Mrs. Drummond noticed.

"Pull the blinds," she commanded Margaret with mock urgency. "We don't want to make the neighbors hungry."

That made me chuckle. Mrs. Drummond was *okay*. She knew this was a terrible excuse for a meal, but she was not going to feel sorry for herself or her family. Still, it embarrassed me to have to share such measly vittles, and it didn't help when Rach decided to pick a fight. I'm not sure which of the silly things I had said that night or earlier got him riled up, but he turned on me with sarcasm.

"If you get any darker, Emma," he said, "you'll pass for one of the Grubbses."

It was true my skin always turned a rich, dark color in the summer, and it seemed to go well beyond an ordinary tan. I wondered for the first time if this was how people accidentally became black. And I wondered whether I was next. What if my dark skin didn't fade this time at the summer's end? What if I ended up poor like the Grubbses? Tommy Bern would call me a nigger. I retorted, "Well, if you got any more sunburned, Rach, it'd look like paint peeling off a cigar store Indian."

This got a tiny laugh out of Margaret, who immediately lowered her eyes to her plate. Mrs. Drummond stepped in and said, "Rach. Emma. That will be enough."

"Tell him to shut up, then," I said, forgetting all my manners.

That's when John B. put a hand on my arm, like a hobble anchoring a horse. I glared at Rach, who held his spoon with all of his fingers wrapped around the handle as if it were a shovel, the way Thaney told us we couldn't. I felt like telling him he should learn some manners.

That night, I fell asleep praying with all my heart that our house would be all fixed up before Mrs. Drummond could put another paltry dinner on the table. My prayer was not answered. We were still there the next night when she served a "rabbit stew." I couldn't eat it. I'd seen Rach earlier with two dead squirrels.

I began to wonder if I was darkening my skin past the point of no return as I watered Thaney's flowers and weeded her garden every day in the sun (not that I'd have sought out shade indoors if I hadn't been in the garden; I'd a just played across the street with my friends). Every time I was tempted to set down the hoe, however, a picture of Thaney doubled over beneath the fireman's ladder, trying to catch her wind, came to mind and it drove me back to my work.

I had the chickens to tend to as well. It was a duty I usually shared with Eileen and Sue-Sue, but I didn't mind doing it alone. I took the eggs directly to the Drummonds, pleased with each clutch I presented. It felt good to have something to share. And it meant there was something Mrs. Drummond could serve that I could eat, too. "They'd just go to waste at our house," I told her.

Mostly, the Drummonds were nice to us and looked after our comfort, but I missed everything about being home and in my own bed. Whenever I could, I snuck off to use our indoor biffy rather than the Drummonds' stinky outhouse. Guiltily, I'd peel back the chintz curtain when I went in to see if I'd been noticed. As the nights passed, I even began to miss Sue-Sue following me around and Eileen's bossiness. And I grew tired of my best friend, Margaret, whose superiority took full reign, now that I was her captive.

"Here, read this," she said, thrusting a library book at me.

"What is it?"

"A Western. I think you'll find that real cowboys live in Texas or Wyoming or Colorado. Not *Ohio*."

My family finally returned on Saturday, and John B. and I got to move home. Thad pretended I was invisible, but Thaney wasted no time seeking me out to yell at me, even after all my hard work. "Why did you pull up all the new carrot shoots in the garden?" She pointed at a bare patch of earth. "What were you thinking?"

"I thought those were little weeds!" I said.

She harrumphed in disgust.

For a homecoming celebration, Mama fried up two plump chickens on her new stove, just the way we liked them with all the fixings.

By Sunday afternoon, everything was nearly back to normal. We read the funnies in our Sunday paper, and I suggested to Sue-Sue we pay Max Nix a visit next and see the strips in the other paper.

Sue-Sue was still so little then with the cutest turned-up nose. Max fussed over her like a little doll. She had just turned six that summer, and she didn't seem bothered when Max would pull her between his knees to hug her. It made me uncomfortable, though. I would always tell Sue-Sue it was time to go home when it happened.

Max had only a few strands of long, black hair to cover his whole round head, and his mouth had a valentine shape, the upper lip drooping in the middle like a teardrop. His eyeteeth showed like dog fangs when he smiled. His chin and nose were long and sloping, and the jowls on either side hung like a hound dog's.

It was a beautiful day that Sunday so we sat out on Max's porch swing. He plopped between us and put his arm around Sue-Sue. We'd only finished the Katzenjammer Kids when he began taking Sue-Sue's hand and patting it up and down his body, as if it was a game. I hadn't seen him do this before, and I took my eye off the words and pictures to watch. When he moved her hand toward his crotch, I jumped down off the swing and grabbed Sue-Sue away from him. I yanked her arm practically out of the socket as I lit off down the porch steps. "Ouch!" she complained.

"Where you go?" Max called after us. "We moose finish!"

"My mama is calling," I claimed. "She's been watchin' us out the window."

I wanted to scare him, put the threat of an adult into it. Truth was, I didn't think Mama had a clue about what went on over at Max Nix's house. Neither did Max's wife, who often stayed in her kitchen when we came over. I wondered if I should tell Mama, but I wasn't sure I knew the words or how to say them. And I didn't want her to say we couldn't go back again. Sue-Sue and I would miss reading the other funny papers.

When we got close to home, I turned to look back and see whether Max had followed us. But there he sat, still gliding on that swing, looking crestfallen. Later, I looked over again and saw him poke a hole in his newspaper and bring it up to his face like he was reading. But I could tell he was spying through the opening he'd made as Sue-Sue and I turned cartwheels in our front yard.

Two other things happened that summer that stick in my memory, although the significance of neither was clear to me at the time.

Tommy Bern unexpectedly cut across our grass one evening just after dusk, and John B. came out of the shadows to intercept him. He grabbed Tommy by the shirtfront and practically lifted that tub of lard off the ground.

"You stay out of our yard, Tom Bern. You hear me? I don't want to see you anywhere around here." Tommy had a funny little grin and lifted his hands in mock surrender. I assumed Johnny was defending me because of the incident with Roberta on the way to school, and I was proud of him.

Then, a few nights later, a shotgun blast cut through the dark as I lay in bed counting sheep. The concussion was accompanied by the sounds of shredding leaves and splintering wood. I imagined pellets scattering and finding their marks. Then I heard huffing and rapid footsteps as someone ran through our yard. The sounds all seemed magnified in the dark. Afterward, there was complete silence. I lay there listening, waiting for the next noise. A dog barked down the street and Sue-Sue ground her teeth and smacked her lips and rolled over in her sleep.

I got up and looked out the window, but it was too dark to see much. I knew the vague gray shapes of the houses and trees and fences that stood out in the odd silvery light of the stars. But I watched for something that wasn't supposed to be there and didn't see it.

Our back door creaked after a moment and I pressed closer to the glass to see who had gone out. Suddenly, John B. was at my side, looking out, too, and there was Thad moving through the yard in his nightshirt with a flashlight.

"What's going on?" I asked Johnny.

"Nothing." He put an arm around me and steered me away from the window. "You get back to bed. The excitement's over. With any luck, this will be an end to it."

Twenty-Five

ven after all these years, I can recollect the utter panic and sense of doom that gripped me as I approached the start of third grade in 1924. It was as if I were being shoved to the edge of the earth for a stomach-jolting drop over the side. Below was a bed of fiery hot coals known as The Gutch. My only hope was to scramble as best I could across to the safety of summer vacation on the other side. It was my year to suffer Mrs. Gutchow, the battle-ax who ruled third grade like a banana republic tyrant. Having run this gauntlet themselves, my big brother and older sister got a perverse joy out of scaring me with horror stories about her before school began that fall.

"You're lucky you're not left-handed," Johnny said. "The Gutch made Herbert Lovejoy use his right hand for everything, including writing. Then she kept him in from recess for failing penmanship."

Eileen did one of her impersonations, which I thought sounded a lot like her Thaney voice. "Gum chewing will not be tolerated in this classroom!" She gave me a squint. "Honestly, if she catches you, she'll make you spit it into your hand and put your hand on top of your head and then she'll mash your hand down to get the gum in there good. I saw her do it to Morty Freeman, and he had to come to school after that with a big hole in his hair where his mama cut it out."

I had passed The Gutch's classroom many times in my years at South, and I would glance in as one might check carefully for a troll before crossing a bridge. You never knew when she would come flying into the hall, grab someone by the collar, and march them to the principal's office for doing the smallest thing.

The Gutch was the very model of stern probity. Where she got her dark dresses I don't know, but these garments were twenty years behind the times and chosen, it seemed, to strike terror into any child who thought of crossing her. Her braided, iron-colored hair was wound up with little sprouts sticking out of it like coiled barbed wire.

That first day, I was numb with fear. My hands were cold as ice and my armpits already damp when Margaret and I entered her room and scuttled quietly toward the back. I was wearing the dress Eileen had worn on her first day of third grade.

"Where do you think *you're* going?" The Gutch's voice intoned.

I turned and saw her eyes burning a hole in my forehead as she sat behind her desk. Her name was written on the blackboard in chalk letters as perfectly formed as those in a book or on a billboard. "We were just going to sit down," I said.

"Are you the Starkey girl?"

"Uh, yes, ma'am?"

She had a seating chart in front of her, but she didn't have to look at it. She pointed at the center desk in the front row. "Right there." From her expression, it was clear that she intended to keep me under special watch. My heart sank. Had I done something already? Why single me out for a hot seat?

Margaret got a knowing nod of the old lady's head, and was directed to a desk in back. "You will be one of the row monitors this year, Margaret," Mrs. Gutchow said. "You remember how that works. You pick up everyone's papers in your row and bring them forward when I tell you."

I wanted to look back at her. She'd been kicked out of The Gutch's class the year before, and it had done nothing to soften The Gutch's fearsome reputation. But I didn't look at her because Margaret had warned me about rubbernecking. "You'll get a check mark in her book."

"What happens then?"

Margaret just shook her head.

"There's no talking!" Mrs. Gutchow bellowed at the other children as they filed into her room. "Raise your hand if you want to speak, and then speak only *after* I acknowledge you."

Finally, when everyone was settled, she stood up and her knees cracked like ice in the river during a January cold snap.

"Good morning. I am the third grade teacher at South School, Mrs. Gutchow. I am to be addressed at all times as Mrs. Gutchow. I don't want to hear anyone yelling, 'Hey, teacher!'"

Somebody made the mistake of laughing.

"Who was that? Who laughed? Whoever it was, stand up. Right now!" She scanned the room. "I'm waiting." No one budged. "Well, all right. If no one will admit to it, everyone will stay in at recess." Heads swiveled toward the offender, Elmer Tripp. Elmer was a puffy figure of a boy with the backbone of a marshmallow. Sensing no escape, he got uncertainly to his feet.

"Come up here," The Gutch commanded. She consulted her sheet. "Elmer Tripp?" When Elmer reached her desk, she ordered him to stick out his hand. He reached out as though she were going to hand him something, and as he did, a ruler materialized to smack him hard across the palm and wrist. He yelped like a stuck pig. "Next time it will be your knuckles. Now, return to your desk, and let's have no more of that!"

It got very still in the room. Every squeak of the chalk on the blackboard sent a shiver through me. My eyes riveted to Mrs. Gutchow's hand as she wrote in her precise letters "Topeka, Kansas," the capital of our state, and "Sunflower," the state flower. I didn't mean to provoke her, but as it turned out, I seriously underestimated the acuity of her hearing.

Before we turned out the light that night, Sue-Sue asked to see the back of my hand one more time. The throbbing had stopped, and the swelling was down and the redness faded. The start of a mottled bruise was visible.

"And all you did was whisper to the kid next to you?"

"I said I couldn't believe nobody had warned Elmer about The Gutch."

"That's what she made you stand and repeat to the whole class?"

"And she smacked me a good one with the ruler after I did. But she wouldn't let me sit down. She said that I hadn't told the class exactly what I'd whispered."

"Really?"

"I left out the part where I called her The Gutch. On purpose."

"Oh."

"She hit me three times before she got me to say it. And then she hit me again."

I hardly slept a wink that night and my stomach was so jumpy in the morning, I couldn't eat my breakfast. My journey across the hot coals had barely begun, and already I was badly singed. I was sure that I could never get up the nerve to go back to school ever again. And if I didn't, I knew The Gutch would track me down. It was hopeless. I was doomed.

"Which black dress do you suppose The Gutch will wear today?" Eileen smiled as she crunched on her marmalade toast.

I was in no mood. "What are you talking about?"

"Black dresses. It's all she owns. She's mourning the death of Mr. Gutchow."

"He died?"

"Only thirty-five years ago."

Obviously, this was a woman with a long memory. What shred of hope did I have?

Eileen added, "Legend has it he drowned in a fishing accident."

"Likely story," John B. said with a smile. He had his hand cupped around the side of his mouth for a harsh whisper. "After being married to The Gutch a couple of years, the poor man probably jumped overboard with his tackle box tied to his ankle."

"Johnny," Mama cautioned.

The smile got bigger on Johnny's face. He spoke up. "Yeah, you're right. He should have tied the tackle box to *her* ankle."

"Johnny!"

"Alls I'm saying," Johnny concluded.

My hands were sweating as I crossed over the threshold into Room 113 for the second time. I kept telling myself I'd already managed to escape the clutches of the loony teacher on the bus to Joplin the spring before. I ought to be able to figure a way to escape this one, too, particularly since I knew the landscape.

Mrs. Gutchow had written a funny assortment of numbers and x's on the blackboard, like 2x3=6. It was multiplication, she informed us, and we were going to learn how it was done. I concentrated with all my might on what she was saying, never even flinching through a terrific pang that was bloating my empty stomach. Suddenly, the pressure released with a ferocious growl that could be heard in the far corners of the room.

The Gutch wheeled around, eyes wide. I immediately lowered mine, looking up again only after I heard the clack of chalk against the board. "Now, when you multiply two numbers, you come up with a total that would be the same as if you added each of those numbers up as many times as ..."

A second report came from my stomach, louder and stronger than the first, a sort of descending note like a cat's howl with a little flourish at the end. A titter of laughs rippled through the room that was snuffed out when The Gutch gave us the evil eye. Again, I lowered my head and tried to will my stomach into silence as I waited for her to resume. Only she didn't, and I heard her footsteps stop next to my desk. "Is that rude sound coming out of you, Emma Starkey?"

I stared up at her. She had that searing expression in her eyes again. I was saying "I guess so" just about the time my stomach rumbled with a sound like our bathtub made when the last of the water drained out. "I mean, yes, Mrs. Gutchow. I mean, sorry. Excuse me."

"It's distracting!"

"I don't mean for it to happen."

"No? Perhaps it would be better if you stepped into the hall."

"I don't see how that's gonna stop it." Again, there were restrained titters.

"Get up from your desk this second and step out into the hall!"

I felt my classmates' mocking eyes turn on me, and my face grew hot. Then a cold sheet of perspiration spread across my back and under the arms of Eileen's old dress. Mrs. Gutchow stepped to her big desk, opened a spiral notebook, and made a check mark, gesturing me toward the door with her free hand.

I hadn't been in the hall a minute when she came out and leaned down into my face. Her breath was warm and smelled unaccountably like cinnamon. "Listen to me, you little troublemaker, I had nine months of your brother, and you are not going to put me through another year like that one, I assure you."

"I didn't mean anything. It just happened. It's not my fault."

"Quiet. You stay outside this door until I return for you, have you got that?"

"Yes, ma'am."

In less than a minute, I was too antsy to stand there any longer. I was feeling scared and hopeless. I knew I could not go back in that room, even if she was ready to take me back, not if my stomach wasn't going to stop. And it wasn't. At the sound of another growl, my eyes welled up with tears. This was too horrid. I was in a fix. I wiped my eyes angrily and ran toward the sunlight pouring in through the outside door at the end of the corridor.

Twenty-Six

*T*he magnitude of my mistake hit me like a mud brick the second I dashed out that door. There was no place to run. I'd left the school building and jumped into even deeper trouble. I couldn't go home. Mama and Thaney would see I was playing hooky and drag me back. I couldn't go back inside because if The Gutch caught me now, I'd probably get slapped with a ruler across the face. I couldn't hang around the school yard, because I'd be seen. What was I going to do?

Then I saw it, a home bordering the school that was not fenced. I ran for it, pushing through some thick bushes and into the backyard where I stopped to think over what to do next. The branches had scraped my arms and I thought I'd heard something rip, but at least I was shielded and safe for the moment. I sat down next to a pink birdbath, scooped my dress over my upturned knees, and wrapped my arms around my legs. It all seemed utterly silly. All this fuss was over a gurgling stomach, which had stopped now—naturally.

The sun went behind some darkening clouds, and I got goose bumps, so I wrapped my arms tighter around my legs. I thought about staying there in a stranger's backyard until school ended. Then I could walk home and pretend nothing had happened. But I was hungry and my lunch was in my desk in the classroom.

By the time morning recess began, my stomach was growling again and a drizzle had begun falling from the gray sky. I knew I needed a different plan. I could hear the shouts and squeals of children on the other side of the shrubs as they ran around on the playground without me. Why did school work out fine for everyone else but not for me?

Amidst the noise, I heard Margaret's voice calling my name.

"In here!" I called back. I bent back some branches to help her crawl through. She caught a few dry leaves in her hair. I plucked them out as she stooped to brush off her knees on the sheltered side. "How'd you know where to find me?" I asked.

"There aren't that many places you can go to hide, and I already checked the boiler room." The boiler room. I didn't even know where that was. Boy, Margaret never missed a trick. She asked, "What are you going to do? Mrs. Gutchow is fixing to brain you."

"Yeah, I've been thinking. What about this? What if I go back and tell her I had to go to the bathroom—and that's why I wasn't in the hall when she came out to get me? I could say I got sick, and I had to sit on the toilet all this time."

"She sent Roberta to check for you in the bathroom and Roberta said you weren't there."

"But what if I was in a stall Roberta didn't look in?"

"I don't know, Emmy. You might be better off telling the truth."

I decided Margaret wasn't so smart after all. *Tell the truth?* Like that wouldn't get me expelled or something. I said, "Okay, what about this? What if you bring me my lunch at noon—it's in my desk—and I go to the public library with it? I could wait there until school is over and I hear from you that it's safe to go home."

"I think I'll have to start calling you Jane," Margaret said.

"Jane?"

"Calamity Jane."

"That's not funny, Margaret." I'd read one of those dime novels myself.

Margaret folded her arms across her chest. "Well, you have to admit, you keep hopping out of the frying pan into the fire."

I wanted to argue with her, but I couldn't get past the thought that my life *was* a parade of calamities.

Margaret said, "Why in heaven's name did you run off? You'd have only gotten a scolding if you'd stayed in the hall."

"I don't know. I just couldn't stand it. I can't stand her." I shrugged. "Don't you get on her sour side, too, Margaret, on account of me. I'll figure something out here on my own. I'll send you a note or something about it later."

Margaret's eyes suddenly got big, and I turned my head in time to see that a stern man in a dark suit had come through the side yard and was walking directly toward us.

"Emma Starkey?" he said. I froze. "Emma Starkey, get up and come with me. And you, young lady, you get back on that playground." Margaret recognized the principal before I did, and she was back through the bush like a shot.

Mama arrived at the principal's office in her housedress, a large purse clutched under her arm and her best Sunday hat hastily pinned in her hair. We sat in slippery wood chairs facing the principal's desk. Mama was sucking on her lips so hard they disappeared. I was ashamed of the embarrassment I'd caused, but also angry at the injustice of my predicament. I wanted to explain, but I couldn't help myself. It made me want to cry. "It's no fair," I blubbered. "I didn't do anything. My stomach growled."

Word of this was bound to be everywhere before school was out that day since the principal had phoned our house, and I was fairly certain that the operator at central, who was my friend Dema's aunt, had listened in, as was her habit. She'd have told Dema's mother by now, and Dema's mother would have told the neighbor and then it would have gone everywhere.

The principal spoke evenly, gravely, to Mama, not to me. "Mrs. Gutchow wants her suspended from school. For disobedience. For truancy. For being a disruptive force in the classroom. I have to say, sneaking out of school this morning was a serious matter."

"I'll take her home and talk to her," Mama said sweetly. "We'll get it all straightened out. I'll see this doesn't happen again."

Even though we were hurrying because of the drizzle, the walk home seemed much longer to me than usual. Mama took her time before she broke the silence. "What in the world am I going to do about you, Emma Faye? And because of you, I suspect Sue-Sue is going to be wilder still."

What could I say? "Margaret says I'm like Calamity Jane."

It surprised me to hear Mama laugh. I looked over to see her shaking her head.

We traipsed another block in silence, thunderclouds gathering above. Then she said, "Emmy, there are people in this world that you just have to step lightly around. Mrs. Gutchow is one of them. She won't put up with your rambunctious shenanigans." I felt like saying something about John B. setting me up, but I didn't. "This may be the year you have to grow up and take some responsibility for what you do or you will suffer severe consequences. I can't protect you if you're determined to be a wild and undisciplined child your entire life."

"Yes, ma'am," I said, although I hadn't planned to be a child my whole life.

"When we get home, you are going to sit down and write a letter of apology to Mrs. Gutchow. You are going to apologize for every single thing that's happened. And you will say you are very sorry. And you will promise her that it won't ever happen again. Is that understood?"

"Yes, ma'am."

"Now let's hurry along before we get any wetter."

I was penciling out the words of an apology on a practice tablet after lunch when I heard a commotion in the front yard and the sound of feet stomping rapidly across our front porch. Then the doorbell rang twice and someone knocked real loud on the screen door. There were excited voices.

I was surprised to see Margaret and Roberta were responsible for making all the commotion. Why weren't they in school? Margaret was bursting with excitement. "Wow! Did you miss it, Emmy! Wow!"

"You should a seen her!" Roberta said. "It were somethin'!" I'd never seen Roberta so animated, either. Or so talkative.

"Seen who?" I asked.

"Mrs. Gutchow!" they chimed together.

"Yeah? What'd she do now?"

"You won't believe it!" Margaret exclaimed. "She got all crazy and fell down at the blackboard."

"She what?"

"It's true. She started reeling around like she was having a dizzy spell or something, but she was talking gibberish all the while she did. It was like she was speaking the way those holy rollers do at a tent revival. Only she turned sort of purple when she did it, not pink, and her feet scooted out from under her, and then she was on the floor."

I could scarcely believe my ears. "You're making this up!"

"No!" Margaret said. "Honest injun! Ask anybody. It's the gospel."

"And she fell down?" I asked Roberta, seeking confirmation. "On the floor?"

"Made a little puddle," Roberta said, her eyes staring back at the memory.

I had to think a second. A puddle. "No-o-o-o!!"

"Yep," Roberta said. "No mistaking it. Smelt."

"Girls!" Mama called from the kitchen, where the sound of her and Thaney peeling potatoes had slowed to a halt. "That'll be enough about that." I could hear them moving in our direction.

"We couldn't believe our eyes," Margaret said, plunging on. "So we all just sat there for a few minutes. I guess everybody was waiting for her to get up again. And when she didn't, we thought she might be dead."

"My heavens!" Mama said. "She isn't, is she?"

"I don't think so, Mrs. Starkey. She groaned once when she was lying there. And Tubby—I mean Elmer—ran out into the hall and started screaming bloody murder. Eventually the principal came. And a janitor. And they sent another teacher off to fetch a doctor, and then they herded us off to the gym. Then we stood around in there while Elmer played with the lights. Then they sent us home."

"Really?" Mama asked. "Just now?"

"*Really.*"

"Boy, you're right," I said. "I really did miss it. But you're sure she didn't croak?" I felt guilty, like it might be my fault, causing all that trouble accidentally.

"Big ol' white ambulance come," Roberta said. "Then she open one eye."

"Wow!" I was flabbergasted. "This is unbelievable." I started to pace as I thought about it. "Gosh, what happens now?" Was I still suspended? I looked at Mama and didn't ask. I could see she was sizing it all up still, too.

Margaret said. "We'll be having a sub, I s'pose."

"You s'pose?"

"Couldn' be no worse than The Gutch," Roberta said, and looked anxiously at Mama and Thaney. "I mean Miz Gutchow."

Twenty-Seven

y fortunes had pivoted on a microscopic hinge. It was incredible. One tiny blood vessel deep in the brain of a hardened old woman failed and everything about one girl's third grade year turned around in the next heartbeat. Back then, I didn't understand the medical pathology, but I recognized the word *stroke* being murmured by the adults. Somehow, it left me as light as a feather. I jumped off the front porch three times, each jump arcing higher than the last. Joy should not grow out of another's misery, but I did not let that stop me. I didn't give a fig for The Gutch, not after all of the suffering she'd dished out first.

The best was yet to come, however. I will never forget the first time I laid eyes on him. That smile. Those blue eyes. I thought he was some good-looking high school boy the principal had sent in to keep an eye on our class until our substitute could show up. Then, he introduced himself as *Mister* Smallwood, our new teacher, and you could feel a rush of excitement surge through the room. This *boy* (he was barely a man) was actually going to teach us. *Our* class! Who would have thought such a crazy, wonderful thing was possible? And, really, he didn't seem that far removed from the athletic boys we had watched the previous summer doing calisthenics on the high school field.

He was devilishly handsome. When he smiled at me as I reached my desk, my knees went all mushy, and I had to put a hand out to brace myself and sit down quick.

"He's dreamy," Margaret said at recess. "Will you trade places?"

"Not on your life." Suddenly being stuck up front was a very good thing indeed. I liked staring unabashedly at Mr. Smallwood's fresh, smooth face. He had the most perfect nose I had ever seen. His golden hair was not parted in the middle, as had been the style for years, but to the side where it paid compliment to the contours of his cheekbones. His eyes were quick and intelligent, hungry for anything of beauty or interest. And his manner of speaking to us felt like a gentle caress after The Gutch's barked orders.

"Good morning. I am pleased to see so many obviously bright faces in my class." Our nervous and self-conscious laughter reminded me of Elmer Beck's dog, a mischievous mutt that circled and cowered whenever it approached strangers. Suddenly, Mr. Smallwood looked as if he felt sorry for us. "I am sure you have all suffered a great shock, but I am pleased to be able to report that Mrs. Gutchow is recovering nicely in the hospital." The energy in the room evaporated like gasoline on hot pavement. Did he mean she was coming back? Mr. Smallwood seemed to sense he had said something upsetting, but obviously, he didn't know what because his next comment only underlined the point. "She is expected to be all right, class!" Only then did it seem to come clear to him that we were not rooting for her full recovery.

"I see," he said uncertainly.

"I hear Mrs. Gutchow wants to come back," Margaret told me as she eased back into the hay and stared up at the barn's rafters the next afternoon. "Trouble is, her face has gone all crooked."

It scared me to hear it. She was already the subject of nightmares, reading my apology letter in a hospital bed, crumpling it up, spitting on it. Next, she appeared on our porch, bent on a vendetta and carrying a ruler that whipped like Mama's hickory switch. So vivid were these dreams that I had to peek out the parlor window before opening our front door the next time the bell rang.

Mama had insisted on my finishing the apology letter and delivering it to the principal, even though it was all a pack of lies and Mrs. Gutchow was no longer around to spit on them. "It's important that the principal read it, too," Mama said. When he did, as I watched in the slippery chair, he nodded. "You may go back to your class, Emma."

Margaret's suggestion that The Gutch might return someday made me anxious. I reached up to the shelf in the barn where John B. kept his old slingshot, loaded a marble into it, and shot it across at a galvanized washtub that hung on the opposite wall of the barn. It thudded off the nearby wood.

"I'd have to quit school if The Gutch came back," I told her.

Margaret adopted a cowboy drawl. "This school ain't big enough for the two of us." She laughed at her own wit. She said, "Don't worry. It's never going to happen. The Gutch is through. She'll never come back."

"It'd be a double whammy if she did," I said, consumed by the threat of it. "We'd lose Mr. Smallwood and we'd be trapped in her awful jail again." Mr. Smallwood was like a dream come true, and the object of a dozen crushes among the girls in my class. In the privacy of the haymow, Margaret and I began writing him mash notes that we read to each other with giggles and shrieks before stuffing them into a coffee can we hid up high.

In one, I begged him for a strand of the hair that often slipped down onto his forehead, and which he raked back into place with his long, elegant fingers. "That golden lock that pesters you?" I wrote. "I would treasure it all my life."

I resolved to Margaret now, "If Mr. Smallwood leaves, I'm going with him."

The next marble out of my slingshot clanked off the tub. Bull's-eye.

"Ma! I'm gonna knock Emma into the middle of next week if she doesn't stop hogging up this bathroom every morning before school!" Eileen stood just outside the locked door as she yelled this.

I pulled back the razor and hurriedly wiped Thad's shaving cream off my forehead with a towel. "All right, all right!" I yelled. I quickly folded the straight edge and put it back in the drawer. "Keep your bustle buttoned!" My eyebrows would have to wait. I'd been unhappy with them ever since Margaret made a remark about how bushy they always were. I'd tried using Mama's tweezers to pluck them into shape, but I had to stop. The sting was more than I could stand. Plus I found one of Thaney's gray mustache hairs caught in the tweezers.

I'd never worried much about my looks before, but Margaret and I had come to the conclusion that appearance was vital to getting noticed in the right way by Mr. Smallwood. In the hayloft, we cleared out the can of marbles, the slingshot and the other junk from John B.'s shelf and replaced them with lipstick, face powder, and cold cream that Margaret stole from Reno's vanity when she wasn't looking. Reno had long since moved home after her marriage failed and she threw the Bull out of the house Mr. Drummond had bought for them across the street. Mr. Drummond had sold it and made her move home, but the Bull liked to sneak back to spy on Reno. He became an elusive phantom whose cigarette smoke we could smell in the air around the neighborhood from time to time.

Mama gave me a leaky perfume atomizer from the attic and an old mirror, which we also propped up on the shelf. Before long, we added hairbrushes and stiffening goop.

Reno's oxblood lipstick made us look more like clowns than grown-ups, but we could never wear it to school anyway. In the dim light, I could make Margaret's freckles seem to disappear under the face powder, but I put so much on her that it set off a sneezing fit, and she had to go home and wash up. She came back a while later with a fashion magazine she'd borrowed from Reno's room.

"This is what we should be doing," she said, opening it and pointing to an article on hairstyles. "This could make all the difference. And these, we could wear to school!"

The current styles were all quite short to accommodate the snug cloche hats that were all the rage. Women pulled cloche hats so far down over their heads that they had to tip their faces back to see. "The forehead is completely out of fashion," Margaret said. She brushed her dark hair forward and looked at it in the mirror. "I think mine's long enough."

"Long enough?" I asked.

"For bangs."

"Look, here's a style like Natalie wore," I said, pointing. "If they're cutting it that way in Joplin, it's got to be right. That's what I want." I turned the page to see if there were others. "Hey, what's this?"

It was an article on flattening your bosoms to make them disappear with a Symington side lacer. Margaret and I giggled. We weren't going to be needing one of those.

The scorching heat of the curling iron made me wince.

"If you don't hold still, you're going to get burned," Mama warned me. And she was right. The fiery metal did touch my scalp, and I jumped up as if I'd been shot. I danced around the chair in the kitchen, shouting and patting at the spot on my head until the stinging passed. I could smell burned skin now along with my singed hair.

"Would you like to stop?" Mama asked.

And ruin my chance? No! I pictured again Mr. Smallwood dancing with me in his arms. He was not that tall in my fantasy. My face was expertly made up from our secret stash of cosmetics and my hair was perfect. Mr. Smallwood couldn't take his eyes off me.

"No," I said. "I'll be still."

I needed that wave in my hair. Mama picked up the picture I'd torn out of Reno's magazine and studied it again for a moment. "We're almost done," she said. She had cut my hair this once rather than Thad, who liked to use a sheep-shearing motion for speed. The last time I had asked Thad to cut my hair in a special way—shingled up the back and long on the sides—I ended up looking like one of those dogs with the long, floppy ears.

Mama took her time now with the final waves. When she was finished, she handed me a mirror.

My new hairstyle wasn't a match for the picture in the magazine, but the dramatic change in my appearance put a charge in me anyway. I was on Cloud Nine. Finally, I looked grown up. "Wow!" I exclaimed. "That's something!"

And I got noticed, all right. Mr. Smallwood didn't exactly appear smitten, however, as he stared at me the next day for a long moment. I tried to read the expression in his eyes, knowing it wasn't the reaction I was looking for, but unwilling to see a hint of amusement there. I was just happy to be noticed.

And just as happy three days later when Mama washed my hair and my waves vanished.

Twenty-Eight

*T*he skies over Cornucopia, Kansas, turned slate gray on schedule that November as the winds blew bitterly out of the North. And, on schedule, Mama dug out the long underwear and ugly black wool socks. We hated this stuff. But matters got worse this time because she introduced an obnoxious new weapon in the fight against the winter elements—a stink bomb in a tiny cloth bag that was fastened to a loop of string.

"Eeew," Eileen complained. "What *is* that?"

"It's an asphidity bag," Mama said.

"More like an asphyxia bag, you ask me," John B. said, backing away.

Mama smiled. "This one's yours, Johnny. Go on, take it. Now put it around your neck and tuck it into your shirt."

"What the Sam Hill for?" he demanded, holding it at arm's length.

"It wards off humors and miasmas," Mama said. "It will keep you well."

"I don't get it," I said, taking up the torch of resistance. "How can it keep you well if the smell alone makes you sick?" Johnny had gotten a smile. I got a frown. But I dug in my toes. Itchy long johns and ugly socks were one thing. A stink bomb was quite another—like illegal mustard gas. I'd gotten a whiff of one the year before from under Hubert Jones' plaid flannel shirt and the smell like to wore my nose out. I told Mama, "I'm not doing it. And that's final." I handed mine back to her.

"You *are* going to wear it," she said, "like it or *not*." She handed it back to me.

The vile vapors spoiled the taste of my oatmeal that morning. I added another spoonful of brown sugar and turned my face over my shoulder to gasp in some fresh air. John B. was in a sour mood, too.

"I found a bunch of makeup and girl crap on my shelf in the haymow," he announced to no one in particular. Then his eye scanned his sisters around the table. "Fer cryin' out loud! Where's my slingshot? Tell me that." He scooped the last of his cereal and said, "Isn't it bad enough that I have to put up with that stuff cluttering up all the space in the bathroom? Do I have to trip over it out in the barn, too?" He didn't look directly at me, but *he* knew that *I* knew who he was yelling at.

By the time I found where he'd thrown everything, the lipstick was frozen and crumbled, the powder had spilled, and the mirror cracked. I guess I had it coming, not respecting his stuff. By then, cold weather had driven Margaret and me back indoors anyway. We idled our afternoons with Reno's fashion magazines, learning all about rising hemlines and the allure of the naked arm while reclining on Margaret's bed.

The first time I got sweaty playing basketball in P.E.—and it didn't take much in those long johns—Mr. Smallwood's eyebrows shot up and his head jerked back when I walked past him. My face blazed hot. I'd been betrayed by Margaret's reassurances and by my classmates' abominable senses of smell. The truth was that I stunk. I hurried away from my teacher as fast as I could and turned my face. I couldn't bear to look at him.

He recovered enough after I'd cleared off to show us the proper technique for shooting a basketball. And something else too, something he called his signature shot. He lay flat on the floor, his back against the wood, and tossed the ball up and over his head in a perfect arc through the hoop. We cheered. We all had to try it, too, of course, but we really needed our legs to make the ball go that high.

None of us could get it to go more than four or five feet off the floor when lying on our backs.

"It takes a lot of practice," Mr. Smallwood said as we struggled.

Later, when our beloved teacher was pacing back and forth in front of the class teaching us Kansas history, his favorite subject, he stopped suddenly right in front of me. You have to understand, it was sometimes hard for me to pay attention to his words when he smiled and made little jokes. I would notice his perfect teeth and the lovely shape of his mouth and get lost in a daydream, which was what I was doing right then when he stopped talking suddenly and his nostrils flared. His eyes cut me a look. I sunk lower in my seat. It was that awful smell again.

Just before the bell, as everyone rolled up the day's art project to take home, Mr. Smallwood approached me to say he was switching Sarah Meyer's and my desks. Sarah had one in the back next to Margaret. "I thought you'd like to sit with your friend," he told me.

For the first time, his beautiful smile looked shrewd and cold. The truth was he couldn't stand the smell of me, and that was that. I thought about throwing the asphidity bag into the sewer on the way home, but how would I explain it to Mama later when she noticed it was missing? I just knew I had to get back into Mr. Smallwood's good graces, however, so I could get back up front where I belonged.

The next morning, I spritzed myself good with Mama's best perfume and ran out the door before she could notice. This time when I sashayed past his desk, Mr. Smallwood got a good whiff of Masque Rouge. I could see his head swivel my direction as I watched him out of the corner of my eye when I passed his desk. My plan appeared to be working. When it came time for P.E., I made sure to take off the asphyxia bag and leave it on the floor under my desk so it wouldn't get all sweaty and kick out more vapor. That part worked, but then I discovered the stink of my long underwear rising up.

I was trapped in a stewpot of gagging smells, a predicament I was giving serious thought to at lunch when Margaret interrupted, breathless after running across the lunchroom. "You're not going to believe this."

"Believe what?"

"I've discovered where Mr. Smallwood lives!"

"What? Really?"

"Yes." She drew herself up slightly and glanced back over her shoulder. Then she leaned toward me and gave me a conspiratorial whisper. "What do you say we go over after school and spy on him?"

I could hardly sit still all afternoon.

Mr. Smallwood's address was a red brick apartment building with black shutters and a sign out front that said, "Modern Apartment to Let. Inquire Within." It was just a block or two from Rex's house, but he wasn't chained up outside on that cold day.

We edged slowly around Mr. Smallwood's apartment building, peering into windows. Lights had been turned on in a few of the rooms, but many were shadowy dark. Other than an old woman in a basement apartment who had fallen asleep with her knitting in her lap, I saw only empty furniture. In the upper rooms, only the ceilings were visible along with houseplants on windowsills and tall lamps. I got a little, secret thrill when I imagined seeing Mr. Smallwood with his suit pants and shirt off, walking around in his underwear, like John B. after church.

"Are you sure he lives here?" I asked.

"Yes. I just don't know which apartment it is, that's all," Margaret said. "Come on." The front vestibule was empty, and it was safe to dash over to the door to go in.

"Wait," I said. "I got to take this off." I pointed at my chest where the asphidity bag dangled. I was worried that the fumes might linger and that Mr. Smallwood would figure out that I'd been there. I unbuttoned my coat and drew on the string to lift it out of my dress and slip it over my head. Then I hung it on the branch of a bush. I nodded. "Okay."

The outside door made a heavy scraping sound as it closed behind us in that cramped, hot room. There were more than a dozen mailboxes in three rows. One said, "Smallwood, Russell—2D," and my heart leaped. It was true. This *was* where he lived. And he had a first name! "Russell!" I said out loud and giggled. I wanted to repeat it again and again. "Oh, Russell!" I twittered in a flirty, squeaky voice. "Let's run away. What do you say?"

Margaret smiled and shook her head. She lowered the pitch of her voice into manly range as best she could. "Sorry, Emma, I got my eye on Margaret Drummond."

I punched her playfully, but I had begun feeling as if we had just run over the edge of a high cliff and were floating in midair, waiting for the inevitable, crushing pull of gravity to spoil the fun. I had always trusted that beneath Margaret's silly chatter and moony behavior that she understood Mr. Smallwood was not interested in us eight-year-old girls or willing to wait for one until she turned sixteen. After all, he was not like that creepy Max Nix. "We don't know where 2D is," I said. I was about to add, *let's go*, when Margaret said, "Only one way to find out."

She twisted the knob and pushed on the door and her shoulder bounced off the glass. Locked. Thank goodness. No way in. This would have to stop now. I thought it'd gone far enough. Margaret looked back at the mailboxes, and before I could grab her hand, she pressed one of the buttons in a stack next to what looked like a country telephone built flush into the wall. Then she pressed another and another and another.

In a moment, there was a buzzing sound in the doorframe and Margaret's eyes got very big and very smug. She pushed on the door again, and it unlatched and swung open. "Come on," she said.

I followed reluctantly, ashamed and scared rather than excited. I just wanted to run away. But in the face of Margaret's confident enthusiasm, I'd look like a chicken. Why was it easy for me to see when Margaret was going haywire, but not when I was?

We entered on what felt like a landing with a half flight of stairs up, and a half flight down to the basement apartments. "Up, I imagine, don't you?" Margaret said in a hushed voice.

I nodded. She took the steps with light, quiet feet and I followed suit. We found ourselves outside 2A on one side and 2B on the other in a dim, quiet corridor that led to the back of the building, where a window lit another set of stairs. "This way," Margaret said, pointing, "probably on the right."

She slipped off her shoes and began tiptoeing down the cold, speckled floor in her stocking feet. I took fewer steps and slower, hanging back, all my senses on alert. Margaret stopped outside a door marked 2D and after a moment, she pressed her ear to the wood. Her eyes got wide and she motioned me urgently to come.

I edged closer and heard low murmurs. Then I heard Mr. Smallwood's voice. "Well, that all depends, doesn't it?" he said. And it was clear to me that he was with someone. Then a woman laughed, and my spirits plunged further. It was worse than hearing him say The Gutch was recovering. Was there a Mrs. Smallwood?

I took off and ran, not caring about the racket, Margaret on my heels after she had jumped back into her shoes. We took the stairs in a clatter, banged out the door, and didn't stop running until we were all the way home. That's when I remembered that I'd left the asphidity bag hanging in the bush. "Oh, no!" I told Margaret. "What am I going to do?"

"That's your problem, isn't it?" She was indignant over something.

"My mama will kill me if I don't wear it. What's wrong with you?"

I could see she'd turned crabby. "What's wrong! What's wrong? There's a woman. Didn't you hear? It's horrible! He's horrible! Oh!" And she stomped off.

Twenty-Nine

I found Margaret in our barn the next afternoon, huddled under a ratty old blanket, asleep in her winter coat. A book lay open in the straw next to her. She had not been at school. I felt a rush of relief when I was able to rouse her, but then a vast expanse of bare forehead rose up and it startled me.

"What happened to your bangs?" I asked, forgetting all the other questions that had been bouncing around in my head. Gone was the long, shaggy hair that had hung in her eyes like a sheepdog. The change did not suit her at all. She had cut off her nose to spite her face, as Thaney would say.

"Men are never trustworthy, are they?" she replied, and asked if I'd fetch her a cup of water from the pump house. I did. I was still speechless upon my return. Where did she pick up such four-bit words? And such angry notions? She must have sensed my reaction because she said, "You know what Reno says? Reno says men are shits."

I gasped. "Margaret!" A nervous laugh shot out of me. I could practically taste soap, as if hearing forbidden words might prompt the same punishment as saying them.

"They're only interested in one thing, little girl, she says, and don't you forget it."

I wanted to forget it. Right that second. But I couldn't. The idea attached like a leech. "Margaret, wait. You know it was all just pretend about us and Mr. Smallwood," I said. "I mean he likes us. Just not, you know, as ..."

"I know that!" She made a little snort of disgust. "Don't be stupid. But I thought he was different. I thought he was special. He's *not!*"

"Come on! He *is* special! Why are you so angry?"

"Tell me, Emma. Didn't you think he went home and read great old books and listened to fine music—like operas and symphonies? Maybe practice the piano. Or the cello. And once in a while, when he needed to stretch his legs, he'd go out and play basketball with other men."

She couldn't be serious. Before Margaret found his apartment, I never thought about Mr. Smallwood being anywhere but at school. I said, "Maybe he does do all those things, Margaret, and we just caught him at a bad time."

"No, Reno is right," she said. "It's no good pretending he's someone he's not."

"Wait, Margaret. We don't know who the woman was," I said. My mind scrambled for something that could put everything right. "Heck, maybe it was his mama!"

"Ha," she said. And then a second later she laughed, for real. And once she started laughing, it was like she couldn't stop. So I threw what was left of the glass of water in her face like I'd seen someone do in the movies. It worked. She stopped instantly. "Hey!" she shouted indignantly. "Wha'd you do that for?" Her lip quivered then and she sobbed.

That night, I got another of my earaches, which quickly turned into a sore throat and a high fever. I went down for the count, monsters poking into sweaty dreams, leaving no room for worries over Margaret. I missed four days of school.

Then Mama bared my chest to put on some Vicks, and I was in trouble.

"Where is your asphidity bag?" she asked, as if I'd flushed it down the toilet.

"I don't know. Honestly, I lost it."

"You lost it? Lost it how?"

I couldn't very well answer that. "Playing."

"You lost it playing?"

"Yes." I moaned. My ear hurt like the dickens and now I felt ashamed again of what Margaret and I had done—a trespass I was not prepared to confess just then to my mother. Telling her wouldn't change the fact that the asphidity bag was truly lost. I'd gone back to the apartment building the morning after our spy adventure to look for it, but it wasn't there. Mama probably figured I brought this illness on myself by not wearing it. Perhaps I deserved to suffer. "I'm sorry," I said. "Really. I'm really sorry."

Even sick at home, I was not beyond the reach of Mr. Smallwood. Eileen shocked everyone with news about him on my first night out of bed for supper in almost a week.

"What do you think about this?" she said, standing next to Johnny, holding a bowl of red potatoes. She was nearly as tall as my brother, despite being two years younger. Soon she would shoot past him and there would be trouble. John B. was a proud boy and not likely to tolerate his argumentative, athletic sister lording anything over him. Eileen said, "Emma's teacher is courting my teacher."

I nearly choked. "What?"

"That's right. Mr. Shortwood is courting Miss Granger."

"Smallwood. His name is Russell Smallwood." I felt my face turn pink at letting it slip that I knew Mr. Smallwood's first name. I added quickly, "I know that because that's the way on he wrote it on the blackboard." Conversational chaos at the supper table swept my transparent lie neatly under a rug. Still, I lowered my eyes to Thaney's plate as she cut her green beans into tiny pieces. She seemed to be off in her own little world, not listening to anything or anyone. But I was too, picturing the mousey Miss Granger and thinking about what crazy thing Margaret might do next.

"He's calling on her," Eileen insisted. "I believe that's the way it's said in proper company. Kids have seen them together. He'd be quite a catch if she could land him. He's going places. You can tell. The great Mr. Softwood."

"Mama! Eileen's making fun of a teacher's name," Sue-Sue said in singsong cadence. Eileen shot a warning look, like she'd deal with a dirty little tattletale later.

John B. changed the subject. "Tallulah was favoring her left front hoof when I walked her home this afternoon," he told Thad. "She milked okay after I rubbed some liniment on her leg. But I think we should see how it's doing in the morning."

Thad grunted. He was attacking the calf's liver and onions on his plate as if it were the only meal he'd eaten all week. I wanted to gag just looking at it. Nothing appealed to me but the potatoes, and those only after I had salted them down good. I wished we were having cornbread and beans.

"If they get married," Eileen went on, "they'll make Miss Granger quit teaching, of course. They couldn't take a chance on her belly swelling up in front of impressionable children with their incessant questions."

Where was she getting this stuff, I wondered.

John B. spoke up again. "Dick Burke made varsity," he said. Thad stopped sawing on his liver and looked up. This was hardly news. Dick Burke was the star of the basketball team. "I think they're going to be good this year," John B. added. For some reason, he winked at me. Had I missed something?

"Eileen," Mama said. "Perhaps you could refill the milk pitcher, please?"

"I think it's unfair," Eileen said.

"What?" Mama asked.

"Making a woman quit because she might get in a family way," Eileen said.

"Oh, that," Mama said. Her eyelids fluttered.

John B. cleared his throat. "The team'll be good because the pep is sure to be up. Dick Burke's little sister, Kathy, made the cheerleading squad." Suddenly Eileen got very silent, and her face got very red and she did a very unexpected thing. She picked up a handful of her green beans and threw them in Johnny's face. I watched in disbelief as Thaney idly snatched one up, put it on her own plate, and cut it into tiny pieces. Everyone else started shouting. Mama's voice rose above them all.

"Eileen, you'll excuse yourself and leave the table! This minute!"

"You didn't hear about it 'cause you had the night sweats," Sue-Sue told me later. "Eileen went out for Pepper Shakers on Tuesday." Which was what junior cheerleaders were called. "So I guess she didn't make it." Sue-Sue had slept in Eileen's room while I was sick, and she must have picked up on the dirt.

"What else did you hear?" I asked her, just as our front doorbell rang. It was 7:30 on a school night. John B. called, "I'll get it," and ambled to the door.

"Is your mother or father home?" said a man. I knew that voice, and it gave me a jolt. Mr. Smallwood.

Johnny must have recognized him, too, because he didn't holler out his usual summons. Instead, in a very polite tone he invited Mr. Smallwood into the front hall, where he asked him to wait while he went in search of Mama. Quietly, I crept out of my room toward the top of the stairs on my hands and knees, my heart pounding. Teachers never came to your house, unless . . . . I closed my eyes so I could listen harder. Had he figured out that it was Margaret and me who were outside his door last week? Had he come to tell my parents? How could he know it was us? Unless he'd found my asphidity bag hanging in the bush! Had he come here to confront me with it?

I heard footsteps from the kitchen. Then Mama said, "Yes?" Her tone was uncertain. She had not met my new teacher.

"Mrs. Starkey, I am Russell Smallwood, Emma's teacher. How is she doing?"

Mama hesitated before replying. He had caught her off guard. "Oh, Mr. Smallwood. She's better. Yes, definitely. She ate with us tonight for the first time. Is everything all right?" It had become very still in the house. Thad stopped turning the pages of the newspaper, but I could hear the sound of Thaney's cross-stitch thread tugging repeatedly through the cloth stretched tight like the skin of a drum.

"Oh, yes, certainly. Only ..." He hesitated, and I held my breath. "I'm just a little concerned. Emma is a very good student, as I'm sure you know. But I just thought, well, she would find herself far behind in the lessons when she returned. And, well, I've taken the liberty of putting together a packet of spelling words and marked some problems in her math book here. Perhaps you or someone else could give her a hand with it."

I let out a breath. But just as quickly I had to suck it back in again. "I am going to Drummonds' next," he said. "Margaret has been gone all this time, too. Those girls are such good friends. You haven't by any chance heard how Margaret is doing?"

Mama sounded uncertain. "No. I hadn't heard she was sick, to tell you the truth." There was a pause. Then Mama said, "Emma's gone to bed already, Mr. Smallwood." It took a moment to realize that either he had been looking past my mother to try to spot me in the house or he had tried to walk farther in. Mama said, "I'll just take those."

"Well," Mr. Smallwood said, "yes. Here you go. Tell Emma Godspeed."

"Thank you. I'll surely do that, Mr. Smallwood. Good night."

"What a handsome teacher you have, Emma," Mama said, when she came upstairs and found me under the covers. There was a trace of a smile in her eyes. "And so young! You never told me." She brushed my hair back with her hand and felt my forehead for a fever. "You know, it's funny. I think Mr. Smallwood has an asphidity bag, too." Mama's nose was almost as keen as mine.

I tried to smile. "Really," I said. "That's nice. Well, Mama, I think I need to go to sleep now. I'm real tired." I quickly closed my eyes.

She tucked me in and bent down to kiss my forehead gently.

"He said to wish you Godspeed," Mama said.

"Mmm-hmm," I replied softly, as if I were already drifting off when in fact I was listening intently for the sound of the light switch and praying for the cool seclusion of darkness. I was glad

Mr. Smallwood hadn't told Mama what us girls had done. I should have thanked him my first chance. Only I didn't realize that the opportunity would be limited, that both he and Miss Granger would vanish without notice from South School right after Easter, to where, we never learned.

Thirty

One day in late March, Thaney brought a handful of bare, misshapen twigs into the house. She stuck them in a vase and filled it with water, and she set the whole thing out on a table in the front hall—further evidence, I thought, that she had gone completely off her rocker. *Thaney Insane.* She had spent the winter mostly in her own room, as dormant as the peonies in her frozen garden. Sue-Sue and I were giggling over her handiwork in the hall when she unexpectedly strolled through.

"Thaney," I said, "what is this?"

"Forsythia." Like that explained it.

"Oh," I said, and Sue-Sue giggled again. After Thaney left, Sue-Sue whispered, "They're imaginary flowers, you see." And I had to laugh out loud.

Several days later, the branches sprouted with delicate yellow blossoms, shaming us both. April fools. The flowers reawakened our stale house with something fresh, and they seemed to jar Thaney back to life, as well. I heard her and Mama planning a trip out to the farm to bring in seeds and bulbs that would be needed for the garden that year. The sweet scent of spring had yet to arrive, but from the warmth of an early April day, you could practically feel nature gathering its forces, getting ready to burst out.

On the first nice day, John B. and Rach got out the bats and baseballs and began playing catch across the creek in the backyard. Their feet wore out the brown grass where they landed in the soggy turf and ripped open slicks of mud. When Eileen came out with an old mitt to join them, Rach chuckled and said, "Sure, why not?" But Johnny scowled at her and told her to get back in the house or he'd drill her with his bean ball.

Rach's face had become more angular, and he had grown noticeably taller over the winter, while stocky John B. remained stuck with his old height and baby face. He always threw harder than Rach and played with more intensity, and Rach never seemed to mind having a shrimp for a friend.

The blooming of Thaney's forsythia got me thinking about spring, and how it liked to sneak up and burst through. One minute the trees were bare and the next they were full of leaves. You might see buds, but you never actually saw them form. And you might notice the first leaves while they were still tiny, but you didn't see them come out. At least nothing ever got bigger while I was staring at it. I wondered if that was the way it would be with the changes that would happen to me someday. Would I just wake up one morning with hair in places I hadn't had it before and breasts sprouting out to there?

It seemed to be the sixth grade when the girls I knew first developed. I could see the little swells under some of their blouses at school and the thickening of legs and hips. Buds about to leaf out. At least on some. Not all. It was as if growth was a lottery distributed at random. I dreaded the day that fate would point at me, particularly the onset of that mysterious ailment I'd heard girls whisper about—*the curse.*

Eileen had begun subtly moving in a way that said she was changing. She'd already gotten taller than John B. I began surreptitiously studying her body, looking for signs, knowing I would be next in only a couple of years. I was curious how it went and how it was going to feel.

Eileen wasn't one to confide in me. She was actually closer to Mama than Sue-Sue and I. I was fairly certain Mama told her things that she didn't tell the rest of us since Eileen was oldest, and I wondered how we were expected to find out if Eileen kept it all to herself. From time to time, Margaret shined a garish light into the blackness by passing along some peculiar fact that Reno had blurted out. But I ignored most of it since Reno was hardly someone I trusted or wanted to model myself after.

Changes were coming to Thaney's body, too. She looked like a wasp that was shriveling up. Her eyes sunk, her spine curved, and her shoulders stooped. She constantly rubbed the knuckles of her gnarly old hands, and her ankles puffed out when she was on her feet for long. But it was the drift of her personality that was most striking. She wasn't so much bossy anymore as she was surly, all mutters and sighs. All winter long, I'd heard her talk to herself when she was in her room alone. Like everyone else, I pretended nothing was different until the day came when it could no longer be ignored.

"Emma, go tell Grandma that dinner is ready," Mama said one late July afternoon.

"Where is she?" I asked.

"In her room, I expect."

"No, I just went past there. Maybe she's out in the garden."

But she wasn't. And she wasn't on the porch.

"Did you check the barn?" Mama asked.

"Why the heck would she be in the barn?" I wanted to know, but I went. No Thaney. Just Tallulah chewing hay and the Saxon making ticking noises as it cooled. I returned to the kitchen bewildered. "I don't get it," I said. "Where could she be?"

Mama turned everything off on the stove, wiped her hands on her apron, and slipped it off. "Go get your father. Hurry now. We have to find her."

After a few minutes of random searches on our street and adjacent blocks, everyone turning up in the same spots shrugging with frustration and failure, Thad rounded us all up in the driveway and took charge. "John B., you and your mother go look in the shops downtown. Eileen, you take Sue-Sue and see if she's gone to First Methodist. Emma, you come with me. We'll all meet back here in half an hour."

Thad got out the Saxon and we drove up and down streets, looking out the car windows. I waved to my friend Dusty Oates and yelled out to him, "Hey, Dusty, you seen my grandmother?" He called back, "No, did you lose her?"

Why she would wander off without saying something, no one seemed to know. She had just disappeared. Before the half hour was up, my imagination had conjured up all sorts of awful disasters. I felt sorry for every mean thing I'd ever said or done to her.

On one of our swings through the neighborhood, we drove past the Methodist Church, where Eileen was coming out with a shake of her head. I'd thought there was a good chance she'd be there, what with Thaney being a Methodist *and* a Republican. *And* a widow, I thought. Pa Joesy's funeral had been there on a day very much like this one. I asked Thad, "Has it been a year already since Pa Joesy died?" He looked over at me with a surprised expression, and without saying a word made a hard turn onto Sycamore and sped out to the cemetery, slowing only when he got to the narrow, winding lane to Grandpa's grave.

And there she was, an astonishing sight, not sitting or kneeling by the grave, but perched atop Pa Joesy's tall tombstone, as if she had been deposited there precariously by a flood. How she could have clawed her way up was a complete mystery. Her eyes were closed and her lips were quivering.

I watched Thad go to her and lift her gently off the tombstone, cradling her in his arms. "He wants me to join him," Thaney insisted. "I should have gone first."

"There, there, Mother," Thad said. "Calm yourself. That's enough now."

Aunt Fern arrived two days later. Thad took a half day off from work and picked her up at the train station and brought her to the house. Thaney had vacant eyes when her daughter hugged her, and her arms hung limp in passive acquiescence at her sides.

Mama sent us outside. Later, when I went past Thaney's room just before dinner, I could hear Aunt Fern speaking quietly, and Thaney moaning. "But my garden! My garden!"

Fern said something that I couldn't hear, her tone low and soothing. And then Thaney spoke again in a sharp whine. "What about Pa? I can't just leave him!"

"They're shipping her off to a home," Eileen informed me.

I tried to remember what life had been like in the house before Thaney and Pa Joesy arrived, and I could not. Still, the possibility of returning to a time without them held the promise of enormous relief, not unlike summer break from school. I stood silently cheering Aunt Fern on as Thaney voiced another objection. "But they haven't found my glasses yet."

John B., Eileen, Sue-Sue, and I had all walked different routes Thaney might have taken to the cemetery looking everywhere for her missing glasses, but without success. I would happily do it a thousand times over if finding them meant she would actually leave. That was hateful, I know. My conscience already told me. But so be it.

"No! You can't make me! I'm *not* seeing any small-town doctors!" Thaney howled. I wondered whether they were reconsidering.

Mama had taken it as a personal failing that she had allowed Thaney to wander off.

"I'd have taken her out to the grave myself, but I lost track of the date. How could I? My God, it's a wonder she didn't go the wrong way and end up in the river! How she made it all the way out there on her own I'll never know. She might have died!"

John B. put his arm around her. "Come on, Ma, this isn't your fault."

To calm Thaney, it was decided not to rush into anything. Rather, Mama suggested, we would stick to our routine until the weekend, give Thaney a chance to settle herself. On Saturday, our elderly neighbor, Sadie McLune, came over and kept her company, as usual, and the rest of us went to the band concert at the square downtown, which was our custom.

Fern had a harrowing day with Thaney on Sunday, however, and emerged from her bedroom at lunchtime completely exasperated. She asked John B. where she could find Thad. Johnny led her to the barn, and he overheard her say, "You must keep a bottle stashed somewhere, Thad, don't you? Come on. Don't be that way. I could use one."

My dad had a bottle of bootleg booze in the house?!

It didn't take long for John B. to circulate that news. Even so, we didn't expect what happened next.

Thirty-One

Jumping rope in the hot afternoon sun with Margaret, Dema, Sue-Sue, and Alice had made my tongue as sandpapery as a cat's. Since Mama always kept a pitcher of Kool-Aid in the icebox in hot weather, I went in for a glass. But the second I walked in the door, I could smell that whiskey. And there sat Thad and Fern staring at each other across the kitchen table, a bottle open between them and a plume of smoke rising off Thad's cigar. I spied on them stealthily as I poured out some Kool-Aid and hastily chugged it down. But the smell and the silence made me jittery. So I turned to run back out.

"Whoa!" Thad barked as I turned to leave, and I nearly jumped out of my skin. "What's your hurry, little girl? Come over here and sit down a minute." I couldn't believe he was talking to me. He scooted out the chair right next to him. My hands went clammy, and the whiskey smell made my eyes burn. Years before, Mama had gargled whiskey for a sore throat or some other ailment. The room smelled like a hospital to me.

"You probably already know that this one's a whippersnapper," Thad said to Fern, like he was introducing me to a visitor who had dropped by to size up the family. "John B. says she's got the nose of a bloodhound. But that wasn't how she figured out where her grandmother wandered off to, I don't expect." He chuckled.

It was unusual to be given credit for anything but mischief by Thad, particularly something that was clearly a stretch like this. My heart sped up, his malarkey giving me the idea he was trying to pawn me off, too. Get Fern to adopt me when she took Thaney away—kind of a package deal.

I'd never seen my father drink. I hadn't even known that he did. Indeed, liquor was illegal! At church, it was demonized as a tool of the devil—and Thad was the treasurer of the church! The room spun a little as I watched the glass go to his lips. My dad was breaking the law! The ooky brown liquid slid back into his tipped-up mouth. He drained the glass and banged it down on the table, and promptly poured out more. I remembered Mama always spat it out when she used it.

Thad wiped his lips with the back of his hand. "She and her grandmother are close," he said, and mussed my hair with his calloused fingers. "What do you think we should do about her?" I thought he was asking Fern about me when he said that, but there was a pause and I went against my better judgment and looked at him. He said, "Your grandmother, little girl? What's best, do you think?"

I was supposed to know this? I sensed something menacing behind Thad's smile. He wanted Thaney out, and he must have figured he had an ally in me. But all I could think of in the pressure of the moment was how Thaney's false teeth clattered when she chewed popcorn and how she slid those plates out when she was finished and licked the small salty pieces out of the cracks to everyone's disgust.

"Go on," Thad ordered. "Speak up. It's all right. Your grandmother won't hear you; she's napping."

"Don't browbeat the girl, Thad," Fern said. A chunk of ice clinked in her glass as she picked it up. I noticed the brown liquid in hers wasn't as dark. "Can't you see she's squirming? Leave her be. You're not fooling her anyway. She knows what's up." She turned to me. "I am taking Grandma Thaney for a while. It's true. If she'll go …"

"That's good," I said. "I guess I mean …" I scooted my chair back hoping to make a getaway.

"Park your butt a minute longer, scamp," Thad said, his callused hand landing hard on my shoulder. "We're not done here. Your grandmother is worried sick about her garden, savvy? It's up to you to convince her it'll be taken good care of if she leaves."

"Oh, yes, sir." This was a relief. I could certainly do that. I smiled reassuringly.

"Otherwise, your father can't dump her on me," Fern said with a scowl.

Thad frowned back. "Change of scenery is what she needs."

"I'd say. It's obvious she's not happy here. And why she'd want to continue staying someplace that makes her unhappy is something I'll never understand. But that's it in a nutshell."

Thad grunted. They were missing the point, I thought. Thaney *liked* being unhappy.

"What are you playing out there?" Fern asked.

"Jump rope."

Fern smiled. "You know, I skipped rope as a girl."

The way she put it, I thought she was angling to join us. "You'd have to wait your turn," I said.

Fern had a laugh like music. "Of course, I'd expect to. No cuts for old ladies. Besides, it would take me a while just to catch on again." She would need more than that if she hadn't skipped in years, I thought. Still, I warmed to the idea—my Aunt Fern out there chanting and rope skipping with the girls, trying to keep up. It sounded like fun. I wasn't exactly sure Margaret and Dema and Sue-Sue and Alice would go for it, but I supposed they'd have to. Fern swallowed some whiskey, jiggled the ice in the glass, and took a final sip. "Well, there's no time like the present."

Thad followed us out after putting on a straw skimmer I'd never seen him take down off the shelf in the front hall closet except on the Fourth of July. I guess he was of a mind to see Fern try this, too. The girls were across the street on the sidewalk. They froze when they saw us all coming.

"Aunt Fern wants to jump rope," I announced. Margaret glanced at Thad and then shot me a look. I just shrugged. The girls started up again, Alice hopping into the whirl of the rope twirled by Margaret and Dema.

Strawberry shortcake
Huckleberry pie
Who's gonna be your lucky guy?

A!
B!
C!

When the rope caught Alice's ankle, the girls all shrieked. "C! C!"

"His initial will be C," I explained to Fern. "Like Charlie or . . . or . . ."

"Clarence," Fern said.

"Not Kway-wence," Alice objected. "Chaw-ee!"

With Alice out, it was Sue-Sue's turn, and she called, "Postman."

The rope started up again, and Sue-Sue made a couple of feints toward it before she finally jumped in. The girls chanted.

Postman, Postman, do your duty,
Here comes Sue-Sue, the American beauty.
She can wiggle,
she can waddle,
she can do the splits.
She wears her dresses *around* her hips

"I'm not wearing a dress!" Sue-Sue shouted, and kept going.

"No fair! No fair!" Dema called, and stopped the rope. "You still have to make the moves. You didn't do the splits so you're out."

"Okay," I said turning to Fern, "that's how it's done. Sort of."

"I see," she said. "All right." She slipped off her shoes. Then she lifted up the hem of her skirt and bent her knees in a deep squat several times, the dips setting off firecrackers in her joints that made us have to stifle laughs. She smiled bravely. "Okay, I think I'm all ready."

As the two tallest, Margaret and I took the ends of the rope and started the twirl, arcing it up extra high by lifting our arms to give Fern space to maneuver. We looked like a couple of windmills. The motion felt odd and reinforced my notion that adults were queer, oversized creatures. Fern hunched a bit looking into the space we were creating and she listened to the rope slap the pavement a few times, shoulders bobbing to the rhythm.

"Red hot pepper," I called out.

Suddenly she skipped in and hopped over the rope in well-timed jumps as we chanted.

Red Hot Pepper
in the pot.
Gotta get over
what the leaders got.
Ten!
Twenty!
Thirty!
Forty!

We sped up the rope with every revolution and Fern's face turned red from exertion. But she was managing a smile now where there had been total concentration before. When she skipped out without fouling the rope, a cheer went up from the little kids, who ran to her and wrapped her in their arms.

Thad had been quietly observing the whole thing with a disdainful look, arms folded across his chest. He said, "Here now, that looks easy."

"That's 'cause you weren't the one in there doing the jumping," Fern said, and bent at the waist, puffing for breath.

"Well, kiss my ... Okay, girls, let's go. Crank it up. My turn."

Thad had a scary smile, his teeth all even and perfect. Fern had told me long before that a horse had kicked them out when Thad was still in high school. But his false choppers never clicked or stunk like Thaney's. Still, something about them embarrassed me now. I wanted to stop him from making a fool of himself in front of my friends, but there was no way I could do it. He had that determined set to his jaw. What had happened to the cranky, stodgy old Thad? Maybe that drinking all afternoon had stopped him from thinking straight.

"Let's go," he said. "What are you waiting for?"

His movements were slightly ponderous. I smelled disaster, but Margaret and I started up with the rope. We reached up high as high as we could, but we couldn't get it over Thad's head on his first move in, and the rope clipped him, knocking his hat off. It promptly rolled away. As I expected, his temper flared. I dropped the rope, ready to run. Thad snatched the rope out of Margaret's hand. "Give me that," he snarled. The girls cowered. They probably thought he was going to string us all up for embarrassing him.

Thad began twisting the rope with quiet ferocity, like he had a grudge against it. Soon, a knot and loop emerged before our riveted eyes. It looked a little like a hangman's noose until he flicked his wrist and set it to spinning. The circle it formed got wider and wider. Our jump rope was now a lariat, and Thad twirled it faster and faster in front of him. Then he hopped into the circle and hopped back out again.

Nobody was more surprised by this agile move than Margaret, who had come to believe that Thad had never been a cowboy. Yet here was my dad in a straw skimmer and city clothes—not chaps or a cowboy hat—doing a rope trick with a lasso.

He kept the rope a-twirl and hopped back in, elevating the lariat up his body so it was circling his chest. Then he lowered it again and stepped back out. He switched hands and repeated the trick. The lariat wobbled a couple of times, but he always recovered.

Each time he hopped back into the circle he lifted the lariat a little higher and a little higher until it was circling above his head, a halo of hemp, big enough for a giant. He permitted himself a smile when it reached the apex, and in the blink of an eye, he sailed the loop over Fern's head, and it settled on her before she could react. Thad drew it tight, pinning her arms.

Then he lifted the boater off his head and swept it in front of him in deep bow. When he came back up, he was holding his teeth in his hand, which scared Alice so much she ran. I was mortified, but everyone else laughed until they practically peed their pants. The memory of that big toothless grin will be with me always.

Thad probably had second thoughts about his little exhibition, because he quickly turned and hightailed it back into the house.

Perhaps he just didn't have an encore.

Thirty-Two

In the end, Fern took Thaney away on Monday morning in a somber gray shirtwaist dress and hat, her head tipped down like a prisoner being marched off to be shot, stubbornly refusing to acknowledge any of the farewells we bid her. Perhaps it was unfair, sending her away. As she walked to the car, her gait was a bit unsteady and I wondered if Thad had slipped some whiskey into her prune juice. At the street, Thad held the car door. Thaney stopped and turned. Then she kissed her fingers and patted her behind with them, the meaning of which was lost on none of us.

"Did you see that?" Sue-Sue exclaimed. She sounded as if she couldn't decide whether it was hilarious or insulting. Maybe both.

We mimicked that gesture for weeks, joyously giving it right back to her in absentia. The house became wonderfully light and happy once again, cut loose from the old ball and chain.

Since no one had to escort Thaney to First Methodist, we all went to church together that Sunday for the first time in several years. Mama bought us girls new pairs of Mary Janes, and we gratefully threw out the old ones that had begun to pinch.

Without Thaney's grouchy view of the world around to color everything, even Thad's attitude seemed to improve.

"I'm going to pitch some horseshoes," he said to me one evening after supper. "Want to come along?" He had his hat in his hand, ready to go.

A wave of panic swamped me. It was a dingy old barn where strange men played in sweat-stained fedoras and worn suspenders smelling of ripe B.O. Plus, Thad was not my idea of fun company either. "Could Sue-Sue come, too?"

He scowled and shifted his weight. "Certainly," he said after a moment.

Once we arrived at the grimy arena on the outskirts of town, it became obvious we were to be a novelty for Thad's old farming cronies amidst the arc and spin of metal shoes. The iron stake was like a prize bell clanging at a carnival, and Sue-Sue and I were the bright Kewpie dolls those men couldn't help fussing over.

"How you girls doing this fine evening?" they asked us.

"Tell your daddy to go easy on us now, y'hear?" they said.

"Is he using magnets out there?" they complained.

I had to admit, Thad was pretty good. With a chaw bulging out his cheek, he could lay one ringer in on top of another. He'd punctuate his victories by spitting a gob of brown juice into the dust. Mama had forbid tobacco chewing in our house after she found Thad was silently killing her houseplants.

Sue-Sue couldn't have cared less about horseshoes. Out of boredom or nervousness, she began bobbing and weaving and shuffling her feet. The next thing I knew, she was humming the tune of the Charleston under her breath and flapping her arms and pivoting on her toes like the song was actually playing. The disturbance attracted the curiosity of men waiting their turns.

"Hey, girlie, do that again," one old boy called. "What was that you was doin'?"

"Ain't you never seen the Charleston, mister?" Sue-Sue said impertinently.

"Is that what that is? That's the dangdest thing I ever saw. Do it again."

So she did it, belting out the song this time and adding another dance step. There was a smattering of applause afterward, and Sue-Sue's eyes brightened like a vaudeville performer's with a standing ovation. The man said, "Hey, that's pretty good. Your sister dance too?"

"Sure, mister. Come on, Emma."

Something about Sue-Sue's eagerness to please these disgusting men and the way she had shimmied her shoulders to their encouragement brought out a streak of stubbornness in me. Everyone had always fawned over her, and she loved it. I felt my body thrum when all those eyes turned on me, and I stood stock-still, glancing anxiously at Thad. He had a puzzled and unhappy look on his face. He rubbed his chin and worked the bulging chaw around to the other cheek.

"Maybe the girl just needs some encouragement, Hollis," a man called out.

I couldn't believe it when the old boy called Hollis reached into his pocket to produce a coin and flipped it into the dust at our feet. Soon, other coins came out and landed near us from other men's pockets. It would have been rude to refuse in response. Yet the extortion scared me more, and Hollis's crude, whiskery face made me recollect the one I'd seen the previous week in the *Cornucopia Beacon* alongside the picture of a young girl with pretty braids. The man in the paper had eyes that seemed dead. There was a third photo, too—a snowy picture taken on a summer night of a blanket thrown over a small body in a clearing in a woods outside some tiny Kansas town called Easterwell. You couldn't tell much from the grainy ink on the news page. It forced you to use your imagination. The story with the pictures told how the man had taken and harmed the girl. I read every word, driven not just by empathy for a child's terror but by the puzzling mind of her attacker too. For the first time, I realized that unexplained evil lurked in everyday places in the world, and that it moved silently and dangerously among us. It transformed me, and for years afterward, I could not walk through the woods between our house and the river. I always ran.

"Thad! You never told us you had such cute girls!" Hollis shouted as we danced. Thad deposited another squirt of tobacco juice into the dust as Sue-Sue and I raised some of our own doing the Charleston in our bare feet on the dirt floor.

"Emma, did you ever see so much loot?" Sue-Sue said as we pocketed the coins. "We can buy candy *and* firecrackers."

"Yeah," I said. "Sure."

Maybe it was cause for celebration like Sue-Sue thought, but at that moment, I was strangely sick at heart, still thinking about that newspaper article. I wanted to tell Sue-Sue about wickedness in the world, but I didn't want to spoil her fun, or explain to her why I would turn and run away as fast as I could if I ever saw that old crony of Thad's on the street. I didn't want my picture to be in the paper someday.

Margaret, Alice, and the girls were playing hopscotch on Dema's front sidewalk when we got home, and we rushed over to try to get in a turn before Mama could call us in at dark. It felt good to get back to something fun and familiar and uncomplicated. I wanted to put dancing for old men out of my mind.

"Hey, where you been?" Dema asked.

Sue-Sue reached into her pocket to show the girls the coins.

"Wow!" Dema said. "Where'd you get those?"

While Sue-Sue told them the story, I stood around feeling antsy, wanting to start a game of hopscotch. The questions took some time and then Sue-Sue spoiled it for me further by saying we should play Run Sheepie Run. "Yeah!" everybody else yelled. The gathering gloom of the evening held no boogeymen for Sue-Sue.

"I'm out," I said. "Anybody want to challenge me to a game of hopscotch?"

Nobody did. Not even Margaret. "It's getting too dark." Dema said, "And we been playing all night." Before I could argue the point, John B. showed up with Rach and Zeke Wilhite and Eileen and some others also clamoring to play Run Sheepie Run. The ruckus drew still more kids, including Dema's older twin brothers, Harvey and Harlan.

"Come on, Emma," John B. said. "Don't be a party pooper."

John B. and Rach were named captains. I decided I would be safe if I stuck close to either boy, so I agreed. We fanned out to be counted off, and I was happy to land on the fox team, which meant I wouldn't have to hide in some prickly, spooky bush with the sheep.

But first I wanted to get John B.'s ear and ask if he thought somebody we knew might be secretly wicked or if someone in Cornucopia could do something unspeakable someday, like that man in Easterwell. The newspaper story said the girl's attacker was a friend of the family. The girl *knew* her killer. Johnny was standing right next to me. But everyone would have heard me if I'd asked him, or butted in if I'd pulled John B. aside. It would have to wait until we could talk in private.

Somehow when the sides were picked, Eileen ended up on our team rather than on Rach's, and I was surprised when I heard her speak to Zeke in that same flirty, high-pitched tone of voice she usually reserved for Rach. Eileen put a hand on Zeke's arm and said, "If you go after Margaret, I'll tag Alice." Zeke was a good-looking boy with intelligent eyes and an easy smile. John B. loved to tell the story of Zeke getting the guys at school to shuffle their feet anytime he had to fart so the shoe scuffing would cover the sound. Because of Zeke's size and speed, Margaret and Alice would be easy prey. Eileen didn't need to be making any special arrangements.

I was thinking about that as the sheep team ran off to hide and our fastest counter peeled off the numbers from one to one hundred at a rapid clip. Was Eileen sweet on Zeke now in addition to Rach? Or had she thrown Rach over?

A gust of wind whistled in the branches of the Z Tree above our heads and gave me a shiver. For as long as we'd ever played this game, home base for Run Sheepie Run was the Z Tree in Woodses' yard. The tree had been badly pruned years before, and one of the main horizontal limbs was hacked off partway out. A branch from there extended up and back toward the tree and abruptly stopped at a second cut, where a third branch extended away from the main trunk. The result formed the letter Z. We thought the tree had magical properties, and we would lie on our backs under it for hours, looking for more hidden letters and numbers.

"Ninety-seven, ninety-eight, ninety-nine, one hundred!" We uncovered our eyes as the counting stopped and John B. led us out on the hunt. The boundaries for Run Sheepie Run had long ago been agreed upon, and there were a limited number of places to conceal a group of the size that Rach led. John B. knew them all, and he began a cautious spiral out from the tree toward the closest of them. As the captain of the other team, Rach followed us, watching John B.'s every move. When Rach saw a big-enough opening for his sheep team to run home safely to the Z Tree without being tagged, he would call out, "Run, sheepie! Run!" Then the sheep would take off for home and we had to try to catch them as they scattered and zigzagged on their mad dash. Touch one before they could touch the tree and they were converted to our team.

With more older kids playing than usual, including the Woods twins, the little kids had no chance that night. It was the big kids who would be hard to catch.

I was near the front of our pack helping to scout and staying close to John B. when little Alice sprung out from behind a tree. Her sudden, unexpected movement so close by startled me, and I shrieked.

Everyone turned my direction and saw Alice scampering away. But where were the others? I thought she must have hidden there after failing to keep up. Then Rach called, "Run, sheepie! Run!" and the pack broke from cover at our backs. It had been a ruse, a cleverly concocted deception, and it appeared it would work.

I was running toward the dispersing pack, screaming and yelling like everyone else, when Zeke and Eileen shot past me. Zeke was making a beeline for Margaret and Eileen was chasing down Alice, as they had planned. But before Zeke got to Margaret, Rach shot out of nowhere and threw a shoulder into him, knocking him down in violation of one of our unwritten rules. Zeke popped back up, yelled an oath and took a swing at Rach. Quickly, the two of them hit the ground in a twisting, rolling heap, grunting and punching as they called each other piss cutters and queers. I'd never seen two boys quicker to fight over something that didn't really matter. Or to fight with such animal abandon, punching and kicking like they wanted to kill one another.

It took some time to stop it. John B. plunged into the fray and tried to pull Rach away in a headlock as Harlan worked to wrap his arms around Zeke in a bear hug to subdue him.

I looked at Eileen. Even in the dark, you could see that her face was flushed and that she was thinking hard about something, maybe something she'd done. I was angry with her, but I couldn't figure why.

Once John B. and Harlan pulled Rach and Zeke apart, they steered them in opposite directions. Rach and Zeke continued to struggle with the peacemakers and shouted names, threats and insults at each other. I had goose bumps that didn't go away until I crawled under the covers that night and Sue-Sue gently stroked my back under my nightie.

Thirty-Three

I haven't told you anything about Frances Boggs, since we weren't all that close. But it was from her that I first learned the true depth of Tommy Bern's depravity.

You see, Frances knew stuff most kids didn't know. And she did stuff other kids didn't do. Mama like to say that whenever Frances turned up at our door, mischief couldn't be far behind. Frances had reddish-blond hair and a face full of defiant freckles. She was between Sue-Sue and me in age and went to our church. I figured she was wild because she didn't have a mother around to bawl her out every time she got out of line. Her dad, who played cards in the group with my folks, wasn't married. He had a young housekeeper living with them to fix the meals and look after Frances.

Frances arrived on our porch one July afternoon with the usual sneakin' look on her face and suggested we take a walk. I thought she was going to propose ringing someone's doorbell and running, but she said, "No, something better," and dragged us clear across town to the railroad tracks before she'd tell us what it was.

"This better be good," I warned her. I'd been planning to do something with Margaret.

She reached into her pocket and pulled out a handful of square foil packets that were lumpy and wrinkled and said Trojan on them.

"What are those?" Sue-Sue asked.

"Safeties."

"Safeways?" Sue-Sue said.

"No, silly. Safeties are for avoiding babies."

"I don't get it," Sue-Sue said.

To my great annoyance, Frances launched into a quick and crude synopsis of the mysteries of the marriage bed as I watched Sue-Sue's eyes grow big.

"You're making that up," Sue-Sue said, and looked to me as if for confirmation that such a crazy thing could *not* be true. I refused to look her in the eye. I wasn't even sure I understood what a Trojan was. Was there something inside the foil you swallowed?

"Where'd you get 'em?" I asked Frances.

"My dad keeps a box of them in a drawer next to his bed."

Now there was some news. Her dad wasn't even married. Sue-Sue and I were quiet a minute, me thinking about what Mr. Boggs might be doing with safeties, and Sue-Sue, I suppose, completely lost and aswim—maybe a little scared—in an unfamiliar sea. Frances interrupted our reveries by ripping open a foil packet and unrolling the contents to full length. It was thin and wrinkly, like a skin that a short snake had shed. Stretched out, the crude, peculiar thing left no doubt what would fit inside. There was a moment of shocked understanding. It was like a one-finger glove.

"But it's huge!" I said. We all laughed.

"My, what big ears you have, Grandma," Frances said, eyes twinkling.

And what big privates, she meant for us to think. And I did. In fact, the Trojan horse of history came to mind, because I now pictured Phelps with his long, wet, pink business scooting out, as it did at the oddest times. I said, "Honestly, your dad had that?"

Frances shrugged and smiled wickedly. Nearly all her baby teeth were missing in front, and she had a tendency to lisp.

"Here," she said, "blow one up. It's just like a balloon. Go on. It won't bite you."

She showed us. It puffed out dangerously, stretching almost to the bursting point before Frances released her pinch on the opening and the safety rocketed out of her hand and squirted around us crazily, like a renegade Fourth of July firework. It made farting noises the whole while, and Frances yelled "Poontang!" as the sound of the safety got juicier and juicier.

Sue-Sue couldn't help herself. She wet her pants before she could catch another breath, she was laughing so hard. She stopped abruptly with a look of abject horror. Then she took off for home with the dark circle of humiliation in the crotch of her dungarees. I couldn't imagine what she was going to tell Mama.

"Why'd you have to go and spill the beans like that to Sue-Sue?" I was mad at Frances now for the trouble she'd caused. I'd have to deal with the consequences.

"Heck, how was I supposed to know she was a virgin?" Frances said.

"A virgin? You mean like Mary, mother of Jesus?"

Frances laughed. "Don't you know nothing? A virgin is someone who doesn't have the knowledge yet. Heck, somebody had to tell her." Like I'd not been a good sister.

I was done talking about this and wanted to get away from Frances, but I decided I had to wait for Sue-Sue to return, and I lay back on the grassy embankment next to the tracks. Who knew what trouble was brewing at home after Sue-Sue got there? Only Frances wouldn't shut up. She told me she didn't have any idea what *poontang* meant (it was just something her daddy said once when he thought she wasn't listening), and then she too lay back and we watched the clouds tumble by in the gusty Kansas sky, picking out shapes that reminded me of things.

"That one looks like a cow," I said, and pointed. Frances gestured to a small white blob nearby and said, "Cow pie."

In addition to being a complete cutup, Frances Boggs was a dyed-in-the-wool gossip. She said, "I hear Zeke Wilhite is sweet on your sister."

"Yeah," I said, "maybe."

"Is your sister sweet on him, too?"

I wasn't sure how to answer that, or if I should. "Jeez, Frances, I don't know."

"Sure you do." She was quiet a moment. "Okay, here's the deal. You tell me about Eileen and I'll tell you a good one in return."

"Yeah, like what?"

She thought a minute. "You know that boy Billy Swenson whose mother dresses him up like a girl?" I nodded. "Well, she's making him take violin lessons now. That's one skirt Tommy Bern won't be trying to peek up."

"Tommy Bern?"

Her eyes said *gotcha!*

"What's this about Tommy Bern?" I pursued. The thought of him being up to something gave me the willies. Who knew what he was capable of? Frances raised her eyebrows as if to say, *I'm waiting.* She still wanted me to swap gossip with her, but I didn't really know what was in Eileen's heart. I shook my head. "Never mind," I said, concealing my disappointment. "It doesn't matter."

"Aha! Eileen *is* sweet on Zeke Wilhite! I thought so!" How she figured that out, I couldn't understand. She exclaimed, "Eileen and Zeke are in love!"

"Hold on, I didn't say that."

Frances ignored me. "So, here's the news. They caught Tommy Bern peepin' again."

"Peepin'?"

"Window peepin'. You know, lookin' in windows when some girl is taking off her underwear?" It surprised me. Then again, Johnny had run Tommy off that time, threatening him if he ever came into our yard again. He must have known or had reason to suspect. Frances said, "One of these days, his old man won't be able to protect him, and Tommy Bern is going to get the snot kicked out of him." She shook her head. "Hey! Do you want to run downtown and spin real fast in Cashman's new revolving door?"

"Huh?" I'd stopped listening. I was thinking about what Roberta Grubbs told me long ago about her dad getting out his shotgun to scare Tommy off.

"Emmy?"

"What?"

"Cashman's?"

"Oh! Naw, you go on. I better go see about Sue-Sue."

On the way home, I stopped by Grubbses to ask Roberta about Tommy Bern.

The Grubbs place was little more than a cottage, the narrow part and a short front porch closest to the street. There was practically no front yard. In the back, the Grubbses kept chickens and a hog pen that I could smell from the street. At the edge of town, where we lived, farm life and city life seemed to overlap.

I'd never once been in the Grubbs place or met any of Roberta's family except her mother, who answered my knock on their screen door. The air coming through the screen was succulent with the smell of something good in the oven. Nothing was visible in the dark interior, however, but the thick, scuffed leg of an old table.

Mrs. Grubbs wiped her hands on a dishtowel and tossed it onto her shoulder. "Well, if it ain't Miss Emmy. Good morning to you, child. How's your fambly?"

"Morning Mrs. Grubbs. Oh, they're fine. I was wondering, could I speak to Roberta?"

"I'm sorry, Miss Emmy. She not here."

"She's not? Oh. Should I come back a little later?"

"Reckon that won't do. See, she gone almost up to the day school take up." I wanted to ask why and where she'd gone, but Mama had told us such questions were not polite. Mrs. Grubbs didn't volunteer anything further. Instead, she said, "I's fixin' to have a fritter. Would you care for one and a nice cold glass of lemonade?" It sounded good, but I was caught up in trying to think of a way to ask Mrs. Grubbs about Tommy Bern. Before I could think of one, she said, "Tell you what. Sit yourself down on that step, Miss Emmy, and I'll bring you one."

And she did. She handed me a plate with a piping hot fritter and a perspiring glass of lemonade. She sat down on the step next to me and drank lemonade from her own glass.

"Mmmm, this is delicious," I said, stuffing my mouth. I washed some down while Mrs. Grubbs watched. I couldn't figure a way to just start asking about Tommy Bern or Mr. Grubbs toting a shotgun. I took another big bite. "Real good."

Mrs. Grubbs spoke. "Miss Emmy, Roberta is at her grandmammy's helping with the pickin'. She go every summer."

"She does? She just goes off by herself?" I asked.

"Heavens no, child. She all together with her brothers and her sisters."

I couldn't resist. "How many she got?" I watched Mrs. Grubbs's brow pinch.

"Three brothers and three sisters." No names. No ages. No details.

"Are they picking strawberries?" I asked. It's what we picked when Sue-Sue and I went to Grandma Hainline's for a week in the summer to earn some pin money. I didn't think that could be it or Roberta wouldn't be gone up 'til school started.

"Berries, peaches, even cotton, if it's ready."

"Cotton?" I'd heard that was hot, backbreaking work. "Jeez."

"'Round here, everybody pitch in," Mrs. Grubbs said, "and pull their weight."

Out of the corner of my eye, I saw someone climbing in the tree in our side yard. And it looked like Eileen, who hadn't been up in a tree in years. Eileen was acting a little strangely since the night of the fight. She'd dropped out of our evening games, and if she spoke to either Rach or Zeke later, it was when no one else was around. Yet on the surface, she appeared cheerful and untroubled, as if nothing had ever happened.

How that was possible, I couldn't understand. Particularly since the bad blood between Zeke and Rach had forced John B. to choose between his two best friends every time he did anything. He could do something with Zeke. Or he could do something with Rach. And each was after him to be loyal to them alone. This had greatly intensified John B.'s irritation with Eileen.

"Everything okay, Miss Emmy?"

"Would you 'scuse me, Mrs. Grubbs?" I said. I couldn't get over seeing Eileen up in that tree, and I couldn't think of a way to get Mrs.

Grubbs to talk about Tommy Bern. "I think I hear my m[...] I set down the plate of greasy crumbs and the lemonade g[...] "Thank you kindly," I called back. "I sure enjoyed it."

Once I was in our side yard, Eileen noticed me but [...] She pretended to be surveying the neighborhood from [...] was standing on, shielding her eyes with her hand like she [...] ranger looking for fires or something.

"Next time, maybe you ought to bring a telescope, [...] her.

"Very funny," Eileen said. She worked her way d[...] swung on the lowest limb and dropped. She wiped her [...] pants. "What do you want, Emma?"

"I was just wondering what you were doing is all."

"Nothing. I was trying to find out if I could see th[...] up there."

"Maybe I'll have a look, too," I said, watching her c[...]

"Go right ahead," she said and turned to leave. A[...] away, she called over her shoulder, "But I'll tell you now, [...] it. It'll be a lot of work for nothing."

Oh, I was going up there, all right. Only I was going [...] Eileen couldn't see me do it. In the meantime, I picked [...] backyard where I could see her bedroom window on the [...] the house as the tree. Sure enough, a minute hadn't gone [...] face appeared there, her eyes anxiously scouring that tre[...] stopping on something else close to where she'd been p[...]

Thirty-Four

"Watcha doing? Bird-watching?"

The sound of Margaret's chirpy voice startled me. I felt jumpy after a quarter hour of spying on Eileen as she periodically popped into her window, forcing me to duck for cover in the yard. I gave Margaret the eye. "Didn't anybody ever tell you not to sneak up on people like that?" *Bird-watching.* What a wiseacre.

"Where have you been?" she asked. "You got a corn kernel on your shirt and crumbs on your face."

I brushed them off. "Okay now? Fine. Listen, this is important. What have you heard about Tommy Bern?"

"Tommy Bern?" she said with a face like I'd asked her about Gunga Din. "Nothing. I stay as far away from that boy as I can."

"Me too. But I still *hear things.*"

"That he's a bully, you mean? Or that he's ugly?" She smirked.

"Very funny." I smiled, and then went back to business. "So you haven't heard any bad stuff he's done."

"I'm not deaf, Emma. What stuff are you talking about exactly?"

"A friend of Sue-Sue's claims he's been peepin' in windows and he's got himself in a whole lot of hot water."

Margaret thought about this moment. "Which friend of Sue-Sue's? Not the twit they caught playing with matches behind the gas station." She was contemptuous of silly people.

"Yeah, it's her, but she does know some pretty strange things."

Margaret looked disgusted. She shook her head. "Did you ask Dema?"

Dema! Why hadn't I thought of that? Dema's two aunts worked as operators at Central and spent most of their day listening in on other people's phone calls. Boy, did they know the dirt! (And word got around.) "I was just about to go talk to her," I lied.

We ran to the Woodses' house. The mystery of Eileen in the side yard tree would have to wait. There was no telling how long my sister was going to stay up in her room keeping lookout.

"Dema went off on her bike a bit ago, girls," Inez Woods told us. "I don't expect she's gone far. You could wait for her in the yard." I was pretty sure Dema's mother knew all about Tommy Bern, too, but I didn't have the nerve to ask her.

We did a few cartwheels on the Woodses' grass once I'd checked to be sure Max Nix wasn't watching from his porch.

"I wish I had a bike," I said, thinking how I'd go looking for Dema. I'd forgotten for a moment that Margaret's family was worse off than us Starkeys by a long shot, and she probably didn't dare even wish for one.

"Not me," Margaret said. "Bikes are dangerous. Walking is better. It gives you time to think."

We took up on an old hopscotch layout, the chalk smudged and faded on the Woodses' sidewalk. Margaret went first and quickly made it to three. She was sizing up the jump to No. 4 when she asked, "Where did the twit think Tommy Bern was peepin'? It wasn't around here, was it? Oooh, that gave me a shiver."

It was reassuring somehow that Margaret was scared of Tommy Bern too, that I wasn't alone in being a 'fraidy cat. Plus Margaret was scared without knowing John B. had shagged Tommy from our yard or that Roberta's father used a shotgun to scare him off. I thought about telling her but decided not to. She looked worried enough already. Instead, I lied with the truth.

"Frances—the twit—didn't say where he was peepin'." Next, I made a nervous joke to throw her further off the scent. "Hey! You s'pose he was peepin' at Cynthia LaFevre? She's got the biggest, fattest fanny in the whole school!" I laughed.

When Dema didn't come home by the time we'd finished hopscotch, we gave up and left for Margaret's house to play dress-up. But just as we were about to cut through my yard, Eileen rushed out the front door, sheet music in hand, late for her piano lesson, as usual. "Hold up, Margaret," I said, watching Eileen run off. "There's something I want to check."

The side yard tree had never been a climbing tree. Not a single limb or branch was within my reach, even when I jumped. I had to push an old crate over to the trunk to get started.

Eileen had been midway up when I spotted her, higher than I had ever climbed in my life. I went up cautiously, and quickly lost my bearings a few branches skyward. Everything looked different up in the leaves. Which limb had she been out on? I glanced back to try to figure out where I was, and saw how far down the hard ground was already. It took my stomach a few seconds to settle, and then I caught sight of all the revolting white splotches on the roof of the hen house. *Bird dogger*—that was what John B. called it. I had to close my eyes and take three deep breaths before I could inch out onto the narrow limb where I hoped I'd seen Eileen. My sweaty hands squeezed the branches and my toes curled around the limbs.

Margaret had volunteered to stay below. "To keep an eye out for Eileen," she said. I figured she was probably afraid of heights. "You finding anything?" she called up.

"Hush up, Margaret," I said. "You want the whole neighborhood to know I'm up here snooping around?"

Too late. Sue-Sue came running a minute later. "Hey! Watcha doin'? Wait! I'm coming up." It only scared me more to have my sister climbing around below me, trapping me out on a limb, but I couldn't stop her.

It put me completely at sixes and sevens. My arms and legs turned rigid and the bark cut into my bare feet. I wasn't even sure what it was I was looking for. It was all hopeless, I decided, watching as my sister blocked my way back down. But then, my vision caught on a small, broken branch dangling by a shred of bark in the breeze. Inches away from it was something shiny, glinting in a shaft of light. It was a tobacco tin nailed to a branch. I took a breath and edged that direction. This had to be what I was looking for, Eileen's little secret. The tin said *Velvet Tobacco,* which was Thad's brand. I thought I knew what I would find inside, and it wasn't tobacco. I inched over, anchored one arm securely around a thick branch and carefully pried open the lid. It yielded with very little effort, but there was nothing inside except the lingering scent of tobacco.

"It's a mailbox," I called down. "But it's empty."

The kids who lived next door to my Grandma Hainline in El Dorado Springs, Missouri, nailed tobacco tins to their tree and called them mailboxes, passing each other notes for fun. I wondered if Eileen was swapping notes with a boy, and which boy it might be. Climbing the tree wouldn't pose a problem for either Rach or Zeke. They were both tall enough to jump and grab the lowest branch. Rach had strong shoulders, and could probably get around a tree as effortlessly as a gorilla. I had once watched him do twenty chin-ups on a length of pipe rigged up in their basement.

Had Eileen chosen him or Zeke? Zeke was better looking and more polished. But if it had been me, I would have gone for Rach. His swagger had verve, and his rough edges made me all mushy.

I climbed down and explained to Margaret about the mailbox. Then I asked, "Rach ever talk to you about his fight with Zeke?"

"Uh-uh," she said. "Don't you think it was over Eileen?"

I nodded.

There had been a time when the three of us Starkey girls would stand around at the sink doing the dishes and drop hints about boys we liked, using only first initials as the others guessed. Now Eileen had gone completely boy crazy and shut us out of her thoughts entirely. I wondered if she knew what she was doing or if she was headed for trouble. She was so pretty. And, somehow, that seemed dangerous.

John B. had the straight skinny on Tommy Bern. He spilled it all to us when Margaret and I cornered him in the barn and told him what Frances had said.

"Yeah, that boy's in trouble," John B. said, keeping his head pressed into Tallulah's flank as he worked her udders. "His folks had to agree to send him away to some military academy back East. He's leavin' soon." Margaret and I looked at each other and listened to the sound of the milk squirting into a pail. "So he won't be around to pester anyone."

"Who was he peepin' on?" we asked. "Do you know?"

"Cheryl Lindskog," John B. said. She was an eighth grader, the only daughter of the family that owned the local Chevrolet dealership and easily the prettiest girl in town.

"Just her?" Margaret asked. "Nobody else?"

John B. hesitated. "I couldn't tell ya. The important thing is he's going away. I say, good riddance! Time we were rid of that creep."

Eileen came into my room and shoved a wadded-up paper at me that night.

"Did you do this?"

I opened it up and spread it out on the dresser. It was not my writing. It was Sue-Sue's. She was down the hall in the bath.

Eileen —
Wach ur step.
Sined, The FANTUM

"No," I said, miffed that Eileen would think I couldn't spell or write cursive, treating me like toe jam. "That's Sue-Sue's writing," I said. I wondered how the word *fantum* was actually spelled. And that made me wonder what Eileen might write to a boy, and what a boy might say in reply. Was it all kissy-kissy mush?

"You told Sue-Sue about the tree, didn't you?" Eileen said.

"I didn't mean to." I hadn't really told her, but Eileen was sort of right. Where she was all wrong was in everything else. "What do you think you're doing anyway, Eileen?" Couldn't she see she was messing things up for everyone, playing Rach against Zeke?

"Emma Faye, you don't know when to mind your own business!"

"Everything okay in there, girls?" It was Mama.

Eileen flushed. "Yes," she said quickly. Her eyes cut toward me to say I'd better keep my yap shut or she wouldn't be finished with me. "I was just talking to Emma."

"Well, Emma has to get ready for her bath," Mama said, arriving at my door. "We've got church in the morning. Let's go, girls. Eileen, you need to straighten up your room."

Thirty-Five

I'd gotten so completely wrapped up in my cat-and-mouse game with Eileen that it came as a nasty shock to have Thaney suddenly turn up at our door.

Sue-Sue and I ran home when we saw Uncle Walter's car pull up. He leaned on the horn and drove straight onto our lawn, right up to the front porch. He got out and hustled around the side to help Thaney out the passenger door. He held her up as if they were limping away from a car accident. Her hair under a tilted hat was in a state, and her pallor was as gray as a December day. I couldn't have been more stunned. What had happened? Why was Thaney with Uncle Walter? What were they doing at our house?

Mama was at the front door in an instant with Eileen, and she hurried down the front steps, calling out, "Oh, Thaney, you poor dear! The long drive has exhausted you." Eileen's expression seemed to reflect something calamitous as well, but I suspected it had less to do with Thaney's tortured face than with the upset of our grandmother returning. There was no question that Thaney looked bad, however, far worse than before she had left us. She was hunched over, her movements feeble, and she acted as if she were wracked with pain. Mama put an arm around her and dispatched Eileen to ring up Thad at the lumberyard. "Tell him they're here," she said.

Tell him they're here? You mean they *knew* Thaney was coming? With Walter? They weren't surprised? It was like a sucker punch to my solar plexus.

Mama helped Thaney into the house, responding with clucking sympathy to her endless groans and whimpers. Then she led her slowly up the stairs to the bedroom my brother had only recently reclaimed. If memory serves, the summer sun ducked behind a massive dark cloud bearing down on Cornucopia, Kansas, just then.

They settled Thaney into bed. Later, the adults gathered for a powwow in the kitchen. The rest of us were shooed outside to play. The gist of the conversation, which could be overheard in splintered fragments beneath the kitchen window, was that Thaney was back for good.

My uncle's gruff voice was low, and only some of his words, "surgery" and "convalescence" and "relapse," drifted clearly through the window. Thad's voice, pitched higher than Walter's, could be heard to ask, "Is she really awful sick?" The next word, *malignant*, silenced all discussion for several seconds, and then my uncle grunted, "Fern says you keep a little whiskey in the house." At that, I went racing off to Margaret for an explanation of the word *malignant*.

"I don't know it," Margaret said, "but we can look it up." She untied the string around her dictionary and flipped back and forth through the loose, dog-eared pages near the middle. "I don't see it," she said. "Wait! What was it again?"

I was so discombobulated that my recollection became blurred in all of the rush. "Mah-lig-ner, I think, or something like that." If I'd seen my uncle's lips move, I'd have been more certain. "It got real quiet after he said it."

"Mah-lig-ner?"

"That's what it sounded like," I said, squeezing my toes under.

"Wait, *malinger* maybe?" Her finger held her place in the long column of gray.

"Yeah, maybe," I said. "I'm not sure." It didn't sound exactly right to me, but if that's what the dictionary said, then maybe my uncle hadn't pronounced it correctly. "Yeah. Malinger."

"Mah-ling-er," Margaret read. "It says, 'To feign illness in order to shirk duty or avoid work.' Why, your grandmother's goldbricking!"

I shook my head in disgust. What a devious old woman!

Around dusk, as Eileen helped Mama unpack Thaney's things, I snuck out to the side yard again and up the tree to the mailbox, still determined to learn Eileen's secret. Again, Margaret acted as my lookout. And again, the tobacco tin was empty.

"Still no luck?" Margaret asked, sensing my discouragement. I shook my head. Then Margaret said, "I'll keep an eye on Rach. See what he's up to."

"Would ya?" I said. "That'd be a big help."

The distant crackling of the approaching thunderstorm and a sudden gust of cool air chased us in for the night. There was nothing quite like a thunderstorm in Kansas. The deep booming thunderclaps could rattle the timbers of even a solid house like ours, and the raindrops would come fat and heavy. But the dark, boiling, ominous clouds are what I remember today. Was there a girl growing up in Kansas at the time who didn't wonder if a cyclone was coming for her when a storm like this approached, just as one had come for Dorothy and Toto in L. Frank Baum's book?

"Don't pull the covers off my head!" Sue-Sue yelled as I joined her in bed.

"Don't you want to make up a story?" I asked. Lightning flashed and thunder boomed, rattling our window and setting off dozens of crinkly echoes that spread slowly outward through the trees. It sounded like everything around us was being shredded.

"I can do it just fine with the covers where they were!" Sue-Sue shouted.

"Okay." I arranged myself into a comfortable spot on the sloping mattress after Sue-Sue had ducked back under. "Want to make up another trip to Oz?" I asked. It had been a tradition on stormy nights to imagine ourselves transported to some magical Emerald City or other world. In our stories, crazy relatives and neighbors populated the landscape. Thaney was often a wicked witch. Max Nix was a sneaky wolf. Little Alice barked like Toto. Some nights, I was Dorothy. Some nights, Sue-Sue was.

"Once upon a time," I began. "Your turn ..."

I awoke to brilliant sunshine early the next morning and quietly got myself out of bed. I tiptoed down the stairs and out through the wet grass into the side yard to climb the tree again. Cold drips fell from leaves onto my face and arms and spotted my nightgown, making me shiver. I was pretty sure nobody had gone up that tree in the rainstorm, but I needed to check anyway. I could have just taken Frances's word for it that Eileen was sweet on Zeke Wilhite and let it go at that. But I was as determined to learn Eileen's secrets as she was to keep them.

The tobacco tin was empty again, and I felt like ripping it off the branch. So I gave it a hard yank, and my foot slipped on the wet bark. The panic of impending disaster shot through me as I went down hard on my rump on the limb, still hanging on for dear life to the slender branch above as it bent and swayed forward but didn't break. I gasped and righted myself with a quick kick of my legs. Then I cussed out loud. The sound of it did nothing to calm me. In fact, it made me jitterier. Eileen might look out her window at any second and see me. I quickly gathered myself and climbed down.

Later that week, Mama sent me to Thaney's room with a tray of hot cocoa and graham crackers. "Take this up to her right away." That had become a common phrase in our house. Thaney hadn't been out of bed yet, even though she no longer looked or acted like her next breath might be her last. Still, we waited on her hand and foot. How was she getting away with this, I wondered. I tried to be grateful that she had at least put her false teeth back into her puckered mouth and that she was postponing the inevitable lecture on the state of her garden until she could get outside to see it. In trade, I was doing backbreaking maid service.

Thaney wore a locket around her neck that morning, and I could tell she wanted me to notice.

"My, that's pretty," I said, trying to muster some sincerity.

She slipped it over her head and handed it to me. "Open it."

I fumbled with the latch at the edge and released it. Inside was a tiny picture of a round-faced girl. Her long coils of curls and frilly clothes were very old-fashioned, and her expression seemed somewhat vacant, as people often did in old photos. But she looked pleasant.

"Who do you suppose that is?" Thaney asked.

It fell on me then like a load of bricks. "You?"

She nodded. Although I'd guessed it was her, I still thought it queer. Who carries a picture of herself around in a locket, I wondered. "This locket belonged to my mother," she said, as if reading my thoughts. "When she died, I passed it on to my only daughter, Fern. She has had it until now. She suggested that I give it to you."

Swell. What in the world was my aunt thinking? That I'd want some silly old locket or stupid picture? It was just the sort of ridiculous gift that made me mad. It wasn't like I really needed to be reminded that I was related to Thaney. I bit my lip and tried to remember my manners. But it annoyed me somehow to see her as a young girl. I wanted to believe she had always looked like a wasp. For an instant as she stared at me now, I saw someone younger hiding out in her old face. It was only a flicker, and then it vanished.

"You have to grow up sometime, Emma," Thaney said. It surprised me. That was not what I had expected her to say, and my mind rebelled at the idea that I needed a shove from her toward adulthood. She was right about one thing, though. I didn't want to grow up. Or old. Why did adults always push that idea? *Grow up!* Why? Who wanted that? Adults were dull and grotesque. Who'd want to give up the carefree days of childhood for that? Thaney said, "It's unavoidable."

"No, it isn't," I said, angry over her taunts of inevitability, yet unsure how to counter them. "Margaret and I have a pact," I lied. "We're going to be children forever!"

Thaney smiled. "Everybody grows up."

A nasty thought crossed my mind. "No, they don't! My sister Mary Ellen? She didn't!" I wanted to hurt Thaney, pierce her smugness, and my remark seemed to. She frowned and sniffed. I was about to add on something about that dead girl with pigtails in the paper, murdered by that man, but a wave of shame washed over me and I lowered my eyes.

Thaney lay back on her pillow, her eyelids drooping, and waved me away, the locket firmly back in her grip. I thought it was one of her tricks, wanting me to beg or apologize and agree to take it, but I wasn't about to. Let her keep her old locket.

After dark that night, Eileen headed for the bathtub and I snuck out of the house to climb the tree in the side yard again. I couldn't stop myself. I moved the crate into place, and something large startled me by dropping down next to it out of the tree. I yelped with surprise, just before a hand full of hard fingers clamped tight around my throat and lifted me, squeezing the sound into a tiny squeak. My knees buckled and my eyes shot to the face of the attacker. A faint light spilled from an upstairs window. In it, I saw the shadowy features of Tommy Bern. He loosened his grip slightly as I frantically waved my arms, trying to suck in another breath.

"You tell anybody you saw me," Tommy snarled, "and I'll come back for you. I swear I will." His hateful eyes glared into mine. And then he threw me onto the ground with such force, it knocked the rest of the breath out of me. By the time I looked up, I was alone in the dark.

I lay there trembling, in no hurry to move, the world suddenly very different. I touched my neck where Tommy had grabbed it. My throat felt hot. I was going to cry. Tommy Bern had scared the dickens out of me. He had been up in our tree where Eileen had her mailbox. But not to look for a note from her, I suspected. No, he was there just as Eileen had been getting ready for her bath. I closed my eyes, thought about that, and heard myself sob quietly.

Thirty-Six

I was still for what seemed a long time, trying to pull myself together, wanting irrationally to race to the barn before Tommy Bern could come back and finish me off. Surely, he'd figure out that I couldn't keep such horrid news from bursting out of me. And after he'd gone and killed me, Eileen would be devastated. And mortified that some stupid, awful boy had been peeping in her window! I wrapped my arms around me and prayed things wouldn't get messed up even more.

Tommy may not have choked the life out of me, but he had choked me off from my life for the moment. I was frozen to the damp grass that pressed against my arms and legs, listening to the noises from the house that seemed indifferent to my suffering. In time, I had to sit up and face the world. What use was it lying there wishing none of it had ever happened? It had.

"What's wrong?" Sue-Sue asked the second I got back to our room. I quickly turned my face away to conceal my red eyes. Then I pulled our window shade against the horrid night. In the glow of our bedside lamp, blotchy grass stains stood out like accusations on my nightgown. No good could come of telling Sue-Sue anything. John B. would find out, and he'd try to hurt Tommy. Then he'd be in trouble too.

"Nothing's wrong," I said, "so don't ask me again."

"You climbing in the tree after dark?"

"Not another word, Shag!" She hated being called that. It was a name John B. had given her after a particularly bad haircut from

Thad. A pillow came flying my way, hit the wall and plopped to the floor.

"Stay out of this bed!" Sue-Sue said in her bossiest voice.

I started to yell, "Try and make me!" and stopped. I wanted to knock her silly with the pillow she'd thrown, but a noisy row would attract Mama and there would be questions that came with traps. So I offered up an olive branch of sorts.

"Hold on. Hold on. I'm sorry." I lowered my voice and leaned in toward Sue-Sue. "I was outside chasing around with Margaret, and I stubbed my toe and fell and got all dirty after my bath. You know if Mama finds out, she'll give me the switch. Could you please help me keep it quiet?"

I lay awake for a long time that night wondering if I was doing the right thing. It was way too big a secret to keep. But with Tommy Bern going away to military school anyway, I could save everyone a lot of grief by keeping it to myself. Eileen would be spared knowing about Tommy, and John B. would not be consumed by vengeance. No use crying over spilt milk, Thaney always said. "What's done is done." It seemed to fit.

If only I could really have agreed with that deep in my heart.

The following afternoon, my troubled conscience had been rubbed raw by righteous lessons at church and Sunday school, and I was afraid I might burst if I didn't say something to someone. So I pulled Margaret aside at the first opportunity and dragged her up to the hayloft in the barn.

On the way up the ladder, I said, "You gotta promise on a huge stack of Bibles that you'll never whisper a word of this to a soul, 'cause it'd kill Eileen if she found out." When I gave her the news, Margaret swallowed hard like the idea had caught sideways in her throat and she needed to force it down with some spit to make it go away.

"Holy cripes!" she whispered, once she did.

"So do I tell someone or don't I?"

Her face clouded. "Gosh! How should I know?" She tipped back in the straw and stared up awhile. "It's a nasty business. But I s'pose if Tommy's leaving . . ."

"Are we sure that's true? How do we find out?"

"I'm not going to ask him, if that's what you're hinting at."

We went instead to see Dema, who was playing jacks with her cousin in the Woodses' driveway. I said, "Is it true Tommy Bern is leaving town?"

"Why you askin' that for?" Dema wanted to know. She stood up and put her hands on her hips.

"No reason," I said. "Just asking is all."

Dema squinted one eye and leaned in. "What are those funny marks on your throat, Emma Starkey?" she demanded. "Your neck looks like a blue and yella zebra."

"Don't be so darn nosy, Dema," I warned her.

"Who's being nosy?"

"You are."

Dema stuck a finger in my chest. "No, you are. Coming over here asking about Tommy Bern. What do I know about Tommy Bern? Did he do that to you? He did! Didn't he!"

I had to think to shut my mouth when nothing came out.

"Why would he want to choke you?" she demanded. "You know something, don't you?"

"No. I don't know nothing. Leave me alone. Come on, Margaret, let's go!" And away we scuttled like bugs headed for a rock.

It wasn't long after that that John B. came looking for me. He grabbed my arm roughly and spun me around and tipped my chin up to look at my neck.

"Did Tommy Bern do that to you?" he demanded. I tried to think up a plausible lie. Johnny yelled, "Tell me! He did, didn't he? That fat, stupid *piss cutter*. Why? Why'd he do it?"

I knew if I could only think up a good lie, I might still spare Eileen some anguish. I said, "I called him a name is all. I called him a . . . a creep. I'm sorry! I shouldn'a."

"Was he in our yard?" Johnny demanded. He was going too fast for me to think up fresh lies. Johnny said, "He *was*, wasn't he?"

"Yes!" I said, miserably.

"Last night?"

"Yes!"

Johnny's face got red, his jaw jutted out, and he turned on his heel and stomped off in the direction of Tommy Bern's house.

"Johnny, wait! Don't do this!" I called after him. "He's an awful bully! He fights dirty! He never loses—least not that I ever heard of." I didn't say he was a couple inches taller than Johnny, and quite a few pounds heavier. "He'll corner me when you're not around," I pleaded, tagging along after him. I meant it. "He'll beat the tar out of me."

Johnny slowed for a step or two, and then went on.

He pounded on the Berns' door like he was about to break it down. There was flex in his short, angular body, as if all his springs were wound up tight now, and he had to shift from foot to foot to stand still. The porch at the front of the fancy brick house was little more than a landing, but it had two massive Roman columns like something for a courthouse. The stubby wood posts held up a ridiculously tiny roof. I felt terribly exposed standing there, and I didn't want Tommy Bern to see that I had told Johnny. But there was no place to hide nearby. I might have run away, I suppose, but I was too worried about Johnny. So I turned sideways and sort of shriveled up right where I was.

"They ain't home, John Starkey," the neighbor called from her front porch next door. "And if you're there looking for Tommy, you're too late. His folks is already hauling that boy to the train station in Kansas City."

Johnny glared at the woman, Mrs. Wheaton, and kicked over a flowerpot on the Berns' porch. Mrs. Wheaton shook her head and let herself back in her house.

I took a ragged breath, letting go of the fear that had gripped me, grateful that a descent into madness had been prevented. Somehow, everything was going to turn out all right. There wasn't going to be a fight. Tommy Bern truly had left town. I didn't have to worry about him bothering us again. And I had managed to stall John B. just long enough that he might never know what really happened. Still, I have sometimes wondered in the years since how events might have turned out differently if Tommy had been there that day and opened the door when John B. knocked and Johnny had flattened him with a sucker punch. I think Tommy was secretly scared of Johnny. As Thad liked to say, *it's not the size of the dog in the fight; it's the size of the fight in the dog.* But these thoughts were in the distant future. Right then, I was just happy that there wasn't going to be a fight, that Tommy wouldn't be coming after me and John B. was not going to get himself into trouble. Johnny was not similarly mollified, however. Just the opposite.

"That piss cutter's got one comin'," he seethed, balling his fist near his chest. The seed of anger I'd planted had grown to the sky like Jack's beanstalk. John B. was geared up for a fight, and it would take him a while to cool down and let it go, I thought. He had a serious case of Starkey anger and stubbornness. "He's gone now, Johnny," I assured him. "He won't bother us no more."

Max Nix was weaving his Model T backward out his driveway as Johnny and I headed home. He brought his clunker to a halt in the street. There was the sound of gears clashing. Then he lurched forward and drove past us. I watched, wondering what he would do when he saw us, but he only glanced in our direction a second with an indifferent look and then turned his eyes back to the road. No wave. No smile.

I was so happy to be standing next to my brave brother just then. And I was so pleased that Johnny was safe that I just couldn't help myself. I threw my arms around him and hugged him right there on the spot.

"Hey!" he yelled, shrugging loose. "What's with that?"

"Can't a girl hug her brother?" Then I remembered some change I'd stuffed in my pocket from the loot Sue-Sue and I had made dancing the Charleston for the horseshoe players. "Say, Johnny. How about we get ice cream sodas? My treat."

John B. grinned at me then like he'd just heard a sneaking joke, and we turned and walked in the other direction toward town.

Thirty-Seven

*T*he summer seemed to wind down slowly after Tommy left. We frittered away dog day afternoons at the swimming hole below the dam, floating on our backs, letting the warm river current gently carry us along. My ears bobbed in and out of shallow swells and my eyes saw only blue sky and arching trees. Was there anything more peaceful? An hour before, I'd been disgusted at emptying Thaney's bedpan. Now, suspended between earth and sky, it was just the fishy aroma of the languid green river and me drifting farther and farther from the others, letting the sounds of their voices vanish, not lifting my head to go into a dog paddle until I was completely alone, then taking my time returning, swimming a lazy sidestroke toward the dam and the bridge. When I got back, they were all squealing like thrill riders on a rollercoaster.

Rach and Johnny were taking turns shooting Eileen into the air. They would duck her under and use her buoyancy for leverage. Of course, it had become a competition to see who could send her higher.

"New record!" Rach boasted. "Her ankles came out that time!"

"Doesn't count!" Johnny argued. "She bent her knees! And her back went in before her ankles came out! Play fair, Eileen!"

Eileen beamed at her own mischief. She was getting prettier and prettier, I realized. Such a dazzling smile! I'd overheard the ladies whispering at church. "That girl is going to break some hearts," they said. "And that little Sue-Sue! *She* is *such* a doll!" No mention of

Emma. Not even as an afterthought. I had to wonder as I catalogued my faults in the mirror—plain nose, pinched-up mouth, mousy brown hair—had I come from bad seed? It hurt to think there might be a germ of truth in it when Johnny told me (in his kidding way) that I was pretty ugly and pretty apt to stay that way whenever I asked if he thought I was pretty. I knew he was belittling me for asking, but it didn't help a girl when she was being completely overlooked, when she was the "other" sister in the hand-me-down clothes, the dog-eared dime novel between bookend beauties.

"Tiebreaker," Rach called to settle the argument over who had thrown Eileen higher out of the water. The boys exchanged challenging glances, swam out to deeper water, took in several gulps of air, and dove under together. I hated this game. See Who Can Stay Down Longest. It made me terribly anxious, waiting for them to break the surface again. When they did, their first breaths were always desperate gasps. The river had grown so murky by August that their tanned bodies vanished as they went deep. They always did too, I suppose as a way of making themselves stay under longer.

An excited hush fell over us while we waited. Sue-Sue and Alice stopped splashing each other and looked toward the spot at the surface where the boys had slipped down. Bubbles rose to the surface. They were getting better at this, and making us wait longer.

Johnny finally surfaced, slapping the top of the water hard as he fought for a rasping, frantic breath. His head jerked around, looking for Rach, and he cussed when his opponent was not in sight. He churned his legs and used his arms to turn in a circle, watching. "Hell," he muttered. His brow pinched. I saw red splotches on his skin, spider bites from sleeping in the cellar. The time lengthened, and Johnny's face clouded. Rach had been down too long. "Jesus wept!" Johnny said. He gulped another big breath and went back under. Eileen followed, the splash of her leg kick thwoping urgently.

Margaret, who had chosen this of all days to get her nose out of a book and join us in the river, panicked. "I'm going for help!" she shouted. She tried to run through the waist-deep water, awkwardly churning up chop with every energetic stride toward shore. Rach broke the surface at the opposite bank before she could. He laughed raucously. He'd tricked us by coming up for a quick breath someplace behind us, then ducking back under before Johnny had come up. He was a clever cheat.

As John B. resurfaced, Rach mocked him with catcalls. Johnny glared back. "Dammit, Rach!" he yelled. "Are you crazy?" Rach laughed, and Johnny began swimming toward him, cussing with every stroke. In a minute, they were both up on the opposite bank, Johnny chasing the bigger, lankier boy as he ran toward the bridge. Rach was laughing and whooping. Johnny, spent from effort, sucking wind, padded along on his flat feet, losing ground with every stride. In a few seconds, Rach was well ahead, up past the dam, cutting through some trees to the road and the bridge.

Eileen had stayed down a long time and was still catching her breath. She let out a little yelp when Rach hoisted himself up onto the bridge's railing and stumbled slightly getting to his feet. We all watched him bend his knees and grab the superstructure beam for support. With one hand firmly planted on metal, he gathered himself, stood, and smiled. Johnny stopped running. "Hey!" he yelled. "What do you think you're doin'?"

"Second tiebreaker," Rach called out. "First to jump. Or biggest splash."

"No!" Johnny said. "Nothing doing!" He and Rach had argued before about diving off the bridge, Rach always pushing Johnny to risk it with him. "I won the tiebreaker fair and square," Johnny shouted. "No need for a second."

"You conceding?" Rach let go of the beam then and crouched, extending his arms over his head, as if he were actually preparing to dive. I gasped. Then he grinned to show us he was only playing around. He was a-taunting Johnny and showing off for Eileen, and I should have been mad, but I liked Rach too much to blame him. Was I sweet on him? Maybe. But if I was, it was only a ridiculous crush, and I preferred to hide it even from myself. What hope did I have, a little kid hanging around an older boy who was starting to grow sideburns? As I gawked at his beautiful body, he seemed to change in the way a familiar word transforms when you stare at it too long. He'd always had a cocky nature and an unpredictable way about him. But he was beginning to look like one of the toughs who hung around the square downtown smoking cigarettes as they lounged in a parked touring car, often sitting on the running boards. As strange as it was, I liked that, but he suddenly seemed more like a stranger, like someone I'd never really, actually know.

"Rach!" Johnny yelled, sounding annoyed now. "Cut it out!"

Alice had been trapping minnows in the shallows near the sandbar with a pail. She started to bawl and Margaret shouted over her wailing, "Rach, you get down from there right this second or I am running home and telling Mama!"

This got a laugh from the daredevil atop the bridge railing, but I noticed that he did rise back up out of his crouch and put a hand on the beam. My toes clenched at his every move. I felt a cramp coming on in my calf, and I headed for shallower water, where I could stand on the mucky bottom. Why, I wondered, did somebody always have to spoil it every time things started smoothing out? I wanted Eileen to stop her tramping with boys because that would probably keep Rach from climbing up on the bridge railing any more. I wanted to get Margaret to forget about getting her father back and stop mooning about him all the time and missing out on fun stuff. But how would I ever get anyone to listen to me? I was just a kid standing in the river feeling goose bumps rise on my neck and back.

A horn blared as a truck approached the narrow bridge. The driver motioned at Rach out the window. He slowed to rumble across the planks. "Get down, kid," you could hear the driver shouting. "You wanta break your neck?"

Rach waved at him in a friendly way, and stayed atop the rail as the truck rolled on, the driver shaking his head. Then Rach pivoted out over the water with one foot planted on the rail and his hand gripping a beam. Alice shrieked. Rach waved again at the departing truck, then shouted to us, "I could slice right through that surface!" and pointed down at the river before pulling himself back in.

John B. sat down in the grass and hugged his knees, keeping his eyes fixed on Rach, waiting him out.

Margaret sloshed up onto the riverbank now, and began running into the woods toward home. "I'm telling!" she called. Rach, apparently more afraid of his mother than heights, hopped down off the railing onto the bridge deck and chased after her.

Thirty-Eight

I never thought anything could make me hate school more than The Gutch had, but the week before classes started that fall, a typewritten letter arrived at our house from the Cornucopia Superintendent's Office announcing that something could.

"What's it say?" I asked Mama as her eye darted along though the gray text, her lips moving slightly. She didn't answer until she got to the bottom and had flipped the page over to glance at the blank back side, as if something might be cleared up there.

"They moved the South School boundary," Mama said, and pulled off her reading glasses to gaze at me. A pinch of worry squeezed the skin between her eyes, and the letter crinkled slightly in her hand. "It says you and Sue-Sue have been reassigned to North for the coming year. It seems there's been a change in enrollment."

I didn't understand. Whoever heard of such a thing? How could the compass needle in your life suddenly be yanked around to point in the opposite direction from your church, your regular school, your friends? This was still the same block in the same neighborhood, wasn't it? We hadn't moved. And now they could send me to North? Just like that? After a dumbstruck moment, I asked, "Does that mean I won't be having Mrs. Stark like Johnny and Eileen did for fourth grade?"

"I expect," Mama said.

I about flipped on the spot. "They can't do this!" I shouted.

"Calm yourself. Yes they can."

The prospect of a strange school terrified me. I shouted, "I won't go!"

Mama shook the paper in my face. "If they say you must, then you must."

"Not if I'm sick!"

"You're not sick," Mama said calmly.

That did it. I said, "Neither is Thaney, but we all pretend that she is!"

Mama's eyes got very big. She looked like I'd hauled off and slapped her square across the chops. A tick later, her face folded into an angry scowl. "Where did you get such a hateful idea, Emma Faye Starkey?"

"I heard Uncle Walter tell on her. He said Thaney was malingering."

"He said no such thing! What you are talking about?"

"I heard him. I was standing right outside that window!"

"You were what?" Mama clucked her tongue. I could see right off I'd made a serious slip. She said, "We'll come back to that in a minute, young lady. In the meantime, I want to know what it is you *think* you overheard—*exactly*."

I stared down at the grimy nail of my big toe and nudged it along a crack in the linoleum. "I only heard a couple words 'cause I just happened to be walking by, you see, and the window was open at the time, and Uncle Walter, he was talking kind of loud—"

"—Emma! Tell me! *What* did you hear?"

"Only a word or two, that's all. And one of them was that whopper. I'd never heard it before. Then it got all quiet in here, you know? So, me and Margaret looked it up."

Mama's voice huffed with exasperation. *"Malinger."* The pinch in her brow deepened, and her eyes appeared to search for the missing memory.

"That's right," I said, and immediately felt my confidence in that particular word slip again. I said, "Only it sounded more like *mahligner* when he said it."

"Malig-ner?" She looked puzzled. "That's not a word." She blinked a couple of times and said "Ohmigod!" before turning a hard eye on me. "It isn't mahligner you heard, Emma. The word is *malignant.*" I had to admit, that sounded more like it. Mama put a hand up to her mouth. Something bad was coming, I could tell. She said, "Uncle Walter was saying that Thaney has malignant tumors."

"Malignant tumors? What are those?"

"Those are nasty growths inside your body that aren't supposed to be there."

This was too much. *Growths?* Bad stuff could just start growing inside you like mushrooms on a stump? "Does that mean Thaney is really awful sick, like Thad said?" I had completely lost my composure, betraying everything I'd heard.

Mama lifted her eyebrows and tilted her head toward me as she spoke. "Thaney is the kind of sick where you don't get well."

I knew what that meant. It meant I'd messed up big. And all thanks to Margaret, I thought uncharitably. Eating squirrel for dinner had probably shrunk her brain.

"I didn't know!" I pleaded, shamefaced. How awful! I'd been mean to Thaney just when I should have been kind because she was going to die from icky rotten stuff growing inside her. I hadn't meant to do that any more than I'd meant to laugh on Pa Joesy's deathbed. Still, I had, and it was just as disrespectful, if not more. But how was I to know? Thaney had always been tougher than a callus and as prickly as a weed. "I thought she was puttin' on an act," I said.

"She is not." Mama's eyes raked across me. "Have you said something to her?"

I thought of the locket I'd rudely refused to accept. "I got to go talk to her," I said, and I ran for the stairs and Thaney's room before Mama could say another word.

That locket would dangle around my neck for a long time after that, and its thin silver chain felt heavy against my skin. It made me think of poor, dumb Rex chained to his tree. Only my necklace chain tied me to an old woman full of rotten mushrooms. It was like she'd captured and belled me like a cat with her locket and her picture and her cranky old advice. As I took it from her and put it on, a smug smile of triumph lifted her sagging face. Oh how she relished her victory. I hope you're happy, I thought, 'cause your plan can never work. I would never be able to be a faithful, obedient, loving granddaughter to her, no matter how hard I tried and no matter how sick she got. It was like trying to make a pet out of a porcupine. And that locket was just about as much fun to wear as an asphidity bag.

The night before school was to start, John B. offered to walk me up to North to have a look around and ease my nerves. It was four blocks farther than South, but it seemed much farther than that.

We walked past unfamiliar houses and yards, past streets with Indian names like Osage and Neosho, past things I'd never seen before. All the while, John B. tried to keep up the chatter. He'd point to a metal stick attached to a chimney and say, "Look, they've got radio." Or "Step on that crack and you'll break your mother's back."

For whatever reason, our family seldom went north of Bridge Street, which ran across the center of Cornucopia like the Mason-Dixon Line. Beyond it was foreign territory. It felt like trespassing, walking in these other people's neighborhoods, even on the sidewalks. On one of the blocks, a dog rushed out of nowhere, barking ferociously at us from behind a tall wire fence. The hair on my arms and neck stood up.

"It's only for a couple years," John B. said, trying to sound soothing. "Once you're in junior high, like Eileen, you get to go to South again." The junior high school occupied the top floor of South. For high school, you rode the bus to the county seat.

We passed a group of children in one yard who stopped playing to stare silently at us. I didn't recognize a one of them, and I slowed down without meaning to, preparing to run the other direction if they came at us. Then I noticed that John B. hadn't changed his pace and I had to skip a couple times to catch up. His shoulders were straight and he paid those kids no mind. I felt safe at his side, John B. walking as if he owned the street, all confident and cocky. I tried straightening

my shoulders, too, and mimicked John B.'s easy strides. But it occurred
to me right then that he wouldn't be there with us every day when we
walked to school, when I'd be responsible for protecting Sue-Sue, and
it left me feeling more scared than I had been before.

"Are you paying attention?" Johnny asked suddenly. "You gotta
walk Sue-Sue in the morning, remember?"

"Course I'm rememberin'," I said, checking the sign at the next
intersection to see where we were so I could memorize the street
name and find my way to this corner. You couldn't really get lost for
more than thirty seconds in Cornucopia with its square blocks and
numbered north-south streets, but I promised myself I'd pay closer
attention on the way back.

North School looked so much like South once we got there that
I couldn't tell them apart. John B. could. "Look, it's got lions at the
corners."

I looked up at the stone carvings and said, "What's South got?"

"Pigs," he said, and flashed a grin. "Naw, it's bears."

I laughed grudgingly. He took me over to a window to peek in.
Three milky glass globes hung from the ceiling unlit. The blackboard,
George Washington's picture, and the United States map were in
shadows. The walls had a familiar green color up to the height of
a man and became white above that. The round-faced clock said
a quarter past seven. I'd never seen a school clock with its hands
pointing that way—and I'd stared at plenty. School clocks stopped
at three-fifteen and jumped ahead to eight o'clock before everyone got
there the next morning, didn't they?

"Look," Johnny said. "It's not so different."

Then why did I feel all tingly and anxious peering in? Like
peeking under the flap of a circus tent before the clowns and wild
animals and high-flying acrobats came busting out from secret places.
"What about my friends?" I said. See what he said to that.

"Roberta will be going to North, too. And Dema."

"But not Margaret!" I whined. "And lots of others!"

"Not unless they change the boundary again from right behind
our house."

I let out a ragged sigh. "Johnny! What am I going to do? I'm so scared!" It was embarrassing to have to say it, and I tried to hide my face.

He caught and held my arms. "Sometimes you just got to buck up and do what you got to do," he said, giving me a little shake. "You're brave enough. I heard about you climbing all over the side yard tree." I didn't know what his smile meant.

"You never get scared, do you?" I said.

Johnny took his time answering that. "Not about school, no."

"Would you even be scared if Mama and Thad died?"

He frowned. After a minute, he shook his head. "Everybody gets scared sometimes, Emma." Like being scared to jump off the bridge with Rach, I thought, even though that didn't count because it was reckless and stupid. Anybody'd be scared of that. John B. said, "Listen, you can't let Sue-Sue see you act like this. It'll frighten her. You have to be brave. She's in the same boat, you know."

"Hey, that ain't my fault!" I said. "I'm not making her go there! Maybe the dumb superintendent ought to walk her to school." When Johnny gave me a look, I said, "Why do I have to be brave when you know I'm just as scared as she is?"

"The only time you can truly be brave is when you *are* scared," Johnny said. "If you're not scared, then you're just doing what comes easy."

I looked back in at the picture of George, all sober in his silly white wig. Why were there suddenly fewer students at North than at South, I wondered. What had happened to them? Had they been rounded up, shoved down into the boiler room, and clamped to the wall? And what about the nasty boy who used the *F*-word on me? Was he down there? If anybody deserved to be thrown in a dungeon, it was him.

"Hey," John B. said, and pointed to a playground. "They got swings. How about I give you a real high push?"

"Sure," I said a little uncertainly.

So off we went.

Thirty-Nine

When I think back on that first year at North School, I recall most clearly a note being passed in class that Decker Dugan wadded into his mouth after I tried to grab it away from him. His jackass smile said that his buddy had written hateful things in it about me, and the note would soon be reduced to little more than pulpy, non-incriminating mush. I wish that's what had happened to all my memories of that year.

On the other hand, I can't for the life of me remember the name of my fourth grade teacher. I can't even picture her face when I try. I think she had a little mustache—or was that the Sunday school teacher? I don't remember her ever interceding on my behalf. Instead, she would order me to sit down and be quiet. Once, after I'd foolishly walked to school in the rain without a coat, she had me stand in the hall until I stopped dripping. Even after all these years, I occasionally dream that I am walking to North School with Sue-Sue, Dema and Roberta. We arrive to find it's not there. There's a train depot where it should be instead. We jump on the first train to get to class, but we have to hide from the conductor because we can't find our tickets as it goes on and on and on.

It's silly, yes. But it was a troubling time for me, a time when even moments of pleasure could sour unexpectedly. At North, I met Lillian Burgess, and she became a good friend. I loved to visit her house, which was in a woodsy area near the river. It always smelled so nice and new. Unfortunately, Decker Dugan, the *F*-word boy, lived nearby, and he would ambush us from the trees with an air rifle until the sting of BBs drove us back inside. My troubles with that worm seemed endless.

On the first day that year, I walked to school in roomy hand-me-down shoes that flopped around and blistered my feet. Still, I took great pride in being able to say, "Follow me. I know the way." We moved along in a nervous pack, and while I had the foresight to steer everyone across the street before we got to the house with the vicious dog, the stupid mutt barked at us anyway, and we ran like frightened rabbits.

"Jeez, it looks just like South," Dema said when we arrived.

"Except for the lion carvings," I said, pointing.

"South has lion carvings," Dema said.

"No it doesn't!" I said. "It has—"

"—Look! There's swings! Come on. Let's go before they're all taken!"

"—pigs."

Sue-Sue never once complained about going to North School, and immediately she fit right in. But it was like a prison for me, two years of confinement while life went on without us south of Bridge Street. I escaped the tedium only by daydreaming about the future. At first, my mind would jump ahead to three o'clock and the freedom that awaited me when school finally let out. Later, I began thinking about what would happen after my return to South School in two years. Then, gradually, as the weeks wore on, I began to think about what was in store in the distant future when I had completed school. What would I do then? I tried to picture myself in a nurse's uniform. But at the thought of Thaney's bedpan, I scrapped that and began to dream of teaching. I'd be a kind teacher, a friendly one, I thought, except to bullies like Decker Dugan, whom I'd whip into utter humiliation in front of the whole class every day. Eventually, I could picture my face disfigured into a hard, crooked scowl like The Gutch's, and once again my dreams moved on. I thought I could be a secretary, like our neighbor Mrs. Sterns, who could take dictation right on a typewriter and boasted shamelessly about her remarkable skill any time the opportunity presented itself. But that idea faded too. What

I really wanted in the future, I decided, was to have babies—beautiful, pink, gurgling babies as precious as my sister Mary Ellen had been while she lived. It was God's plan for me, I told myself. My destiny. I would replace Mary Ellen on this earth with my own sweet infants. Something our minister said from the pulpit one Sunday seemed to confirm this. "We must not let the capricious circumstance of daily travail mar the true happiness of life," he said. "Rather, we should put our faith in God's love and God's plan."

God's plan. Yes! I began playing games to predict how many babies I'd have, writing numbers between my knuckles and reciting a rhyme or the Pledge of Allegiance as I tapped the markings in time to the words. When the words ran out and my fingertip was resting on a three or an eight or a five, I'd spend hours dreaming up what to name my beautiful brood and I would write my choices down on my penmanship practice tablet. I loved the look of names like Natalie and Fern for girls, William and Glen for boys. I absolutely refused to consider the names Tommy, Decker, or Thad. So too Reno, Bethany, and Eileen.

I had asked Margaret to keep an eye on Eileen for me at South in my absence. It was a time when my sister had grown positively obsessed with her appearance—and with boys. Every morning the smell of singed hair from curling irons fouled the upstairs hall outside her room. To spy on Eileen's locker and the boys who congregated there, Margaret had to sneak part way up the top flight of stairs at school. But she did it. Then she told me the boys that Eileen chose to walk home with and those she brushed off. Rach and Zeke weren't in either group because they'd moved on to high school along with John B. Increasingly, John B. and Rach avoided us younger ones, smoking cigarettes on the sly in the barn as they held hushed conversations in deepening voices.

When John B. got a job pumping gas and patching car tires at a garage, one of the first things he bought with his meager pay was a little Kodak. He brought it home one day and began taking pictures of us in the yard and on the porch. I recently found one of the small, square snapshots of us girls in our funny hairstyles and old-fashioned clothes. Except for the proud, prominent bumps of her developing breasts, Eileen's graceful body was as narrow as a boy's in her Pepper Shaker uniform when she made cheerleader on her second try. She was almost a head taller than me. I had Thad's gangly limbs and gloomy face. If anybody had told me at the time that I favored my dad, I'd have probably spit in their eye. Thad's mouth was disgusting with its tobacco stains and perfectly aligned false teeth. His smiles were all clinkers, which is probably one reason he attempted so few of them. In the picture, you can tell that Eileen inherited Mama's sunnier disposition. It was another reason to resent her, this brainy, beautiful, popular girl.

I worked for a time during this period at trying to make myself more cheerful, to see if that might improve my prospects, but "the capricious circumstances of life" were as sneaky as that jackass, Decker, and kept realigning in fresh ways against me. I must say Mom was willing to listen patiently to my daily recitation of complaints about North School, but she always replied with the same suggestions instead of the sympathy I craved. She'd say, "Just try to make the best of it."

"You don't understand," I argued. "Decker's mouth is filthier than a sewer worker's boots and he won't stop pinching me. It's torture."

"Pinch him back," she replied. "When life deals you lemons, Emma, you make lemonade."

There was a bit of Thaney in all of us, apparently. I knew Mama was really on my side, but it appeared that she felt a stronger obligation to steer me off the path of self-pity, which she said would only lead to more misery. What she didn't seem to understand was that my little world was under siege, that I only wanted a grown-up for an ally, one who would fold me in her warm arms and say, "There, there. It'll be okay."

How pathetic it was to crave such babying when you're about to turn ten.

"I'm not going to spy on Eileen anymore," Margaret informed me one afternoon as she painted my toenails with polish we'd taken from Reno's room. An early frost had driven us inside and etched brilliant patterns on Margaret's window.

"Why not?" I demanded.

"I'm tired of that game. It's a waste of my time. One day it's this boy. One day it's that. So what? She's head cheerleader. What do you expect? Who cares if she's walking home with boys?"

"I do!" I said, rather too strongly. I wasn't sure why it was so important to me, but it had always been important to keep an eye on my big sister to see how she handled each new challenge of growing up. I just didn't feel like following her over this cliff chasing boys. I asked Margaret, "What's this fascination she's got with boys? I don't get this whole boy thing." I couldn't silence the sense I had that boys were cocky fools and a waste of time.

"Boys are a pain," Margaret agreed. She snickered, and added softly, "But some of them are kinda cute." Then she said something very softly. Margaret liked to whisper when she said really interesting things. I couldn't believe what I thought I'd heard.

"What's that?" I leaned forward, straining, watching her lips. Margaret dipped her face toward her toe painting and mumbled again, even softer. I said, "I can't *hear* you!" My own words almost made me laugh. It was the exact phrase that Thaney used on us when she pretended she couldn't hear some snotty remark we had made about her.

"It's nothing," Margaret said, speaking up.

"You said, 'Like John B.,' didn't you!"

She blushed. I'd never seen Margaret blush. Was it true? Did she have a secret crush on my older brother like I had on hers? "Never mind!" she said sharply. "You want to have a family, don't you?"

"What? Oh. Yeah."

"How many spinsters do you know who have children? You gotta get married if you want a family. So you're going to have to say 'I do' to somebody someday. Better get used to the idea."

Of course, she was right. But I wasn't about to concede the point. "There must be some other way."

"No, there isn't. And you'll feel differently about it when puberty comes."

"Puberty?"

She looked at me like I was a complete moron and went for her crumbling dictionary. She opened it to the middle, found the right page, and handed it to me with her finger on the word so I could read the definition for myself.

> **puberty** (pyoo'ber te) n. the state or quality of being capable of getting or bearing offspring—the period at which sexual maturity is reached. The age of puberty is commonly designated as 14 for boys and 12 for girls.

"Twelve!" I exclaimed. "Girls can't have babies when they're twelve!"

"Yes," Margaret said, shutting the book. "Some girls can."

"Some?" I said. "Some? Exactly how are you supposed to know if you can or you can't?"

"Believe me, you'll know." She looked away.

I'd been so shocked to see the words *sexual maturity* printed boldly in a book that I almost missed seeing Margaret struggle with the temptation to say something more, perhaps about her sister, Reno. I asked, "Is the word sex listed in your dictionary, too?" I wanted to look up all sorts of tantalizing smut just then—body parts, crude functions. Safeties. *Poontang.* I'd never realized what a treasure trove a dictionary could be.

"Yes," she said. She pulled the rubber band about the book again, as if the contents were none of my business. "If you think Eileen's gone crazy, you should have seen the goofy things Reno did when she reached puberty," she said.

I stared at her. What was she talking about? I was almost afraid to ask. Then I suddenly wondered if Margaret someday could be completely transformed by puberty and follow in Reno's wayward footsteps. What about little Alice? Was that why they were keeping that girl practically under lock and key?

"When Reno developed breasts," Margaret said without my asking, "she came into my room one day and took off her blouse and showed them to me. I was little, but I could see she was proud. She made me squeeze one. I hated it and I laughed. Reno said, 'Wise up, twerp, you'll have them, too, one day.'"

"Really!" I said, trying to put the story directly out of my mind. I wanted to change the subject, but I drew a blank as I fought off that goofy picture of Reno with her blouse off.

"So I wouldn't be too worried about Eileen," Margaret was saying. "All she's doing is seeing which boys she can twist around her little finger."

I thought a minute about what she'd mumbled about my brother, John B. "Margaret, would you ever be tempted to kiss a boy?" I hoped she'd say no. I wanted an ally in her, and I didn't want a picture in my head of Margaret kissing my brother.

"It would depend on the boy," she said. Then her hand went up like a traffic cop's. The discussion was over.

Forty

*M*alignant tumors were no match for Bethany Sain Starkey. She did not die that year. Or the next. Or the next. In fact, her strength had soon improved enough that she could get herself out of bed, down the stairs, and into the most comfortable chair in the parlor. For my part, I was just happy she was making it down the hall to the biffy again. Only slowly did it dawn on us that she was not going to the grave quickly—or quietly. She came back to our dinner table groaning, sighing, and muttering, often upsetting one or another of us with one of her random remarks. Years would pass before she fell and broke her hip, and finally departed this earth. Her endurance was stunning, and it left me with wrongheaded ideas about the virulence of cancer that I still haven't shaken to this day.

At the time, her ability to cheat death confused and annoyed me. My vibrant baby sister had died from a touch of fever one winter and my withered old grandmother with malignant tumors growing in the forest of her innards could linger like a bad odor? I used up prayer time each Sunday morning at church asking for answers.

Dear God, I know it's none of my business, but why would you take Mary Ellen when she was so young, and then spare Thaney, who is practically a fossil? The harder I prayed for enlightenment, the greater my suspicion grew that *I* was being tested. If God had even the slightest hint that I wanted Thaney to die, I was in deep trouble.

"Why do you wear that ugly old thing every day?" Eileen asked one morning at breakfast as I rearranged the chain on Thaney's locket around my neck. Eileen's eyebrows looked darker to me somehow. Was she doing something to color them?

"I, uh," I said, "I like it."

"You don't," Eileen replied flatly. "You're just wearing it 'cause you're scared of Thaney."

"That ain't true," I said, but I didn't argue long. It was more like I was scared of God. It was as if that little silver locket was a talisman that gave me the power of life and death over my grandmother. Absurd, I know, but it didn't seem so at the time under the spell of my tortured, superstitious logic. Thaney was sure to notice the minute I took the locket off and threw it in a drawer, and it would just be my luck that immediately afterward—in some cosmic, unacceptable twist of spite—she'd give up the ghost and die. Once again, I'd have to live with the blemish of disrespecting an older person near death. So I kept the ding-dang locket on, and Thaney stayed alive and ornery. Stalemate.

"Your grandmother Thaney is nuttier than a fruitcake," Margaret told me one winter's afternoon as we played Parcheesi under the dining room table. Margaret was never shy about sharing her opinions. Then again, neither was I. Sometimes, when I heard Margaret blurt comments like that, it made me think that maybe, just maybe, things might go easier on me if *I* did a better job of keeping my trap shut once in a while.

"When you went to the cupboard to get the game," Margaret said, "Thaney wandered through and gave me the eye and said something about 'everybody has an anus.' Then she said, 'Did you know that the anus is the puckered flower of the alimentary canal?'" Margaret shook her head. "I mean, good God!"

I winced but I was not surprised. "Thaney has taken to talking about unmentionable body parts," I said apologetically. "It's a phase." Like her sudden robust appetite for mushrooms, which she bought from a German-speaking woman next door who handpicked them in the woods in the summer and dried them meticulously on screens. This German woman was the mother-in-law of Mrs. Sterns, the boastful, lightning-fast typist. Thaney had also started snatching up handbills off our front door and carrying them up to her room. It would be months before I realized why.

"I thought you told me she was deathly sick," Margaret said.

"She is," I replied. "Only you can't kill a weed is what she says."

We clamped ice skates onto our boots that winter and skated on the river where the stagnant water between the bridge and the dam had frozen over completely. At first, we were cautious on the uneven surface. But after some practice, we began improvising games of hockey and pompom pull away. One day, Rach organized crack the whip and I foolishly positioned myself to be on the end to be whipped.

We formed a line and joined hands with Rach and John B. and Eileen together and the younger children like me at the end. I was next to little Alice, whose runny nose had left crusty deposits on her mittens that I couldn't bear to touch, even wearing mittens myself. I grabbed the elbow of her coat, which was one place she couldn't reach with that streaming river of snot, and then we all began to skate slowly in unison. Rach picked up the pace at the front before making a sudden left turn, pivoting in a way that whipped the end of the line where I was in a snapping motion.

The rush of speed I got from it was as exhilarating as I'd hoped, and I laughed as I saw Alice's mittened hand disappear up her coat sleeve from my fierce tugging down on the elbow. The speed got so great, however, that I lost my hold on Alice's jacket sleeve as it was about to rip off.

Suddenly, I was zipping along alone, the cold wind in my face, moving faster than I'd ever gone in my life on my own two feet, headed directly toward the spillway of the dam at the southern edge of our pond, beyond which was an abrupt five-foot drop onto thin ice below. I tried to turn, but my blade caught in a crack and twisted the clamp right off the sole of my boot. I went down and my head struck hard on the ice. I skidded across the pond on my chest and one arm, drawing closer to the dam by the second. In a panic, I shot my arms out and kicked my legs, but to no avail. The ice slid relentlessly under my knit mittens, coat, and dungarees. Finally, I curled into a ball and closed my eyes, just waiting for the fall and the bath of ice water that would follow. But something grabbed hard on my right ankle and abruptly spun me around, and I stopped. When I opened my eyes, I was peering over the edge. My stomach rose up.

"Shit on a stick," I heard Rach yell, and I laughed in spite of my shock and pain, or perhaps because of them, feeling a rush of relief over the disaster averted. I heard the scratches of fast-approaching skates, but I lay still, like a possum, listening to my own heartbeat and watching the breath from my mouth make reassuring little clouds.

When Rach bent over me to pull me away from the edge, I smiled bravely. There was soft sympathy in his eyes that I'd never seen beneath that rough and tumble exterior. It was as if he were truly noticing me for the first time, the girl behind the big mouth and crazy shenanigans. The Calamity Jane he'd declined to get to know. But there was a gulf between us too in that look, like I was just the little sister of the girl he was mad for.

"You okay?" he asked.

"I think so," I said. "Thanks." But when I tried to get up, a sharp pain shot up my leg and instantly dispelled all complacency.

"What is it?" Rach asked.

Fear had taken a break, but it caught up with me again. Something must be seriously wrong, I thought. I was mad at Rach now. I could have *drowned*. I wanted to yell at him, but I remembered about keeping my trap shut. After a moment, I sensed an opportunity. I said truthfully, "I think I twisted my knee. I'm not sure I can stand."

"Here," he said, sliding his hands under my hips and back, granting a secret wish I'd hardly dared to hold. "I got you."

I felt my face go hot as he lifted me off the ice in his strapping arms. I smelled cigarettes and sweat in the wool of his dark coat as he skated awkwardly with me clasped to his chest. The tug of muscles through the layers of our winter clothes yielded up shapes and contours of him that I can still recall today. I boldly laid my face against his shoulder and neck, where the thud of his heart pulsed loud and fast. Or was it my own I was hearing? It remains a mystery to me.

John B. skated alongside and said, "I'll take her."

I was happy to hear Rach refuse. "Naw. Let me get her to shore. It'd be too hard to hand her off."

He set me down gently in a snowbank at the river's edge. "I could carry you home, if you want," Rach said. My heart raced.

"I'll do it," John B. said. I'd always craved Johnny's attention, but for once I wished he'd butt out. I started to groan like Thaney about my injury and I looked pleadingly at Rach, who I sensed was feeling guilty for what had happened. But then the others skated up and gathered around to watch, so I had to behave. I felt Eileen's and Margaret's eyes bore in on me.

"What happened to your skate?" Sue-Sue asked. It was dangling from its leather strap around my ankle. She scooted forward and released the clasp.

"It hit a rut or a crack or something and tore off," I said. "That's why I took the spill." For the first time, I noticed my ankle was throbbing with pain as well.

"That loose skate saved you," John B. said. "It jammed into the ice when you curled up and turned your leg, just before the dam."

"It was all pretty spectacular," Rach said, and laughed. "Bet you can't do it again."

John B. was slipping out of his skates, and preparing to hoist me up for a piggyback ride.

I was disappointed. Margaret's words—"it depends on the boy"—returned and bounced around in my head. Maybe I did understand what all the fuss was about boys.

Rach nonchalantly skated backward away from us and I turned to wave "thank you" to him. His smile was like an apology. But for what? For the incident? For yielding me up to my brother?

I had a lump the size of a goose egg on the side of my head, and my knee and elbow had strawberry bruises from smacking the ice through my clothes. You could see in a long, straight red mark where the skate strap had twisted around my ankle. It hurt to walk, so Mama let me stay home from school the next day.

I was happy to miss school, but I couldn't stop the scene at the river from replaying itself again and again in my mind as I lay in bed. I was desperate to see Rach, even if he would only put me back in my place when we met again. How cruel that my one special moment had come and gone so swiftly and unexpectedly, that it could not be re-created. Sadly, I feared it would be the only time that Rach would ever hold me in his arms.

Forty-One

My obsession with Rach Drummond overpowered me after that. To this day, I can't look at the cover of a romance novel without blushing. The lurid art lays bare all of the secrets from my girlhood daydreams and fantasies.

At various moments of this silliness, I imagined Rach shirtless, swaggering down our street, a sheriff with a gleaming revolver at his hip. At other times, his powerful, glistening arms flexed the levers of a locomotive racing across the Kansas countryside.

I told a girl I was envious of at school that an "older boy" had saved me from drowning when I fell through the ice at the river the previous winter, and that he planned on courting me one day.

"He says if you save someone's life, you're responsible for them after that. So, we'll get married when I'm a little older. That way, he can keep his promise and be responsible for me."

Rach's muscular arms and chest flexed deeply in my fantasies about him, but I did not imagine him touching me. Instead, he acted as a shield against all that was wicked and dangerous in my small and sometimes fearful world. Rach came to mind when the mongrel dog snarled at me on my way to school. I pictured him making that hound whine pitifully and turn tail with just his steely stare. When Decker Dugan's sassing got ugly on the playground, it was Rach's fist I saw knocking him down. And when a stranger knocked at our door after dark, it was Rach I summoned to mind to answer the bell. Other boys were just frail specimens. Take Orville Jacobson. He was sweet and funny, a friend, but when I caught him looking at me in class, I gave him no encouragement. He was skinny and jittery with a perpetual cough. Bobby Beckerman, on the other hand, was big for his age, but I spurned him because he lacked Rach's square jaw and broad shoulders. Bobby was a sissy to someone like me, a worshipper at the altar of strength. Rach alone had the kind of raw electricity that lifted the hairs on my arms.

During this time, I studied myself closely in the mirror, futzing with ways to look more alluring to the object of my affections. Should I comb my hair this way or that? I experimented again and again with the curling iron, making changes toward an ideal that existed only vaguely in my mind.

"Are you trying to look like Eileen?" Sue-Sue asked me one day. "Because that's just the way she's doing her hair now too, you know."

Sue-Sue had seen a truth that eluded me. I was out to steal Rach from my sister by beating her at her own game. And me walking around in Eileen's old clothes, not realizing it. "She copied me," I lied. Sue-Sue snorted.

Secretly, I applied faint dabs of rouge to my cheeks one morning when I was supposed to go to the Methodist Church with Thaney. The Drummonds would be there, of course. But when I saw my grandmother's heavily blackened eyebrows and the specks of powder that had showered onto her dark dress, two maroon circles of rouge standing out like bull's-eyes on the skin sagging at her cheekbones, my own efforts suddenly felt just as crude and obvious. Rach would not be fooled. I raced upstairs and scrubbed my face clean before we left. I didn't want him to see me like that. I needed a better plan.

I thought I'd found it as a damsel in distress when I saw him out our kitchen window one Saturday chopping firewood in his backyard. I hurriedly put on a jacket and ran out to the barn to get our ax. Rach paused, looking amused, when he saw me emerge with it in my hands. He lifted his chin silently in a companionable greeting from across the creek that divided our lots. I selected the biggest piece of firewood I could find in our pile and lugged it over to our chopping block, where I stood it on end the way I had seen Rach do it. Then

I hefted the long, awkward ax in both hands. With so much weight down at one end, I had to cant my hip and slide my right hand up the long handle to manage it. Rach watched all this, as I had hoped he would, staring as I bent my knees and lifted the blade over my head, swaying under its weight. I fixed my eye on that log and with every ounce of strength I possessed, I arced the blade over to bring it down. At the last second—with the heavy head racing on its uncertain course—I shut my eyes, afraid of what might happen next, scared that a splinter might fly up into my face. Only after I'd closed my eyes did I consider what that might do to my aim. If I missed, the ax blade might fly past the wood and into my leg or foot instead. I had hoped to mess up enough to get advice, not medical treatment. With the ax continuing down, I jerked one leg back before anything could skitter off the block and hit it. To my surprise, the blade sunk deep into the grain of the log and stopped with a sharp splitting sound. I opened my eyes wide.

"Hey! Not bad!" Rach yelled. "Where'd you learn to do that?"

I tried not to smile as I turned away. "Watching you," I said, not really wanting him to hear. I tried to lift the ax again, but it was now wedged tight in the wood. No amount of rocking or wiggling would release it, and suddenly everything tumbled off the block with me hanging on like a girl holding a dog straining at a leash. I cursed. I heard Rach laugh and then he was coming my way. I felt weightless. The slightest puff of breeze could have lifted me like a kite. I was afraid to open my mouth and speak, fearful I might make a fool of myself. Months of fantasizing had not prepared me to deal with success.

"Here, let me give you a hand with that," he said, as he drew close. "Why isn't John B. doing this?"

"He's busy helping Thad." It was a lie. I had no idea where he was. I had hoped to choose my words more carefully, but the good ones, it seemed, had completely flown out of my head. My skin hummed at the thought that Rach might touch me, but disappointment supplanted anticipation when he pushed me brusquely aside with the back of his arm and took the ax out of my hands. He returned the wood to the block, gripped his own ax near the blade and drove mine the rest of the way through with a single crack. He started to hand me back my ax, and then didn't.

"You sure you know what you're doing here?" he said.

I giggled. "No."

"An ax is a dangerous thing, huh?"

"Could you show me how it's done?"

"It ain't about that. You just don't have the muscles for it." I felt my advantage slipping away. I must have looked crestfallen, because he said, "How about I do a few for you?" He was all business now, but it did not diminish the glow of having him to myself.

"Sure," I said. "That'd be great!"

I found myself making up a story about Thaney catching a chill and how we needed a lot of wood for our parlor stove. I fetched fresh logs from the woodpile as quickly as Rach could drive his ax through each piece. He never missed. I knew there was a chance that Eileen or John B. might come out and unmask my little charade, but I let it continue anyway as the split wood piled up and steam puffed out into the frigid air from the grunts of Rach's exertion.

"I want to have lots of babies when I grow up," I said. It was like somebody else had spoken, some stupid child who had commandeered my voice and mouth just to blurt out these embarrassing words. I turned my face away.

"As soon as I'm old enough," Rach said, apparently not sensing my shame, "I'm enlisting in the Army. I'm going to learn to fly. When you fly a plane, you can soar above everything and everyone and practically touch the sky." A dreamy smile came to his face and lingered. "Put this hick town behind me forever." He nodded. "John B. and me both are enlisting on the same day." I took a sharp breath, and Rach said, "Hey, you can't tell nobody I said that, okay? Johnny'd bust me one if he knew I squealed on him. He thinks your ma will try and stop him."

Of course, she would. "Ma won't be the only one!" I said. I couldn't believe it. Johnny join the Army? I said, "Johnny can't do that! Somebody might try and shoot him!"

Rach laughed. "The war's over, in case you hadn't heard. And *we* won."

I'd heard. On Armistice Day each year, I'd watched men from Cornucopia who'd fought in the Great War marching around the town square in their old Army caps with colored ribbons and bronze medals pinned to their cotton shirts. A few remaining veterans of the War Between the States marched with them. One had the empty sleeve of his shirt folded neatly and pinned up. But it was the man I'd never seen that I thought of now. The hermit, the one some said was yella. Tetched, according to others. He hadn't come back whole, Mama told me. Developed a bad case of *war nerves*. He lived in a long, narrow white house three blocks from us. It looked like an army barracks I'd seen in Uncle Walter's pictures. Only his front curtains were always drawn tight and his front door always closed. On the porch hung an American flag, placed there by his family, like the ones on coffins when a soldier is brought home to be buried.

"War is bad," I said. I wanted to run to John B. and tell him that he couldn't go. But if I ran right then, Rach would figure out what I was doing and I could forget about ever being his girl. So I decided to argue with him instead. "Besides, what do we need an army for when there ain't any war?"

Rach shrugged and smiled like it was a stupid question. "If there wasn't any army, some other country could march over here and take whatever they wanted, any old time."

"That doesn't have anything to do with John B.," I shot back. "The Starkeys don't have anything worth stealing, Rach Drummond, and neither do you. It's no fair dragging John B. into this!" He was forever trying to make Johnny do something crazy and reckless.

"Nobody's making him," Rach said. "It was his idea to begin with."

I felt my mouth go dry. Was that true? Did John B. want to leave? I could see how he might want to get away from Thad. But Mama and the rest of us? Is this what he and Rach had been talking about when they hunted rabbits and smoked their cigarettes in the barn? Joining the Army? How could he make a decision like that and not tell anyone? I prayed Rach was making it up, making idle chatter to impress me.

"I can't see Johnny shooting nobody," I said. Then another thought surfaced. "Could you? Shoot somebody, I mean?"

Rach took his time answering. "Depends," he said gravely. I stared at his eyelashes. They were curly and thick like a baby's and they softened the hard lines of his jaw and cheeks and forehead. "Listen," he said, "I told you a secret. Now you gotta tell me one. Who is that sister of yours sweet on?" He stared over my shoulder now toward the house, as if by looking hard enough, he might see Eileen and read her thoughts.

I started to say, "What's so great about Eileen?" But I stopped, knowing the answer might cause me pain. There was a weight hanging around my heart now. I felt like a fool.

"You're fixing to get hurt, Rach Drummond," I said, bitterness rising. "Eileen toys with you like she does with all the boys. Only you don't see it." The only person Eileen loved was herself. I said, "You're too stupid to tell when a girl really likes ya."

Rach looked down at me a second, then pushed his cap up and wiped the perspiration off his brow with his sleeve. "So, tell me the answer. Who's her favorite?"

I wanted to spit on him. Or punch him. But he was too big and I was a coward. I turned and stormed away toward the house. "Hey," Rach called after me. "Where you going?" I ignored him. "What about all this firewood?" he yelled. Not my problem, I thought. He yelled, "Hey! You're forgettin' your ax."

The next time I saw Orville Jacobson look my way, I made a point of smiling back at him.

Forty-Two

While Rach continued to pine for Eileen, she was turning her back on him for good. The words, "You can have him for all I care," popped out of her one day as I walked past her room. Telling me she knew I was making a play for her boyfriend. And while it was true, I resented her saying it, knowing she intended it as a slap, a snake, gift-wrapped in tissue paper with a fancy bow. Rach wasn't *hers* to give away anyway!

I took a breath. "Who?" I asked.

Eileen had turned her fluttering eyelids and her musical laugh on a dark-haired boy in the eighth grade who had the best two-handed set shot on the school basketball team. "Rach," she said to me. "That's *who*." She made a face like something left a bad taste in her mouth. "Good luck. Now help me with these buttons in back."

I suppressed a smile. In her mind, she'd done me a favor. Now I must do her one. It was a beautiful new dress. The fabric felt soft and satiny beneath my fingertips. Mama had made it, and I'd be wearing it in two years after its luster had faded in the wash and it had started to fray at the hem. I wondered if I pulled hard enough on the collar, I could choke off Eileen's air. But a lighter mood surfaced.

"Not interested in Rach, thanks," I said cheerfully and ambled away, leaving three random buttons in the line unfastened as she studied herself in the mirror. I didn't want Rach. I'd moved on, boldly leaving a homemade basket of wildflowers, gum, and peppermints dangling on Orville Jacobson's doorknob on May I, just to see how this shy, skinny boy would react to the encouragement of a May basket. As it happened, Orville wrote a rapturous poem and passed it to me with a pink face and downcast eyes on the playground. I have since misplaced his lovely tribute, but I remember distinctly it was smart and tightly rhymed. *Cupid's dart has pierced my heart* . . . It was the first time any boy had paid me that sort of notice. It was sweet of him, but still my attentions toward him never rose above amusement, and I took perverse joy in tormenting him. It tickled me unduly to tell him one thing and then do another. Then I'd accuse him of not listening carefully, just to see how patient he would be with me. I don't know why I didn't feel any empathy for his plight. I guess it's hard to take someone seriously when they have a drooling crush on you, and making fun of Orville's puppy love seemed the right thing to do. I thought he'd have a good coughing fit someday and get over it. In the meantime, I continued to snickeringly accept his tender attentions.

Eileen and Mama had not picked up on the Orville development, however, despite my telling Sue-Sue all about it.

Mama said, "Do you really think Rach is a suitable boy for you?"

Of course, she would believe what Eileen told her before she believed anything Sue-Sue or I said. But I was miffed that I was of so little consequence that she wouldn't bother to ask me whether I had a boyfriend or not. I said, "You don't mind that John B. is Rach's friend."

"Well, John B. happens to be a boy, and he also happens to be four years older than you."

"Thad is eleven years older than you."

Mama's chin rocked back at this jab. She sputtered. "That's different."

"How?"

"It just is, Emma." Then, as if suddenly hitting on something to rescue her from her predicament, her face brightened. "We were both adults when we met." Which I found out later was not exactly true. They had met when Mama was still in high school. John B. had been born when she was just nineteen. But I got her point. And she got mine.

In the end, I stopped tormenting Orville. His heartfelt earnestness was just too much. He'd wanted to hold my hand, and not seeing any harm in it, I let him. But it was clammy, and a dreamy expression spread over his face that alarmed me. I couldn't look him in the eye after that. And then, Bobby Beckerman offered to walk me home via downtown after school, and he bought me an ice cream cone. So it was over with Orville.

Meanwhile, I forced all thought of Rach into the background, hoping that the spell I'd been under was completely broken. But when I saw him outside again in the spring and he ignored me, I was surprised by the dull ache that formed in my chest, like something precious had been stolen—something that had never been mine to begin with.

"Aren't boys the most ridiculous creatures?" I asked Sue-Sue in bed one night after I'd concocted a yarn for her about a boy who dressed up as a girl kissing himself in a mirror and turning into a frog.

"Boy, howdy," she agreed. "You said it."

"Why do you suppose Mama married Thad?" I asked. No sooner had the words passed my lips than the question struck me as the most profound riddle of the twentieth century. And I couldn't drop it. It was like a celery string caught between my teeth.

"Jeez!" Sue-Sue said. "I never thought of that! Yeah, why did she?"

I shook my head. "I'm stumped." They were so different. Thad was as dull and rough as scuffed shoe leather. Mama was a warm, soft biscuit with honey. For every smile of encouragement we got from her, we got a grumpy frown and a thump on the neck from him. Besides, why would Mama marry a man with no teeth?

Sue-Sue said, "Maybe Mama likes rope tricks." She giggled. "Maybe Thad lassoed her heart."

I groaned. "Could you be serious for a minute?"

"Well, I don't hear you coming up with anything."

"That's 'cause I don't have any idea. That's why I asked you the question to begin with, or did you forget?"

I knew we were missing something, some hidden fact on which it probably all hinged. But how could we find out what that was? You couldn't come up with it thinking about Thad, I was pretty sure. He was a mystery, a man with a concealed personality. A hint of it bubbled to the surface in off-color, barnyard stories that earned him laughs on occasion when he told them at the weekly card games or at the horseshoe pits. Nights when I lay awake waiting for sleep, I sometimes heard Mama chuckle from behind their closed bedroom door after they'd gotten into bed. It was a deep, throaty chuckle, full of appreciation and warmth. But if Thad had such a good sense of humor, why didn't he share it with us children or laugh at any of our jokes?

Was it that he was smarter than the rest of us? No question he was smart. Otherwise, Mr. Osborne wouldn't have trusted him to run the lumberyard. The people at church wouldn't have elected him treasurer.

"Maybe we should ask her," Sue-Sue said.

"Ask her?" I repeated, hoping to put Sue-Sue out front on it.

"Mama. Why she married him."

"Hey, that's a good idea. Tell me what she says."

"Me? No, you ask her."

Sue-Sue had the better chance, I thought. As the baby of the family, she had the freedom to innocently venture into sensitive topics. I was quiet a minute, thinking if I added to the mystery, it might move her into action. "You suppose Thad forced her?" I asked. Sue-Sue knew how hard and unbending Thad could be. "You know, I'll bet he did!"

"How would he do that?"

"That's what you gotta find out. You know how he is, always getting his way, even when Mama doesn't like it."

Sue-Sue's "mm-hmm" sounded uncertain.

I said, "I mean, how about when he decides to take the strap to John B.'s hide? She doesn't like that at all. But what does she do? Nothing. She goes away and cries." Whippings were sometimes scary things to hear, as if some deep, unstoppable rage surfaced in Thad that might never be put back. I had witnessed a streak of similar anger in Rach once, when little Alice didn't do something he told her to immediately. He lifted her up fiercely by her hair, and the poor girl screamed bloody murder.

"Men are the bosses," Sue-Sue said.

"That's true," I said. "Only, Mama can usually figure ways around Thad's bossing when she wants. She gets him to back down sometimes when she looks at him a certain way." I laced my fingers together over my belly and sighed. "You don't suppose she married him just because he was the first to ask, do you? You don't suppose she thought a better offer might never come along?"

Sue-Sue didn't answer. There was no telling whether I was pushing her to the brink of giving in or she was silently digging in her toes against being the one to ask.

I waited her out, wondering whether Thaney might know. She hadn't seemed to care lately what dirt she blabbed. But if we asked her, there was a risk she'd take umbrage, as the question contained the hidden suggestion that her son was not good enough for our mother. She'd light into me good if she took it that way.

Eileen might also be enlisted to ask Mama or Thaney. Eileen felt entitled to answers, which often got her somewhere. I, on the other hand, had always been content gathering up only the informational crumbs that happened to drop within my reach.

"I don't know. It just seems odd when you think about it," Sue-Sue said. "I mean, he's not the least bit handsome." She seemed to be trailing the discussion badly. I wondered if she were losing interest or becoming drowsy.

"Come on," I said. "Mama will tell you if you ask."

Sue-Sue lifted her hand in the dark and appeared to study her fingers. "Maybe," she said. "Maybe not." She was quiet a minute. "Is it true your fingernails only grow at night?" Without waiting for a reply, she rolled over and turned her back on me.

I closed my eyes and silently said my prayers, remembering to ask God to find a way to keep John B. from enlisting in the Army. And

if He thought it would help me understand about real love, to unveil
the mystery of Thad and Jesse.

Forty-Three

*T*hey sounded like hornets as big as tractors. The noise built beyond belief as one slipped over the top branch of a tree across the street. I had pictured what it was going to look like before it roared into view—two stacked wings with a coffin-shaped fuselage clamped in between. I could scarcely have imagined its speed, however, or how it could twist like a corkscrew in the air as it thundered by. It was terrifying and exhilarating all at once. I dropped the garden hose and pressed my hands to my ears, a grin spreading across my face.

The Jennies—that's what they called them—turned around somewhere west of the river and made another pass over Cornucopia, not so close to the ground this time. Yet the growl of engine and propeller again sent dogs yapping and rabbits scurrying for cover.

I put a hand up to block the sun and saw light glint off the goggles of a helmeted pilot looking down. He lifted his arm out of the cockpit, and I waved, thinking that was what he was doing. But he was tossing out a sheaf of paper that fluttered like big snowflakes in the bright sky, the pages spreading and floating on a north wind, dipping and diving. I ran a zigzag up the block chasing after one that eventually wedged against Max Nix's front fence.

"What's it say?" Dema shouted as she came running. Children descended on us from all directions.

I read it aloud: "Announcing the Gilmore Bros. Air Show and Plane Rides at Rehkamp's farm on County Road 6, 2 PM. Saturday June 12, 1926." I looked up. "That's today!"

As I got to the kitchen, Mama was sprinkling cinnamon on custard cups she'd set out to cool. The sweet scent of vanilla tickled my nose. I shoved the handbill at her. "Can we go? Can we?"

Mama held the paper at arm's length and tipped her head back slightly. "Is this what all that dreadful racket is? Barnstormers?" She frowned. "I'm not sure my ears could put up with it."

"Aw, Ma! Come on. It'd be great!"

"Let's wait and see what your father says."

She hadn't any more thrown down that roadblock than Thad walked in the back door with a gleam in his eye. "Grab your hat, Ma," he said. "Can't miss this. Whole town is gonna be there."

Cars and trucks crawled out County 6 weaving past people on foot and around vehicles that had stopped along the road. Sue-Sue and I were in the backseat of the Saxon with Thaney, who insisted on coming along, maybe so she could mutter under her breath the entire way about the lousy springs and Thad's sudden moves on the accelerator and brake. I wearied of her grousing and the fumy traffic jam. Sue-Sue and I were quick to hop out and join Margaret and Alice when we spotted them walking beside the highway.

"Ever seen a flying circus?" Margaret asked.

"Never. Never saw a real airplane before today. Not with my own two eyes."

"The stunts are incredible! We saw a show once in Michigan. A wing walker jumped from one plane to another in midair!"

There were three Jennies parked in a line on the trampled grass of the Rehkamps' pasture, swallowed up in the chattering crowds that touched the planes' wings, struts, and fuselages and kicked the wheels. Children swarmed a pilot who emerged from the barn in an unzipped leather jacket and silk scarf. He moved along holding a small crate over his head until he got to the center of the gravel drive, where he set it down and stepped up. He hadn't shaved and there were circles of white skin around his eyes. His goggles were pushed up onto his leather helmet. He called out for attention, but didn't get it until he drew a pistol out of his jacket and fired it into the air. At the crack of the gunshot, a hush fell over everyone.

"Ladies and gentlemen! All you little warts, too! Welcome to Gilmore Brothers Flying Circus! Following this afternoon's exhibition of barrel rolls, loop-the-loops, and a plethora of death-defying aerial acrobatics, you, too, will be able to experience the thrill of flying up there with one of our aces. Just see Mr. Atanapolous over there for your ticket." A fat man sitting in a convertible with the top down gave a little salute. The pilot shouted, "For the small cost of *one* dollar, you can take the most memorable ride of your entire life. That's a special price, today only, just for you good folks of Kansas County, Kansas. Don't miss your chance to see your hometown, your house—or your neighbor's privy—from a bird's-eye view!" Spectators began shoving hands into pockets and lining up next to the automobile. I blinked hard when I saw who was among them.

"Margaret, look!" I pointed.

"My God! Tommy Bern! Why isn't he at military school?"

We hadn't expected him home for summer vacation. Everything about it seemed out of place. Tommy's trousers were gray uniform pants with a dark stripe down the leg, and his dark hair was cut severely close. His once lumpy body was trim now, the baby fat melted away. Two hard eyes stared out of his angular face.

I said, "This is bad. I gotta find John B. We got to make sure he doesn't see Tommy. God knows what he might do."

It wasn't long before I spotted Johnny. He was with Rach near the barn talking to one of the pilots. The announcer behind me was shouting that the show would begin in a few minutes. Rach was pointing his thumb at his own chest and talking a mile a minute as the pilot rubbed his chin and looked him over. Then the pilot smiled, put an arm around him, and walked him into the barn. John B. followed.

"What's going on?" I asked.

Rach emerged a couple moments later from the barn wearing a bright yellow jacket with the Gilmore Bros. name spelled out on the back and a leather aviator helmet.

"Wait! He's not going flying with them, is he?" I asked Margaret.

We ran up as they made their way to one of the planes.

"Rach! Wait!" Margaret called. "Whatcha doin'?"

Rach turned and gestured at the jacket. "They're giving me a try as a wing walker!"

I felt my heart leap in my chest and my stomach jump up after it.

"Rach Drummond!" Margaret shouted at him. "Just you wait 'til Ma hears. She'll skin you alive." She turned to me. "I gotta find Alice. She's gonna be real upset."

The sound of the first plane starting up made me jump, and I looked around as it taxied off, shooting back a blast of its own wind. A mechanic with his collar turned up on a pair of oil-stained coveralls walked quickly to the second plane, put two hands on its propeller, and yelled, "Throttle up!" to the pilot before pulling down hard on the blade. The engine sputtered and roared to life. The mechanic stood aside then, his fedora clamped down low over his eyes. The Jenny bounded swiftly across the open field after its mate and lifted off, rocking slightly as it went up. Then it righted itself and flew out toward the horizon, where it turned back, side by side with the other. As the two planes reached the Rehkamps' field again, they shot up and made a huge circle in the air like a somersault right over the crowd.

I glanced over to where Margaret had been standing, wondering about her reaction, forgetting she was off looking for Alice.

"Double loop the loop!" someone shouted. I turned all the way around to see if Margaret had found little Alice, but it was impossible to see through the crowd.

Again, the Jennies raced toward the horizon. Only one returned this time, twisting like a corkscrew through the air. "Barrel roll!" someone shouted. Then the second came down from high in the sky, plummeting toward the ground at a steep angle, twisting like a posthole digger about to drive into the earth. There were shrieks all around just before the pilot pulled out of the dive and shot across the field, barely clearing the Rehkamps' wire fence. Was it a *death spiral?* I wondered.

"Okay, boy, climb up," the mechanic shouted to Rach over the noise as he set a stubby ladder down near the wing. The mechanic had his head down, looking toward the ground. He shouted, "Hang onto the struts, put your feet in the clamps at the front of the wing, and don't step on the aileron."

Rach had his back to the mechanic, facing the crowd, up on his toes trying to peer over the heads of the people in front, staring as he had that day in the yard, looking over my shoulder to see if Eileen might materialize. There was an aura of imminent tragedy to him now. Why was it so important to show off for her, I wondered.

The mechanic checked the tension on a wire connecting the two wings and turned a thumbscrew as the other Jennies roared by again and a cheer went up from the crowd. I turned in time only to see them going away.

The pilot yelled, "Hey, Drummond, let's go. I gotta get up there."

"I can't start the plane until you're on the wing, boy," the mechanic said to Rach's back. There was something familiar in the man's Yankee accent and rich baritone voice, but I couldn't see his face beneath his down-turned hat brim.

I prayed that Rach would reconsider. It sickened me to think he would risk his life like this. I wanted to tell him that Eileen would think he was a crazy fool, but I bit my lip because I knew from his grim expression that he had probably seen her with another boy.

I tugged on John B.'s sleeve until he looked at me with eyes that were hollow with worry. I shook my head and frowned. *Don't let him do it.* John B. shrugged like someone feeling a pitcher of milk slip from his fingers. He turned back to Rach.

"You sure?" John B. asked him. Rach nodded, and the two boys shook hands.

Then Rach stepped onto the ladder. John B. called, "Hey, Rach. Good luck!" The mechanic's head shot up at these words and he bolted forward and grabbed Rach's arm, yanking him off the ladder. "Jesus!" he yelled. "What do you think you're doing?"

Again, the planes roared past low with an ear-splitting racket, dust gushing up in their wake. Rach and the mechanic stared at each other.

"What the hell!" Rach yelled.

The pilot began shouting. "Dammit, forget the kid! Let's go! Start me up!"

Rach gave the mechanic a shove. "You got nothing to say about this!" he shouted. He went for the ladder again. But the mechanic kicked it out from under him and then grabbed Rach's collar as he tried to climb onto the wing anyway. "Let go of me!" Rach yelled. "Leave me alone!"

"I won't, and I'm not starting this plane until you've cleared out."

Rach threw a punch that knocked the man down, and his fedora fell off and rolled away in the dirt. "You stay away from me!" Rach yelled. "I don't ever want to see you again!"

Then he turned and ran into the crowd, which continued to watch the planes in the air rather than the drama playing out near the third Jenny. John B. shot me a look before running after Rach. I turned to the fallen mechanic, who sat up and rubbed his jaw. He glanced around for his hat as he ran a hand through his matted hair. Although he looked older and not as cocky as I remembered, I knew I recognized him.

"Mr. Drummond?"

Forty-Four

"You're Emma, right?" he said. "Emma Starkey?" His eyes were bloodshot and puffiness was gathering beneath one eye. Three years had passed since he'd fled Cornucopia, and his wrinkles had multiplied and gotten a whole lot deeper in the meantime, I thought.

"Yes, sir," I said.

"Is Margaret with you?" His eyes darted around.

"She was," I said. "She's off corralling Alice. You want me to go find her?"

"No, I got to get this plane started." He gently touched the swelling beneath his eye. "You seen my hat?"

"Yes, sir. I'll get it." It had tumbled into the rut of a plane tire in the soft soil.

"Damn it all, Drummond, let's go!" the pilot yelled. "Crank the son of a bitch."

"Keep your damn shirt on," Mr. Drummond muttered. He turned to me. "Stand clear, okay? A propeller can chop you into a million pieces." My head ducked like a turtle's into my shoulders. Margaret's dad moved around to the front of the plane and called, "Throttle up!" Then he yanked hard on the blade and the engine chugged and sputtered. The propeller whirled with a whopping sound until it caught hard and roared.

"Let's go," Mr. Drummond shouted over the noise. I handed him his hat. He pulled it low over his eyes the way he'd worn it before.

He glanced around as furtively as a criminal and nudged me toward the barn. "In there!"

"I think I better go look for Margaret!" I shouted.

"Not yet! Come with me." He grabbed my arm. "Who else is here?" From his family, I thought he meant. I told him what I knew as we made our way to the barn, where he quickly slid the door closed behind us. The airplane growls were quieter and deeper now. Damp hay and cow pee choked the air. A horse snorted and shifted in a stall.

"I can't believe that boy," Mr. Drummond said. He dug a Thermos out of a satchel and poured out a cup of coffee. It sloshed in his shaky hand. "Tell me, what's come over Rach? Did he suddenly turn stupid?"

I wasn't sure what to say. Fortunately, I had my own question. "Why was that pilot gonna let him do it, for heaven's sake?"

Mr. Drummond slurped some coffee and gripped the cup now in both hands, staring over it. "The show's old acrobat—some hotshot who went by the name of Dusty Diego—he walked off last week. He got wind the government was going to outlaw most of the stuff he did because of all the accidents that keep happening. I guess he didn't want to wait around for the ax to fall. Roger's been recruiting locals on the fly ever since. One show at a time. Amateurs can't do tricks, of course, but it excites the folks to see one of their own up there." He sipped his coffee. "I should have left with Dusty. I didn't want to come here, face this town. People haven't forgotten, have they?"

Once more, I was at a loss for words. How could anybody forget how he ran around smooching a woman with notoriously bad breath, and one of the homeliest women in Cornucopia to boot? Okay, that might be an exaggeration. But she certainly was ugly compared to his wife.

"How is Mrs. Drummond doing?" he asked, almost as if he'd read my thoughts.

"Fine, sir," I said. My face turned hot at this lie. Anger welled up in me too. He'd abandoned his family and run off with all the money. What did he expect? She was living the life of Riley? My eyes dug down into my dirty toes. I thought of a question I could ask that would change the subject. "There's something I don't understand. Why do you work for a flying circus anyway?"

He stopped staring at the steam coming off his cup and looked at me.

"Long story." For a moment, I thought he was going to drop it at that, but after a time he said, "I'll give you the short version. I was working at a filling station near Salina when the show came through. I love airplanes. So I went out to watch. I heard something in Bud Gilmore's engine I didn't like when it started up, and I walked right up to him and told him so. He went out anyway. Then it conked on him."

"You mean it stopped running? While he was up flying? Holy smokes! What happened?"

Mr. Drummond laughed. "Down he and that plane came. In some farmer's field. Gravity takes over real quick. Anyway, Gilmore ran all the way back to base and hired me on the spot." He laughed again.

"How'd you know it was gonna conk?"

"I worked before as an engineer, you know. In Michigan. Car companies, mostly. Anyway, the engine sound? It's like when a piano's out of tune. Some people hear it. Some don't."

I felt antsy. I wanted to run and find Margaret, give her the startling news that her dad was here. Being with Mr. Drummond was making me uncomfortable, as usual. I wasn't sure how I was going to explain this to my folks either. They'd probably be unhappy I hadn't come find them and let them handle it.

"I think I better get going, Mr. Drummond," I said.

"I'm making you nervous, aren't I? I'm sorry. It's okay."

"No, it ain't that. I'm just supposed to be, you know, keeping an eye on my sister."

He nodded. I turned to leave. "Emma," he said softly. I turned back. "Tell Margaret ... tell her, well, I won't be traveling forever. Someday I'll get settled. Then ..." He stopped and shook his head. "—No, forget it."

I asked, "Are you really thinking about leaving the show, Mr. Drummond?"

He shook his head with a sigh of resignation and drank the dregs of the coffee, which must have been bitter, considering the face he made. "I don't know. Out of my hands, probably. They could shut us down any day. The government. Making all these new rules."

"Where would you go then? If they did?"

"Wichita, probably. They're building airplanes there now. I met a man in Rago, Kansas, when we played there. Nice fella. Clyde Cessna. He works for one of the Wichita outfits. Told me he's thinking about going off on his own. Said he'd take me."

He glanced up and stopped to listen to the planes scald the air above the Rehkamps' farm again, and he nodded to himself. "They're getting near the end. They'll need to be gassed up for the customer rides in a couple minutes." He gestured toward dozens of large red gas cans that were lined up near the door. I nodded, thinking I had an opening to say good-bye now, that he was about to get busy. Before I could, he said, "Is Margaret still the smartest pupil at South School?" He smiled a bit.

"Why don't you ask her yourself?" I said. "I'll go get her."

"No, don't. That's not such a good idea." He shook his head and stared across the open space in the barn wall for a second before looking at me sharply. "In fact, I'd prefer that you didn't tell her you talked to me. All right?"

"She's going to find out," I argued. "Rach'll tell her you were here."

"That's true, I suppose," he said, and looked away. "But I'll be gone by then. So, just let it go for now. *Please?*"

"Yeah. Sure." I lingered by the door, surprised that I felt sorry for him.

He got up and walked over, and he grabbed my arm. "You gotta promise me."

I looked down at his hand. I had goose bumps.

"All right, Mr. Drummond, if that's what you want. It's a promise." I shook his hand, too, for good measure, hoping that would be an end to it. I said, "Well, good luck!" I pulled hard on the door. It weighed a ton and slid slowly, ponderously, fighting my hurried movements and my flimsy arms. As soon as it was open a crack, I squeezed through and let myself out into the yard, and there was Margaret, standing right there in front of me, practically in my face.

"Here you are! I've been looking all over!" She sounded mad.

I put my arms back to block the opening and tried to slide the barn door shut.

"What were you doing in there?" she demanded.

"Nothing."

"Nothing?" She made a face. "Who were you talking to?"

I wasn't sure how Margaret would take it if I told her. And I'd just promised not to. And the man I promised was still within earshot. I had to keep my word. Besides, Margaret had run away from home once to try to join her father. And when that ended badly, she tore his picture to bits for her trouble.

"I wasn't talking to nobody." I tried to change the subject. "Where's Alice?"

"My mom took her home. Don't change the subject. Who is it you're hiding? Is Rach in there?"

"No! Course not. He and John B. left. Long time ago."

"Who is it then?" Criminy, she could be persistent.

I wanted to move away from the barn, away from Mr. Drummond and the whole business, but I needed to hold my ground or Margaret could push past me. I grew angry with Mr. Drummond for putting me in such a spot. Only a coward would refuse to see his own daughter or put a girl between himself and the girl's best friend. It was unfair making a kid do an adult's dirty work. The harder I fought Margaret, the more determined she was going to become to find out what I was concealing. When she found out later I'd been hiding her dad, well . . . Suddenly, a light went on in my head.

"You can't go in there," I said flatly, waving a red cape before a bull.

"What! Emma Starkey, you move aside this minute or I'm going to haul off and knock you flat on your can. Move!"

I did.

She zipped past me into the dark barn. I followed. She froze when she saw him standing there, twenty feet away. I wondered what would happen next. Would she walk toward her long-lost father or shout at him and run out the door?

"Hello, Meg. How are you?" Mr. Drummond said.

"Dad?" she said uncertainly. Her father's eyes misted up as Margaret moved forward. It was my clue to leave.

I let John B. tell the part about Rach and wing walking as we set the table for dinner, but I got to tell the part about Mr. Drummond being the mechanic for the Gilmore Bros. Flying Circus, and how he'd gone home with Margaret after I got them together.

"Nobody knew it was Mr. Drummond—except Rach, that is— because his father grabbed him," I said. "I'd a never knowed myself if Mr. Drummond's fedora hadn't flew off when Rach clocked him."

"Is Mr. Drummond planning to move back in with his family?" Mama asked.

"What?" I said. The question took me by surprise. I didn't understand. Why would they take him back even if he wanted to come home? Wasn't he just stopping by for a visit? A notion of something permanent made me scared again for poor Margaret. It would bust her world into a million pieces if her dad came home only to run off again. Had anybody thought about that? I was holding a soup spoon for my place setting. I saw the fuzzy reflection of my face upside-down in it.

"I sure hope not," I said.

Forty-Five

ommy Bern had completely slipped my mind in all of the crazy events that day until he lay bleeding to death in our side yard.

The sound of a gunshot outside the house jolted us just as Sue-Sue and I were climbing into bed. I thought of the pilot firing his pistol into the air and the sudden hush that followed it. There was a shout in the house, Mama yelling to Thad, "What was that?" A moment later, we were all outside in our nighties, staring at a body dressed in dark clothes on the lawn beneath the side yard tree.

Thad kneeled down with a flashlight. Something black like charcoal or shoe polish was smeared on the boy's hands and face, like a singer in a minstrel show. Thad told Mama to call Doc Becker and the police department. "Tell them there's been a shooting," he said. Then, to the fallen figure, "You hold on, son."

"Who is it?" Eileen called out.

"Looks to be the druggist's boy, _____ Bern?"

"Tommy," John B. said. He sounded irked. "Tommy Bern." He folded his arms over his long johns, which Johnny always wore to bed.

Thad stared in my brother's direction a moment, and I wondered if I should have told Thad last year about Tommy in our side yard tree, and whether I was in a mess of trouble now because I hadn't. Thad growled, "You children go back in the house."

Tommy's raspy, ragged breathing labored in the darkness as we edged away. Then a siren started howling in the distance. I knew it would get louder and louder until its wailing stopped directly in front of our house, announcing to anybody with ears that something awful was going on at the Starkeys'.

Four policemen piled out of two patrol cars, and I ran to Eileen's room, hoping to hear at her window what Thad said to them. Eileen stayed downstairs in the kitchen with Mama, who answered the phone when our one-long-two-short signal rang on the party line. I heard her tell the bad news to somebody on the phone. Then the phone came alive with all of the different bell signals of our neighbors.

"There was some trouble about a year ago at Grubbses'," Thad told the chief, who wore a nicer cap with a special badge on the front. "Tommy Bern might have been prowling around over there, I don't know. Not for a fact."

The chief dispatched one of the officers to Grubbses' house. "It's the nigger place across the street," he told his man. "Take Collins with you. You boys watch your step." I wondered what Roberta would say if they talked to her. Had her dad shot Tommy?

"Whose room is that up there?" the chief asked, suddenly pointing right at me in Eileen's window. Too late, I ducked into the shadows.

"That's my daughter Eileen's," Thad told him.

"Do you keep guns in the house, Mr. Starkey?"

Thad made John B. show him Pa Joesy's old rifle that he used for hunting. The chief brought it out of a closet and into the hall light upstairs. Policemen rocked on their feet as they stood there watching, thick bodies filling up space, leather squeaking. Sue-Sue and I peeked out from our room, where I'd gone after I was spotted. Thaney gawked from her door, too, her hand clutched at the front of her dark cotton robe. "It's a Winchester .22," she volunteered. The chief checked the chamber and the mechanism and then sniffed the barrel of the old rifle. He handed it to the other officer. "Going to have to keep this for a while," he told John B. "You understand."

Without turning his head my direction, John B. answered my pantomimed questions with another of his shrugs.

"Son, the Bern boy is dead out there," the chief said. It seemed to jolt John B, and his eyes went into a distant stare. "Is there anything you want to tell me?"

"No, sir. I'm real sorry."

"Sorry?" The chief's voice was gruff. "You're *real* sorry?" He laid the words out, like the pieces of a broken plate. "Exactly what is it you're sorry for? Tell me that."

"Sorry he's dead, I meant. That's all." I thought Johnny was acting kind of hard-nosed, considering the circumstances.

A silence stretched out a minute before the chief asked, "Was there bad blood between you and Tom Bern?" John B. hesitantly mumbled a respectful *no, sir.* The chief said, "You don't sound so sure. You want to try that again?"

John B. took his time. It got very still in the hall. "Tommy ... Tom, well, he was nobody I ever cared for very much, you might say."

"I see."

"His parents didn't send him away for no reason," John B. said.

This seemed to catch the chief by surprise. "Is that right? Why's that?"

My brother sounded exasperated. "'Cause he's a peeper. Was. Everybody knows it! *Sir.*"

"And you saw him peeping in your sister's window, did you?"

"Nope. Never did," Johnny said flatly. "I'd a ..." He stopped. I knew. He'd have beaten him to a pulp, if he had. Only Johnny must have decided not to say it.

"Okay," the chief said after a moment. "Here's what I'm gonna do. I'm gonna talk to your dad here, and I'm going to make a phone call, and I want you to go downstairs and sit in your parlor, and I want you to just wait for me there. Is that clear?"

"Yes, sir."

"All right," he said turning once again to Thad. "Are there any more guns?"

My eyes went directly to the whopper holstered at the chief's hip. It was a dark, bulky contraption—mean looking—and I cowered where I stood thinking he could draw it and point it at anyone he pleased, anytime (him being chief of police and all).

"No," Thad told him. "No other guns."

"You're sure."

"Yes."

Without anybody noticing, I slipped down the back stairs to see my brother.

"What's going on? Why are they taking your rifle?"

"No idea," John B. said. He seemed distracted, preoccupied.

"What are you thinking?" I asked.

"Nothing."

I scoffed and started to argue, but Mama was calling from the kitchen. "Girls! In here, please." I touched Johnny's shoulder lightly as I left. Mama was making cocoa. A row of cups and saucers sat at the ready on the counter. Eileen and Sue-Sue looked dazed and didn't speak. Mama said, "We're going to have to get some sleep around here once the police leave. This will help."

I didn't like the police in our house, and I said so. What had we done? I was scared for John B., too, and I told that to anyone who'd listen. I felt a good rant coming on just as Mama interrupted.

"John B. hasn't done anything, Emma. He was in his room when Tommy was shot. I know that for a fact. Let's keep that in mind." Johnny's "room" was in the basement. Could he have shot Tommy from there? "Now, can someone please tell me what Tommy Bern was doing in our yard?"

"Yeah, that's kinda strange," I said, and squinted menacingly at Sue-Sue, who was giving me the eye.

"I've heard some nasty chatter about Tommy Bern," Mama said. "I hear that he is not a very nice boy, that he does ... did ... what? ... disturbing, unpleasant things." We all shrugged. Mama soldiered on. "Eileen, were your lights on when this happened?"

Eileen's vacant stare didn't change. She nodded very slightly. I looked at her closely now, and I could tell that she had added it all up and discovered the ugly truth.

"Did you have your shade pulled?"

This time she shook her head very slightly, and spoke in little more than a whisper. "I don't know. I think so." I'd found the shade up when I went to spy on Thad. Plus, more than once I'd seen her brushing her hair without a stitch on, door ajar, studying her round little breasts in the mirror, the black of night filling the panes of her window.

"If you ask me," I said, rising to Eileen's defense anyway, "Tommy Bern had it coming." I knew Mama would light into me for that one, and she wasted no time.

"Emma! What an awful thing to say! And you know it! *Thou shalt not kill.* Or had you forgotten? That boy may have done rotten things, but that doesn't mean he deserved to be shot by somebody who decided to take matters in their own hands. That's not done in a law-abiding society. Now the police will have to sort things out, and whoever took that boy's life is going to pay dearly for it."

"Seems to me, the police shoulda did something about Tommy Bern long ago," I said. "Then this never woulda happened." The sound of my own words made me angrier, but I clamped my jaw shut when I heard the chief's heavy footfalls announce that he was coming down our stairs.

He came into the kitchen and lifted the receiver on the phone without so much as a howdy-do. His leather belt squeaked around his tubby middle when he took a deep breath and let out a sigh. "You need to get off this line," he barked at someone. I heard squawking in the earpiece when he held it away from his head. "Chief Rogers, that's who." His belt squeaked again, and there were clicks on the line before central picked up. "Lucille, it's Clem." He spoke loudly into the mouthpiece. "I need you to roust a couple of the boys and have them cover the station. That's right. I'll call down there in a bit. Yeah, the boy's dead. We're going to need a conveyance out here. New York. The Starkeys, yes. Oh, and call the coroner and tell him we got one for him, will ya?"

We sipped our cocoa in silence.

"Lucille?" the chief said. "Before you start on all that, I need you to hook me up to Arlen Bern's house. What? No, I'm not likely to forget that, Lucille. No, ma'am. Yeah, thanks. I will. I got the feeling it's going to be a long night."

Sometime after midnight, I was roused from a fitful sleep by the smell of smoke drifting in my window. I'd been dreaming that Tommy was yelling "Nigger" and breaking windows in our house, taunting John B. with shouts. "Come on out, you cowardly niggah!" I lay there in the dark and heard crackling like a wood fire spitting sparks and men talking in the street outside my window. I got up and looked out. Everything in the yard was shrouded in thick smoke, like a fog. There was a fire truck silhouetted against some burning embers, and only stove chimneys stood where the Grubbses' place had been. Sour cocoa curdled in my stomach. Thad stood in the yard, hands on hips, suspender straps puckering his nightshirt, which he had tucked into his trousers. I ran downstairs in my nightgown and out onto the cool, dewy grass of the front lawn.

It surprised me when he reached down for my hand and wrapped it in his. I saw charred stains and pinholes in his nightshirt where sparks had burned through. He had a soot streak across his cheek and flecks of ash in his hair. It startled me when he spoke. "Never would have believed it possible. Not here. Not in Cornucopia." He shook his head sadly. "Police never did come."

Only then did I think of Roberta's terrifying night. It was like noticing the pain of a cut only after you'd seen the blood. Had she been trapped in a house that was on fire? Had I slept right through her ordeal? I felt a pang of shame.

"The Grubbses?" I said. "Are they okay?"

"Everybody got out," Thad said.

"They did?"

"I saw them going in the direction of the river on foot."

"I gotta go find Roberta," I said.

Thad tightened his grip on my hand. "Leave it be. They've gone. Nobody here can help them now."

I was confused. "Where would they go?"

"Cousins, probably. I don't know. Family."

I felt small and helpless in a world I didn't understand. "But who would do something like this?"

Thad was silent a moment. Then, "Cowards who hide in robes and hoods."

We stood watching the flames lick at what was left as firemen sprayed water over the surrounding grass and trees. "But why? Why did somebody do it?" I asked.

"They got the idea that Mr. Grubbs shot that boy." I could tell from the way he said it that he was blaming himself for pointing his finger that direction, steering the police away from us, never thinking of the harm it might cause elsewhere.

"Do *you* think Mr. Grubbs shot Tommy?"

"No," Thad said flatly. "Wasn't a shotgun killed Tommy Bern. It was a rifle."

I couldn't hold back a sob or the tears. "Oh! It's all so awful!" I wailed. Thad dropped my hand. I felt his arm go around my shoulder, and I ducked, expecting to be smacked upside my head. But he drew me to him and held on, stroking my hair and listening to my tears.

Forty-Six

I awoke to brilliant sunlight and the sound of a window shade shooting up and clattering. I squinted. Light scoured the bedroom floor and walls in places it didn't reach until midday. "What time is it?" I mumbled. I was stiff and groggy, plucked too fast from a fog of dark dreams into brutal daylight. The feeling of catastrophe weighed on my chest. Sue-Sue stood at the window. The little stinkpot. Pretending the runaway shade was an accident.

"Past noon." She adjusted and refastened the straps of her overalls, as if to say, *notice how I'm dressed and you're not.* The house was oddly quiet.

"Where is everybody?" I asked. "Church?"

"Mama and Thad are. Mama said we could sleep in."

"And John B.?"

"I don't know. Mama says he walked Tallulah to pasture first thing and didn't come back."

This news nipped my restoring yawn and stretch in the bud. Air rushed out of my lungs. My arms fell limp. Where had Johnny gone? Could you join the Army on Sunday? I glared at Sue-Sue, "Have you checked the barn?"

"Course I did. I 'magine he just went hunting with Rach."

"On a Sunday morning?" I kicked the covers off, annoyed to have slept through everything and be hearing about it secondhand from Sue-Sue, who never properly got anything straight. I said, "Besides, how can he go hunting when the police have his rifle?"

"Oh." She rubbed her nose with the palm of her hand, like she might be trying to push her brains back in. "Hey! I almost forgot!" she said. "Grubbses had a fire!"

Like it was thrilling news. Like it was me who had slept through the whole thing.

"Ding-dang it, Sue-Sue. A LYNCH MOB *set* their house on fire! It's gone! They're gone! And lucky if they are alive! If it hadn't been for Thad, I don't know ... Honestly, you can be such a doodle head fart sniffer sometimes!" She looked ready to cry or to punch me or both. I asked, "What about Eileen? Where is she?" This was one of those rare times when I felt my big sister would be preferable to my little one.

"Thaney woke her up and made her go to the Methodists'." A noticeable pout had crept into Sue-Sue's voice.

I asked, "Are they saying who killed Tommy?"

"Ma says they're hunting for Mr. Grubbs. So I guess he musta."

Wrong again, I thought.

"Criminy! You don't know spit!" I jumped out of bed and yanked off my nightgown. "Not plain spit!"

"I just told you where Eileen was." She watched me pull on my shirt and my overalls, muttering, "Boy, somebody got up on the wrong side of the bed." Then, under her breath, she added, "And not all that early, neither."

"Yeah, well who never woke me up?" I demanded. "Huh?" The day was nearly half over and events had rapidly run away on me. "What in tarnation did you think you were doing, lounging around all morning with John B. missing?"

I could hear her mutter the words "crabby" and "fault" as we came down the stairs. I grabbed a cold biscuit off a plate in the kitchen on the way out the door, just to quiet my sour, empty belly.

"Where are we going?" Sue-Sue wanted to know.

"To find Johnny."

"How we going to do that?"

"I don't know," I admitted. Mama and Thad and Eileen and Thaney would be home from church shortly, but I didn't feel like waiting around. I was too worried. I took a bite of the biscuit and tried to think, but dry powdery dough sucked every drop of spit out of my mouth and biscuit plastered itself to the roof of my mouth. I tried to work it loose, but when a chunk broke off, it stuck in my throat. I threw the rest on the ground and ran for the garden hose to wash it down.

It was then that Dema and her little sister came running out of the woods in swimsuits yelling. "Rach is gonna jump! Rach is gonna jump!"

"From the bridge?" I yelled.

"He's gone off his rocker!" Dema yelled back. She and her sister ran on toward home. Sue-Sue and I dashed toward the river. Wherever Rach was, John B. could not be far away.

Scampering along the footpath through the woods, Sue-Sue shouted, "Is he really gonna do it this time?"

"How should I know?" I snapped. Sue-Sue had gotten on my nerves. You couldn't think with her yapping all the time. Why was this happening? Tommy. The Grubbses. Now Rach was threatening to jump?

We emerged from the trees into sunlight and looked toward the bridge.

"There he is!" Sue-Sue yelled, as if I wouldn't see him.

"Could you just shut up for one ding-dang minute?" I said.

"Holy smokes, Emma, what did I do?"

Rach was seated on the bridge railing, head down. It startled me to see him in his dungarees, not his swimsuit. This wasn't the playful, cocky Rach. This was someone else entirely. John B. stood next to him, staring at the horizon, saying something. Talking Rach out of it, I thought. You couldn't hear them. Water rushed down the spillway of the dam and bathers stood below in the water staring up at the boys on the bridge. It was a hot day, and a weekend crowd had formed along the riverbank. Groups of children shivered in dripping swimsuits, wrapped in towels, waiting and watching with their mothers, some with toddlers balanced on canted hips.

"What do you suppose they're saying?" I asked, without thinking. Then it hit me. Rach, a crack shot with a rifle. Rach, stuck on Eileen. Had he seen Tommy climb the tree in our side yard that night? It was too awful to comprehend. I said, "Come on."

"Where we going?"

"See if we can help John B. talk him down."

We approached the concrete abutment to the bridge by edging along the steep embankment, limping like cripples, one foot lower than the other. I thought John B. would be happy to see us. Instead, he began vigorously waving us back. *Get away! Don't come over here.* Rach turned and looked at us then, too, and he hopped up onto his feet on the railing with one hand on a girder for balance. There was that whiff of tragedy about him that I had seen the day before at the air show, which felt like ages ago.

"What do we do?" Sue-Sue asked.

"We gotta get back. Come on! Move!"

Rach's eyes released us and turned to the cut where Sue-Sue and I had emerged from the woods, as if someone else were expected. Of course. *Eileen.* Even now, she was the one he wanted to see. Had he shot Tommy thinking he was protecting her? Shot him through the heart in a moment of anger with no regard for the consequences? Oh, Rach! Doomed boy! I wondered whether Eileen could talk him down if she came.

I turned my back to them, unable to bear watching this play out.

The order seemed to have gone out of the world, like a desk drawer pulled out too far and the contents spilled and scattered. Did Rach know he was not suspected of shooting Tommy—that the police were after Mr. Grubbs? I hoped John B. had told him. Or did it matter? Could Rach's conscience stand the idea of getting away with murder? Would that be worse than prison? I believed now that Rach had killed Tommy, and that John B. had figured it out last night. And that was why my brother looked distressed then and why he stood by him now.

I turned to face the bridge again, my nerves tingling. What was happening? Rach looked skittish and uncertain on the railing, a shadow of the brash boy I adored. I tried telling myself that everything would work out, that John B. could talk him down. I saw how hard my brother was trying, gesturing with his hands, working his shoulders. I tried telling myself that even if he jumped, Rach knew what he was doing, that he was athletic and strong. Only, something at the very core of me refused to believe any of it.

Soon, a caravan of cars rolled out along Bridge Street from town, slowing in the distance, and stopping along the shoulder a hundred feet away. The first one out of a car was Mr. Drummond.

Rach must have seen him too, because he pointed that direction and shouted something that stopped Mr. Drummond and everyone else in their tracks. Mr. Drummond gave him a shrug with splayed hands. Then he lifted a hand to his mouth and called out to Rach, taking a cautious step forward as he did. Again, Rach's arm shot up as he shouted at his father. John B. reached toward Rach and spoke, but Rach's head swiveled toward the edge of the woods where Eileen now emerged, followed by Dema, her sister and a small pack of neighborhood children. Rach raised his fingers in a tentative and melancholy greeting. He stared at my sister a long moment. And then—just like that—he was off the bridge and in the air.

Sue-Sue cried out, but I was stupefied. A boy that I cared the world about was diving headfirst toward the river in jeans, arms extended out over his head, flinging himself away from the safety of a rusting steel girder bridge. It was a long way down, and Rach's feet scissored ever so slightly in the air, toppling him out of vertical just before he hit the water.

A silly cheer went up from the children in swimsuits along the shore as he knifed through the gray surface, his off-kilter legs kicking out a huge spray. Bubbles and concentric ripples marked the place he'd gone down into the murk. There was silence as the gathered waited for him to break the surface again. When his head didn't bob up after a moment, I thought of the trick he'd played on us before. Above, I saw John B. scan the deep pool between the bridge and the dam, then climb up onto the railing, I thought for a better look. But when he bent his knees to jump, I shouted, "Johnny, no!" But it was too late. He was already hurtling toward the water, feet first, his arms circling and waving to stay upright.

Sue-Sue and I scooted down the hill fast on our rumps, but Mr. Drummond slid past us, throwing off his jacket and ripping open his shirt as he went. Just as he reached the water, he tossed everything aside and jumped in. He was a pretty good swimmer. Sue-Sue and I could handle ourselves in the river, too, but neither of us had ever been in the deep pool above the dam. "Just wait!" I said as we reached the water's edge. "Watch for John B."

Tears welled in my eyes when Johnny finally popped up, gasping for air. He shook the dripping water off his face, gulped down a big breath and dove back under. Mr. Drummond broke the surface shortly after Johnny, and did the same. If they had to fight for breath already, I thought, how long could Rach survive under there?

Others began diving into the water now. Mothers called their children to them and hurried away from the river. Everything inside me started to shake, and nothing I tried could stop it. I couldn't sit still. I couldn't jump in either. I just couldn't. I'm not sure why. I paced the shore and listened to a siren in the distance.

On the third time down, Mr. Drummond pulled Rach's lifeless body to the surface. His eyes and mouth were open, but his expression was as empty as the face of a ghost. There were howls of anguish from women who stood watching from the bridge and men began shouting.

"Somebody get a doctor!"

"We need an ambulance!"

"Get some help down there!"

I could barely see through my tears as Mr. Drummond, with Johnny's help, pulled Rach's body ashore. Mr. Drummond pushed repeatedly on Rach's chest while Johnny crawled away and retched up river water. When he was done, my brother lay back in the grass and stared at the sky. Water rolled down the sides of his face.

Then, suddenly, Thad had hold of my arm, pulling Sue-Sue and me away from there.

Forty-Seven

*J*ohn B. was the last to come home from the river that day. Mama had one of her arms wrapped around Sue-Sue and the other securely around me on our navy velour divan in the parlor. I'd cried myself out, but my lungs were heaving up hot, shivery sighs as my fingers idly straightened and smoothed the doily on the arm of the divan.

Our mantel clock ticked along, Mama not saying much. Us neither. What was there to say? "We've all had a nasty shock," she'd already said, underestimating the mountain of calamity and heartbreak that had bullied up out of the earth overnight. None of it seemed possible.

Eileen slunk in and plopped down in Thaney's favorite chair. Grandma had gone upstairs after finishing her cottage cheese and Melba toast. She had delivered a single acerbic comment. "Boy never had a lick of sense." Eileen refused to look at us. She was bent at the waist, silently examining her slender hands, like there might be blood on them. Dr. Becker, she'd told us, had covered Rach's body and face with an old lap robe from an automobile trunk. She left the river after that. What could she possibly be thinking, I wondered.

When the spring to the back door screen stretched with a twang and banged shut, I thought perhaps it was Thad with some news. After dropping us girls at home, he had gone to Mrs. Sterns' house next door to find someone to stay with Mrs. Drummond through the next several hours. But it wasn't Thad returning. It was John B., whose clothes were damp and hair still tangled from river water. There was a wild, angry look in his eyes. He wasted no time going for Eileen, jabbing a finger at her as he shouted, "This is *your* fault! He's dead because of *you.*"

Mama lifted her arm off my shoulder and rocked herself, struggling to get up off the divan and onto her feet. Eileen shot up out of Thaney's chair. My brother and sister usually waited until Mama and Thad weren't around to pick serious fights with each other, but there was no stopping them this time. Eileen raised her hands to her hips and took a step toward Johnny with her chin jutting out. "It has nothing to do with me!" she yelled in his face. "Just a crazy boy doing one last crazy thing."

John B.'s fist came out of nowhere, flying smack into Eileen's chin. It made a sound like a chicken bone breaking off from Sunday dinner and Eileen's head snapped back hard. She went down with a shriek followed by a whimper. I felt a peculiar rush of satisfaction watching this until I saw the seething look on Johnny's face. Shades of Thad. Mama must have seen it too because she threw a bear hug on him, pinning his arms to his sides before he could hit Eileen again while she was down. Johnny danced like he was trying to wriggle free, but Mama held him tight.

"Stop this!" she ordered. I was sure Johnny could bust loose if he really tried, but I think he loved Mama too much to disobey.

Eileen was curled up on the floor, working something around in her mouth. She pushed to her knees and spit a tiny object into her hand. Her eyes got as big as saucers. It was a bloodied chunk of tooth. "My God!" she wailed. "Look what you've done!" She thrust it toward John B. Then she clapped her other hand over her mouth and hid the new gap in her precious smile.

For once, Mama did not side with her beloved son. "John B. Starkey," she said angrily, giving him a shove out of the parlor. "I want you out of this house! This instant!" John B. allowed himself to be rousted, but not before he had called Eileen a fool and a tramp. She started to get to her feet, but Mama stepped between them, and Johnny stormed out. Mama tipped Eileen's chin up to examine the damage and said, "Well, missy, let's see what that smart mouth has earned for its trouble."

Before she could, Eileen ran to the bathroom and slammed the door. I heard the hook click.

I'd seldom seen Mama so weary or disgusted. "And on the Sabbath, too," she said to Sue-Sue and me.

I went up the stairs to my room on wobbly legs and quietly shut the door behind me. I didn't want to listen to any more crying or cussing or name-calling. I had slept until noon, but I crawled back under the covers, closed my eyes and hoped to push the world far away. I felt all trembly and weak and my stomach ached.

I tried to make my mind go blank, but it was impossible. Everything ached too much for Rach. Why did he have to go and jump? What an awful price to pay for mistakes he alone was not responsible for. I groaned and immediately wished I hadn't, because I knew by the sound that I was feeling just as sorry for myself as I was for the lost boy.

I opened my eyes and stared at the light coating of ash on the windows, a souvenir of the Grubbses' fire. Outside, the hot mid-afternoon sun beat down with unrelenting intensity. It seemed to bleach the world white, as if Judgment Day had arrived.

A dozen boys turned up to mourn Rach's passing two days later at the Drummonds' house, Zeke Wilhite among them. Had he and Rach buried the hatchet after their vicious fight? Had they spit into their hands and shaken on it? I pictured John B. there handling the negotiations. And I wondered what both boys could have said to make peace about Eileen.

The Starkeys bowed their heads at the sad, somber occasion. All except Eileen. She had barricaded herself in her room at home, a hostage to her own vanity. The dentist hadn't finished outfitting her with a cap for the broken front tooth, and she was wearing humiliation like sackcloth. She barely mumbled for days, fearful I suppose that the gap in her teeth would show and someone might gaze upon such imperfection. Not that her silence bothered us. In fact, it suited the mood in the house. We all but stopped visiting with each other at dinner. Thad probably welcomed it.

Honoring a request from Mrs. Drummond, John B. got up in a white shirt and starched collar at the funeral and gave a short eulogy. His voice cracked when he spoke of his best friend, and he got to swallowing pretty hard and couldn't finish. He sat back down and hung his head. The boys around him reached over and clapped him hard on the back. Later, they wolfed down a spread of sandwiches and cakes that Mama and the other neighbor ladies had made.

On the afternoon Rach died, Mr. Drummond had made a plea to the Methodist minister for a church funeral for his son. Thaney said it was only because the silly fool wasn't welcome to set foot in the Drummond house ever again. The Methodist preacher declined Mr. Drummond's request, however, saying that the church was already reserved for Tommy Bern's funeral and there were weddings scheduled that week as well. I wondered who spoke at Tommy's memorial and what on earth they could have said. As to Mr. Drummond, he ended up outside on a bench in the yard during Rach's service smoking cigarettes under an umbrella in a steady drizzle while some family shirttail relative who was a preacher read The Word.

Nearly everybody lined up that afternoon to speak to Mrs. Drummond as she sat beside the casket with Margaret and James. It took me twenty minutes to get up the nerve to go into the same room with Rach's body, and when I did (after I heard the casket was closed), Mrs. Drummond looked like a person who was asleep with her eyes open. Hardly a flicker of recognition showed in her face as I gave her my condolences. I think she'd gone off to a place where she hoped trouble couldn't find her anymore. Margaret shook her head as a warning to me when I raised an eyebrow and started to say something.

"My family and I thank you for coming," Margaret said, a line she repeated to everyone who stopped by to pay their respects. The words sounded like she hardly knew me at all, like we hadn't been best friends since the first grade. I'd barely seen Margaret since the accident—which was what everybody was calling it now, a diving accident—but until that moment, I had figured she was laying low because her family came first. I spent hours in the haymow expecting her to turn up and talk about things. But I saw her just once, and that was when she went out to their privy. Her wave was a perfunctory sort of gesture. Then she disappeared back into the house.

Margaret hadn't seen Rach dive off the bridge. She was lucky. She wouldn't have to carry that horrid image around. I wished to God I hadn't been there. I might have slept right through it too if Sue-Sue hadn't jerked up the window shade right when she did. Now I couldn't get Rach's gray, lifeless face unstuck from my head, even when I tried to remember his smile as he lifted me off the ice and carried me in his arms. That special winter's day memory was a darting jackrabbit now that I would chase around for weeks until I doubted it had ever really happened.

Sue-Sue had found me in the barn the morning after the accident and bedded down next to me in the straw. I could see she was troubled, so I put an arm around her, pulled her in close, and stroked her hair. Then I gave her an extra hug, trying to squeeze the words out of her.

"I keep thinking, what if Johnny had drowned too?" she said finally.

How odd that struck me. She was scared about something bad that *didn't happen*. And me? I knew suddenly that I wasn't scared anymore because something bad did. I had been scared for a long time until then, I discovered. Now with Rach dead, God rest his soul, I wouldn't have to worry anymore about his crazy recklessness.

I said, "You know Johnny promised me he'd never jump off that bridge. Still, I don't blame him. I'd have jumped myself if it had been Margaret down there. Or you." Sue-Sue buried her face in my neck and cuddled up. And I felt my throat go hot again.

I stared a long time at Rach's coffin down in the damp hole where the men lowered it. I thought about Rach never becoming a man. And I thought about my brother standing a better chance of growing up to be one now that his buddy was gone.

The indestructible boy was dead. Rest in Peace, Rach Drummond.

Forty-Eight

*M*ama had assured us things would get better after the funeral. Nothing could have been further from the truth. A heartache I'd sensed coming on for days arrived the morning after the funeral as Margaret knocked at our back door. The flash of pleasure I felt at seeing her withered in the shadow of the dark look on her face. I told her to come on in. But she folded her arms over her chest and just stood there looking off to the side.

"I need to tell you something," she said.

My neck muscles knotted up. "Uh-huh? Let's go out in the barn."

"No," she said and turned to face me. She squinted up one eye like she'd just bit into a lemon. "Here it is: My mom and dad and me, and Alice, you see, we're all moving to Wichita."

Her words left me so numb, I asked her to repeat them. Then I made her stop because it was stomping on my chest until I couldn't breathe. I whispered, "You can't mean it ..."

"I'm sorry," Margaret said, sounding formal, polite, and final, not sorry. "The movers'll be here on Saturday. Reno and James are gonna stay behind, but the rest of us can't stand to be here a second longer."

Can't stand to be here?

It was like a stranger there on our stoop, saying these words, an emissary of a girl I once knew. I remembered suddenly that I hadn't seen her cry when her brother died, and I wasn't sure what that meant. A buzz got going in my ears. I thought I might be sick. I managed to hear the end of what she said next, something about needing a book that she'd lent me. She said, "I have to have all my stuff in boxes tomorrow."

"But why, Margaret?"

"The movers are gonna tote up the job and give my dad a price."

"No—why do you have to go? Honestly? Wait! You could stay here and live with us! Remember, like that time when I stayed at your place after the fire? Come on! We'll ask my mama when she gets back."

She like to jumped down my throat. "You think I'd stay here when my mom and my dad need me with them?" It took a moment for the steeliness in her eyes to soften. After a breath, she found a different pitch for her voice too. "I'm sorry, but that's just plain dumb. I want to be with my family. My mom's not well. And my dad's promising to take care of her. He's got a new job. So it's all settled. We're leaving."

This was the Drummond way, I thought. *Run!* Every time something went wrong, you could count on Mr. Drummond to take off. He ran away from Michigan when Reno had baby Alice. He fled Cornucopia after his wife found out he'd been stepping out with Ada Jensen. And now he was doing it again, ashamed that his son had killed a boy in Cornucopia and taken his own life the day after.

I wanted to argue. I wanted to give Margaret a thousand reasons why she shouldn't go.

She said, "So, can I get my book back?"

I just stared. I couldn't get past the annoyance and confusion. Why was Mrs. Drummond forgiving Mr. Drummond? Had she taken pity on him just for making him sit out in the rain at Rach's funeral? I didn't get any of it. How had this man gotten his foot back in the door, let alone figured out how to force everybody to hightail it to Wichita?

"Well?" Margaret said. "Do you have it? My book?"

"Yeah. Okay. Come on in." She stood there like a stick for a moment then nodded. We tromped up the stairs together, me saying,

"Margaret, listen, please, honestly, what am I supposed to do if you leave?"

"How should I know?" she said. "What did you do before I got here?" Like that was an answer. Fact was, I couldn't remember a thing about life without the Drummonds. And a fat lot of hooey that selfish Margaret Drummond seemed to care about it.

I should never have said this, but I did. "Dang it all, Margaret, what makes you think you can just go running off any old time like some ding-dang pack of gypsies?" I wasn't very tactful when I was ten. Or very smart.

It was all Eileen's fault, I decided. She had ruined it for everybody. She'd fixed it so the Drummonds couldn't stand to be our neighbors anymore. She'd gotten Rach killed. If she had only treated him a tiny bit nicer—and kept her shades pulled—none of it might have happened.

"Let's cut up all of Eileen's dresses," I suggested to Sue-Sue after Margaret went home.

"What?" Sue-Sue's eyes got big. "What'll you wear to church next year then?"

"I'd sooner wear rags than something that's been on her back!"

Sue-Sue hadn't been interested in anything I'd suggested for days, but this appeared to excite the living devil in her. And nothing stood in our way. Eileen was off at the dentist. The doors to her room and closet were wide open.

In we went and pulled her best Sunday dress off its hanger. I stabbed the point of the scissors through the bodice, hatefully picturing Eileen inside it as I did. Then I worked the scissors and tore a piece off as Sue-Sue squealed happily. Her silly, undiscerning merriment sobered me somehow. I'd been in an angry, bitter trance since my first impulse for revenge. Now I had second thoughts. I stared at the chunk of fabric in my hand. Was Eileen turning me into a spiteful person? Was cutting up her dress really going to change anything? In fact, wouldn't it make that despicable nature of hers even worse? I set the scissors down, and Sue-Sue picked them up immediately, continuing where I'd left off, slashing out a fresh hole and then another and another.

"Okay, that's enough," I said when she'd made a half-dozen cuts. "That'll do."

"No!" she shouted as I went to take the scissors away. She held to them firmly. "Stop it! Let go!" she demanded. "This is fun." She was starved for destruction.

I wrestled the scissors away, told her Eileen wouldn't have a dress left to notice if she didn't stop, and we hung the tattered remains back up. Then I pushed my sister on out of there. Eileen couldn't miss the message. Pieces of her dress were scattered around. I just wondered what she would do to retaliate—besides tell Mama.

I heard her come in a half hour later and storm up to her room, slamming the door. Mama explained that the tooth the dentist made was silver and Eileen felt she looked like a pirate. How much more were we going to have to endure of Eileen's vanity? I stopped on the stairs when I heard her shriek. "Oh, my God! My dress! Mom!" She came roaring out.

I stood in her path on the landing, hands on hips, ready to face the music and eager for a fight. Eileen shouted, "You did this, you little brat, didn't you!" When she snarled, I saw her new capped tooth. A big hoot of a laugh erupted out of me. That silver thing practically shouted *Yo-ho-ho, matey.*

"You know, Eileen," I told her, "you look more like Thad every day."

She slapped me hard. My sister was strong and big, but I landed a punch to her belly and one to her eye before Mama could arrive and pull us apart. I had to rub my hand where Eileen had bitten it. I yelled, "You're just lucky I didn't bust another tooth out!" I wanted to hurt her real bad. I swear I'd have uncorked a good one if she'd said anything back.

It was another silent meal that night at the Starkeys. I fumed over the sting of the switch that Mama had applied to the back of my legs. Sue-Sue wet her pants before her full punishment had been administered, so she obtained an unfair reprieve. The girl could pee like a racehorse.

I didn't care about that. It was Mama's reaction that I still seethed over. "What's gotten into you, Emma?" she'd demanded. I wondered, what kind of question was that? Where had she been all this time?

"What's gotten into me? Eileen! Eileen's gotten into me. I hate her!"

Mama looked at me like I was not any daughter of hers. Which only made me madder. "Honestly!" I screamed. "Why don't you ever punish Eileen?"

Forty-Nine

*M*onths would pass before I could work up the courage to ask John B. about Rach's death and the stunning events leading up to it.

Instead, our conversations got stuck on how Thaney was going off her rocker. And she was. I watched from the hall more than once as she wrote intently on the back of a handbill in her room. Curiosity finally got the best of me, of course, and when she wasn't around, I snuck in there to have a look. I discovered a large pile of old circulars in her dresser, handbills for trusses and patent medicines and hardware store novelties. She had filled the backs of every one in a small neat hand, writing out mean, distorted things, telling hateful lies about all of us. It filled page after page. Thaney in Miseryland.

"She swears that Eileen stole four pairs of her drawers!" I reported. "And that Thad spies on her in the biffy!"

We laughed raucously. But the outrageousness of some accusations, claiming that Mama secretly fixed to send her away because she hoped to run off with Mr. Shackleforth, the butcher—raised my hackles. It lit a fire in me. The rot of self-pity over all of the recent misery burned away. I was immersed now in the strange, lonely world of my grandmother's paranoia, and it roused me out of a funk, outrageous poison an antidote for melancholy.

I knew I was taking a chance that day in the barn when I told John B. something I'd seen Thaney wrote about Rach, but I trusted that I'd always be friends with John B. It was just Eileen I wasn't so sure about.

First, I asked to make sure it was okay to bring it up. Then I said, "Thaney thinks Rach had it in his mind that he was shooting Mr. Drummond the night he killed Tommy."

John B. stopped pitching hay. Usually his retorts to Thaney's drivel came sharp and quick. This time, he looked at a loss for words. He rubbed his jaw and leaned a moment on the handle of the pitchfork.

"Huh," he said with a shrug, and went back to distributing the straw.

I figured I'd struck out, that I'd have to get him to talk about Rach some other time. But then Johnny spoke up again as he pitched hay. "I gotta say, maybe the old gal still has a marble or two left."

This surprised me. "What's that supposed to mean?" I asked.

After hiding out in our barn the night of the shooting, Rach had confided everything to Johnny. Johnny told Thad and the police about it later. According to the story, Rach had packed a bag and left his house for good after getting into another fight with his father. Then Rach saw Tommy come into our yard and start to climb the tree outside Eileen's room after her light came on. Rach's anger boiled over at it all—Tommy, Eileen, his father, his life. He aimed his rifle at Tommy Bern and shot him dead as he climbed our tree. He figured nobody would see him do it, and everyone would be glad, because Tommy was a bad apple. "Who was ever gonna put a stop to it?" he'd asked. Later, when he saw the men in hoods and robes come and shout names and accusations at Mr. Grubbs and set fire to his house, he realized he had done a terrible, terrible thing.

After John B. related Rach's confessions to Thad in the tormented hours of that terrible Sunday afternoon, Thad took him down to the police station to repeat it to the chief. While it cleared up suspicions against Mr. Grubbs, it did nothing to rebuild the Grubbses' house or undo the night of terror inflicted on that poor Negro family. The Grubbses never returned to Cornucopia, and I don't know to this day where my childhood friend Roberta is.

"You're not saying now that Rach thought he was shooting his dad, are ya?" I asked Johnny. "Is it really true what Thaney wrote?"

"I'm saying, if Tommy hadn't turned up to climb our tree that night when he did, it might have been Mr. Drummond who was dead right now."

I had to puzzle that one out a minute. "So Rach had the rifle with him in our yard 'cause he was really fixing to kill his own dad and then run away?" I asked.

"He was hiding behind the privy. I don't know that he'd a done it. Not really. How could I?"

John B. went back to his pitchfork.

This aspect of the story had never made it into the papers. I'd read all the articles about the shooting and about Rach jumping off the bridge. (There was one tiny story about the fire at the Grubbses' house that night, too, a single paragraph that related how a blaze of "undetermined origin" burned down a cottage on New York Avenue and how the family had relocated elsewhere.) I took the papers up to my room every day, but I didn't clip any of it out.

There were stories galore. It went on for days. It was obvious that the reporter wasn't acquainted with Rach or Tommy. You'd have thought Tommy never did anything wrong in his life the way he was remembered in the fine words of friends and relatives that were printed. There seemed to be some complete misunderstanding at the center of things. Here was all this praise for Tommy's accomplishments at military school, too, and nothing about why he'd been sent there. No words of tribute were paid to Rach, of course. He had admitted murdering Tommy Bern. He was a villain, plain and simple. He probably even deserved what happened to him.

It made me angry. Mostly, I hated how Rach would be remembered forever in Cornucopia as a murderer and not as a faithful friend of my brother or a boy who dreamed of flying, a someday hero who would not have been afraid to stand up and protect his country against enemies that rose against it.

Speaking of which, my brother kept his pledge to Rach a couple years later and went off to enlist in the Army. He took it hard when they turned him down because of his flat feet and a heart murmur. They wouldn't be so picky in the months after Pearl Harbor. His enlistment in 1942 upset Mama no end, as I had expected. She had a premonition, I think, that Johnny would be lost to us all. And he was, in April 1943, off on some remote island of the Pacific. Why we were fighting like roosters with the Japs over a speck of land in the middle of a vast ocean I couldn't begin to understand.

From the newspaper articles about Rach's death, I learned the coroner had ruled that he perished from a broken neck caused by impact with the water. But I knew he was dead because he couldn't live with himself. His heart never was in that dive. He'd radiated resignation as he stood there on that corroded girder before he leaped, the same way he'd looked prepared to die on a wing walk at the Gilmore Brothers air show the day before. The cockiness had drained out of him. You could argue about this conclusion, of course. You might even say it was God's hand that tipped him off balance before he hit the water, just to be sure he paid for his sins.

I put it that way because of something John B. said that afternoon when I mentioned that Mama had told someone on the phone that Rach jumped because he was despondent.

John B. said, "Rach told me he was putting everything in God's hands. *Making this dive leaves it up to the Lord.* That was what he said." I shook my head and shrugged. I felt all aswim, lost in Rach's notions of justice. John B. put his arm around me and pulled me close. He must have known his words would shock me. "Honest, Emmy, just be happy Rach didn't turn the gun on himself."

My chat with Johnny happened months after Margaret had left. We'd long since watched the movers wrap the Drummonds' old furniture in ratty quilted blankets, roll up their rugs and box their dishes, seen them carry out the lamps and tables and footstools, and load all that junk onto a big truck at the street, regret and sorrow a secret part of the methodical process.

We said our good-byes in the Drummonds' front yard with James and Reno standing by to see the rest of their family off. James hugged Mrs. Drummond as she got in the car, but he refused to shake his prodigal father's hand.

"I'll send you my new address once we get settled," Margaret told me as she hoisted her small suitcase into the trunk.

Other than the thank-you notes I was forced to write at Christmas and the mandatory letter home from El Dorado Springs when we stayed at the Hainlines' for a week in the summer, I knew next to nothing about letter writing. What on earth would I have to tell Margaret about if she wasn't around?

I tried to say the word "good-bye" and found I couldn't. I threw my arms around my friend and hung on for dear life. She hugged me back and then pushed me away and climbed into the backseat.

I remember the rear of the Drummonds' car had an oval-shaped window. Margaret's head popped up in it halfway down the block. Her hand followed next. The small, tentative wave she made was an odd echo of Rach's final gesture before he'd jumped from the bridge. Then Margaret closed her eyes for a second and when she reopened them, her pupils were gone, crossed completely out of sight. I laughed with tears brimming in my eyes, pain gripping my chest, and a lump in my throat.

I stood there long after the car disappeared around the corner, wondering how I might have changed things to make it all turn out differently. More than eighty years later, at the end of my life, I still don't have the answer.